I0583477

In loving memory of my Aunt Gina, who loved The Wizard of Oz and left us too soon. Your spirit and love will always stay in my heart. I miss you so much.

"'You have plenty of courage, I am sure,' answered Oz. 'All you need is confidence in yourself. There is no living thing that is not afraid when it faces danger. The true courage is in facing danger when you are afraid, and that kind of courage you have in plenty'"
-L Frank Baum

Chapter 1: Something's Coming

Mochi's tongue drags across my cheek, warm and slobbery, yanking me from dreams I can't quite remember. I blink at the ceiling of the hotel room, disoriented for half a second before yesterday crashes back—FanCon, the crowds, the electric buzz of being surrounded by people who get it.

"Off, Mochi." My voice comes out scratchy. He whines, tail thumping against the bedframe.

Ariana groans from the other bed, her arm flung dramatically over her face. "What time is it?"

I grab my phone from the nightstand. "Eight-thirty."

"Ugh. Why are we awake?"

"Because today's the autograph." My heart does this stupid flutter thing just saying it out loud.

Ariana peeks from under her arm, one brown eye visible. "Tristian day. Of course." She stretches, and I catch a glimpse of the ink curling up her ribcage. "You're gonna be insufferable."

"I'm not—"

"You absolutely are." She sits up, hair escaping from its bun in wild chunks. "You've had it bad since that indie thing."

"*Dans l'Ombre*." The French rolls off my tongue, probably butchered. "It was brilliant. Dark and unsettling and—"

"And he could read the phone book and you'd swoon." Ariana grins. "That accent does something to you."

Heat creeps up my neck because she's not wrong. There's something about the way Tristian speaks—mostly British, crisp and proper, but certain words get touched by French, softened at the edges. It started with *Dans l'Ombre*, this psychological horror film nobody stateside watched, where he played a man slowly unraveling. I found it by accident on a streaming service at 2 AM during a particularly bad foster home stint. His voice—God, his voice became this anchor.

Then *Quantum* happened, and suddenly everyone knew him, but I'd been there first. Not that it mattered.

"Bethany's gonna be there too," Ariana says, swinging her legs out of bed. "From the theater?"

My stomach drops. "Perfect Bethany."

"Don't start."

"I'm not." I wheel toward my suitcase, where Alice waits—blue dress, white apron, black headband. "She's just... she's everything I'm not."

"She's vapid."

"She's beautiful." I pull out the costume, smoothing wrinkles that aren't there. "And walks. And probably won't stutter when she meets him."

Ariana crosses to me, crouches down so we're eye-level. "You're beautiful. Also, your costume's better. I saw hers on Instagram—Spirit Halloween clearance rack vibes."

That startles a laugh out of me.

"There she is." Ariana taps my nose. "Now go shower before Mochi decides your face needs another bath."

The bathroom's cramped, but I manage. Water streams over my shoulders, and without thinking, I start humming. The melody builds, and then I'm singing, full voice, letting it echo off tiles.

Dorothy. I've wanted to play her since I was twelve, stuck in a group home, watching the musical on a battered laptop. The hope in her voice, the yearning for something better, somewhere better. It lived in my chest like a secret.

My voice cracks on the high note, but I push through. Dreams don't come true for girls like me—foster kids, wheelchair users, people who apologize for existing. But here, in this shower, in this costume, for one weekend, I can pretend.

Today I meet Tristian Lambert.

Today I pretend I deserve my dreams.

"You sound amazing, Em!" Ariana's voice carries through the bathroom door.

I shut off the water, wrapping myself in a towel. "Just warming up."

"For what, Broadway auditions in the hotel hallway?"

"Maybe." I transfer to the shower chair, beginning the careful process of drying off. My fingers work automatically, muscle memory from years of practice.

The singing started with Martha Hendricks. Foster home number seven, or maybe eight—they blur together. She had this thing about noise, about children being seen and not heard, which meant any sound I made earned me hours in the hall closet. Dark. Cramped. Smelling of mothballs and her stale cigarette smoke.

So I sang. Quietly at first, then louder when I realized the closet muffled everything. The Wonderful Wizard of Oz became my escape—Dorothy's voice replacing Martha's shrill complaints. I'd close my eyes and picture yellow brick roads instead of wire hangers digging into my shoulders.

The clothes hanging around me sparked something else. In the darkness, I'd run my fingers over textures— polyester, cotton, the occasional silk blouse Martha saved for church. I started imagining alterations, embellishments, transformations. By the time I left that house, I could picture a garment's construction just by touch, could mentally map where embroidery would elevate cheap fabric into something special.

Martha thought she was punishing me. Instead, she gave me my two greatest passions.

"You okay in there?" Ariana's tone shifts, loses its teasing edge.

"Yeah." I wheel out, dressed in my underwear. "Just thinking."

She perches on the bed edge, reading my face the way she's learned to over three years of friendship. "Martha closet thoughts?"

"How'd you know?"

"You get this look." She stands, grabs the Alice dress. "Plus you only sing that intensely when you're processing old shit."

Ariana Garcia appeared sophomore year like some tattooed guardian angel. I'd been eating alone in the cafeteria—again—when she dropped her tray across from me and announced we were friends now. Just like that. No preamble, no awkward small talk.

She's tough in ways I'm not. Calls out professors who forget accessibility, tells off guys who stare at my wheelchair like it's a tragedy, once threw a drink on someone who called me "inspirational" for existing in public. But she's also the person who researched labradoodle breeders for weeks, who showed up at my dorm with an eight-week-old fluffball and said, "His name's Mochi and he's yours."

That was almost two years ago. Mochi changed everything—gave me something to care for, something that needed me.

"Arms up." Ariana helps me into the dress, her hands gentle despite the barbell through her eyebrow, the skull tattooed on her wrist. "You're gonna kill it today."

"It's just an autograph."

"It's *Tristian Lambert*." She fastens the apron. "The guy whose voice got you through the worst shit. That matters."

I smooth the blue fabric over my lap, adjusting the white apron. Something flutters in my chest—not anxiety, surprisingly. Something lighter. Hopeful, almost.

"I have this weird feeling." The words come out soft. "Like today's important."

"Course it is. You're meeting your celebrity crush."

"No, I mean—" I can't explain it. This sense of standing on the edge of something, of my life splitting into before and after. "Something good's gonna happen."

Ariana grins. "Damn right it is. Now let's finish your transformation."

Light bleeds through the suite's curtains, harsh and immediate. The pillow beside me still smells faintly of last night's conquest—floral perfume and desperation. She left hours ago, after the obligatory selfie and whispered promises I've already forgotten.

I roll over, grabbing my phone. Six-thirty. FanCon day two starts in four hours.

The shower runs scalding, the way I learned to like it at the Lambert estate. Dad always said cold water built character, which meant Jean got the hot water first, Michelle second, and me—the accident, the afterthought, the triplet nobody planned—got whatever remained. Usually ice.

Steam fills the bathroom as I trace the tattoos mapping my torso. Each one a role, a transformation, a version of myself that worked better than the real thing.

Dad never understood acting. Pierre Lambert deals in policy, legislation, proper behavior for a family representing Angoumois in the Assemblée. Jean followed that path perfectly—same sharp suits, same measured speeches, same ability to smile while lying through his teeth. Michelle took the acceptable alternative, becoming the face of French fashion, gracing *Elle* covers with Mum's delicate features.

Then there's me. The embarrassment. The one who ran.

I was raised mostly by Alfred Dupont and his wife Collette. Dad couldn't be bothered with a third child—Jean was the heir, Michelle the beauty, and I was... there. Alfred taught me accents while polishing silver. Collette snuck me pastries and listened when I'd practice monologues in the kitchen.

"You have a gift, Tristian," she'd say in her soft Angoumois lilt, that British precision wrapped around French warmth. "Don't let them take it from you."

Dad tried. God, he tried. Twenty-six years of disappointment etched into his medium-brown eyes every time he looked at me. The son who preferred stages to policy meetings, who memorized Molière instead of voting records, who wanted to *feel* instead of calculate.

The blowup happened at nineteen. Some gala at the estate, politicians and wine exporters discussing Angoumois's economic future. Dad introduced Jean as "my son, following in my footsteps," Michelle as "a testament to Angoumois' beauty." When he got to me, he said, "Tristian is still finding himself."

Still finding myself. Like I was lost. Broken. Incomplete.

I left that night. Took Alfred's emergency cash stash—he replaced it the next day, the note said—and caught the ferry to Marseille. Slept in hostels, auditioned for anything, lived on bread and spite.

Dans l'Ombre changed everything. A psychological horror about a man slowly losing his grip on reality, shot in black and white in Marseille's seediest districts. The director, Claude Mercier, saw something in me—probably recognized the barely-contained rage of a politician's son playing at poverty.

The film played at Cannes. Richard Kellerman, head of Starlight Studios, watched me embody Laurent's descent into madness and saw dollar signs. He found me at the after-party, offered me a contract, a visa, a future that didn't involve disappointing Pierre Lambert.

"You're wasting yourself here, kid," Richard said, his American accent jarring against the French chatter. "Hollywood needs a face like yours."

So I became Tristian Alexandre Lambert, Hollywood's Angoumois darling. Quantum jumpsuits and Victorian waistcoats, charming interviewers and collecting tattoos. Each role another layer between me and the boy who never fit the Lambert dynasty mold.

Dad calls once a year—my birthday, April twenty-fifth. The conversations last exactly four minutes. He asks about my "hobby," I ask about the Assemblée, we both pretend we're not strangers.

The water scalds my shoulders, turning skin pink. I lean against the tile, letting heat work through muscle tension.

"There's this thing," I say to the steam, to nobody, practicing the explanation I've never given an interviewer. "The Lambert Curse."

Sounds dramatic when I say it aloud. Like something from one of my films.

But it's real. Ask anyone who knows the family history. Lamberts don't date casually. We don't do flings or trial periods or sensible courtship. We meet our person, and something clicks—primal, immediate, terrifying. Then we become obsessed.

Dad saw Mum across a crowded assemblée meeting thirty-two years ago. Proposed three weeks later. She said yes before he finished the question.

Jean met Levi at some Hollywood party I dragged him to. One month later, they eloped in Vegas. Didn't tell anyone for two weeks. Dad nearly had a stroke—his heir, his perfect son, married to an American actor in a tacky chapel. But Jean didn't care. He'd found his person.

Michelle spotted Marcus at a photoshoot last year. He was there covering fashion week for some Louisiana tabloid, and she walked right off set mid-shoot to introduce herself. They're engaged now. Mum cried for three days— happy tears, she insisted.

Me? I've dated. Collected phone numbers and fleeting connections, filled hotel rooms with people whose names blur together by morning. I've played the part of boyfriend, lover, companion. Gone through the motions.

Never felt it. That switch everyone describes.

But I want to. God, I want to.

I shut off the water, towel off, run product through my hair until it sweeps back perfectly. The mirror reflects Hollywood's version of me—sharp jawline, calculated stubble, eyes that know how to smolder on cue.

My phone connects to the suite's speakers. Classic rock floods the bathroom—Thunder Valley's "Midnight Rider," all grinding guitars and raw vocals. I sing along while pulling on jeans, my voice hitting notes I never get to use anymore.

"Can't chain me down, won't wear your crown, I'm a midnight rider, baby—"

Acting stole my music. Directors want my face, my accent work, my ability to disappear into characters. Nobody cares that I spent my Angoumois childhood singing in Alfred's kitchen, that Collette said I had "the voice of angels and the soul of a rebel."

The Crimson Hearts comes on next—"Revolution in My Veins"—and I'm halfway through the chorus when someone pounds on the door.

"Tristian! You decent?"

Roger. My assistant, my keeper, my connection to reality.

"Define decent," I call back, buttoning my shirt.

The door opens. Roger walks in first—clipboard already out, efficiency personified. Simone follows, my publicist, phone pressed to her ear, finishing some crisis management call.

"You're singing again," Roger observes, eyebrow raised. "Good mood?"

"Maybe." I switch tracks. Show tunes now—something from an obscure Sondheim revival. My voice softens, finds different colors. *"Isn't it rich, are we a pair—"*

"Save it for the stage you'll never have," Simone cuts in, ending her call. "We've got three hours before FanCon.."

"Sounds thrilling."

"It pays for this suite." She gestures around the hotel room. "Try to look grateful."

But I don't feel grateful. I feel... restless. Electric. Like something's building just beneath my skin.

"Weird question," Roger says, watching me too closely. "You okay? You seem different."

"I'm fine." I grab my jacket. "Just have this feeling."

"Feeling?"

"That something good's going to happen today."

Simone snorts. "At a fan convention? Doubtful."

But the feeling persists, warm and certain in my chest.

Chapter 2: The Foyer Invitation

The second day of FanCon stretches before me like every other convention—an assembly line of faces, markers, and practiced smiles. Celebrity Row hums with controlled chaos. To my left, some action star flexes for selfies. To my right, a sci-fi actress debates whether dragons could realistically breathe fire.

I sign another headshot. Smile. Next.

Then I see her.

She's maybe six people back in line, navigating the crowd in a pink power wheelchair. Alice costume—blue dress, white apron, black headband holding back blonde waves that catch the fluorescent lights. But it's not the costume that makes my pen freeze mid-signature.

It's her face.

Delicate. Oval. Fair skin with this luminous quality, like she's lit from within. And her eyes—even from here I can see they're green. Striking, expressive green that seems to hold entire worlds.

My chest tightens.

Don't be ridiculous.

I'm twenty-six, not some thirteen-year-old with a crush. I've met thousands of beautiful women. This is nothing. Just another fan in costume, another autograph, another—

She moves closer. Three people away now.

My hand trembles slightly as I sign the next photo. The person doesn't notice, too busy gushing about the Hatter's tea party scene.

"Thanks so much," I manage, voice steady despite the strange flutter beneath my ribs.

Two people.

I can see her better now. The way she holds herself—shy but determined. Something vulnerable in her expression, like she's bracing for disappointment but hoping anyway.

Get it together, Lambert.

But my accent's already shifting, British lilt creeping in around the edges. It always gets heavier when I'm nervous, when control slips.

One person.

Then she's there. Right there. Looking up at me with those impossible green eyes, and something in my brain just—*clicks*.

Oh.

Oh no.

"Bonjour," she says, and her voice—Christ, her voice. Mezzo-soprano, warm and musical, wrapping around the French syllable like silk.

I blink. Recover. Smile, though it feels different than the practiced one I've worn all morning.

"Bonjour," I reply, leaning forward slightly. "Tu parles français?"

Her cheeks flush pink. "Un petit peu. Just a little."

The accent's American—Utah, probably, given the location—but she tried. Most people who attempt French with me butcher it, treat it like a party trick. She sounds... genuine. Nervous but genuine.

"That's more than most manage." My voice comes out softer than intended, British edges pronounced. "What's your name, love?"

"Emily." She fidgets with the edge of her apron. "Emily Silver. I just—I wanted to say I love your work. Especially *Dans l'Ombre*. It's... it meant a lot to me."

Dans l'Ombre. Not Quantum Divergence or Erik's Phantom. The indie French film nobody stateside watches.

This girl—Emily—she saw Laurent. My first tattoo. My raw, desperate beginning.

The feeling in my chest expands, terrifying and certain.

No. Absolutely not. This is insane.

But the Lambert curse doesn't care about logic.

I reach for a headshot, hands steadier now despite my racing heart. "How'd you find it? The film, I mean. It's not exactly easy to locate."

"Streaming service algorithm." She smiles, and it transforms her whole face. "Right when I needed it most."

I should sign quickly. Move on. Maintain professional distance.

Instead, I uncap my marker and write carefully:

Emily—Meet me outside the Grand Ballroom in 15 minutes. Please. —T.L.

I add my phone number below. Circle it twice.

"Here you are." I hand her the photo, fingers brushing hers briefly. Electric.

She takes it, glances down, eyes widening as she reads.

"I—what?"

"Fifteen minutes," I repeat, British accent thick now, undeniable. "I've got a break before photo ops. Will you come?"

She nods, speechless.

I watch her wheel away, heart hammering.

What the hell am I doing?

"Peter," I call to my security. "Need a word."

This should be interesting.

Peter leans in as I gesture him closer, eyes already scanning the crowd with professional efficiency.

"Curse," I whisper, accent so thick the word comes out *kuhrs*. "It's the curse."

His expression doesn't change, but something shifts in his posture. Alert. Ready.

"You sure?"

"Look at me." My hands shake as I gesture vaguely at my face. "I'm twenty-six, not seventeen. I don't—this doesn't happen."

"Location?"

"Grand Ballroom foyer. Fifteen minutes."

Peter nods once, already speaking into his wrist comm. "Need the foyer cleared and secured. Twenty minutes. Yes, now."

The code word—half joke, half genuine contingency plan—originated three months ago in Vegas. Jean, normally composed and political, met Levi on set and within a month dragged him to Nevada with the impulsive desperation of a man possessed. Michelle's curse followed two weeks later with Marcus, though at least she waited for a proper engagement.

Mum called it *la malédiction Lambert*—the Lambert curse. When we fall, we fall completely. Catastrophically. No warning, no sense, just absolute certainty.

I briefed my entire team afterward, laughing while I explained. "If I ever use that word, assume I've lost my mind but take it seriously anyway."

They'd nodded, amused but professional.

Nobody's laughing now.

"Color?" Peter asks.

"Blue. Alice costume. Pink wheelchair with—Christ, with stickers all over it. Blonde hair, green eyes." I'm babbling. "Her name's Emily."

"Simone needs to know."

"Tell her." I straighten my jacket, trying to look less unhinged. "Tell everyone. Emily Silver. She's—"

She's mine.

The thought lands with terrifying clarity. I can already see it—summer wedding, probably outdoors because those green eyes deserve natural light. She'd want something intimate, not the massive production my parents would demand. I'd wear gray, maybe charcoal. She'd look stunning in white, blonde waves pinned up with—

"Boss?"

I blink. "Right. Yes. Just... make it happen."

The fifteen minutes crawl. I sign three more autographs on autopilot, British accent so pronounced people keep asking if I'm method-acting. My phone buzzes—Simone confirming the foyer's secure.

When I reach the Grand Ballroom foyer, it's empty except for Emily, positioned near the windows where afternoon light streams through ceiling glass. The convention heat gives way to blessed coolness, air conditioning a relief against my flushed skin.

She's even more radiant here. The natural light catches every strand of blonde, makes her fair skin luminous, turns those green eyes absolutely devastating.

I kneel, bringing myself eye-level with her chair, close enough to catch the faint scent of vanilla and something floral.

Her head tilts, studying my face. Then her hand reaches out, gentle.

"You still have eyeliner under your eyes." Her smile's soft, teasing. She retrieves a wipe from her blue crocheted purse, other hand catching my chin with careful fingers. "I didn't know The Phantom of the Opera wore eyeliner."

The touch—skin against skin, deliberate and tender—sends electricity straight through me.

I chuckle, voice rough. "He had deep-set eyes, *non*?"

"I suppose." She stifles a giggle that makes her whole face glow.

This woman's going to be my wife.

The certainty doesn't scare me anymore.

It feels like coming home.

She leans closer, concentration etched across delicate features as she wipes beneath my eyes with gentle precision. This close, I catch details—faint freckles dusting her nose, the way her blonde waves catch afternoon light streaming through overhead glass, how her tongue peeks between her lips while she works.

Does she feel awkward? This close, with me kneeling beside her chair like some desperate supplicant?

The Quantum lanyard dangles from her wheelchair handle, my face printed on glossy promotional material alongside the lightning bolt logo. Another lanyard loops around her chair—multiple pins clustered together and a name badge. *Emily Silver, Cineplex Theatres*. A ticket taker.

She's been watching my films from behind a podium, tearing stubs and directing crowds.

The realization makes my chest ache.

"There." She sits back, examining her work with a satisfied nod. "Much better. Though I imagine it's difficult keeping that makeup from smudging all day."

"The price of method acting." I flash a grin, watching pink bloom across her cheeks. "Though I confess, Erik's aesthetic requires significant maintenance."

"Worth it." Her voice drops, almost reverent.

Not just a fan. Someone who *sees* the work.

I settle more comfortably on my knees, unwilling to break this bubble we've created. "Tell me something about you. Something real, not just... this." I gesture vaguely at the convention chaos beyond our secured foyer.

She worries her bottom lip between her teeth. "I'm a fashion design student. Utah State University. Graduating in June, actually."

"Fashion?" Interest sparks genuine and immediate. "Specialization?"

"Adaptive wear, mostly. Clothing that's functional and beautiful for people with disabilities." Her fingers trace patterns on her armrest, almost defensive. "The industry ignores us. I want to change that."

Of course she does.

"That's brilliant." The words come out rougher than intended, French bleeding through British precision.

"Genuinely brilliant, Emily. The world needs designers who understand that fashion should be accessible, not exclusive."

The smile she gives me—radiant and surprised—could power entire cities.

"What's your favourite flower?" The question tumbles out unbidden, desperate to know everything about her.

"Poppies." No hesitation. "Red ones. They're delicate but resilient, you know? Beautiful despite—or maybe because of—their fragility."

Red poppies for the wedding.

"Boss." Peter's voice cuts through, apologetic but firm. "Photo op session starts in five. We need to move."

Bloody hell.

I stand reluctantly, already mourning the loss of proximity. "I need to go. Professional obligations and all that rot."

"Of course." She starts wheeling backward, creating distance I don't want.

"Wait." I catch her hand, warmth spreading from the contact. "Your phone. Please."

She blinks, confusion giving way to understanding as she retrieves a pink-cased device from her purse. I input my number quickly, fingers clumsy with urgency.

"I'll text you tonight." Not a question. A promise. "We'll talk properly. Without security hovering or convention schedules dictating every bloody minute."

"You don't have to—"

"I want to." The accent thickens, French overtaking British completely. "*Je veux te connaître.* I want to know you, Emily Silver."

Her emerald eyes widen, lips parting in surprise.

Peter clears his throat. "Boss. Now."

"Are you attending the panel?" The question escapes before Peter can drag me away completely. "The Q&A session?"

"Yes." She tucks blonde waves behind her ear, gesture unconscious and captivating. "With my best friend Ariana. We've been planning it for weeks."

Weeks.

She's been anticipating seeing me, hearing me speak, for *weeks*.

The possessiveness that floods through me—hot and immediate and utterly foreign—must be what Jean feels when Levi walks into a room. What makes Michelle's entire face transform when Marcus texts.

The Lambert curse, alive and thriving in my chest.

"Until later, love." The endearment slips out naturally, accent thick with emotion—British vowels stretched and French undertones curling around consonants. I lift her hand, pressing lips against delicate knuckles in a gesture Dad would approve of. Old-fashioned. Proper.

The sharp intake of her breath makes my pulse race.

Peter practically hauls me toward the photo op room, but my mind's already spinning logistics. General admission panels mean first-come, first seated. Emily and her friend could end up anywhere—back row, side sections, places where I couldn't see those green eyes.

Unacceptable.

"Roger." I snap my fingers the moment we're backstage, surrounded by promotional posters and harried event staff. "Need you immediately."

My assistant appears within seconds, tablet already in hand. "What's happening?"

"Curse." I pace, running fingers through carefully styled hair and destroying the sleek look completely. "It's happening. Emily Silver and Ariana Jennings—find them in the registration system. Move their seats to front row center for the panel. Best sightlines, closest proximity."

Roger's eyebrows climb toward his hairline. "The curse? *The* curse?"

"Don't sound so bloody shocked."

"You've been single for eight months. I assumed you were immune."

"Clearly not." The photo op coordinator waves frantically, trying to get my attention. I ignore her. "Emily Silver. Pink wheelchair, Alice costume, absolute perfection. Make it happen."

"On it." Roger's already typing, professional mask sliding into place despite obvious amusement. "Simone's going to have opinions."

"Simone can schedule around it."

Peter guides me toward the backdrop where fans wait with expensive photo packages, but my phone's already out, scrolling for Gabrielle's contact. The French model I've been casually seeing since the Quantum premiere— beautiful, sophisticated, uncomplicated.

Completely wrong.

Need to talk. Can I call?

Her response comes instantly. **Oui, chéri.**

I step into the hallway, ignoring Peter's disapproving expression. Gabrielle answers on the first ring, voice warm and familiar.

"*Tristian.* Perfect timing. I was thinking we could—"

"I can't see you anymore." The words come out blunt, British accent clipping syllables short. "I've developed feelings for someone else."

Silence stretches painful and heavy.

"Someone else?" Her voice cracks. "We've been sleeping together for months. I thought—*merde*, Tristian, I was falling in love with you."

The guilt hits sharp and immediate, but the possessiveness burning in my chest won't let me backtrack. Can't. Not when Emily's smile is seared into my brain, her vanilla scent still lingering, the warmth of her hand against mine an echo I'm already craving to feel again.

"I'm sorry." And I am—genuinely. "You deserve someone completely devoted. Someone who can give you everything. That's not me anymore."

"Who is she?"

"Someone... unexpected." My free hand traces the Laurent tattoo above my hip, old ink that marked the beginning of everything. "Someone who changes things."

"I see." Gabrielle's breathing turns ragged. "Then I hope she's worth destroying what we had."

"She is."

The certainty in those two words surprises even me.

Gabrielle disconnects without another word. I lean against the wall, phone pressed to my forehead, letting the reality settle.

Twenty minutes ago, I was single, unattached, perfectly content.

Now I'm planning wedding flowers and ending relationships and moving heaven and earth to ensure Emily Silver sits front row center.

The Lambert curse doesn't mess around.

My hands won't stop shaking.

Ariana walks beside me, silent for once, letting me process whatever just happened in that foyer.

Tristian Lambert kissed my hand.

The memory loops endlessly—his lips against my knuckles, accent thick with emotion, those dark eyes holding mine like I'm someone worth seeing.

"Okay." Ariana finally breaks, grabbing my wheelchair handles to stop me mid-aisle. "Spill. Now. Because you're radiating enough giddy energy to power the entire convention center."

"He—" My voice cracks. I clear my throat, trying again. "He asked for my number."

"WHAT?"

Several cosplayers turn to stare. Ariana doesn't care.

"And he kissed my hand, and he called me 'love,' and —" The words tumble out faster, uncontrolled. "His accent got thicker when he said it. British and French mixed together. Ari, I could barely breathe."

"Emily Dorothy Silver." Ariana crouches to my level, brown eyes wide. "Are you telling me that *the* Tristian Lambert is interested in you?"

Don't dream.

The thought surfaces unbidden, sharp and protective. Because this is Tristian Lambert—Hollywood star, international heartthrob, someone who dates supermodels and actresses. Someone completely out of reach for a girl in a pink wheelchair who grew up unwanted.

"He's probably just being nice." I force the words out even though they taste bitter. "Meeting fans, making people feel special. That's his job."

"Did it feel like a job?"

No. It felt like gravity shifting, like finding solid ground after years of falling.

But admitting that seems dangerous.

Instead, I wheel toward a vendor booth plastered with Tristian's face—promotional shots from Quantum, artistic prints from his Mad Hatter role, candid photographs that someone with a telephoto lens captured. My credit card comes out before rational thought kicks in.

"One of each," I tell the vendor.

Ariana laughs, delighted. "You're gone. Absolutely wrecked."

"Shut up." But I'm smiling as the vendor rolls posters into protective tubes. "I've been a fan for years. This is normal."

"You literally met him twenty minutes ago and he gave you his *personal number*. Nothing about this is normal."

She's right. The phone number is proof that something shifted. Changed. Became possible when it should've stayed fantasy.

The thought surfaces cruel and automatic. Because Tristian Lambert could have anyone. Perfect Bethany from theater with her flawless skin and confident laugh. Gabrielle Moreau, the French model the tabloids linked him to. Someone whole, someone who doesn't navigate the world on wheels, someone who fits the narrative of what a Hollywood romance should look like.

"Emily." Ariana's hand covers mine, gentle pressure grounding me. "I can see you spiraling. Stop."

"I'm not—"

"You are." She squeezes once, firm. "And we're going to that panel, and you're going to let yourself enjoy whatever this is. Even if it's just a beautiful moment. Okay?"

My phone buzzes before I can answer. Unknown number.

Front row center is reserved for you and Ariana. Just show up. —T

The vendor hands over my bag of merchandise—Tristian's face repeated across glossy paper, frozen in moments I'll probably frame. My heart hammers against my ribs.

"Ari." I show her the text with trembling hands. "He reserved seats."

"Of course he did." She grins, wicked and knowing. "Boy's smitten."

We make our way toward the Grand Ballroom, weaving through crowds of cosplayers and excited fans. The ADA entrance has a short line—mostly wheelchair users and their companions waiting for priority access. I recognize a few volunteers from earlier, the same ones who helped me navigate the registration chaos yesterday.

One of them—a college-aged guy with a FanCon staff badge—spots me and practically sprints over.

"Emily Silver?"

"Um. Yes?"

"You're on the VIP list." He checks his tablet, grinning. "Mr. Lambert specifically requested front row center placement for you and your guest. Follow me."

Ariana mouths *holy shit* as we're escorted past the general admission line. Jealous stares follow us, but the volunteer chatters excitedly, clearly thrilled to be part of whatever's unfolding.

"He's never done this before," the volunteer confides as we enter the ballroom. "I've worked celebrity panels for three years. They're always professional, friendly, but distant. This?" He gestures toward the reserved section with its perfect sightlines and proximity to the stage. "This is Lambert family possessiveness showing up."

"Lambert family what?"

"Oh, you don't know?" Another volunteer—a woman with purple hair—joins us, eyes bright with gossip. "The Lamberts have this reputation. When they fall, they fall *hard*. Completely obsessive in the best way. It's like a family curse."

My stomach flips. "That's just tabloid nonsense."

"Maybe." Purple-hair pulls out her phone, expression turning conspiratorial. "But he literally texted his girlfriend and ended things. Like, thirty minutes ago. And she already sold the recording."

She turns the screen toward me. Gabrielle Moreau's voice fills the space between us, accented and breaking.

"Who is she?"

Tristian's response comes clear and certain, British vowels stretched with emotion.

"Someone unexpected. Someone who changes things."

"Then I hope she's worth destroying what we had."

"She is."

The recording cuts off. Purple-hair's grin stretches wide.

"Girl, he's talking about *you*."

The sizzle reel plays across three massive screens—footage from my films cut together with precision, building energy. The Mad Hatter's fractured laughter. Nathan Cross shifting mid-battle, bones cracking as raptor DNA rewrites his skeleton. Marcus Reid from Quantum phasing through dimensions, each jump costing him pieces of his humanity.

I watch from backstage, searching the crowd through the gap in the curtains.

There. Front row center, exactly where I asked them to place her.

Emily sits in her decorated pink wheelchair, Ariana beside her clutching what looks like several rolled posters. Even from here, I notice the way Emily leans forward, eyes fixed on the screens, completely absorbed. Her Alice dress catches the light—periwinkle fabric and white apron handmade with a skill that makes my chest tight.

The crowd's energy builds as the reel hits its crescendo. Phantom footage—Erik's mask cracking, revealing scarred flesh beneath. My performance raw and desperate, channeling every moment of feeling like a monster pretending to be human.

The screens cut to black.

Silence stretches for three perfect seconds.

Then the ballroom erupts.

"TRISTIAN! TRISTIAN! TRISTIAN!"

The chant shakes the walls. Two thousand voices united, screaming my name like a summoning spell. I wait for the peak—that moment when the energy maxes out and needs somewhere to go—then step through the curtains.

The roar intensifies. Camera flashes transform the ballroom into a constellation, blinding and beautiful. I find Emily immediately, needing to know if she's really there, if this moment exists beyond fantasy.

She's clapping, eyes bright with something that looks like wonder.

I grab the microphone from its stand, letting the crowd's energy wash over me.

"Salt Lake City!" My voice carries over the speakers, British accent pronounced from adrenaline. "Bloody hell, you lot know how to make an entrance."

Laughter ripples through the ballroom. I pace the stage, feeding off their excitement, letting it ground me.

"No moderator today," I continue. "Just you, me, and whatever chaos emerges. Sound good?"

More cheers. I grin, feeling the familiar rush of performing—except Emily's presence changes the equation. Makes it matter differently.

Questions start flowing. Someone asks about Alice in Wonderland, the darker interpretation I fought the studio to protect.

"May release," I confirm. " This Hatter lived through trauma, survived by fracturing himself into pieces. When Alice shows up, he has to choose—stay broken and safe, or risk becoming whole again."

I catch Emily's expression shift, recognition flickering across her features like she understands something essential.

A teenager asks about Phantom. I lean against the stage edge, close enough that front row attendees could touch me if they reached.

"Just wrapped filming the 1925 remake. We went back to Leroux's novel—Erik as tragic monster, not romantic hero. The Opera Ghost who lives beneath beauty, creating art from darkness." My fingers trace absent patterns on the microphone. "He's a reminder that isolation doesn't make you special. It just makes you alone."

More questions. Quantum sequels. Whether Marcus survives the ninth film. I deflect with practiced charm, protecting spoilers while feeding their enthusiasm.

Then someone brings up Extinction Protocol: Singularity, and the ballroom's energy shifts—younger fans screaming, older ones laughing at the ridiculous premise executed with absolute sincerity.

"Nathan Cross," I start, letting my accent thicken for effect. "Half-raptor shifter paleontologist who becomes pack alpha and claims his brilliant assistant as his mate. Intellectual meets instinct. Science collides with primal need."

"DID YOU KEEP THE CLAWS?" someone shouts from the back.

"CGI prosthetics, love. But the half-transformed state at the end?" I mime claws extending. "That was practical effects. Fangs, scales, claws—Nathan choosing a form that honors both sides of his nature instead of picking one."

Ariana's laugh carries from the front row, delighted. Emily shakes her head, grinning like she can't believe I'm discussing dinosaur shifter films with genuine enthusiasm.

The Q&A line forms. Standard questions about upcoming projects, favorite roles, advice for aspiring actors. I answer on autopilot, watching Emily watch me, wondering what she sees.

Then she's at the microphone.

My heart stops.

"Your characters often deal with isolation," Emily says, voice clear despite the ballroom's size. "The Phantom, Marcus in the Quantum films, and from what you're saying about the Hatter—is that intentional?"

The question cuts through my carefully constructed performance persona, reaching something true underneath. I step closer to the stage edge, needing to see her properly.

"That's..." I pause, British vowels stretching as emotion surfaces. "That's incredibly perceptive."

The ballroom goes quiet, sensing the shift.

"I don't think I realized it until you asked." My grip tightens on the microphone. "But yes. Every character I'm drawn to lives apart somehow. Different. Separated by circumstance or choice or just—" I gesture vaguely. "—being something the world doesn't quite have space for."

Emily's green eyes hold mine, understanding passing between us like shared language.

"Maybe that's what performance is," I continue, speaking to her now instead of the crowd. "Finding the universal in isolation. Making loneliness visible so someone watching realizes they're not the only one feeling it."

Her smile breaks slow and devastating.

The moment stretches. Two thousand people disappear. Just her, and the truth I didn't mean to confess.

Chapter 3: Video Calls and Red Poppies

The hotel suite feels too quiet after the ballroom's chaos. I strip off my shirt, letting it fall somewhere between the bed and bathroom, then pause at the full-length mirror.

The tattoos map my career across my torso like a twisted resume. On my left shoulder blade, "Hatter" curves in Victorian script, still tender from two weeks ago. The artist in Vancouver understood the assignment—making it look handwritten by someone losing their grip on sanity.

"Erik" stretches across my ribs on the right side in Gothic lettering, taking three sessions to complete. The Phantom's real name, not the monster everyone sees. That one bled more than usual, right over bone, but it felt appropriate for a character who lives in constant agony.

My left forearm bears the Quantum symbol—an infinity loop intersected by a lightning bolt—with "Miles Reid" underneath in sleek, futuristic font. Marketing loved that detail when it leaked to social media.

But the one that makes me trace my fingers over it sits just above my hip bone: "Laurent" in faded gray ink that looks older than it is. *Dans l'Ombre*—a psychological horror film I shot in Marseille before Hollywood found me. Nobody stateside has heard of it, which makes the tattoo feel like a secret. Laurent was a lighthouse keeper who slowly realized he'd been dead for thirty years, his isolation the only thing keeping him tethered to existence.

I study my reflection properly. Same dark brown hair, same athletic build I maintain through relentless studio training sessions. Same face that photographs well from every angle, according to Simone's marketing obsessions.

But something's different.

The way my chest tightens when I think about Emily's smile. How my pulse quickened when our eyes met across the ballroom. The certainty settling into my bones like muscle memory from a role I've rehearsed my entire life without knowing it.

The Lambert curse.

Jean fell for Levi after one month. Watched him play the March Hare opposite my Hatter and just—knew. Michelle met Marcus at Jean's engagement party, and within weeks she was texting Dad about wedding venues. Mum swears she recognized Dad the moment he walked into her university lecture hall, grandmère claims grandpère's first words to her rewrote her entire future.

All-consuming. Absolute. The kind of romance that makes logical people throw away logic.

I've been waiting for it. Expecting it. The family legacy I couldn't inherit because I kept choosing wrong partners, kept forcing connections that felt pleasant but never transcendent. Gabrielle's face flashes through my mind— beautiful, sophisticated, completely fine. We had fun. That was the problem. Just fun. Nothing that made my accent thicken from emotion or my hands shake from need.

Emily asked one question and dismantled my carefully constructed performance persona. Saw through to something I didn't know I was revealing.

I step into the shower, letting scalding water pound against muscles tight from maintaining stage presence. My mind keeps circling back to the accessible seating arrangement, how right it felt to make sure she had the best view. How I paced backstage just to catch glimpses of her reactions.

The new tradition surfaces unbidden. Jean's already planning where Levi's name will go, probably something artistic that matches his Hollywood aesthetic. Michelle and Marcus haven't decided yet, but she's been researching artists.

I haven't earned that privilege. Not after three hours and one conversation, no matter how my entire nervous system insists otherwise.

But the thought won't leave.

Where would Emily's name belong?

My ribs already hold Erik's Gothic letters. The shoulder blade claims Hatter's Victorian madness. My forearm displays Quantum's sci-fi precision. Laurent hides near my hip, secret and personal.

Emily deserves something different. Not a character I performed but a truth I'm living.

Maybe over my heart, simple and clean. Maybe along my inner wrist where I'd see it constantly. Somewhere that acknowledges this isn't fiction, isn't a role I'll eventually wrap and move past.

I scrub shampoo through my hair, British vowels slipping into my internal monologue the way they always do when emotions run high.

You've lost your bloody mind. One conversation. One question.

But the Lambert curse doesn't care about logic or reasonable timelines. It just—happens. Recognition like lightning, certainty like gravity.

I rinse off, already planning. Not the tattoo, not yet. That's premature, presumptuous, potentially insane.

But I need to see her again. Actually see her, beyond convention chaos and crowds. Learn what makes her laugh, what she dreams about, whether she feels this same magnetic pull or if I'm just another actor she admired from a distance.

My phone buzzes on the bathroom counter. A text from an unknown number lights the screen.

Thank you for the seating arrangement. That was incredibly kind. - Emily

My hands shake reading it.

Yeah. The curse found me.

Finally.

I flop onto the bed, still damp from the shower, and stare at Emily's text. The words blur as I read them three times, four, searching for subtext that probably isn't there.

Screw it.

I tap her contact—already saved with a little pink wheelchair emoji I added without thinking—and hit the video call button before logic can interfere.

One ring. Two. My heart hammers against my ribs like it's trying to escape. This is ridiculous. I've done intimate scenes with A-list actresses, performed Shakespeare in front of thousands, walked red carpets broadcast to millions.

She answers on the third ring.

The screen fills with blonde hair hanging in damp waves, emerald eyes widening in surprise. She's propped against pillows in what looks like a hotel bed, wearing an oversized gray t-shirt with the Quantum symbol stretched across her chest.

"You're wearing my film."

Pink floods her cheeks. "I—yes. Ariana bought it. Earlier. After we talked."

"Looks better on you than the promotional posters." My accent's thickening already, British vowels sliding into place. I clear my throat. "Just got out of the shower. Needed to wash off the convention grime."

"Same." She touches her wet hair self-consciously. "It's exhausting, all those people."

"You handled the crowd brilliantly. Most people freeze when I kneel down like that, but you just—" I gesture vaguely, searching for words that won't sound completely mad. "You were present. Real."

"I didn't know what else to be."

God, she's going to wreck me.

"Tell me something." I shift against the headboard, trying to look casual despite my pulse racing. "The isolation theme you mentioned. How long have you been analyzing my work like that?"

"Since I first watched *Dans l'Ombre*." Her fingers trace patterns on her blanket, a nervous gesture I file away to remember. "I was sixteen, stuck in a group home with terrible internet. Someone had uploaded it with English subtitles to this sketchy streaming site. Laurent's story just —it resonated."

"Not exactly light viewing for a teenager."

"Neither was my life." She says it simply, without self-pity. "The lighthouse keeper who didn't realize he was dead? Who kept performing his duties in isolation because that's all he knew? I understood that. The routine that becomes prison."

My chest tightens. "Emily—"

The door behind her swings open. A woman with a high bun and visible tattoos on her hands bursts into frame, eyes widening when she spots the phone.

"Ari, no—" Emily starts, but her roommate's already snatching the device.

Ariana's face fills the screen, brown eyes narrowed with protective suspicion. "Tristian Lambert. Hollywood star. Probably dates supermodels."

"Ariana!" Emily's voice comes from off-screen, mortified.

"She's my best friend." Ariana props the phone against something—a lamp maybe—so both of them are visible now. Emily looks like she wants to sink through the mattress. "So here's how this works. You don't get to play with her heart because you're bored between projects."

"I wouldn't—"

"Let me finish." Ariana crosses tattooed arms. "Emily's the kindest person I know. She's brilliant and talented and deserves someone who sees that. Not someone looking for a cute story to tell on talk shows."

"Ari, please—" Emily reaches for the phone but Ariana holds it out of range.

"She's been through more than you can imagine. Foster care, abuse, people who treated her like she was disposable. So if you're just being nice because she's a fan, or because you think disabled girls are easy targets, you can take your accent and your tattoos and—"

"Ariana!" Emily's face burns crimson. "Give me my phone!"

"I'm serious." Ariana's voice drops, deadly serious despite the absurdity of threatening an actor through video chat. "You hurt her, and I don't care how famous you are. I will end you. I know people."

"You know the barista at Beans & Brew," Emily mutters.

"Jason's very loyal. He'd help me hide a body."

I should be offended. Should probably end the call, tell Simone about this bizarre interaction, laugh it off with Roger over drinks.

Instead, I smile.

"You're a good friend." I meet Ariana's eyes through the screen. "Emily's lucky to have someone protecting her like this."

That seems to throw her. "You're not angry?"

"Why would I be? You love her." The words come easy, natural. "I respect that. If someone I cared about was taking calls from strange actors, I'd give the same speech."

"He's not strange," Emily protests weakly.

"I'm definitely strange." I shift so they can see my face better. "I tattoo character names on my body and sing show tunes in the shower. I'm terrified of pigeons. I once cried during a dog food commercial."

Ariana's mouth twitches. "The one with the senior dog and the shelter?"

"Gets me every time."

"Okay." She hands the phone back to Emily, who clutches it like a lifeline. "You get one chance, Lambert. Don't waste it."

"Ariana—" Emily's voice carries warning.

"Oh my God, Mochi!" Emily shoves at something off-screen as a massive white blur launches onto the bed. Both girls groan, then dissolve into giggles as a fluffy labradoodle face shoves into frame, tongue lolling.

"Mochi, down." Emily's trying for stern but ruins it by laughing. "Say hi to the nice movie star."

The dog pants happily at the camera, curly white fur everywhere.

"Why didn't you bring him to the con today?" I lean closer to the screen, studying the labradoodle's friendly face. "He's brilliant."

"Tomorrow's Saturday." Emily scratches behind Mochi's ears absently. "Busiest day. My social anxiety will be out in full force, so he's coming with me. Wearing his 'ask before petting' vest disguised as cosplay to match mine."

"Match how?"

Her smile turns mysterious. "You'll just have to see tomorrow. At three. At the photo op."

"You bought tickets?" Something warm spreads through my chest.

"The second they were available. Five months ago." Pink creeps up her neck. "You were the first major announcement, right after Quantum 3 became a hit. I set three alarms so I wouldn't miss the sale."

Five months. Before we'd ever met, before I knew she existed, she was planning this.

"What hotel are you staying at?" The question tumbles out before I can second-guess it. "Room number?"

Ariana's eyebrows shoot up, but Emily answers without hesitation. "The Grand America. Room 847."

"Same hotel." My mind's already racing through possibilities. "Different floor."

"Fancy." Ariana stage-whispers. "He's probably in the penthouse."

"Presidential suite," I correct absently, still watching Emily's face. "Roger books everything. I just show up."

Mochi shifts, settling his massive head on Emily's lap. She strokes his fur with practiced affection, the gesture so natural it makes my throat tight.

"I should let you go." I don't want to. Want to keep her on this screen, keep hearing her voice, keep watching the way she unconsciously smiles when she's comfortable. "You need rest before tomorrow's chaos."

"Probably." But she doesn't move to end the call.

"Three o'clock then."

"Three o'clock."

We stare at each other through our screens like teenagers, neither wanting to hang up first. Ariana rolls her eyes dramatically.

"Okay, this is painful. Goodnight, movie star." She reaches over and ends the call.

The screen goes dark.

I flop back against the pillows, phone clutched to my chest.

Merde.

I'm in love.

Completely, irrevocably, insanely in love with a girl I've known for less than a day. A girl who analyzed my character choices with more insight than professional critics. Who makes me nervous and excited and desperate to be better than I am.

My phone buzzes. Roger's text lights the screen.

Moved future wife to front of photo op line tomorrow. You have 5 minutes alone time before general admission starts. Don't waste it.

He's seen the curse in person—watched Jean transform from sensible politician to lovesick fool within weeks of meeting Levi. Roger knows the signs.

I pull up his contact.

Send poppies to Room 847, Grand America. Red ones.

Three dots appear immediately.

How many?

All of them. Every red poppy in Salt Lake City.

The dots pause, then continue.

On it. Anything else?

I hesitate, thinking of Emily's emerald eyes, the way she lit up talking about fashion design.

Actually—find a diadem. Made of diamond poppies. Something a fashion student would appreciate. Send that too.

You've lost your mind.

Completely. Make it happen.

This is why I get paid the big bucks.

Chapter 4: Ratatouille for Two

Saturday drags like time itself has decided to mock me. Morning autograph session, panel discussion, press interviews—all of it blurs into background noise. Every time I glance at my phone, it's still not three o'clock.

Roger catches me checking again during a photo with fans dressed as Quantum characters.

"You're pathetic," he mutters as the group files out.

"Aware."

Two forty-five. Fifteen minutes.

My leg bounces under the table. Peter shoots me a look from his position by the door.

"Moving to photo op setup," he announces. "General admission starts at 3:15."

Which means Emily arrives at three. Five minutes alone, Roger promised.

The convention center's photo op area is organized chaos—backdrops, lighting equipment, photographers adjusting cameras. I position myself center frame, running through possible conversation starters. Too eager. Too casual. Too—

"Mr. Lambert?" The volunteer at check-in waves. "Your VIP is here."

She wheels through the entrance, and my brain short-circuits.

Christine Daaé. The 1925 silent film version, complete with drop-waist dress in pale pink, pearls draped across her chest, vintage headpiece catching the lights. But it's Mochi who steals the show—the labradoodle wears a miniature naval uniform, complete with officer's cap perched between his fluffy ears.

"Raoul." I drop to one knee as they approach, addressing the dog with mock solemnity. "You've been promoted to Vicomte, I see."

Mochi interprets this as an invitation. He lunges forward, enormous paws landing on my shoulders, tongue assault commencing.

"Mochi, down!" Emily's laughing, tugging his vest. "You're supposed to be dignified—"

I'm laughing too hard to care about the drool on my shirt. Mochi's tail whips back and forth, entire body wiggling with joy as he bathes my face in enthusiastic kisses.

"Good boy." I scratch behind his ears, earning another wet lick across my cheek. "Excellent judge of character."

"I'm so sorry—"

"Don't be." I straighten, wiping my face with my sleeve. "He's perfect. You're perfect. This costume—Christine from the silent film?"

"You recognize it." Her smile could power the entire convention center. "Most people only know the stage version or the 2004 film."

I move closer, studying the period-accurate details. "You made this?"

"Mochi's uniform too. His vest underneath says 'ask before petting,' but the naval coat covers it for photos."

Brilliant. Beautiful and brilliant.

"Emily." My heart hammers. "The convention ends at seven. Would you—I'd like to take you to dinner. A proper date. Or—" Better idea strikes. "Come to my suite? I'll make you dinner. Mum's ratatouille. We can watch movies in pajamas, no cameras, no crowds. Just us."

Pink floods her cheeks. "You cook?"

"I'm Angoumois. We're born knowing how to cook."

"Then yes." She bites her lip, emerald eyes sparkling. "I'd love that."

"Photo time!" The photographer calls. "What pose are we doing?"

I extend my hand to Emily. "May I?"

She nods, and I gently lift her from the wheelchair, settling her against my chest. She weighs nothing, fits perfectly in my arms. Her hand rests against my shoulder as I gaze down at her, the classic Phantom pose—Erik holding Christine, that moment before the mask comes off.

The camera flashes.

"Beautiful!" The photographer checks his screen. "Mr. Lambert, you want copies?"

"Roger, get me copies of that." I don't look away from Emily's face. "Multiple prints. Digital files. Everything

Seven-fifteen. Emily arrives at eight.

I stare at the ingredients arranged on the suite's kitchenette counter—eggplant, zucchini, tomatoes, bell peppers, garlic, herbs. Everything for Mum's ratatouille. My hands won't stop shaking.

This is ridiculous. I've cooked this dish a hundred times. But suddenly the measurements escape me, the timing feels wrong, and I can't remember if the basil goes in first or last.

My phone sits on the marble surface, screen dark. Taunting.

I snatch it up and open the video call app, selecting Jean's contact. Then Marcus. Group call. My finger hovers over the button.

Three-fifteen in the morning in Grantham Bridge. Eight-fifteen in New Orleans.

I press it anyway.

Jean's face appears first, hair disheveled, reading glasses perched on his nose. His home office bookshelves loom behind him in the dim lamplight. "Tris? What's wrong? Are you hurt?"

"No, I—"

Marcus pops into frame, street lights glowing behind him. He's walking, phone jostling. "Hold up, this better be good. I'm carrying gumbo and it's hot."

"Where's Michelle?" I pace the suite, phone gripped tight.

"Right here." Michelle's face joins the split screen, her model-perfect features relaxed without makeup. Marcus's New Orleans apartment shows behind her—exposed brick, vintage posters. "Tristian, it's the middle of the night here."

"It's three in the morning for Jean!"

Jean removes his glasses, pinching the bridge of his nose. "Yes, which is why I'm assuming someone died."

"Nobody died. The opposite. I—" The words tumble out. "I broke up with Gabrielle."

Silence.

Then Michelle: "Thank God."

"Finally," Marcus adds. "That woman had the personality of cardboard."

Jean leans back in his leather chair, a slow smile spreading. "And you're panicking because...?"

"The curse struck." I set the phone against the backsplash so they can see me properly. "I met her yesterday. Emily. She's a fashion student at Utah State, graduates in June, specializes in adaptive wear, has a service dog named Mochi—this massive white labradoodle who's the friendliest creature alive. Her roommate Ariana has like sixty tattoos and threatened to end me if I hurt Emily, which I respect completely. Emily's brilliant, she analyzed my character patterns during the panel and saw things I'd never consciously noticed, and she made this 1925 Christine Daaé costume by hand that was museum-quality, and—"

"Breathe," Jean commands.

I gulp air. "She's coming here. Tonight. Eight o'clock. First date. I'm making ratatouille and we're watching movies in pajamas and I can't remember if Mum puts the basil in first or last."

Michelle's grin could light up a runway. "What does she look like?"

"Blonde hair, hip-length, these waves that catch light. Emerald eyes—actual emerald, not hazel or green-ish. Fair skin with this rosy undertone. Heart-shaped face, full pink lips. She uses a pink power wheelchair, decorated with stickers. She's beautiful, Michelle. The kind of beautiful that makes you forget how to form sentences."

Marcus shifts his phone, and I glimpse paper bags of food. "Hold up. You met her *yesterday* and you're already at the cooking-her-dinner stage?"

"Yes."

"And you're certain." Jean's tone shifts, understanding dawning. "Not infatuated. Not intrigued. Certain."

"Like Dad was certain about Mum. Like you were about Levi."

Jean sets down his glasses entirely. "Merde."

"It's happening," Michelle whispers. "The Lambert curse strikes again."

"It's not a curse if it's real." But my hands still shake. "I gave her my number after five minutes. Moved her seats to front row. Sent her flowers and a diamond diadem. Today I invited her here instead of taking her somewhere public because I want her to myself. No cameras, no crowds, nobody else looking at her." The possessiveness surging through my veins should terrify me. Instead it feels right. "I want to know everything. Her favorite books, what she dreams about, why she chose adaptive fashion, what made her smile before we met. I want—"

"To keep her." Michelle finishes, voice soft. "Tris, that's how it works for us."

"Dad won't leave Mum's side for more than necessary," Jean agrees. "I follow Levi to sets across the world. Michelle literally restructures her modeling schedule around Marcus's assignments."

"We're possessive creatures when we love," Marcus says. He's stopped walking, face serious despite the beignet-dusted paper bag. "Question is, does Emily know what she's getting into?"

"She knows I'm interested. She said yes to tonight."

"That's not what he means." Jean leans forward, dark brown eyes intense in the lamplight. "Does she understand that once a Lambert claims someone, we don't let go? That you'll rearrange your entire life around her? That you'll be —" He pauses, searching for the word. "Utterly devoted to the point of absurdity?"

Movement behind Jean. Levi appears in frame, wearing pajama pants and nothing else, light blue eyes sleepy but curious. His short dark brown hair sticks up at odd angles, his beard slightly mussed. He drapes himself over Jean's shoulders, muscular arms encircling his husband's chest.

"Are we telling Tristian he's going to be insufferable now?" Levi's voice carries that Ohio warmth. "Because you were insufferable, babe. Still are, actually."

"Says the man who flew to Angoumois every weekend for two months."

"You're proving my point." Levi grins at me through the screen. "Listen, Tris—just be honest with her. Emily, right? Tell her you're intense. Tell her it's a family trait. Give her the choice."

"The basil goes in last," Jean adds. "And use fresh, not dried."

"Seven-thirty," Michelle announces. "You need to start cooking. Go. We want updates."

"Lots of updates," Marcus agrees. "Photos. The whole thing."

The call ends, leaving me alone with vegetables and racing thoughts.

Honest. I can do honest.

I grab the cutting board and start dicing eggplant, letting muscle memory take over. The rhythm steadies me —slice, dice, repeat. Garlic next, minced fine. Oil heating in the pan.

My phone buzzes. Emily: *Leaving now! Should I bring anything?*

Me: *Just yourself. And Mochi if you want.*

Emily: *He's coming. He insisted.*

I smile at the screen, that possessive warmth spreading through my chest again. Mine. She's going to be mine.

The basil sits waiting on the counter. Last, after everything else has melded together.

Some things are worth waiting for.

The knock arrives precisely at eight.

I wipe my hands on a towel and cross to the door, heart hammering like it did opening night of *Dans l'Ombre*. Worse, actually. At least I'd had months to prepare for that premiere.

Emily waits in the hallway, and every coherent thought evacuates my brain.

She wears Dorothy pajamas—blue gingham set that matches her wheelchair decorations. The top buttons in the front, short-sleeved, paired with matching shorts. But it's the diadem nestled in those blonde waves that destroys me. Red poppies catching the light, diamonds glittering against her hair.

She wore it. She's actually wearing something I gave her.

"Too much?" Her cheeks flush pink. "Ari said it was too much for pajamas, but—"

"You're perfect." The words scrape out rough. "Absolutely perfect."

Mochi launches from her lap, white curly fur flying as he bounds toward me. Seventy pounds of enthusiastic labradoodle connects with my chest, tongue swiping across my jaw in sloppy kisses.

"Down, Mochi!" Emily's voice carries mortification. "Sorry, he's—he remembers you from earlier."

"Good boy." I scratch behind his floppy ears, letting him lick my face. "Hello to you too, mate."

Emily navigates inside, wheels smooth against the hardwood. Her emerald eyes sweep the suite—taking in the living area, the dining table set with Mum's good china that I demanded hotel staff find somewhere, the covered dishes waiting.

"It smells amazing." She parks near the table. "Like... herbs and garlic and something sweet?"

"Ratatouille, fresh baguettes, and crème brûlée for after." I close the door, suddenly nervous in my own space. "Nothing fancy, just—"

"You made crème brûlée?" Those eyes widen. "That's not 'nothing fancy,' that's—Tristian, that's incredible."

"Mum taught me." I move to the table, lifting covers. "Said any proper Angoumoisz boy should know how to cook for someone important."

The blush deepens. She's important. The word settles between us, heavier than I intended.

Mochi sniffs toward the kitchen, nose working overtime.

"I made steak and chicken for him." I grab the dog bowls I'd requested. "Figured he'd want proper dinner too."

"You didn't have to—"

"I wanted to." The truth tastes simple. "Everything I do tonight, I want to do."

Emily watches me arrange Mochi's food, something soft crossing her features. Gratitude, maybe. Or surprise that someone thought of her dog as more than an accessory.

We settle at the table—Emily transferring from wheelchair to the upholstered chair with practiced ease. I serve the ratatouille, golden vegetables glistening in tomato sauce, fresh basil scattered on top like Mum always does.

"Bon appétit," I murmur.

Emily takes a bite, eyes closing. A small sound escapes her throat—pleasure and contentment mixed together. That noise shoots straight through me, possessive heat coiling low in my gut.

Mine. She's making that sound because of something I created.

"This is—" She opens her eyes, catching me staring. "Tristian, this is the best ratatouille I've ever had."

"You've had ratatouille before?"

"Once, at this French restaurant in Salt Lake for my birthday last year. Ari saved up." She takes another bite, savoring. "But this is different. Better. There's something... I don't know, warmer about it?"

"Mum's secret is the time. Most people rush it. She lets each vegetable cook properly before adding the next, building flavor." I tear off a piece of baguette. "And love, she always says. You have to cook with love."

Emily's gaze drops to her plate, blonde waves hiding her expression.

"Tell me about your family," I prompt, desperate to know everything. "I know Michelle's engaged to Marcus— saw that in *People Magazine*. And Jean's running again?"

"You follow politics?" Surprise colors her voice.

"Hard not to when it's your family." I sip wine—a Côtes du Rhône that pairs perfectly with the vegetables. "Jean's running for his second term in the Angoumois Assemblée. Dad's up for reelection too, naturally. They want me to come campaign, make appearances, be the 'success story of Lambert ambition.'"

"But you don't want to."

Sharp girl. I love how she reads between lines.

"I left at nineteen to escape that world. Politics, expectations, the dynasty Dad built." The old resentment surfaces, bitter on my tongue. "I never fit. Jean thrives on policy and speeches. Michelle conquered modeling on her own terms. I just wanted to act, to become other people, to disappear into characters."

"That's why Laurent meant so much." Not a question. Emily traces her fork through sauce. "Your first escape."

"Alfred and Colette—our butler and head housekeeper—they raised us more than Dad and Mum did. Nappies, scraped knees, homework help, everything. Alfred taught me to cook, actually. Said I had the hands for it." I flex my fingers, remembering. "When I told him about Marseille, about the film, he slipped me money Dad didn't know about. Colette packed my bags while Dad shouted that I was ruining the family legacy."

"But you went anyway."

"Best decision I ever made." I meet her eyes. "Until meeting you."

Pink floods her cheeks again. She ducks her head, hair cascading forward.

"What about you?" I lean back, deliberately casual. "You mentioned foster care?"

"Since I was five." Her voice goes quiet. "My birth parents died in a car accident. No other family wanted a kid with cerebral palsy, I guess. So I went into the system."

Rage sparks hot in my chest. "Didn't want—"

"It's fine. I'm used to it." But her hands tighten around her fork. "Bounced between homes until I aged out at eighteen. Most were... not great. Some were actively terrible. But I survived, got into USU on scholarship, met Ari freshman year. She's the only real friend I've ever had."

"Emily—"

"It made me stronger." She raises her chin, defiant. "Made me fight for what I want. Like adaptive fashion. Like making clothes that help people feel beautiful regardless of disability. Like—"

She cuts off, but I hear what she doesn't say. Like believing she deserves good things.

I reach across the table, covering her hand with mine. Her skin feels soft, delicate against my palm. And there— raised ridges beneath my fingers. Scars.

Everything in me goes still.

"What's this?" I turn her wrist gently, exposing white lines crisscrossing her forearm.

"Nothing. Old injuries."

"From what?" The growl in my voice surprises us both.

"Foster homes." She tries to pull away, but I hold firm —gentle but unyielding. "Some parents got creative with punishments. Closets, belts, whatever worked. It's ancient history, Tristian. They healed years ago."

Ancient history. As if that makes it acceptable. As if someone laid hands on what's mine and I should just—

Stop. She's not yours yet. Don't scare her.

I release her wrist, breathing through the protective fury searing my veins. "I'm sorry that happened to you."

"Not your fault."

"No." I pick up my wine, needing something to do with my hands besides hunt down every person who hurt her. "But I'm still sorry."

Mochi wanders over, resting his head on Emily's lap. She strokes his ears, grounding herself.

I'll call Roger tomorrow. There are specialists in Beverly Hills who work miracles with scar revision. Laser treatments, surgery if needed. As future Mrs. Lambert—

Christ, I'm already planning that far ahead.

But looking at Emily in my suite, wearing the diadem I sent, eating food I made, trusting me with her past—yeah. Future Mrs. Lambert doesn't seem premature at all.

It seems inevitable.

I clear the dishes while Emily plays with Mochi on the floor, his tail wagging so hard his whole back end wiggles.

Watching them together—her laugh bright and unguarded, his devotion absolute—something shifts in my chest.

"Come on." I scoop Emily into my arms before she can protest, wheelchair left behind. She weighs nothing, all delicate bones and soft curves against my chest. "We're watching films."

"Tristian—"

"Shh." I carry her to the king bed, setting her gently against the mountain of pillows. "Tonight you don't argue. Tonight you let someone take care of you."

Her emerald eyes shine wet. Nobody's done this before, I realize. Nobody's just carried her to bed and tucked her in like she matters.

I pull the duvet up around her, then carefully remove the poppy diadem from her hair. The blonde waves tumble loose, cascading over white pillows. My fingers itch to touch, to see if those strands feel as silky as they look.

"What are we watching?" I grab the remote, settling beside her. Mochi launches onto the bed, curling across both our laps like he owns us.

"You'll laugh."

"Try me."

Emily bites her lip, shy again. "The Wonderful Wizard of Oz. The 1940s Starlight Studios version."

My eyebrows shoot up. "That's your favorite? Not some indie French film?"

"My middle name is Dorothy." Her voice goes soft, vulnerable. "After Dorothy Gale. My mom loved that movie. It's the only thing I really know about her, you know? That she loved Oz enough to name me after it."

Christ. I pull her closer, needing her against my side. "Then we're watching Oz."

She queues it up on the streaming service, and the familiar Starlight Studios logo fills the screen—the same company producing *Alice*. The opening credits roll in that gorgeous Technicolor, vibrant even eighty years later.

Emily knows every line. Every song. Her lips move silently along with Dorothy's dialogue, and when Frances Gale starts singing tears slip down Emily's cheeks.

I wipe them away with my thumb, saying nothing.

"I've seen the stage musical Wonderful on YouTube about a million times," she whispers during a quiet moment. "The 2005 one, based on Jeremy Corbyn's novel? It's beautiful. Tells Dorothy's whole backstory, her life in Kansas, how she becomes this brave hero. There's a prince named Felix who gets turned into the Scarecrow, and he's her love interest, and—" She stops, embarrassed. "Sorry. I'm rambling."

"Don't apologize." My mind spins. Roger's been pushing me to audition for *Wonderful* for weeks. The film adaptation, big-budget musical, perfect follow-up to *Alice*. I kept refusing because musicals felt too far outside my comfort zone.

But Felix. Dorothy's love interest. A prince transformed into something else, finding himself through her.

For Emily, I'd learn every song. Every dance step. Every piece of Oz lore that exists.

"Do you want to perform?" I ask. "On stage, I mean?"

"I dream about playing Dorothy someday." Her laugh holds no hope. "Stupid, right? Girl in a wheelchair playing the most iconic role in musical theater?"

"Not stupid." Fury heats my blood again—at everyone who made her think dreams were stupid. "Brilliant. Dorothy's about finding home, finding courage. You have more of both than anyone I know."

She stares at me like I've spoken a foreign language.

I pull out my phone, fingers flying. Order the fourteen original Baum books—first editions if Roger can find them. The Corbyn novel *Wonderful: The Life and Times of Dorothy Mae Gale*. That index book cataloging every Oz adaptation ever made.

I'll learn everything. Every detail. Every version of this story she loves.

And when I book Felix—because I will book it, I'll make sure of it—I'll bring her to set. Introduce her to directors. Open doors.

"Tristian?" Emily's voice pulls me back. "You okay?"

"Perfect." I kiss her forehead, breathing her in. "Just thinking about possibilities."

On screen, Dorothy clicks her heels. Mochi snores between us. Emily's head grows heavy against my shoulder.

This. This is what the Lambert curse feels like. Not possession or obsession.

Just absolute certainty that I'd learn every story she loves, memorize every dream she's afraid to speak, make every impossible thing possible—if it means keeping her exactly here.

Exactly mine.

The Oz credits roll, Dorothy home in Kansas, and I check my watch. Ten-thirty. Emily yawns against my shoulder, trying to hide it.

"One more?" I stroke her hair, the silky strands exactly as soft as I imagined. "My choice this time?"

"Mmm." She nestles deeper into the pillows, Mochi adjusting his position across our legs. "What's your favorite?"

"The first *Extinction Protocol*." I grab the remote, already pulling it up. "1996. Before they went all franchise and merchandising."

Emily's eyes light up, exhaustion forgotten. "The original Prehistoric Paradise? With Dr. Elena Vargas and the raptor pack dynamics?"

"You've seen it?" Pleasure warms my chest. Of course she has. Sharp girl who loves stories.

"Saw the newest one four times last summer." Pink floods her cheeks. "When they announced you'd be playing Dr. Nathan Cross in number eight, I—I might have screamed in the dorm common room."

The memory hits me. Roger's call, the script courier, reading Nathan's character breakdown in my trailer between *Alice* takes. Paleontologist from Alabama. Former military. Part raptor himself through genetic experiments he doesn't remember consenting to as a child.

Possessive. Protective. Feral when threatened.

I'd cried reading the scene where Nathan discovers Maya nearly torn apart by aggressive raptors, the ones they'd been sent to study. His DNA singing to claim her, protect her, never let her out of his sight again.

At the time, I thought I understood the character academically. The instinct to shield what's yours, the desperation when mortality crashes close.

But holding Emily, scars hidden beneath Dorothy pajamas, her trust fragile as spun glass—now I *know* Nathan. Feel him in my bones.

"They sent me to kill the dangerous ones," I murmur, quoting the script I've memorized. "Figure out why some shift and others don't, why they turned aggressive. All I found was her, bleeding in that bunker, and every violent instinct I've ever buried just—erupted."

Emily shivers. "The scene where he pins her against the wall?"

"Tears her clothes checking for bites, for scratches, for any injury that might—" I stop, throat tight. "Yeah. That scene."

The one where Nathan loses control completely. Shreds Maya's shirt hunting for wounds, hands shaking, teeth bared. Not sexual, not yet. Just pure claiming need, the raptor DNA demanding proof she'll survive.

I press play on the original film. The Prehistoric Paradise logo fills the screen—palm trees and DNA helixes twisted together. John Williams' score swells, that perfect blend of wonder and danger.

"I was seven when this came out," I say. "Sneaked into the cinema in Grantham Bridge five times. Dad was campaigning for his first election, expected me home for photo ops and speeches. I just wanted dinosaurs."

"Rebellion through blockbusters." Emily grins, settling against my side. "Very on-brand."

The film unfolds—Dr. Elena Vargas's wonder at seeing living dinosaurs, the security systems failing, the raptors escaping. That kitchen scene where the kids hide from velociraptors still makes my pulse spike.

"The raptor who claims Elena at the end," Emily says during a quiet moment. "Marcus, right? The beta male who protects her from the alpha?"

"He shifts for the first time because of her." I remember the theater audience gasping, my teenage brain exploding.

"Violence and protection tangled together. The franchise built everything on that foundation."

Seven films later, species added each time. Triceratops shifters. Pteranodon packs. That brutal scene in number seven where a T-Rex shifter ate someone whole on-screen, earning the first R-rating in the franchise.

And now Nathan. My Nathan. Part raptor through experiments, sent to investigate why some dinosaurs can shift to human form while others remain purely animal. Why aggression spiked suddenly.

Finding Maya in that bunker changed everything.

"I need you to understand something," I say, pausing the film. Emily looks up, emerald eyes curious. "When they sent me Nathan's script, the bunker scene—I cried reading it."

"Why?"

"Because I didn't understand him yet. Couldn't feel why he'd lose control like that, why seeing her hurt would shred every civilized piece of him." I cup her face, thumb stroking her cheekbone. "But now, sitting here with you, knowing people hurt you—"

My voice cracks. Emily's hand covers mine, squeezing.

"Nathan tears her clothes off not because he wants to," I continue. "But because he *needs* to see. Needs proof she'll survive. The raptor DNA doesn't care about propriety or boundaries when its mate is bleeding."

"Mate," Emily whispers. "When he bites her shoulder."

"Claiming mark." My teeth ache looking at her throat, smooth and unmarked. Civilized, I remind myself. You're civilized. "Permanent bond in raptor culture. She becomes pack, becomes *his*, and nobody touches her without going through him first."

Emily's breathing quickens, pulse fluttering at her neck.

I force myself back, resuming the film. Watching Dr. Vargas run from raptors, hide, survive. The final confrontation where Marcus shifts—bones cracking, skin splitting, becoming human to save her from the alpha's killing strike.

The claiming comes after. When she's safe and he's still half-feral, DNA screaming mine mine mine. He pins her against the bunker wall, not hurting but not gentle either. Just desperate possession, the need to mark and keep.

"Stay." The word escapes before I can stop it. The credits roll, Mochi snoring between us. "Tonight. Just to sleep, I promise. I just—"

Need to know you're safe. Need to wake up and find you here. Need to not spend the night imagining you alone in some hotel room where I can't reach you.

"Just to sleep," Emily echoes, something unreadable in her expression.

"I'll keep my hands to myself. You have my word." I kiss her forehead, breathing her in. "But please, Emily. Stay."

She nods against my chest, and relief floods through me so intense it's almost painful.

Mine. She's staying. She's safe.

I settle the duvet around us, Mochi sprawled across our legs like a furry chaperone. Emily's breathing evens out first, exhaustion claiming her.

I stay awake longer, watching her sleep. Memorizing the curve of her cheek, the flutter of her lashes, the way her hand curls against my chest like she's holding on.

Tomorrow I'll call Roger about *Wonderful*. About Felix and Dorothy and making impossible things possible.

Tonight I just hold her.

Just keep her safe.

Just let the Lambert curse—or maybe Nathan's raptor DNA bleeding into my real life—settle into certainty.

She's mine. And I'm keeping her.

I extract myself carefully, sliding pillows around Emily so she won't wake. My phone reads midnight—eight in the morning in Angoumois. One AM in New Orleans.

Perfect.

I retreat to the sitting room, closing the bedroom door partway. The video call connects on the second ring.

"Again?" Jean appears first, already dressed for Sunday morning mass. "What happened to 'goodnight, going on a date'?"

"The date ended." Levi leans into frame, hair sleep-mussed. "He's calling because—"

"Because I need to show you something." Michelle joins, Marcus visible behind her in Saints pajama bottoms. "Wait for it."

I flip the camera, angling it through the doorway. Emily sleeps curled on her side, blonde hair spilling across my pillows, the Wonderful Wizard of Oz shirt riding up slightly.

"Merde," Jean breathes.

"She's gorgeous," Michelle whispers.

"Man's got it *bad*." Marcus grins, that Louisiana drawl thickening. "Look at how you framed that shot. Cinematography doesn't lie."

I flip the camera back. "Is it possible? To be in love this soon? Two conversations and dinner?"

"The Lambert curse doesn't operate on normal timelines." Jean straightens his collar. "Grandpère knew in thirty seconds. Dad took two minutes."

"Celebrity-fan relationships crash and burn." The words taste bitter. "She idolized me before we met. How do I know this isn't just starstruck infatuation on her end?"

"Did she act starstruck over dinner?" Levi asks.

I replay the evening—Emily challenging my interpretation of Nathan's character, arguing about Viktor's motivations in Extinction Protocol, dissecting the costume design in Phantom. "She told me the Masquerade sequence needed better historical accuracy. Said the 1881 Paris Opera wouldn't have allowed certain fabric combinations."

"That's not a fan." Michelle grins. "That's someone treating you like a person."

"Mama calls it lightning strike love." Marcus leans forward, expression serious. "Voodoo love at first sight, coup de foudre—whatever you call it, when it hits, you just *know*. My cousin Evangeline met her wife at a gas station. Married three months later. Twenty years strong now."

"But what if—"

"Brother." Jean's voice cuts through my spiral. "You've dated actresses, models, that tech heiress. Did any of them make you call us at ungodly hours just to talk about them?"

No. Gabrielle was lovely, and I'd cared. But I'd ended it with regret, not agony. I'd never wanted to show my siblings photos of her sleeping, never needed their validation.

"She's different," I say quietly.

"She's yours." Marcus points at the screen. "That possessive thing in your voice when you say her name? That's it, man. That's the real deal. Don't overthink it. Don't let fame complications kill something good before it starts."

The Lambert possessiveness, the thing I've witnessed in Dad with Mum, in Jean with Levi. That absolute certainty of *mine*, of needing them safe and close and permanently claimed.

It's settling into my bones, wrapping around my ribs. Emily. My Emily.

"I'm supposed to fly to Toronto tomorrow." I run a hand through my hair. "Alice press tour starts Tuesday."

"So delay." Levi shrugs. "You're Tristian Lambert. They'll wait."

"David will have questions."

"Kellerman knows about the curse." Jean smirks. "He'll understand. And run a background check."

"He runs those on everyone I date." Standard protocol—Kellerman protecting his investment, his surrogate son. "This time I hope he finds everything. Her foster care records, her university transcripts, all of it. I want to know everything she's survived."

To understand how strong she is. To know exactly what I'm fighting for.

"Take her for coffee in the morning," Michelle suggests. "Something normal. No hotel suites, no movie star gestures. Just you and her."

"And then tell her the truth." Jean's expression softens. "That you're falling for her. Fast and probably terrifying, but real."

We say goodnight—good morning for them. I pull up my pilot's contact.

Change of plans. Delay Toronto departure until Monday evening. Will advise.

Derek's response comes immediately: **Understood. Standing by.**

David next. He'll be awake—the man runs on four hours of sleep and black coffee.

Need to push Toronto. Taking an extra day in SLC. Personal matter.

Three dots appear, disappear, appear again.

Her name?

Emily Dorothy Silver.

I'll have the report by noon. Don't do anything stupid.

Too late. Already in love with her.

Christ. Another Lambert down. Fine. Take your time. I'll handle the studio.

I return to the bedroom, sliding back under the duvet. Emily murmurs something, shifting closer. Her hand finds my chest again, settling over my heartbeat.

Mine.

The word pulses with each breath. Mine mine mine.

I press a kiss to her hair, breathing her in. Tomorrow I'll take her for coffee. Tell her I'm canceling flights, rearranging press tours, upending my entire schedule.

For her.

Because the Lambert curse isn't a curse at all. It's recognition—the soul identifying its match, the heart claiming its home.

And Emily Dorothy Silver, foster care survivor and fashion design genius, brilliant mind in a beautiful body, speaker of French and defender of historical accuracy? She's mine.

Chapter 5: Karaoke Under Neon Lights

The Logan winter bites through my jacket as I climb the stairs to Emily's student apartment, heart hammering against my ribs. Five months. Five months of video calls that stretched past midnight, text messages that made Roger raise his eyebrows, rearranging my entire schedule around Utah time zones.

Five months without touching her.

I knock. Mochi barks—deeper now, more authoritative. The training program in Seattle transformed him from enthusiastic companion to certified service dog, complete with credentials that grant Emily access anywhere she needs him. Worth every penny just to hear the joy in her voice when she called to tell me he'd passed.

The door swings open.

Emily sits in her pink wheelchair, emerald eyes lighting up in that way that makes my chest constrict. She wears jeans and a sweater she designed herself—adaptive closures hidden in the seams, cut to drape perfectly around her seated position.

"Bonjour, mon cœur." I step inside, dropping to one knee so we're eye level. "Missed you."

"Five months." Her fingers trace my jaw, and I lean into the touch like a starving man. "You grew a beard."

"For the press tour. Alice marketing wanted the Hatter looking 'rugged.'" I turn my head, pressing a kiss to her palm. "Hate it?"

"No." Her thumb brushes my lower lip. "It suits you."

Mochi wedges between us, tail wagging, service vest perfectly fitted. I scratch behind his ears, grinning at the patch Emily sewed on: *Mochi - Service Dog - Do Not Pet*.

"Look at you, mate. All official now." I glance up at Emily. "He's been brilliant?"

"Perfect." Pride fills her voice. "He alerts before my anxiety spikes, retrieves anything I drop, even learned to open doors with the handle attachment."

I'd watched videos of his training sessions, FaceTimed with his handler weekly. Obsessive? Probably. But seeing Emily's independence expand, watching her confidence grow—worth every obsessive moment.

"Where's Ariana?"

"Girls' night." Emily wheels backward, gesturing me inside. "We have the place to ourselves."

The apartment reflects both of them—Ariana's bold artwork covering one wall, Emily's design sketches pinned to a massive corkboard. A dress form displays what looks like adaptive formalwear, the construction sophisticated enough to rival Parisian couture houses.

"That's stunning, darling." I move closer, examining the hidden magnetic closures, the strategic seaming that allows for seated wear while maintaining elegant lines. "New commission?"

"My thesis collection." She wheels beside me, pride and uncertainty mixing in her expression. "Adaptive evening wear. I'm showing it at the university fashion showcase in April."

"I'll be there." No question. I'd cancel a premiere if necessary.

"Tristian, you don't have to—"

"I'll be there," I repeat, turning to face her. "Wouldn't miss it for anything, love."

Pink floods her cheeks. Five months, and I still haven't kissed her. Waited, because distance makes everything complicated. Wanted our first kiss to be real, present, not separated by screens and time zones.

"So." I settle on her couch, Mochi immediately claiming the spot beside me. "Where are you taking me tonight? You've been cryptic all week."

"It's a surprise." Mischief dances in her eyes. "But you can't wear that."

"What's wrong with this?" I glance down at my designer jeans and button-down. Classic, appropriate for Logan nightlife—not that I've experienced it.

"Too Hollywood." She wheels to her bedroom, emerging with a bundle of fabric. "I made these for you. For tonight."

I unfold dark wash jeans—perfectly fitted, I can tell from the cut—and a deep blue henley, soft fabric that will move well. Both pieces modified with her signature hidden details: reinforced seams, strategic stretch panels, closures designed for easy movement.

"You made these? For me?"

"Your measurements are public knowledge." She shrugs, but her smile betrays her pleasure. "I might have studied your red carpet photos. Analyzed your movement patterns."

"Stalker," I tease, standing to press a kiss to her forehead. Still not her lips. Not yet. "Thank you, mon trésor. They're perfect."

"Bathroom's through there." She points. "I need to change too."

I grab the clothes, pausing at the bathroom door. "Emily?"

"Mm?"

"I'm really here. Actually here."

"I know." Her voice softens. "I keep thinking I'll wake up and you'll still be in LA, or London, or Toronto..."

"Not going anywhere tonight." I catch her gaze, hold it. "Promise."

She disappears into her bedroom, and I change quickly. The henley fits like it was tailored—which, technically, it was. Emily understands bodies, movement, the way fabric needs to work with someone rather than against them.

I emerge to find her transferring to the couch, Mochi attentive at her side. She's changed into black jeans and a deep red top that makes her blonde hair seem to glow.

"Gorgeous," I murmur, earning another blush.

"We should go." But she doesn't move, eyes tracing my face like she's memorizing it. "I missed you."

"Missed you too, sweetheart." I crouch in front of her chair again, taking her hands. "So bloody much."

"Then let's make tonight count." She squeezes my fingers. "Trust me?"

"Always."

She grins. "Good. Because we're going somewhere you've definitely never been."

Melody's sits wedged between a tattoo parlor and a vintage bookshop on Main Street, the kind of place I'd walk past without noticing. Neon sign flickering pink and blue, bass thumping through brick walls.

"Karaoke?" I grin at Emily as she navigates the ramp. "You've discovered my secret."

"YouTube leaked footage from your Phantom cast party." She throws a smile over her shoulder. "You murdered Bowie. In the best way."

Inside, the bar pulses with life—college students claiming tables, a bachelorette party commandeering the stage, locals who treat this place like a second home. Nobody glances twice at us. Just another couple on a Thursday night.

Emily waves at the bartender, a woman with purple hair and sleeve tattoos. "Hey, Mel!"

"Emmy! Haven't seen you in forever, girl." Mel leans across the bar, then spots me. "Holy—"

"He's with me," Emily says quickly. "Can we get the usual?"

"On it." Mel's already mixing something pink and fizzy. "And for your friend?"

"Whiskey neat." I slide onto the stool beside Emily's chair. "Whatever you've got that's decent."

"We've got excellent." Mel pours Jameson, neat, slides it across. "On the house. Anyone who makes Emmy smile like that earns free drinks."

The mocktail arrives in a hurricane glass, garnished with fresh strawberries and mint. Emily sips, eyes closing in appreciation.

"What is that?"

"Trade secret." She offers me a taste. Strawberry, basil, something citrus underneath. Bright and clean and perfectly Emily.

We claim a table near the stage, Mochi settling beneath with practiced ease. The current singer butchers Journey, enthusiastic if not talented. Emily hums along, fingers tapping rhythm against her glass.

"So." I lean close, speaking near her ear to be heard over the music. "What are we singing?"

"You'll see." That mischievous glint again. "I signed us up already."

Three songs later, the DJ calls her name. Emily wheels to the stage, accepts the microphone with the confidence of someone who's done this before. The opening notes hit—heavy guitar, driving bass, pure grunge energy.

Then she opens her mouth and destroys me.

Her voice drops low, smoky and rich, before leaping octaves into this soaring belt that shouldn't be possible. The lyrics—something about seeing through masks, knowing someone's truth beneath the surface, recognizing beauty in the broken pieces.

You see the girl I hide / Behind these emerald eyes / You know my heart's design / Better than I know myself

The note jumps are insane, mezzo range pushed to extremes. Everyone in the bar stops talking, watches this blonde girl in a pink wheelchair command the stage like she owns it.

I'm halfway in love with her already. This might finish me completely.

She holds the final note, lets it soar and crack and resolve, and the bar erupts. I'm on my feet applauding before I realize I've moved.

"Your turn, Hollywood." She wheels past, breathless and glowing.

The DJ grins, reading my selection. "Ballsy choice, man."

The opening riff of "Midnight Rider" by The Renegades fills the bar—classic rock, driving rhythm, built for a tenor who can growl. I grab the mic, find Emily's eyes, and let loose.

Singing in bars feels different than stages. Rawer. Real. I pour everything into it—the months apart, the wanting, the certainty that this girl is everything.

Emily dances in her chair, hands raised, lost in the music. When I drop to one knee for the final chorus, singing directly to her, her smile could power the whole damn city.

The song ends. I'm breathing hard, adrenaline singing through my veins. Emily reaches for me and I take her hand, pulling her close as the next song starts—something slow, perfect for swaying.

My phone buzzes in my pocket. I ignore it.

It buzzes again.

"Check it," Emily murmurs. "Might be important."

I pull out my phone one-handed, keeping the other around Emily's shoulders as we move together.

Triplets + Marcus

Jean: Mate, kiss her already! We can see the sexual tension through your Instagram story

Marcus: For real tho. That girl is GONE for you

Michelle: Jean's not wrong. Make a move!

I glance up. Emily's watching me, question in her eyes.

"My siblings are meddling." I pocket the phone, cup her face with both hands. "They think I should kiss you."

"Do you?" Her breath catches. "Want to kiss me?"

"Since the moment you said 'Bonjour.'"

"Then stop talking."

I lean down, she tilts up, and when our lips meet it's like every song I've ever sung suddenly makes sense. She tastes like strawberries and mint, soft and sweet and perfect. Her hand fists in my shirt, pulling me closer, and I'm drowning in her, lost and found simultaneously.

My phone slides from my pocket, hitting something.

We break apart, both breathing hard. Emily's lips are pink and swollen, her eyes dark with want.

"Wow," she whispers.

"Yeah." I rest my forehead against hers. "Wow."

My phone lights up on the floor.

Voice memo sent to Triplets + Marcus

Oh no.

"Your siblings just heard us making out." Emily's face flushes crimson.

"Brilliant." I scrub my hand over my face. "They'll never let me live this down."

My phone erupts with notifications. I silence it without looking.

"Next round?" The DJ's voice crackles through the speakers. "Emily and Tristian, you're up again!"

Emily grins, wheels toward the stage. "Ready?"

The opening beat drops—heavy, hypnotic, all sultry bass and promise. Emily takes the mic, and her entire demeanor shifts. Gone is the sweet girl who sang grunge. This is pure confidence, sensual and commanding.

She moves with the rhythm, voice dropping low and dangerous as she sings about control and surrender, about knowing exactly what she wants and demanding it. The lyrics paint pictures—chains made of choice, pleasure wrapped in power, submission as its own kind of strength.

Heat pools low in my stomach. She's performing for me, emerald eyes locked on mine, and every word feels like a promise.

The crowd goes wild. I'm rooted to the spot, blood pounding in my ears.

"Your turn." She wheels past, fingers trailing across my shoulder. "Let's see what you've got, Hollywood."

The opening synth fills the bar—electronic, pulsing, pure swagger. I grab the mic and channel every dominant character I've ever played, letting the persona slide over me like a second skin.

The lyrics flow, all about taking charge, about knowing exactly how to make someone come undone. I prowl the small stage, eyes never leaving Emily's, singing about pleasure and power and the beautiful blur between them.

Her breath catches. I can see her pulse racing at her throat.

I drop to a crouch in front of her chair for the final verse, voice going rough and low, making every word a promise. When the song ends, the silence stretches for a heartbeat before applause crashes over us.

I'm on my knees, breathing hard, inches from her face.

"Okay," she whispers. "You win."

"No contest." I stand, extend my hand. "Come outside with me?"

We claim a quiet corner of the patio, heaters glowing orange against the March chill. Mochi settles at Emily's feet, ever vigilant.

"I want to take you on a real date." The words tumble out faster than planned. "New York. Fashion Week is next week—I can get you into any show you want. Front row. And 'Wonderful' just started revival previews on Broadway. I can get tickets. Backstage access to both."

"Tristian—"

"I know it's fast. I know we barely know each other. But I've been thinking about you every day for five months, and I—" I rake my fingers through my hair. "I want this. Us. Whatever this is."

Emily stares at me, eyes wide. "That's... that's a lot."

"Too much?"

"No. Just..." She pulls out her phone. "Let me make some calls."

She dials. "Hey, Derek? It's Emily. I need someone to cover my shifts this week... Yeah, all of them... I know it's short notice, but something came up... Thank you! You're the best."

Next call. "Hi, this is Emily Silver, I'm in the ensemble for 'Chicago'? I need to arrange time off for next week... Family emergency... Yes, I'll send the formal request tomorrow... Thank you so much."

Third call. "Jordan? Hey, can you take notes for me in Advanced Construction next week? I'll owe you coffee for a month... You're amazing, thank you!"

She looks up at me, biting her lip. "I need to call Ariana."

The phone barely rings once.

"WHERE THE HELL ARE YOU?" Ariana's voice carries across the patio. "I came home and you're GONE, your location says some random bar, and—oh my god, is he there? Is Tristian Lambert there?"

"We're at Melody's. And yes, he's—"

"PUT ME ON VIDEO."

Emily switches to FaceTime. Ariana's face fills the screen, makeup half-removed, eyes blazing.

"Tristian Alexandre Lambert." She points at the camera. "If you hurt her, I will hunt you down. I don't care how famous you are. I will end you."

"Understood."

"Good. Now why are you calling me at eleven PM?"

"He wants to take me to New York," Emily says quietly. "Fashion Week and 'Wonderful' on Broadway."

Ariana's expression cycles through shock, excitement, and suspicion in rapid succession. "When?"

"Tomorrow morning."

"TOMORROW— Emily Dorothy Silver, you cannot just fly to New York with a man you've known for like, five cumulative hours!"

"Seven," I interject. "If you count video calls."

"NOT HELPING." Ariana glares. "Emmy, this is insane."

"I know." Emily's voice steadies. "But I want to go."

Silence stretches. Ariana's face softens.

"Okay. But you check in every day. And if anything feels wrong, you call me immediately. I will fly out there myself if I have to."

"I promise."

After Emily hangs up, I pull out my own phone. "I should probably arrange the jet."

I text my pilot while Emily watches, fingers absently stroking Mochi's ears.

"There's something I need to tell you." I pocket my phone, take her hand. "About my family. We have this... thing. A curse, kind of."

"A curse?"

"We fall hard. Fast. My grandfather saw my grandmother once and knew. Proposed three days later. My father proposed to my mother after a week. Jean married

Levi after a month. Michelle and Marcus got engaged after six weeks."

"That's..." Emily processes this. "Intense."

"I know how I feel about you." I meet her eyes, let her see everything. "I've known since you said 'Bonjour.' And I need you to understand what you're getting into with me. Because I don't do casual. I don't do slow. When I fall, I fall completely."

Her hand tightens around mine. "That's terrifying."

"I know."

"But also kind of beautiful."

I exhale. "So you'll come?"

"We leave tomorrow?" She's already mentally packing, I can see it.

"First thing. Mochi too, obviously."

She laughs, bright and free. "Then yes. Let's go to New York."

Chapter 6: One City at a Time

Emily presses her face against the jet window as Manhattan rises from the Hudson, steel and glass catching afternoon sun. Mochi shifts in his service vest, settling closer to her wheelchair secured in the cabin.

"It's so tall." Wonder threads through her voice. "Pictures don't..."

"Wait until tonight." I lean over to look past her. "The city lights up like stars fell sideways."

She turns, emerald eyes bright. "You've been here a lot?"

"Press tours. Premieres. Jean lives in Brooklyn in the summer with Levi." I pull out my phone, scrolling through location photos. "But I want to show you Angoumois first. My home. The vineyards go on forever, and the coastline— you can see France and England on clear days."

"Your accent gets thicker when you talk about it."

I hadn't noticed. "It's different there. Quieter. No Dadrazzi hiding in the hedgerows."

"Mostly."

The jet banks, beginning descent. Emily grips the armrest, knuckles white.

"First time flying?" I cover her hand with mine.

"First time leaving Utah."

The weight of that settles between us. Twenty-two years in one place, most spent surviving rather than living. And here she is, trusting me enough to cross the country.

"After New York, we'll go everywhere." The words spill out, plans forming faster than sense. "Paris for the fashion houses. You could intern at Dior, Chanel—I know people. Hollywood for the *Alice* premiere in May. You'll walk the red carpet with me."

"Tristian—"

"The Venice Film Festival in September. Tokyo for the *Alice* premiere there. Angoumois for my birthday in April—Michelle's planning some ridiculous party, but the island is beautiful then. Cherry blossoms everywhere."

She's staring at me like I've grown a second head.

"Too much again?"

"You're talking about months. We've had one date."

"Two, if you count tonight." The jet touches down, smooth as silk. "Three after the show tomorrow. Four when we visit Jean and Levi. Five—"

"Okay, okay." She laughs, shaking her head. "One thing at a time."

But I can see it in her eyes—she wants this too. Wants to believe in the possibility of everything I'm offering.

The flight attendant opens the cabin door. Cold air rushes in, carrying the scent of jet fuel and city exhaust. Two SUVs wait on the tarmac, Peter already coordinating with the car service about Mochi's needs.

"Mr. Lambert." The driver approaches, professional smile in place. "Welcome to New York. We have the accessible vehicle ready."

Emily navigates her wheelchair down the jet's ramp, Mochi matching her pace perfectly. Manhattan spreads before us, close enough to touch.

"First stop: hotel. You'll want to rest before Fashion Week starts tomorrow." I climb into the SUV beside her. "Then dinner at this place in the Village—best French food outside Paris. And after—"

"Do you ever stop planning?"

"Not when it comes to you."

She reaches for my hand, threading our fingers together. "For someone who claims to fall fast, you're very focused on the future."

"Because I can see it." I brush my thumb across her knuckles. "All of it. You in Paris, sketching designs in café windows. Walking red carpets. Meeting my family in Angoumois. Every premiere, every city, every—"

"Tristian." She squeezes my hand. "I'm here now. Can we start with that?"

The city blurs past the windows, possibility stretching ahead like an unwritten script.

"Yeah." I smile. "We can start with now."

The Bryant Park tents hum with controlled chaos. Fashion Week transforms Manhattan into something feverish, electric. Models drift past in clothes that won't hit stores for six months, photographers jostle for position, and the air smells like expensive perfume and ambition.

Emily's eyes track everything at once.

"That's McQueen." She points to a model in structural black. "The silhouette—see how it defies gravity? Sarah Burton's signature."

"I see fabric."

"You see art." Her wheelchair navigates the crowded pathway with practiced ease, Mochi guiding around clusters of people in impossible heels. "That construction probably took two hundred hours minimum."

A hand waves from across the tent. Three women approach, all legs and cheekbones and the particular confidence that comes from being photographed for a living.

"Tristian Lambert." The brunette air-kisses both my cheeks. "Michelle said you'd be here. Where is she?"

"Paris shoot. Ran late." I gesture to Emily. "This is Emily Silver. Emily, these are Michelle's friends—Anika, Soraya, and Camille."

"The fashion student." Anika's smile widens. "Michelle mentioned you. Utah State, right?"

Emily's surprise flickers across her face. "She knows about me?"

"Tristian won't shut up about you in the family chat." Soraya crouches to Mochi's level, letting him sniff her hand. "Your work focuses on adaptive design?"

"Adaptive clothing for people with disabilities." Emily's voice steadies as she talks shop. "Most fashion ignores accessibility completely. Magnetic closures instead of buttons, wheelchair-friendly hemlines, sensory-safe fabrics —"

"Brilliant." Camille pulls out her phone. "There's a designer showing tomorrow, Sofia Chen. She's doing exactly that kind of work. Want an introduction?"

"I—yes. God, yes."

They discuss construction techniques I don't understand, fabrics I've never heard of. Soraya mentions someone at Parsons. Anika knows a buyer at Nordstrom looking for adaptive lines. Emily's face glows brighter with each connection, each possibility.

"You should visit Paris." Anika exchanges numbers with Emily. "Michelle can connect you with the major houses. They're finally starting to think about accessibility."

"Finally." Emily's laugh carries an edge. "Only took them a century."

"Change happens slow in fashion." Camille straightens. "Until someone forces it faster. Could be you."

The models drift away to their next show, leaving Emily staring at her phone like it holds treasure.

"They just—they gave me their numbers."

"You impressed them." I wheel her toward the runway entrance. "You know more about fashion than half the people here."

"They're Michelle's friends because they know you're serious about me." She looks up, emerald eyes searching. "Your whole family's talking about me, and we haven't even met."

"They're busy. Jean's in D.C. Michelle's shooting in Paris. My parents are—" I stop. "They're always busy."

"You don't talk about them much."

"Nothing to say." The lights dim as the show starts. "We're not close."

Music pounds through the tent. Models glide down the runway in architectural impossible things. Emily leans forward, absorbing every detail, her hand sketching phantom designs on her armrest.

"There." She points. "That gathering technique—I could adapt that for seated wear. The drape would work perfectly for—"

Her voice fades as she focuses, mind already redesigning, reimagining. I watch her instead of the show, memorizing the concentration on her face, the way brilliance looks on her.

Central Park stretches endlessly under twilight, paths winding through bare March trees. Emily shivers despite the blanket across her lap, her face tighter than it was an hour ago.

"Cold?" I adjust the blanket higher.

"I'm fine." But her jaw clenches, releasing. Clenches again.

We've covered miles today—Fashion Week shows, lunch at that Vietnamese place she loved, the *Wonderful* matinee where she cried. Backstage, she'd met Dorothy herself, gushed about costume construction while pain crept into the corners of her eyes.

I'd noticed. Said nothing. Rookie mistake.

"Emily."

"It's just—" She grips the wheelchair armrest. "My back. It does this sometimes after long days."

Mochi whines, pressing his nose against her leg. The dog knows before she admits it.

"Why didn't you say something earlier?" I crouch beside her chair. "We could've rested, gone back—"

"Because I wanted to see everything." Her voice breaks slightly. "I wanted one perfect day in New York, and I got it, and now my stupid body won't—"

She stops. Breathes through whatever's lancing up her spine.

I switch her chair to manual mode, releasing the power controls. "Hotel. Now."

"Tristian—"

"We're not arguing about this." I start pushing, Mochi padding alongside with his ears back. "You're in pain. We're fixing it."

The path back feels longer than it should. Each bump registers in how Emily's shoulders tense, how her breathing shifts. Mochi keeps looking up at her, worried brown eyes tracking every wince.

"I'm okay, buddy." She reaches down to scratch his head. "Just overdid it."

At the hotel, I bypass the elevator crowds and find the service lift. Less jostling. Emily doesn't comment, but her hand finds mine on the wheelchair grip, squeezing once.

The suite door clicks open. I head straight for her room, already calculating. "Where's your medication?"

"Front pocket of my bag. The orange bottle."

I find it—prescription ibuprofen, 800mg. The label warns against exceeding dosage. Emily's already reaching for it.

"How many?"

"Two. With food." She grimaces. "There's protein bars in my suitcase."

I grab three bars and water, watching as she swallows the pills. Mochi jumps onto the bed, circling until he settles right beside where she'll lie, his bulk a warm presence.

"He always does this." Emily shifts from chair to mattress, movements careful. "Whenever I'm hurting, he knows."

"Good dog." I kneel, scratching behind Mochi's ears. "Take care of your mum."

The labradoodle licks my hand once, then refocuses entirely on Emily. His head rests on her leg, eyes fixed on her face like he's monitoring for changes.

"I'm sorry." Emily's voice comes small. "I ruined the day."

"You didn't ruin anything." I sit on the bed's edge, careful not to jostle. "I pushed too hard. Should've checked in more."

"I wanted to keep going."

"I know." I brush blonde hair from her face. "But you need to tell me when you're hurting. I can't read your mind."

"Yet." The corner of her mouth lifts. "Give it time."

Mochi shifts closer, pressing his warmth against her legs. The dog's devotion is absolute—he'd sit there all night if she needed.

"Rest." I stand. "I'll order room service. Something easy."

"Tristian?" She catches my hand. "Thank you. For today. All of it."

"Get some sleep." I squeeze her fingers. "We've got two more days in New York."

"More adventures?"

"Gentler ones." I smile. "Promise."

Emily's breathing evens out behind the closed door. Mochi hasn't moved from his post—I checked five minutes ago, found the labradoodle plastered against her side like a furry sentinel.

I pull out my phone, scrolling to Roger's contact. Three rings.

"It's midnight, Tristian."

"I need renovations done on the Hills house." I pace the suite's living room, already cataloging everything that needs changing. "Full accessibility retrofit. Wheelchair ramps, wider doorways, the works."

Silence. Then: "You've known her six months."

"Five months, two weeks, three days." I stop at the window. Manhattan glitters below, oblivious. "And I need it done before she graduates in June."

"June." Roger exhales slowly. "That's eleven weeks."

"Ten if we start tomorrow." I open my notes app, typing as I talk. "Master bathroom—install a roll-in shower. Those zero-threshold ones, grab bars at multiple heights. And a soaking tub. Big enough for two."

"Romantic."

"She mentioned loving baths at dinner. Said most hotels don't have tubs deep enough, accessible enough." The memory surfaces—Emily describing the one foster home with a clawfoot tub, how she'd soak for hours when the pain got bad. "I want her to have that. Whenever she needs."

Roger's keyboard clicks in the background. "What else?"

"The gym. Add parallel bars for physical therapy. Treatment table—the kind that adjusts for height. Yoga mats, resistance bands, anything her PT might recommend." I think of how Emily moved today, the careful way she transferred from wheelchair to bed. "She shouldn't have to go to some clinical facility. She should be able to work out at home."

"Home." Roger catches the word. "Your home."

"Our home." It slips out, certainty wrapped in two syllables. "Eventually."

"You haven't even asked her to be your girlfriend yet."

"Working on it." I resume pacing. "The backyard needs leveling. No steps, smooth pathways. And Mochi needs space—build him something. Dog house, maybe? No, bigger. A palace."

"A palace."

"He's her service dog. He deserves five-star accommodations." I picture the labradoodle's devotion, how he'd stationed himself against Emily without being asked. "Climate controlled. Maybe a little fountain? Dogs like water."

"Anything else, Prince Charming?"

I ignore the sarcasm. "Kitchen counters—install some lower sections so she can access them from her chair. Her whole degree is fashion, but she loves cooking. Said her apartment's kitchen is useless because everything's too high."

The typing continues. Roger knows better than to argue when I'm like this.

"Bedroom?" he asks.

"Leave it for now." Heat crawls up my neck. "That's— we're not there yet."

"But you want the bathroom built for two."

"Shut up." I drop onto the couch. "How fast can this happen?"

"With enough money? Eight weeks, maybe seven if I bribe the contractors." Papers rustle. "Permits will be hell. Hollywood Hills has restrictions—"

"I don't care about restrictions. Make it happen."

"This is insane."

"This is the Lambert curse." I think of my grandfather proposing after three days, my father buying my mother a house before their second date. "I'm actually showing restraint."

"God help her." But Roger's smiling—I can hear it. "I'll start calling contractors tomorrow. Accessibility specialists, PT equipment suppliers, luxury dog house architects apparently."

"Roger?"

"Yeah?"

"Thank you." I mean it. "For not questioning this."

"Oh, I'm questioning everything." He laughs quietly. "But I've worked for you long enough to know when you've made up your mind. Send me her measurements—wheelchair width, reach range, anything relevant."

"I'll get them."

"Without being creepy about it."

"I'll try."

The call ends. I stare at my notes app, at the growing list of everything Emily might need, might want, might not even know she wants yet.

Girlfriend first. Then fiancée. Then wife.

The trajectory's clear as film blocking, inevitable as the Lambert curse itself.

I just need her to say yes.

The kitchen gleams, all new lower countertops and accessible workspace. I dip another strawberry in melted dark chocolate, watching it drip before setting it on parchment paper. Seventeen perfect ones already lined up like edible soldiers.

My phone buzzes. Emily's text lights the screen:

Boarding now. Mochi's wearing his flight vest. He looks so professional.

I smile, thumbs flying. *Photo evidence required, mon cœur.*

Three dots appear, then a picture—Emily grinning beside Mochi in his service vest, airport gate in the background. Ariana photobombs from behind, making devil horns.

Tell Ariana she's not subtle, I text back.

She says that's the point.

Another photo follows. Emily's holding up the leather jacket she made for my birthday—black with the Extinction Protocol logo hand-embroidered across the back in stunning detail. I'd worn it to three interviews, bragged about her craftsmanship to anyone who'd listen.

Still my favorite thing I own, I send.

Sap.

Your sap, darling.

The dots dance, stop, dance again. Finally: *Can't wait to see you.*

I lean against the counter—the regulation-height one, not the lowered section I'd installed specifically so Emily could cook beside me. Almost thre months since New York. Ninety-two days of FaceTime calls and text marathons, of falling asleep with my phone propped on the pillow so I could watch her breathe.

Long-distance is torture. Even with daily contact, even with the Lambert certainty thrumming through my veins that she's *mine*, the separation carves me hollow.

I dip another strawberry, thinking about tonight.

The research fills a private folder on my laptop—articles about sex and disability, forum discussions, even a few academic papers. I'd approached it like preparing for a role: methodical, thorough, determined to get every detail right.

Positions that wouldn't strain her legs. Pillows for support under her hips. Communication strategies, pacing, reading her body's signals. One physiotherapist's blog had emphasized creativity over assumption—every body different, every person's needs unique.

I'd taken notes. Color-coded them, actually, which Michelle had mocked mercilessly when she'd caught me studying at Easter dinner.

"You made a spreadsheet," she'd said, peering over my shoulder.

"Research is important."

"It's sex, not a military operation."

"It's Emily." I'd closed the laptop. "I'm not fumbling this."

Jean had been more helpful, surprisingly. A quiet conversation over wine while Levi charmed our parents in the next room.

"The Lambert curse makes us intense," Jean had said. "But intensity without care is just selfishness. Learn her. Listen. The rest follows."

Sound advice. Terrifying advice.

I finish the last strawberry, surveying my work. Romantic and practical—easy to eat, delicious, not too heavy. The champagne chills in the fridge, expensive and perfectly bubbly. Candles wait unlit on the bedroom dresser.

If she wants. Only if she wants.

My phone rings. FaceTime from Emily.

"Impatient?" I answer, grinning at her face filling the screen.

"The gate agent said boarding's delayed fifteen minutes." She's flushed, excited. "Wanted to see you."

"Always want to see you, love." I flip the camera to show the strawberries. "Look what I've made."

Her eyes widen. "Are those—Tristian, those are gorgeous."

"Thought you might be hungry. After the premiere, after everything." Heat creeps up my neck. "If you want to come back here. To the house. You haven't seen it since the renovations."

"Renovations?" She tilts her head. "You mentioned painting."

"Might've done a bit more than painting."

"How much more?"

"You'll see." I flip the camera back to my face. "Ariana still terrorizing the airport?"

"She bought nine magazines. *Nine*. Three of them have you on the cover."

"My face is very profitable."

Emily laughs, and God, I've missed that sound in person. Phone calls don't capture the way her whole expression lights up, the little snort she tries to hide.

"Jean's nervous about meeting you," I say, moving to the living room. "He texted four times this morning asking what to wear."

"He's a politician. How does he not know what to wear?"

"He wants to impress you." I drop onto the couch—the same one from before, but with new cushions arranged specifically for her comfort. "Levi's betting Jean will cry. Apparently, he gets emotional at premieres."

"Will *you* cry?"

"I'm Angoumoisian. We don't cry."

"You cried during Wonderful."

"That was strategic moisture." I smile. "And you were holding my hand. Doesn't count."

Her face softens. "I miss you."

"Eighty-seven days too long, sweetheart."

"You counted?"

"Every single one." I lean back, studying her through the screen. "Tonight's going to be perfect. The premiere, dinner, whatever you want after. No pressure, no expectations. Just us."

"Just us sounds good." She glances off-camera. "Ariana says we're boarding for real now. She's making grabby hands at me."

"Tell her I said thank you. For coming with you."

"She heard. She says you're welcome and also you better have good snacks."

"Roger stocked the entire guest house. She'll be fine." I soften my voice. "Safe flight, mon cœur. Text when you land?"

"Promise." She blows a kiss at the screen. "Love you—"

She freezes. The words hang between us, unplanned, enormous.

"Emily—"

"I have to board." Her face flames scarlet. "Bye!"

The call ends.

I stare at the blank screen, heart hammering against my ribs.

She loves me.

Emily Dorothy Silver loves me.

I'm grinning like an idiot, alone in my renovated house, chocolate on my fingers and hope exploding through my chest.

Tonight. I'll say it back tonight, properly, when I can see her face and hold her hands and make sure she knows I fell first, fell harder, fell completely.

The Lambert curse strikes again.

And this time, she's falling too.

The home gym sprawls across what used to be a guest bedroom—all polished hardwood and floor-to-ceiling mirrors. I changed everything six weeks ago, transforming my bachelor pad workout space into something useful.

The parallel bars gleam in the afternoon light. Emily calls them torture bars, which makes me laugh every time because she's not wrong. I've watched enough of her therapy videos to understand the particular hell of supporting your own weight when your legs refuse to cooperate.

I strip off my shirt, tossing it on the bench beside the yoga mats. Two of them, purple and teal, positioned side-by-side. Emily mentioned doing yoga in one of our calls—stretches her physical therapist recommended, breathing exercises that help with spasms.

"You could join me sometime," she'd said, shy and hopeful.

I'd ordered the mats that night.

The parallel bars call to me. I grip the cool metal, lifting myself up, holding steady. Arms burning, core engaged. Emily manages maybe ten feet on these before her legs give out. Ten feet of pure determination and gritted teeth.

I lower myself, move to the treadmill.

This one cost more than my first car. Accessible treadmill with ceiling harness, specialized grips, speed controls at multiple heights. The salesperson had looked at me like I'd grown a second head when I'd explained what I needed.

"For rehabilitation?" she'd asked.

"For my girlfriend."

The word had felt strange then. Still feels insufficient now. Emily's so much more than girlfriend—she's certainty and future and the reason I renovated my entire house.

I clip into the harness, testing the support. Emily hates walking. She's told me a dozen times, voice tight with frustration.

"It's not real walking," she'd said during one particularly rough call. "It's just... pretending my body works differently than it does."

"Does it help? Physically?"

"Yeah. Muscle tone, bone density, all that fun stuff." She'd sighed. "My PT says pool therapy's best, but the reverse walker or treadmill with support works too. I can manage point-oh-six miles. With breaks. Some days."

Point-oh-six miles. About three hundred seventeen feet of exhausting, painful work.

I'd researched pools after that conversation. Installation costs, heating systems, accessibility features. The backyard has space. Maybe next year, if Emily—

If Emily moves in.

The thought stops me cold, still clipped into the harness like an idiot.

She could move in. After graduation in June. Bring Mochi, bring her sewing machines and fabric mountains and the organized chaos that follows her everywhere.

The whole house is ready. Lower counters in the kitchen, roll-in shower in the master bath, wider doorways, ramps instead of the front steps. Roger had overseen everything while I'd traveled for Wonderland press, texting me photos of each completed renovation.

I unclip from the harness, moving to the therapy mat table in the corner.

This one I'd researched obsessively. Height-adjustable, wide enough for range-of-motion exercises, padded but firm. Emily mentioned her PT appointments—stretches and manipulations that leave her wrung out but functional.

I run my hand along the vinyl surface, imagining her here. Morning stretches while I make coffee. Evening therapy while we talk about our days. Me learning to help, learning her body's language, learning what support looks like instead of just intensity.

The Lambert curse makes us intense. Jean's voice echoes. But intensity without care is just selfishness.

I grab my phone, pulling up Emily's last text. The photo of her and Mochi at the airport, both of them ready to come home.

To come here.

To me.

She loves me. She said it, panicked and perfect, before hanging up.

Tonight I'll say it back. Tonight I'll show her every renovation, every accommodation, every piece of evidence that she's already woven into my life.

Three more hours.

I can wait three more hours.

Raymond circles Emily like a predator eyeing prey, makeup brushes bristling from his belt holster. "Tilt your chin up, darling. Just a touch."

Emily complies, hands folded in her lap. The silver gown catches light from every angle—thousands of hand-sewn crystals cascading down the mermaid silhouette like water frozen mid-fall.

"You made this?" Raymond's French accent thickens with approval. "Couture houses would kill for this construction."

"Custom pattern." Emily's voice carries quiet pride. "Adaptive design. See how the bodice—"

"Opens completely in the back with hidden magnets." Raymond examines the seam. "Genius. Absolute genius."

Ariana sprawls on the hotel couch, already camera-ready in emerald green. "I keep telling her to submit to *Project Runway*."

"Too much drama." Emily meets my eyes in the mirror. "I like creating, not competing."

I lean against the doorframe, bow tie still hanging loose around my neck. She's breathtaking. The silver fabric pools around her wheelchair, transformed into an extension of the gown itself—deliberate design, not accommodation.

Raymond applies highlighter to Emily's cheekbones. "Close your eyes."

She does. Long lashes dark against fair skin.

Five months of semi-dating. Three months official. Eight months total since FanCon, since I'd known with absolute certainty that this woman would change everything.

"Almost done," Raymond promises, reaching for lipstick.

I move closer, catching Emily's hand. Her fingers curl into mine automatically, comfortable as breathing.

"You look—" I stop, searching for words that aren't inadequate. "There aren't words."

Pink floods her cheeks. "You're biased."

"Accurate." I press a kiss to her knuckles. "Devastatingly, objectively accurate."

Raymond snorts. "Save it for the cameras, Casanova. I need ten more minutes."

Ariana catches my eye, one eyebrow raised in silent question. I'd pulled her aside earlier, confessed my intentions for after the premiere.

"Don't hurt her," she'd said, fierce and protective.

"Never."

"Good." She'd smiled then, genuine warmth breaking through the warning. "Because she loves you. Really loves you."

I know. God, I know.

Raymond finishes with a final spritz of setting spray. "Perfection. Don't touch your face, don't cry, and for the love of Dior, don't let Tristian smudge that lipstick until after photos."

Emily laughs, bright and unguarded. "I'll try."

"You'll succeed." He packs his brushes with military precision. "I've worked with actresses who can't resist their co-stars for thirty seconds. You have more self-control than all of them combined."

He's wrong. I've felt Emily tremble when I kiss her. Felt her breath catch when my hand settles on her waist. Self-control isn't easy for either of us.

Eight months. That's long enough to wait, right?

Raymond and Ariana excuse themselves—something about checking on the car. The suite door clicks shut.

Emily turns her chair to face me fully. "They're not subtle."

"Neither am I." I kneel beside her wheelchair, eye level. "Emily, when we get back to the mansion tonight—"

"Tristian—"

"I want to make love to you." The words come out rough, honest. "Five months of semi-dating, three months official—that's long enough to know what I want. You're what I want."

Her emerald eyes widen. "I want that too. I do. But with my disability..." She bites her lip, and I resist the urge to kiss her. "There's a chance I can't. Have sex, I mean. Or... finish."

I cup her face gently. "We'll find a comfortable position. I've been researching."

"You—researched?"

"Extensively." Heat crawls up my neck. "Adaptive intimacy, positioning for limited mobility, communication strategies—"

"You researched sex. For me."

"For us."

The limo door opens to a wall of light and noise. Flash. Flash. Flash.

"Stay close," I murmur to Emily, helping secure Mochi's service vest one last time. The labradoodle sits at attention, professional despite the chaos waiting outside.

Raymond had arranged the handicap-accessible limo specifically for tonight—ramp instead of stairs, wider interior, space for Emily's wheelchair. The studio wanted us arriving together. Good. I wouldn't have it any other way.

Peter exits first, surveying the red carpet like a general assessing a battlefield. "Clear path to the step-and-repeat. No touching Ms. Silver."

"Got it." I squeeze Emily's hand. "Ready?"

She nods, but her breathing already sounds shallow.

The ramp descends. I exit, turn back to help guide her wheelchair. Ariana follows, stunning in emerald, phone already recording.

Then it hits. The wall of sound.

"Tristian! Who's the girl?"

"Look here! Over here!"

"Is that your girlfriend?"

"How long have you been dating?"

"What's her name?"

The questions pile on top of each other, aggressive and relentless. Flashes explode like artillery fire. Cameras thrust forward, invasive and hungry.

Emily's hand tightens on her armrest. Her chest rises and falls too quickly.

Mochi moves immediately, pressing against her leg. His training kicks in—he'd passed his service dog certification three months ago, right before New York.

"Emily?" I kneel beside her wheelchair, blocking some of the cameras with my body. "Breathe with me. In through your nose—"

"Can't—" She fumbles for her purse. The inhaler. Where's her inhaler?

Ariana's already there, pressing it into Emily's trembling hand. "I got you. Four counts in, four counts out."

The Dadrazzi surge closer.

"Back up!" Peter's voice cuts through the noise. "Give her space. Now."

Emily raises the inhaler to her lips, but her hands shake too violently.

I steady them, guiding it. "Slow breath. That's it."

Mochi leans harder against her, grounding pressure. His nose nudges her free hand until her fingers bury in his fur.

The wheezing eases. Slightly.

"One question at a time!" I stand, rounding on the photographers with fury burning through my careful media training. My accent thickens, British edges sharpening. "You lot can't behave like bloody animals. She's a person, not a spectacle."

Ariana steps forward, phone still recording, probably documenting everything in case we need evidence later. "You want a story? Then wait your turn like professionals."

The crowd quiets. Marginally.

Emily's breathing evens out. She meets my eyes, nodding.

"You sure?" I ask quietly.

"Yeah." Her voice carries more strength than before. "I'm okay."

I help her adjust the silver gown, making sure it drapes perfectly. Mochi positions himself on her left side, alert and ready.

"One question," I announce to the press. "That's it for now."

A woman in front calls out, "What's her name?"

Simple. Safe.

"Emily Silver," I say, settling my hand on her shoulder. "Fashion design student at Utah State University. Graduating in June. She designed her own gown tonight."

The cameras focus on the dress. Emily tilts her chin up, confident despite the panic attack moments before.

"One more," Ariana negotiates, fierce and protective. "Then we're moving to the step-and-repeat."

"How did you meet?"

I smile, genuine. "FanCon in Salt Lake City. She spoke French to me at an autograph table, and I was lost."

The cameras continue their assault as we make our way down the carpet. Emily's wheelchair glides smoothly over the specialized surface the studio installed—Roger's doing, no doubt. Peter carves a path through the photographers, keeping them at a respectful distance.

Ahead, I spot familiar faces clustered near the theater entrance.

"Your family?" Emily asks, following my gaze.

"All of them, apparently." I can't keep the warmth from my voice.

Jean waves, dapper in his navy suit. Levi stands beside him, looking every inch the Hollywood star despite technically being here as my brother-in-law. Michelle practically glows in a red couture gown that probably cost more than most people's cars. And Marcus—

"Marcus came from Louisiana for this?" I blink.

"Wouldn't miss it for the world, brother!" Marcus calls out.

We approach, and Mochi's professional demeanor shatters completely. The labradoodle launches himself at Jean with the force of a small missile.

"Merde—" Jean staggers backward, arms windmilling before he topples onto the red carpet. Mochi plants his paws on Jean's chest, tail wagging furiously, tongue swiping across my brother's face in enthusiastic greeting.

"Mochi! Down!" Emily's command lacks bite—she's laughing too hard.

Levi pulls out his phone, recording. "This is going in the family archive."

"Traitor," Jean manages between dog kisses. "Get this beast off me."

"He's not a beast, he's affectionate." I grab Mochi's vest, hauling him back. The dog immediately returns to Emily's side, tail still wagging but posture controlled.

Michelle crouches beside Emily's wheelchair, ignoring the cameras entirely. "That silver is custom, isn't it? The draping accommodates your chair without compromising the line."

"You noticed." Emily's eyes light up. "I had to restructure the entire bodice to—"

"To distribute weight differently," Michelle finishes. "Brilliant. We need to talk about your portfolio. I wasn't going to miss meeting the woman who's got my brother texting French poetry at three in the morning."

"I do not text poetry."

"You absolutely do," Jean says, brushing dog fur off his suit as Levi helps him stand. "Remember the sonnet about her eyes?"

Heat crawls up my neck.

Marcus extends his hand to Emily. "Marcus Butler. Professional third wheel and unofficial family comedian. You must be the famous Emily who's got Tristian here acting like a lovesick teenager."

"Guilty." Emily shakes his hand, grinning. "Though I maintain he's the one who—"

"Showed up at your apartment with groceries and reorganized your entire pantry alphabetically?" Ariana interjects, stepping forward. "Because he definitely did that."

"You told them?" I stare at Emily.

"Ariana tells everyone everything," Emily counters.

Marcus laughs, loud and genuine. "I like her already. Ari, right? You're the one who threatened Tristian over video chat?"

"That was a promise, not a threat." Ariana grins. "Big difference."

"Semantics." Marcus throws an arm around Ariana's shoulders like they've been friends for years. "You, me, and Emily need to form an alliance. Keep these Lambert people in line."

"The three amigos," Ariana agrees.

"I'm standing right here," I protest.

Emily rolls forward, Mochi keeping pace. "They're not wrong. You do need supervision."

Michelle loops her arm through Emily's, already pulling out her phone. "I'm texting you my agent's contact information. She handles emerging designers, and your work deserves representation."

"I haven't even graduated—"

"Details." Michelle waves dismissively.

Peter clears his throat. "The premiere starts in fifteen minutes."

The usher guides us to our row—front section, aisle seats with accessibility space. Studio knew I'd requested it months ago, back when Emily was just a possibility I couldn't stop thinking about.

Cameras still track our every movement. The flash of phones, the whisper of gossip spreading through the crowd.

Emily positions her wheelchair beside the designated seat, locks the wheels. "This part's always fun with an audience."

"You don't have to—"

"I've got it." She transfers the armrest, adjusts her position. Determination settles across her features, the same expression she wore when facing down the Dadrazzi outside. "Just... stay close. In case."

I crouch beside her wheelchair, hands hovering without actually touching. She doesn't need me grabbing at her, treating her like glass. But if she loses balance—

Emily grips the theatre seat armrest with her right hand, braces against her wheelchair with her left. Her core engages as she shifts her weight, sliding across. The silver gown pools around her legs, fabric catching for a moment.

"Here." I adjust the material so it doesn't tangle.

She completes the transfer smoothly, settling into the theatre seat with practiced efficiency. "See? Told you."

"You did." I can't keep the pride from my voice. "Still going to hover."

"I'd be disappointed if you didn't."

Mochi positions himself at her feet, a warm presence against her legs. The labradoodle's already in full service mode, alert but calm.

I reach for her wheelchair, finding the lever underneath to switch it to manual mode. The electronic controls power down with a soft click.

"Sir?" An usher appears, young kid with nervous energy. "I can store that for you. We have a secure area for mobility devices."

Emily tenses beside me. Her hand finds mine, squeezes.

"It'll be safe," I murmur. "Right there when we need it."

"I know. Just—" She exhales slowly. "Feels weird. Like losing a limb."

Michelle leans across Jean and Levi. "I get anxious when they valet my car. Same thing, different wheels."

"Exactly the same," Emily agrees, smiling despite her obvious discomfort.

I release the wheelchair to the usher, watching as he rolls it up the aisle. Cameras catch every moment—probably already uploading to social media. *Tristian Lambert's Girlfriend Uses Wheelchair.* The headlines write themselves.

"Stop thinking about the press," Emily says quietly.

"How did you—"

"Your jaw does this thing." She touches my face, just below my ear. "Tightens when you're stressed."

I settle into the seat beside her, our shoulders pressing together. The theatre fills around us—cast members, studio executives, critics already composing reviews in their heads. Michelle and Jean take the seats to Emily's right, Levi beyond them. Marcus and Ariana grab spots in the row behind us.

"Popcorn?" Ariana thrusts a massive bucket between our seats. "Theater guy gave me extra butter. Think he recognized me from your Instagram."

"You posted?" Emily twists to look at her.

"Just the red carpet entrance. You looked gorgeous." Ariana grins, shameless. "Might've tagged Tristian. And Michelle. And used approximately forty hashtags."

Marcus leans forward. "Forty-two. I counted."

The lights dim. Conversations fade to whispers.

Emily's hand finds mine in the darkness, fingers intertwining. Her thumb traces circles across my knuckles, soothing.

On screen, the Starlight Studios logo appears. Then darkness. Then—

White rabbits racing across a field of red poppies.

Alice begins.

The opening credits roll over a dreamlike landscape— roses painted red, hedgehogs curled into croquet balls, flamingos stretching their necks toward impossible angles.

Then Alice tumbles down the rabbit hole.

Emily's grip on my hand tightens as the girl falls, falls, falls through the darkness. Her breathing stays even despite the tension in her shoulders. Mochi's head lifts, sensing her anxiety, but she touches his ears and he settles.

The film unfolds across the screen. Alice shrinks, grows, navigates a world that makes no sense. The White Rabbit rushes past with his pocket watch. The Caterpillar smokes his hookah on a mushroom, dispensing cryptic wisdom.

Then the tea party.

I watch myself appear on screen as the Mad Hatter, caught mid-laugh with a teacup raised. The costume department outdid themselves—mismatched patterns, a top hat listing at a dangerous angle, eyes slightly too bright with barely-contained chaos.

Levi's March Hare bounces into frame, whiskers twitching. "Clean cup! Move down!"

The theatre laughs. Emily's hand squeezes mine again, different this time. Pride, maybe. Wonder.

The Hatter notices Alice watching from behind a tree. His expression shifts—madness giving way to something sharper. Curious.

"You're not from here," my screen-self says, circling Alice slowly. "The Queen will have your head if she finds you wandering about unclaimed."

"I don't belong to anyone," Alice protests.

"Precisely the problem." The Hatter produces a silver chain from his pocket, a tiny top hat pendant dangling from it. "Wear this. Anyone sees it, they'll know you're under my protection. Even the Queen won't dare cross that boundary."

"Why would you protect me?"

The Hatter's smile goes crooked. "Because, my dear Alice, you're the first interesting thing to happen in

Wonderland in quite some time. And I've grown dreadfully bored."

Alice accepts the necklace. The camera lingers on her fastening it, the pendant settling against her throat.

Michelle whispers something to Jean. He nods, grinning.

The story continues. The Queen of Hearts appears—not monstrous but theatrical, all grand gestures and elaborate gowns. My step-sister in the film's mythology, played by Helena Cunningham with delicious over-the-top flair.

"Hatter!" The Queen sweeps into the garden, her court trailing behind. "Who is this creature you've claimed?"

"Alice," I say on screen, stepping between them. "She's under my protection, Your Majesty. As is her right."

The Queen examines Alice like a particularly interesting specimen. Then she breaks into a radiant smile. "How delightful! We haven't had a proper Alice in ages. The last one was dreadfully dull. This one has spirit."

She takes Alice's hand, declaring her an honored guest.

But shadows move in the background. The Knave of Hearts watches from the rose garden, scheming. The Cheshire Cat materializes in a tree, grin too wide, eyes calculating where everyone else sees only whimsy.

The villains of the piece. Not the Queen with her bombastic threats, but the quiet manipulators working beneath the surface.

Emily leans closer. "They twisted it," she breathes. "Made the obvious villain sympathetic."

"Director's choice," I murmur back. "Said everyone expects the Queen to be the monster. Wanted to subvert that."

The trial of the stolen tarts becomes a mystery instead of absurdity. The Knave framed someone. The Cat orchestrated it. Alice pieces together the truth while the Hatter distracts the court with increasingly nonsensical testimony.

"You're protecting her again," Emily observes.

"Always."

On screen, Alice solves the case. The real culprits revealed, the Queen declares the matter settled. Then asks the question:

"Will you stay, Alice? Wonderland could use someone with your particular clarity."

The camera holds on Alice's face. Decision weighing. Return to the ordinary world, or remain in madness?

She looks at the Hatter. He tips his hat, expression hopeful beneath the chaos.

"I'll stay," Alice says.

The final scene: a wedding in the Queen's garden. Alice in white, the Hatter in an only slightly more organized suit. The March Hare serves as best man. The Queen officiates with theatrical flourish.

"You may kiss your bride," she declares.

The Hatter sweeps Alice into his arms. The kiss lingers, sweet and certain.

The screen fades to black as Wonderland celebrates.

Applause erupts through the theatre. Critics stand. Cast members beam.

Emily's crying. Silent tears tracking down her face, ruining her carefully applied makeup.

"Hey." I brush them away with my thumb. "What's wrong?"

"Nothing's wrong." She laughs, watery and bright. "It's perfect. You're perfect. She stayed. Alice stayed."

Understanding hits. The parallel she's drawing. Alice choosing Wonderland. Emily choosing—

"I'd stay too," she whispers. "If you asked."

The applause continues around us. Cameras flash. But all I see is Emily, emerald eyes shining in the darkness, declaring something that sounds remarkably like forever.

Chapter 7: You Are It

The drive back stretches electric. Emily's declaration still echoes between us—*I'd stay too, if you asked.*

Marcus drives while Michelle and Jean discuss the film's cinematography. Ariana scrolls through her phone, reading social media reactions. Emily's quiet beside me, fingers laced with mine, poppy diadem catching streetlight.

I haven't let go since the theatre.

"Ariana," I say as we pull through the security gate. "Guest house is yours. Fully stocked fridge, hot tub on the deck, Wi-Fi password's on the counter."

She perks up. "Guest house?"

"Separate entrance, total privacy." I meet her eyes in the rearview mirror. "Unless you'd prefer the main house."

"Guest house sounds perfect." Her grin goes knowing. "I'll be fine. Completely. Won't need anything."

Marcus parks near the entrance. Michelle whistles low. "You went full renovation, didn't you?"

"Might've added a few things."

The front ramp flows seamlessly into the landscaping now—nothing institutional about it. Just smooth concrete curves between the rosebushes, wide enough for Emily's chair with space to spare.

Jean helps unload luggage while Ariana explores her temporary quarters. Mochi bounds out, immediately investigating every scent.

"Come here, boy." I lead him through the house. "Got something for you."

The downstairs bedroom—my former guest room—is pure dog paradise. Orthopedic bed bigger than most humans need, toy basket overflowing, water fountain bubbling in the corner. Floor-to-ceiling windows overlook the pool.

"Puppy palace," Emily breathes. "You built him a puppy palace."

"He's important to you." I scratch behind Mochi's ears. "That makes him important to me. Plus he's got the bedroom upstairs too, next to—"

"Next to what?"

Right. She hasn't seen upstairs yet.

"Let me show you."

The elevator gleams, brushed steel and mirrored walls. I installed it where the coat closet used to be, cutting through to the second floor. Barely noticeable unless you know where to look.

Emily rolls inside. "When did you—"

"Started the day after New York." I press the button. "Contractor thought I was insane, demanding it finished before you arrived."

The doors open onto the landing. Everything's wider now—doorways, hallways, even the crown molding redesigned to accommodate the structural changes.

My bedroom sits at the end of the hall. I rebuilt the entrance, removing the double doors for a single extra-wide one. Custom-made, hand-carved mahogany that cost more than my first car.

"Tristian." Emily's voice goes soft.

Inside, the transformation's complete. California king platform bed, lower than standard, with a ramp on one side for easy transfer. The fireplace mantle repositioned, accessible. Bookshelves at reachable heights. Even the light switches lowered.

Mochi's second bed sits near the window, cushioned and ready.

The bathroom makes Emily gasp. Roll-in shower with multiple seats, grab bars that don't look medical, heated tile floors. Dual vanity with one side lower, mirror angled perfect for wheelchair height.

"The tub—"

"Big enough for two. Thought it might help after long days. Your physical therapist mentioned hydrotherapy."

"You talked to my physical therapist?"

"Wanted to get everything right."

She rolls through the space, touching surfaces, testing accessibility. Her reflection multiplies in the mirrors—silver dress, poppy crown, eyes bright with unshed tears.

"This is too much."

"Not possible." I kneel beside her chair. "Emily, nothing's too much for you."

Her hands cup my face. "I haven't even graduated yet. We've only been together eight months."

"Eight months, two weeks, four days." I turn to kiss her palm. "But who's counting?"

She laughs, watery. "You're ridiculous."

"Ridiculously in love with you." The words come easy. True. "The Lambert curse, remember? My family falls fast and stays fallen."

"Your family." She traces my jawline. "Not just you."

"Jean knew Levi was it after their first coffee date. Michelle swears she knew about Marcus the second he walked into her photoshoot. My grandfather proposed to Gran after knowing her seventy-two hours."

"Seventy-two hours?"

"They were married sixty-three years." I stand, pulling her gently against me. "When you know, you know."

Her chair's battery light blinks. Right—needs charging.

"Outlet's by the nightstand," I say. "Had them installed every six feet."

While Emily plugs in, I slip into the bathroom. Matches, candles, rose petals scattered across surfaces— preparation from earlier, when hope felt more fragile than certainty.

The candles flicker to life. Soft light, warm shadows.

When I return, Emily's transferred to the bed. The diadem rests on the nightstand.

She's stunning. Always has been.

"Come here," she whispers.

I do.

My hands shake reaching for the zipper at her back. Months of research, preparation, planning—none of it steadies the tremor in my fingers.

"You okay?" Emily's voice carries warmth, no judgment.

"Terrified I'll mess this up."

"You won't."

The zipper slides smooth, revealing pale skin inch by inch. I work slowly, giving her time to stop me if she wants. The silver fabric pools around her waist, and I help ease it down over her hips, careful not to jostle her legs.

She's wearing simple cotton—lavender panties, soft bra without clasps or hooks. Practical. The kind that goes on and off without complicated maneuvering.

"These make mornings easier," she says, catching my gaze. "Ariana calls them my independence underwear."

"They're perfect."

Because they are. Because she is.

Scars map her body like a different kind of tattoo— evidence of survival, persistence, battles fought in operating rooms instead of on stages. Two thin lines mark her right hip, barely visible unless you're looking. Surgical precision that probably hurt like hell when she was too young to remember.

"Hip tendon release." She follows my gaze. "I was three. Don't remember the surgery, just Mom—my second foster mom—telling me I was brave."

I trace the marks with one finger, feather-light. "These too?"

"Those too." Her hand covers mine. "I've got more. Ankle surgeries at seven and nine. Nothing dramatic. Just... maintenance."

"You don't have to explain."

"I want to." She shifts against the pillows, moonlight catching the curve of her shoulder. "Everyone sees the chair first. The disability. But the scars—they're mine. They're what it took to walk as much as I did, for as long as I could."

My throat tightens. "How long?"

"Until fourteen. Muscles gave up before I did." No bitterness in her voice, just fact. "Some kids with schizencephaly never walk. I got years. The surgeries bought me that."

I kiss the scars, both of them, feeling the slight texture difference against my lips. "Thank you."

"For what?"

"Fighting. Being here. Letting me—"

"Tristian." She tugs me up, eye level. "Stop spiraling. I'm here because I want to be. Not because you renovated your house or bought me poppies or researched adaptive positions."

"Though the research helps?"

"The research helps." Her smile goes wicked. "But mostly I'm here because you're you. And I'm me. And this —" She gestures between us. "—feels right."

Right doesn't cover it. Nothing in my vocabulary does.

I run my hands along her sides, mapping the landscape of her. She's soft where muscles relaxed years ago, firmer where they compensate for what doesn't work. Every curve tells a story—medical history, daily battles, small victories.

"You're staring again."

"Can't help it." My thumb traces her ribcage. "You're extraordinary."

"I'm in my underwear and you're fully dressed. That's what's extraordinary."

Fair point.

I stand, shrugging off the jacket. Bow tie next—never could stand the things. Shirt buttons take forever with fingers gone clumsy.

"Need help?" Emily props herself on her elbows, grinning.

"I've got it."

"Could've fooled me."

The shirt hits the floor. Pants follow. I leave my boxer briefs on—matching her vulnerability, not rushing.

When I return to the bed, she reaches for me.

"Hi," she whispers.

"Hi yourself."

Emily's fingers trace the tattoo over my ribs—Erik in Gothic lettering. "Does this one hurt?"

"Like you wouldn't believe." I shiver under her touch. "Bone hurts worse than muscle."

"Good to know." She grins, shifting onto her side. Her hand trails down, exploring. "What about this one?"

Miles Reid, Quantum's symbol etched beneath. "Less painful. More... tedious."

Her laugh vibrates against my skin. "Tedious? Really?"

"Four hours in the chair. Artist kept taking smoke breaks."

"Four hours?" Her eyebrows lift. "That's dedication."

"Or stupidity." I lean in, kissing her shoulder. "Depends on who you ask."

Her breath hitches. "Who would you ask?"

"No one." I kiss her again, lower this time. "Because no one matters but you."

She smiles, soft and slow. "Smooth talker."

"Just truth."

I reach for her bra, fingers skimming her sides. She lifts her arms, helping me ease the cotton over her head. Her breasts are perfect—small, round, nipples already hardening. I cup one, thumb circling the peak. She gasps, arching into my touch.

"Okay?" I ask.

"More than okay." Her voice goes breathy. "Don't stop."

So I don't. I lean down, taking her nipple into my mouth. Her hands fist in my hair, holding me close. Every flick of my tongue draws a new sound from her—soft moans, sharp gasps, whispers of my name.

When I finally lift my head, her eyes are dark with desire. I hook my fingers in her panties, tugging them down. She kicks them off, impatient.

"Pillow," I murmur, reaching for one. I prop it under her hips, lifting her slightly. She watches me, curiosity mixed with heat.

I part her thighs, slow and gentle. Her muscles tremble under my hands, tense with anticipation. I settle between her legs, shoulders pressing against her inner thighs.

"Tristian—" She starts to sit up, but I press a hand to her stomach, easing her back down.

"Let me," I say. "Please."

She nods, biting her lip. I can see the nervousness in her eyes, the uncertainty. But there's trust too. And that's what matters most.

I start slow, tracing her folds with my tongue. She tastes sweet, musky, intoxicating. Her hips jerk slightly, responsive even with limited movement. I take my time, learning her body, listening to her breath hitch and release.

Every flick of my tongue draws a new sound from her. She's vocal, expressive, holding nothing back. Her hands find my hair again, gripping tight. I slide one finger inside her, feeling her clench around me.

"Oh god," she gasps. "Tristian—"

I add another finger, curling them upward. Her hips lift slightly, meeting my rhythm. I can feel her tension building, coiling tighter with each stroke.

Her orgasm hits hard. She cries out, body shaking as waves of pleasure crash over her. I ride it out with her, fingers moving slower, tongue gentle against her sensitive flesh.

When she finally stills, I press a soft kiss to her inner thigh. She looks down at me, eyes glazed, cheeks flushed.

"Wow," she breathes. "That was... wow."

I grin, crawling up beside her. "Good wow?"

"Amazing wow." She turns onto her side, facing me. Her hand cups my cheek, thumb brushing my lips. "Thank you."

"No thanks needed." I kiss her palm. "That was all for you."

Her smile goes soft. "I've never... I mean, I didn't know if I could..."

"Could what?"

"Feel that," she admits. "I've read about it, obviously. But my body doesn't always cooperate. I wasn't sure if—"

"If you could orgasm?"

She nods.

"Well, now you know." I tuck a strand of hair behind her ear. "And we'll keep learning, together."

Her eyes shine with unshed tears. "Together," she echoes.

I pull her close, holding her against me. Her heart beats steady against mine, syncopated rhythm. This feels right—her in my arms, my name on her lips. Like everything before was just rehearsal, and this is opening night.

"Tristian?" she murmurs.

"Hmm?"

"I want you inside me."

Heat surges through me. But I hesitate, remembering her words earlier. "Emily, we don't have to rush—"

"I'm not rushing." She lifts her head, meeting my gaze. "I'm sure. I want this. Want you."

And who am I to argue with that?

I ease back, searching her face. "You're sure?"

Emily's eyes meet mine, steady and certain. "Positive."

Shifting onto my knees, I hook my thumbs into my boxer briefs, pushing them down. My cock springs free, already hard and aching. Emily's gaze drops, eyes widening slightly.

"Okay?" I ask.

She nods, swallowing. "More than okay."

I reach for the nightstand, fumbling for the condom I stashed earlier. But Emily's hand covers mine, stopping me.

"Don't," she says.

My brow furrows. "Don't what?"

"Don't use that." She takes the packet from my hand, tossing it aside. "I'm on birth control. The patch. And I have PCOS—it's not like I ovulate regularly anyway."

A primal surge goes through me—possessiveness, raw and fierce. Mine. She's mine.

"Emily—" My voice goes low, gruff. "You're certain?"

"Completely." Her fingers wrap around my length, guiding me toward her. "I want to feel you. All of you."

Christ, this woman. She undoes me.

I shift between her thighs, lining myself up. Her hips barely lift, but it's enough. I slide in slowly, inch by inch, watching her face for any sign of discomfort. None comes. Only pleasure, eyes dark with it, lips parted on soft gasps.

"Alright, love?" I murmur, voice gone thick with desire.

She nods, hands gripping my shoulders. "Don't stop."

So I don't. I sink deeper, feeling her clench around me, tight and hot and perfect. When I'm fully sheathed, I pause, letting her adjust. Her breath hitches, nails digging into my skin.

"Tristian," she whispers. "Move. Please."

Bracing myself on one elbow, I begin to thrust—slow, steady, mindful of her body's limits. Her hips don't meet mine, but that's alright. I'll do the moving for both of us.

I lean down, kissing her deep. She moans into my mouth, tongue tangling with mine. My pace quickens, driven by her sounds, her taste, her scent surrounding me.

"You feel incredible," I murmur against her lips. "So bloody perfect."

Her legs barely move, but her arms wrap around me, holding tight. I slide a hand beneath her ass, lifting slightly, angling her hips. She gasps, breaking our kiss.

"There?" I ask.

"Yes," she breathes. "Right there."

I hit that spot again, grinding against her. Her moan fills the room, music to my ears. Sweat beads on my brow, spine tingling with building tension.

"Emily," I groan. "Emily—"

Her name becomes a chant on my lips, a prayer in French and English. *Emily. Mon Dieu, Emily. You're mine, love. All mine.*

Her body responds, clenching tighter, drawing me deeper. I can feel her pleasure mounting, matching my own. But I need more. Need her there with me, tumbling over the edge.

Reaching between us, I find her clit, circling it with my thumb. Her cry echoes off the walls, sharp and sudden.

"Come on, love," I coax. "Come for me. Let me feel you."

And she does. Her orgasm grips her, stealing her breath, pulsing around me. It's enough to send me spiraling, following her into bliss.

I come hard, spilling inside her, claiming her completely. Mine. She's mine.

We lie there, panting, hearts pounding together. I'm still inside her, still hard. Still wanting.

"Tristian," she murmurs, voice sated and soft.

"Hmm?" I nuzzle her neck, inhaling her scent.

"That was... incredible."

"You're incredible." I lift my head, meeting her gaze. "And you're mine."

Her smile goes radiant. "Yours."

Carefully, I ease out, rolling onto my side. Pulling her against me, I reach for the blankets, covering us both. She nestles into my chest, sighing contentedly.

"I love you," I whisper into her hair.

She tilts her head, kissing my jaw. "I love you too."

We lie there, basking in the afterglow. But soon, too soon, I feel her stirring beside me.

"Bathroom," she murmurs, already reaching for her chair.

I sit up, swinging my legs over the edge of the bed. "Let me."

Before she can protest, I scoop her into my arms, carrying her toward the en suite. She laughs, clinging to my neck.

"I can do it myself, you know."

"I know." I set her down gently on the cool tile. "But let me take care of you. Please."

She looks up at me, eyes soft. "Alright."

I help her onto the toilet, turning away to give her privacy. When she's done, I lift her again, setting her on the vanity while I wash my hands.

"Toothbrush?" I ask.

She nods. "I'd like that."

Reaching for the spare toothbrush I kept for her, I squeeze on a dollop of paste. She takes it, smiling. We brush side by side, domestic and intimate.

After rinsing, I carry her back to bed. She snuggles into the pillows, watching as I clean myself up quickly before joining her.

"You're good at that," she says as I slide in beside her.

"At what?"

"Taking care of me." She traces patterns on my chest, fingers light. "Most people... they either do too much or not enough. You're just right."

Warmth spreads through me at her words. "I'm glad, love."

Her hand stills, resting over my heart. "I never thought... I never imagined someone like you."

"Someone like me?"

"Kind. Gentle. Patient." She looks up at me, eyes shining. "Loving."

I cup her cheek, thumb brushing her skin. "I never imagined someone like you either. Strong. Brave. Beautiful." I lean down, kissing her softly. "Mine."

Her smile widens. "Yours."

Emily's breathing evens out, settling into sleep's rhythm. But I'm not done yet.

Sliding carefully from beneath her, I ease off the bed. Her physical therapist's instructions echo in my mind—*warm muscles prevent spasms, gentle movement stops joints from locking.*

The heating pad waits in the bathroom cabinet, right where I stashed it. I grab it along with the massage oil, lavender-scented because she mentioned it helps her relax.

Back at the bedside, I plug in the heating pad, waiting for it to warm. Emily stirs slightly but doesn't wake.

"Shh," I murmur, pressing a kiss to her temple. "Just taking care of you."

When the pad reaches temperature, I drape it across her hips. She sighs, muscles already responding to the heat. I pour oil into my palms, rubbing them together before working the liquid into her thighs.

Gentle pressure, circular motions—techniques I studied from three different physiotherapy videos. Her muscles give under my touch, releasing tension I didn't realize she carried.

"Warm hip is a happy hip," I whisper, repeating what her therapist told me during our phone consultation.

Emily hums, half-asleep. "You remembered."

"I remember everything about you."

I work down to her calves, kneading carefully. Her legs don't respond like most people's would, but that doesn't matter. What matters is preventing the morning stiffness, the spasms that could steal her smile.

After fifteen minutes, I remove the heating pad, setting it aside to cool. Emily's completely asleep now, breathing deep and steady. I clean my hands, then slip back into bed beside her.

She rolls toward me instinctively, nestling against my chest. Mochi lifts his head from his bed near the window, checking on his person before settling back down.

I reach for my phone on the nightstand, thumbs hovering over the Lambert family group chat. Jean, Marcus, Michelle—they've been waiting for updates since we left the premiere.

Tristian: She's the one.

Three dots appear immediately. Then Jean's response.

Jean: We know. You told us eight months ago.

Michelle: And every day since.

Marcus: Man's got it BAD.

I grin at the screen, typing faster.

Tristian: I'm going to propose. Soon. Something Wonderful themed.

The chat explodes.

Michelle: FINALLY

Jean: About bloody time

Marcus: Wonderful Wizard of Oz?? My man's going THEATRICAL

Levi: (Jean's showing me over his shoulder) DO IT. She's perfect for you.

Michelle: When? Where? Do you have a ring?

Tristian: Working on details. Want it perfect. She deserves perfect.

Marcus: She deserves YOU, which is pretty damn close

I set the phone aside, wrapping my arms around Emily. She murmurs something unintelligible, burrowing closer.

"Love you," I whisper against her hair.

In sleep, she smiles.

My mind spins with possibilities—yellow brick road motifs, emerald green accents, poppies everywhere. A proposal worthy of Dorothy herself.

But that's tomorrow's problem.

Tonight, I just hold her.

My future.

My always.

Mine.

Emily's breathing stays deep and even when I slip from the bed. Mochi lifts his head, watching me pad across the hardwood floor. I press a finger to my lips. He settles back down, understanding.

The guest house sits beyond the pool, lights still glowing through the windows. Ariana's awake—probably scrolling through tonight's social media explosion. Pictures of Emily and me on the red carpet already trend across three platforms.

I knock softly. Footsteps approach, then the door swings open.

"If you hurt her, I don't care how famous you are—" Ariana starts.

"I need your blessing to propose."

She blinks. "What?"

"Emily's asleep. You're the closest thing she has to a sister." I meet her eyes, meaning every word. "I won't ask without your permission."

Ariana stares at me for three full seconds. Then she grabs my arm, yanking me inside. "Get in here before you wake the whole neighborhood."

The guest house mirrors my main home's aesthetic— clean lines, warm woods, comfortable furniture. Ariana's laptop sits open on the coffee table, displaying a Twitter feed filled with tonight's premiere photos.

"You're serious." She crosses her arms. "You want to propose."

"During her birthday weekend. August thirty-first."

"That's three months away."

"Ninety-two days." I run a hand through my hair. "I've been planning since New York. But I need your help."

Her expression softens slightly. "What exactly are you planning?"

"Starlight Studios Paris. The Wonderful World section." I pull out my phone, showing her the research I've compiled. "They have a theatre inside the Emerald City attraction. Does a fifteen-minute show every hour featuring songs from the musical."

Ariana's eyes widen. "She's obsessed with that show."

"I know. I've been studying the books—all fourteen Baum originals, plus Corbyn's novel from '94." I swipe to another file. "The musical premiered in 2005. I've read every behind-the-scenes book published, watched every bootleg recording I could find."

"You've done homework."

"I'm auditioning for Felix next month. Dorothy's love interest." I meet her gaze. "The Prince of Oz. Son of Ozma."

"The Scarecrow." Recognition sparks in her eyes. "Emily's favorite character besides Dorothy."

"Exactly." I pull up another document. "In Emerald City tradition, proposals happen during the Festival of Lights. The suitor presents their beloved with a ring made from compressed emeralds and recites a declaration of intent before witnesses."

Ariana sinks onto the couch. "You memorized Ozian marriage customs."

"Every tradition. Every ritual. Every blessing and vow." I sit beside her. "Emily knows this lore better than anyone. If I'm going to do this, it has to be perfect."

She studies me, protective instinct warring with something else. Hope, maybe. "She's been hurt so much. Foster care, abuse, people leaving—"

"I'm not leaving." The words come fierce, absolute. "Ever. That's why I'm asking you first. Because you know her better than anyone, and you'll tell me if this is wrong."

Silence stretches between us. Ariana's fingers drum against her knee, thinking.

"The finale," she says finally. "During the show's finale. That's when you should do it."

"The finale?"

She pulls up a video on her laptop, queuing to the final number. "Emily cries every single time. Says it's about people changing each other, making each other better."

"Perfect," I whisper.

Ariana nods. "I'll help. But Tristian?"

"Yeah?"

"If you screw this up, Mochi will be the least of your problems."

I grin. "Understood."

My phone buzzes. Jean's sent a text.

Jean: Found three jewelers in Paris. Sending links. Michelle says go with Cartier.

Michelle: (replying) DON'T go with Cartier. Too obvious. Try Boucheron. They do custom emerald work.

Marcus: Y'all are thinking too small. Man needs something SPECIAL.

I show Ariana the thread. She laughs. "Your family's intense."

"They're invested." I type a response.

I glance toward the main house, where Emily sleeps in our bed. Our home. Our future stretching out like yellow brick road.

"Thank you," I tell Ariana. "For trusting me with her."

She softens. "Thank you for loving her right."

The ceiling fan rotates in lazy circles. I count the blades —one, two, three, four, five—then start over. Beside me, Tristian breathes deep and even, one arm draped across my waist.

2:47 AM. The clock on his nightstand glows soft blue.

I should sleep. Should close my eyes and drift off wrapped in Egyptian cotton sheets worth more than my entire childhood wardrobe. Instead, I trace the path that led here.

Foster homes. Closets. Pain. Then fashion school, Ariana, survival.

And now... this.

Tristian flew me to New York on a private jet. His family treats me like I already belong. Tonight, cameras flashed while I wore a gown *I* designed, sitting beside a man who researched disability accommodations because he wanted to love me properly.

I should feel grateful. Blessed. Like every dream came true at once.

But there's this weight in my chest. This certainty that happiness this bright burns out fast.

What happens when he realizes?

When he understands I come with doctor appointments and muscle spasms and days my body simply refuses to cooperate. When red carpets become exhausting instead of exciting. When he wants spontaneity—late-night drives, impromptu trips, adventures—and I need predictability, planning, accessible everything.

When he sees I'm not whole.

The thought tastes bitter.

"Emily?"

I freeze. Tristian's voice carries that edge of alertness—instantly awake, instantly concerned.

"I'm okay."

He rises on one elbow, studying me in the darkness. His hair sticks up on one side, endearing and rumpled. "Your breathing changed."

"Just thinking."

"About?" His thumb strokes my shoulder, gentle and persistent.

The words stick. Then unstick. "I wish I could be... whole. For you."

Silence. I can't see his expression clearly, but tension radiates through his frame.

"You are."

"Don't lie."

"I'm not." He shifts, and suddenly I'm cradled against him, his heartbeat steady beneath my ear. "Emily—"

"You say that now. But eventually you'll want someone who can—"

"Stop." Not harsh. Firm. "How about I prove it, love?"

My self-doubt cracks. Just slightly. "Prove what?"

"That you're everything." His lips brush my temple. "Right now. Exactly as you are."

"Tristian—"

"No." He tilts my chin up, forcing me to meet his eyes. Even in shadow, they burn with something fierce. "You think I renovated this entire house on a whim? Spent three months researching adaptive equipment and accessibility features because I was bored?"

"I—"

"I did it because I see *you*. Not what you think you're missing. Not some idealized version without challenges." His voice drops lower, more intimate. "I see Emily. The woman who survived hell and still creates beauty. Who critiques my films and sings grunge karaoke and makes her own red carpet gowns."

Tears prick hot behind my eyes.

"The woman I'm completely gone for," he continues. "Wheelchair, service dog, scars, spasms, all of it. That's who I choose. Every single day."

"But what if—"

"No what-ifs." He kisses me softly. "We handle whatever comes. Together. That's what this is."

Something loosens in my ribcage. Not all the doubt— that'll take time, therapy, proof. But enough that I can breathe deeper.

"Prove it, then," I whisper.

His smile curves against my skin. "Gladly."

Tristian's lips trail down my neck, slow and reverent. Each kiss lingers, igniting sparks beneath my skin. He pauses at my collarbone, then lower, tracing the curve of my breast. I gasp when he takes one nipple into his mouth, arching beneath him as warmth pools in my core.

"You're perfect," he murmurs against my flesh. His hands roam, mapping every inch of me, callouses catching on smooth skin. Each touch erases doubt, replaces it with belonging.

He moves lower, kissing along my ribcage. I squirm, giggling at the ticklish sensation. His chuckle vibrates through me, deep and throaty. Then he reaches my belly button, dipping his tongue inside. My giggles shift to moans.

"You like that?" His voice rumbles against my stomach.

I nod, words stolen by sensation.

He lavishes attention there, kissing and licking until I'm writhing. Then he hooks his hands under my thighs, spreading me wide. Cool air hits hot flesh.

"Tristian..." I half-sit, reaching for him.

"Shh." He grins up at me, wicked and sweet all at once. "Let me worship you, Emily."

His head dips between my legs. At the first touch of his tongue, I collapse back onto the pillow. Pleasure jolts through me, electric and raw. He takes his time, exploring every fold, every sensitive spot. Learning what makes me gasp, what makes me cry out.

My orgasm builds slow and steady. I clutch the sheets, anchoring myself as waves of ecstasy threaten to drown me. Tristian's grip tightens on my thighs, holding me in place as he devours me.

"Oh god," I pant. "Tristian..."

He hums approval, the vibration sending me spiraling higher. Then he slides two fingers inside, curling them just right. I shatter, coming undone around him.

When I finally float back down, he's there, propped on one elbow, watching me. His lips glisten with my release. I reach up, tracing his mouth with shaky fingers.

"Is that enough, my love?" he asks softly. "Or do I need to make love to you for the rest of the night?"

I smile, heart full. "Make love to me, Tristian. All night long."

Tristian carries me to the bathroom, strong arms cradling me against his chest. His heartbeat thrums steady beneath my ear.

"Can you stand?" He sets me carefully on my feet, hands steadying my hips.

"Yeah." I grip the grab bar he installed—one of dozens throughout this house, all placed exactly where I'd need them.

He turns away, giving me privacy. Water runs in the sink while I use the toilet. The mundane intimacy of it strikes me. No embarrassment. No awkwardness. Just... comfort.

"All done?"

"Mhm."

He faces me again, eyes soft. "Bath?"

I glance at the massive tub—deep, with built-in seating and handrails. "At three AM?"

"Why not, ma pitite?"

The French endearment melts something inside me. "You're ridiculous."

"You love it." He starts the water, testing the temperature before adding bath salts. Steam rises, smelling of lavender and eucalyptus.

When the tub fills halfway, Tristian lifts me again. I sink into warm water with a grateful sigh. He slides behind me, legs bracketing mine.

"Lean back."

I settle against his chest. His arms circle my waist, anchoring me. We float together in silence, water lapping gently.

"This okay?" he murmurs against my hair.

"Perfect."

His fingers trace lazy patterns on my stomach. Not sexual—just touching. Connecting.

"Tell me something," I whisper.

"Anything."

"Why me?" The question escapes before I can stop it. "You could have anyone."

"I don't want anyone." His grip tightens slightly. "I want you."

"But—"

"Emily." He turns my chin, forcing eye contact. "Stop looking for reasons I'll leave. I won't."

"How can you know that?"

"Because." He kisses my temple. "You're it for me. The Lambert curse, remember? We fall once. Forever."

I want to argue. To point out all the ways this could fail. But exhaustion weighs heavy, and his embrace feels too safe.

"Okay," I breathe.

"Yeah?"

"Yeah."

We soak until the water cools. Then Tristian dries me with a fluffy towel, gentle and thorough. He wraps me in his robe—too big, sleeves hanging past my hands—and carries me back to bed.

The sheets welcome me like a cloud. I burrow into the pillow while Tristian settles beside me, pulling the duvet over us both.

"Sleep, love."

"Not tired yet." A lie. My eyelids droop.

"Then listen." His fingers card through my hair, soothing. "I'm going to tell you our future."

"Tristian—"

"Shh. Just listen."

I relax into him, letting his voice wash over me.

"You'll move in after graduation," he begins. "Five days from now. No arguments."

I start to protest, but he covers my mouth gently.

"Your studio will be that room overlooking the garden. Perfect light for designing. And you'll take that internship with Michelle's agent—she already loves you."

His vision unfolds like a fairy tale. Me creating adaptive fashion lines. Him supporting every step. Us traveling between LA and Grantham Bridge , building a life.

"Mochi gets a custom doghouse in the backyard," he continues. "With air conditioning. Because we spoil him."

A laugh bubbles up. "Of course we do."

"And when you're ready—no rush—we'll get married. Small ceremony. Just family. Ariana can officiate."

"She'd love that."

"I know." He kisses my forehead. "We'll figure out kids later. Maybe adoption, like you mentioned. Or not. Whatever you want."

My self-doubt quiets. Not gone—it'll return, demanding reassurance. But for now, wrapped in Tristian's certainty, I believe.

"Sounds perfect," I murmur, half-asleep.

"It will be." His arms tighten protectively. "I promise, Emily. It will be."

Darkness tugs me under. Safe. Loved. Home.

The Utah State amphitheater buzzes with pre-ceremony chaos. I stand at the edge of the handicap seating section, watching graduates file in. Michelle adjusts her sunglasses beside me, scanning the crowd.

"There." Marcus points toward the accessibility entrance.

Emily appears in her pink wheelchair, cap gleaming under the afternoon sun. Even from here, I spot the rhinestones—emerald green crystals arranged in patterns across the black mortarboard. Yellow brick road winding toward... is that the Emerald City?

"She bedazzled her graduation cap," Michelle laughs. "Of course she did."

My phone vibrates. Jean's face fills the screen, Levi peering over his shoulder from their Grantham Bridge apartment.

"Can you see her yet?" Jean asks.

"Just arrived." I angle the camera toward Emily, who's transferring from her chair to an aisle seat. Mochi settles at her feet, wearing a tiny green bow tie that matches the Oz theme.

"The dog's more dressed up than I was at my graduation," Levi observes.

"The dog has better fashion sense than you period," Michelle shoots back.

Emily catches my eye across the rows. Her smile—nervous, bright—makes my chest tight. I blow her a kiss. She catches it, presses it to her heart.

"Gross," Marcus mutters, grinning.

The ceremony starts with the usual pomp. Speeches about futures and potential. I barely hear them, watching Emily's profile. She keeps touching her cap, adjusting the rhinestones like they might fall off.

"Department of Arts and Sciences," the dean announces.

My pulse quickens.

Names blur together until—

"Emily Dorothy Silver. Summa Cum Laude. Valedictorian."

The amphitheater erupts. I'm on my feet before conscious thought, shouting louder than anyone. Michelle wolf-whistles. Marcus films everything.

"She didn't tell us she was valedictorian!" Jean's voice crackles through my phone speaker.

Emily wheels toward the podium. My heart hammers. She'll give her speech from the chair—she always does public speaking seated. Easier. Safer.

Except.

She locks her wheels. Grips the podium edge.

"What's she doing?" Michelle breathes beside me.

Emily pushes up. Standing. Hands white-knuckled on the wood, knees locked, every muscle visibly straining.

"Oh my God," I whisper.

She stands there, swaying slightly, and begins.

"Four years ago, I didn't think I'd be here." Her voice carries, strong despite the tremor in her legs. "I didn't think I deserved to be here."

The crowd quiets completely.

"But I learned something in these halls." She pauses, adjusting her grip. "We don't have to wait for permission to chase our dreams. We just have to start walking—or rolling—toward them."

Scattered laughter. Applause.

She speaks for three more minutes. About adaptive design. About creating space for bodies like hers in an industry that ignores them. About fashion as activism, as revolution, as art.

She never sits.

When she finishes, the standing ovation shakes the bleachers. I can't see through the blur in my eyes. Michelle squeezes my hand.

"Your girl's a fighter," Marcus says quietly.

"I know."

The dean steps forward with Emily's diploma—and a second certificate.

"We also recognize Mochi Silver, certified service dog, who attended every class alongside Emily."

The labradoodle's tail wags frantically as Emily accepts both documents, still gripping the podium.

"They gave the dog a degree," Levi gasps through the phone. "I love Americans."

Emily finally sits, collapsing into her wheelchair with visible relief. But her smile blazes brighter than all those emerald rhinestones combined.

And I fall in love with her all over again.

We push through the crowd toward the amphitheater exit. Families cluster everywhere, balloons bobbing, cameras flashing. My chest feels too tight, like my ribs can't contain what's building inside.

Marcus spots them first. "There!"

Emily and Ariana emerge through the accessibility ramp, Mochi trotting between them with his certificate clutched in his teeth. Emily still wears her cap, those emerald rhinestones catching sunlight.

Marcus reaches her before I do, swooping down to lift her straight from the chair. He spins her around, both of them laughing.

"Valedictorian!" He sets her down carefully. "You beautiful genius!"

"You didn't tell us," Ariana mock-scolds, hugging her tight.

Michelle claims Emily next, kissing both her cheeks. "That speech. I'm calling my agent tomorrow. You're designing for Fashion Week."

Then they all step back, leaving space.

I can't move. Can't speak. Every word tangles in my throat.

Emily's smile falters. "Tris?"

"You stood." It comes out broken, thick. The British vowels flood through unchecked. "The entire bloody speech, you stood there."

"I wanted to." Her fingers twist in her lap. "For this. For —"

I'm on my knees before she finishes, face buried against her stomach, arms wrapped around her waist. She smells like vanilla and achievement and everything I've ever wanted.

"Proud of you." My voice cracks. "So impossibly proud."

Her hands thread through my hair, gentle. "You're crying."

"Am not."

"You absolutely are," Jean's voice crackles from Marcus's phone.

"Bugger off," I tell my brother, not lifting my head.

Emily laughs, the sound vibrating through her belly against my cheek. "He flew your whole family in on video."

"We wouldn't miss this!" Levi shouts through the speaker.

I finally pull back, cupping Emily's face. Mascara runs beneath her eyes too. "I'm staying. Few days. Help you pack."

"Pack?"

"You're moving in with me." I brush my thumb across her cheekbone. "Unless you've changed your mind about Los Angeles?"

"I haven't changed my mind about anything." She leans into my palm. "But I graduate today. You didn't have to—"

"I want to. Everything in boxes, sorted, moved. Together." I kiss her forehead, her nose, the corner of her mouth. "Then dinner. Maddox, yeah? Your favorite."

"You remembered."

"I remember everything about you, darling."

Ariana clears her throat. "Should we... give you two a minute?"

"No." Emily catches my hand, intertwining our fingers. "I want everyone here. All of us together."

So we take photos—hundreds of them. Emily in her cap, holding her diploma and Mochi's certificate. Emily with Ariana, with Marcus, with Michelle. Me kneeling beside her chair while she kisses my cheek. Mochi photo-bombing every third shot.

"Tonight," I murmur against her ear while Michelle fusses with her phone angle. "After dinner. Going to worship every inch of you."

Her breath catches. "Tristian—"

"Hours, Em. My mouth between those beautiful thighs until you forget your own name." I nip her earlobe. "Then I'll fill you up, keep you full. Won't let you go until morning."

"People can hear you."

"Don't care." I slide my hand to the nape of her neck, feeling her pulse race. "You're mine. My brilliant, gorgeous genius. And tonight I'm going to show you exactly what that means."

She shivers despite the June heat.

"Okay, lovebirds," Marcus announces. "Steakhouse reservations are in two hours. Emily needs to change, and Tristian needs a cold shower."

"Absolutely not changing," Emily declares. "I'm wearing my cap to dinner."

"With the rhinestones?"

"Especially with the rhinestones."

I lift her from the chair, cradling her close. "Whatever you want, love. Tonight, tomorrow, always. It's yours."

She touches my face, thumb tracing my jaw. "Then take me home."

My phone screams at 5:47. Emily's limbs tangle with mine, her breath warm against my collarbone. I'm still buried inside her from when we woke sometime around three, too desperate to separate.

"Ignore it," she mumbles.

The ringtone persists. Grandmère's contact photo glares from the screen—her in full costume from a 1957 review, feathered and fabulous.

"Can't. She'll send the gendarmes." I shift carefully, reaching for the phone. Emily whimpers at the movement, and Christ, I'm already getting hard again.

"Allô, Grandmère."

"Tristian Alexandre Lambert." Her English carries that clipped Angoumois lilt, every syllable precise. "Your father and brother face reelection in November. The family convenes in Grantham Bridge immediately to campaign."

Emily tenses against me. I stroke her hip, keeping her still.

"When?"

"Now. Jean has already arranged renovations at the château for dear Emily. Bathrooms, your childhood bedroom, the common areas—all accessible. We expect you both by week's end."

My brain struggles through the fog of sleep and sex. "Emily just graduated yesterday."

"Which is why I'm calling this morning rather than last week. Bring her. Bring that charming dog. Michelle and Marcus will meet you there—they're returning from Logan shortly."

Emily's fingers dig into my shoulder. Her emerald eyes have gone wide.

"Grandmère, we haven't—"

"Non, non. No arguments. Your Dad needs his children. All of them." Her voice softens. "Including the one who will soon join us officially."

The line goes dead.

"Tristiaaaann." Emily shifts her hips, and pleasure shoots up my spine. "We're still—oh God—"

"I know, darling." I thrust gently, watching her eyes flutter. "Just give me a minute."

"A minute for what?"

"Arranging our departure." I reach for my phone again, trying to concentrate while she clenches around me. "Then I'm finishing what I started."

I text Derek, my pilot: *Need the jet ready for Grantham Bridge within 48 hours. Two passengers, one service dog, wheelchair accommodations.*

His response comes immediately: *Consider it done. Usual crew?*

Yes. And stock French wine. The good stuff.

I toss the phone aside and roll, pinning Emily beneath me. She gasps, back arching.

"Your family?" She can barely form words.

"Wants us in Angoumois. Campaign season." I kiss down her throat, feeling her pulse race. "Jean renovated the château for you. Every bathroom, my old bedroom, everything."

"Without asking?"

"That's the Lambert way. We renovate first, apologize never." I circle my hips and she moans. "Your things that we don't need will ship to LA. What you need comes with us to Grantham Bridge."

"When?"

"Two days. Maybe three if I can negotiate." I capture her mouth, swallowing her protests. "Michelle and Marcus meet us there."

She threads her fingers through my hair, tugging. "I haven't met your parents yet."

"You will. At the château. In my childhood bed if I have my way." I grin against her lips. "Fair warning—my bedroom's on the second floor overlooking the vineyard. Windows face east. Morning sun's relentless."

"Tristian—"

"And Dad's intense. Gives speeches at breakfast. Mum cries at everything, especially weddings." I kiss her deeper. "Grandmère will love you. She's been calling you 'dear Emily' for months."

"I'm not ready."

"You stood in front of hundreds yesterday and gave a bloody brilliant speech." I pull back, meeting her gaze. "You can handle the Lamberts."

"Your family is political royalty."

"My family are people who love too hard and argue in three languages." I brush hair from her face. "And they already adore you. Jean renovated a château. Michelle's called you family since New York. Marcus sends me memes about our relationship."

"What kind of memes?"

"Mostly Phantom ones. He's predictable." I shift deeper and she gasps. "Now stop worrying about my family and focus on me."

"Demanding."

"You love it."

She does. I can tell by how her body responds, how she pulls me closer, how my name sounds like prayer on her lips.

Afterward, while she dozes against my chest, I text the logistics team: *Need Emily's dorm packed. Ship essentials to Grantham Bridge, everything else to LA. Handle with care—fashion student. Irreplaceable work.*

Mochi whines from his bed in the corner.

"I know, mate," I whisper. "You're coming too."

Emily's phone buzzes from the nightstand while she's folding one of her adaptive dresses. She glances at the screen, frowns, then keeps packing.

It buzzes again. And again.

"You going to check that?" I ask, shoving my toiletries into a duffel.

"Just notifications."

The tone in her voice makes me look up. She's gone rigid, dress clutched against her chest.

I cross the room and grab her phone. The screen displays a flood of YouTube alerts, Instagram tags, Twitter mentions. Michelle's posted photos from graduation—Emily standing at the podium, mortarboard sparkling, me kissing her cheek afterward.

"Oh, bloody hell."

"It's fine." Emily snatches the phone back, but her hands shake.

"Darling—"

"I said it's fine." She wheels to her closet, grabbing hangers with jerky movements.

I open YouTube on my own phone. The top recommendation makes my stomach drop: *TRISTIAN LAMBERT'S MYSTERY GIRLFRIEND: Who Is She?* Three million views in twelve hours.

I tap play.

"—spotted at the Wonderland premiere with fashion student Emily Silver, and guys, I'm not crying, you're crying." The vlogger, some twenty-something with pink hair, displays screenshots. "She designed her own gown. DESIGNED IT. And look at how he looks at her—"

Comments flood past:

She's in a wheelchair and he still looks at her like she's the only person alive I'M SOBBING okay but did you see the accessibility modifications at his house? king behavior

Michelle Lambert posted grad photos! Emily graduated summa cum laude in Fashion Design!

Then the other kind:

gold digger vibes ngl

she's using her disability for sympathy points

how long until he trades up?

"Stop reading them." Emily's voice cracks.

I look up. She's staring at her phone, tears streaming down her face.

"Emily—"

"They're right." She swipes at her eyes. "I'm not—I don't belong in your world. Look at these comments. Half think I'm manipulating you, the other half think you're some saint for dating the 'poor disabled girl.'"

I drop to my knees beside her wheelchair. "That's rubbish."

"Is it?" She shoves her phone at me. "Read this one: 'She's pretty but he could have anyone. Why settle?'"

"Because everyone else isn't you."

"Tristian, your family is political royalty. You're a movie star. I'm a girl from foster care who can't walk properly and has scars all over her arms." Her breath hitches. "What happens when you realize you made a mistake? When the novelty wears off?"

"Novelty?" Heat flares in my chest. "You think this is novelty?"

"I think you're a Lambert. You fall fast and hard. But what if—what if I'm just another role you're playing? The devoted boyfriend, the guy who renovates his house, who—"

I kiss her. Hard enough to stop the spiral, gentle enough not to overwhelm.

When I pull back, her eyes are wide.

"I have eleven tattoos," I say quietly. "Characters I've inhabited. Roles I've played. Not one of them matters compared to you."

"But—"

"Read the supportive comments. The ones saying how brilliant you are. How talented. How you stood up to give that speech and the entire auditorium went silent because you commanded that space." I frame her face with my hands. "That's who you are, Emily. Not what some jealous stranger types from their mum's basement."

Her phone buzzes again. This time it's Marcus in the family chat: *YouTube vultures found her. Em handling it okay?*

Michelle: *Send her my agent's number. We're burying the negativity with professional opportunities.*

Jean: *Dad wants to issue a statement supporting her.*

"See?" I turn the phone so Emily can read. "Lamberts protect their own."

She hiccups a laugh through her tears. "I'm not a Lambert yet."

"Yet." I kiss her forehead. "Now finish packing. We have a plane to catch and a family to scandalize."

"How are we scandalizing them?"

"By being nauseatingly in love. Dad hates public displays of affection. I plan to hold your hand through every campaign dinner."

This time her laugh sounds genuine. "You're impossible."

"You love it."

"I do." She wipes her eyes. "God help me, I really do."

My phone chimes as Emily stuffs another sweater into her suitcase. I glance at the screen.

Mum: The dress Michelle posted. Emily designed this, yes?

I type back: *Yeah. And her mortarboard. Why?*

Three dots appear. Disappear. Appear again.

Mum: I want her to design for the campaign. All of us. Dad, myself, your siblings. Professional, of course. We will pay her rate.

"Bloody hell."

"What?" Emily looks up from folding a pair of jeans.

I turn the phone toward her. "Mum wants to hire you."

She reads the message. Goes pale. Reads it again.

"She's joking."

"Celeste Lambert doesn't joke about fashion." I scroll to show Emily the follow-up text. "She's already asking about your portfolio."

"I—no. No, I can't. I need measurements. Fabric swatches. Theme concepts. Color palettes. What kind of events? Formal? Semi-formal? Outdoor rallies? Indoor galas?" Her voice climbs higher with each question. "Does your father prefer modern cuts or traditional? Does your mother have color preferences? Skin tone considerations? Body type—"

"Darling—"

"—and the timeline! Campaign season is what, three months? Four? That's barely enough time for proper fittings, let alone design iterations and—"

"Emily—"

"—fabric sourcing, which is different in Angoumois, I don't know suppliers, what if I can't get what I need—"

"Breathe."

She gasps, hand pressed to her chest. Mochi immediately pushes his nose against her leg.

"I can't—this is your family. What if I mess up? What if they hate everything? What if—"

I drop to my knees, gripping her shoulders. "Look at me."

Her eyes are wild, unfocused.

"Breathe with me. In for four." I demonstrate, slow and exaggerated. Mochi whines, pawing at her knee.

Emily's breath shudders in.

"Hold for four."

She clutches Mochi's fur, knuckles white.

"Out for four."

The exhale trembles, but it comes.

"Again." I keep my voice steady, counting through three more cycles. Mochi leans his full weight against her legs, grounding her.

Finally, her shoulders drop. Color returns to her face.

"There you are." I smooth hair back from her forehead. "Better?"

"I freaked out."

"Bit, yeah."

"Your mom wants me to dress your entire family for a political campaign." She laughs, high and slightly hysterical. "That's—that's insane."

"That's Mum recognizing talent when she sees it." I pull up Michelle's Instagram on my phone, showing Emily the premiere photo. "Look at the comments on your dress."

She scrolls, reluctant.

Need to know the designer ASAP

the draping on that gown is EVERYTHING

wheelchair accessibility AND high fashion? where has this designer been all my life

"Seven hundred thousand likes," I point out. "Michelle's agent has already messaged asking for your contact information. Three fashion bloggers want interviews."

"That's different from dressing a politician's family."

"Is it?" I tilt her chin up. "You created adaptive formal wear that's gorgeous and functional. You stood in front of hundreds of people to give a speech. You can handle six Lamberts and a campaign."

"Six very important, very visible Lamberts."

"Who already adore you." I kiss her nose. "Mum wouldn't ask if she didn't believe you could do it. She's particular about appearances."

"That's not helping."

"You'll be brilliant." I pull her hands into mine. "But if you truly don't want to do it, I'll tell her no. Your choice, darling."

Emily looks at Mochi, who wags his tail. Then at her phone, where Mum's message still glows.

"Can I think about it on the plane?"

"Take all the time you need."

She nods, breathing still uneven but steadier. "Okay. Okay. Finish packing first. Panic about fashion empire later."

"That's my girl."

I'm helping Emily transfer sweaters from her dresser to the suitcase when her phone rings. The caller ID reads *Adam - Manager*.

She grimaces. "I forgot to text him about Grantham Bridge ."

"Put it on speaker."

She does. Adam's voice crackles through, sharp and irritated. "Emily, you're scheduled Thursday through Sunday. Where's your availability request?"

"I need two weeks off. Family emergency."

"Two weeks?" He snorts. "Denied. We're short-staffed for the summer blockbuster season. You know this."

"Adam, I'm sorry, but I really need—"

"Not my problem. You're on the schedule. Show up or find another job."

My jaw clenches. Emily's face drains of color, that panicked look creeping back.

I pluck the phone from her hand. "This is Tristian Lambert."

Silence. Then: "Mr. Lambert. I—hello. Big fan."

"Clearly not that big." I keep my voice pleasant, deadly. "Emily's coming to Grantham Bridge with me. Her family will pay her triple her usual rate for the time missed."

"That's—look, I appreciate the offer, but company policy—"

"Let me be clearer." I move to the window, watching Ariana load boxes into the U-Haul below. "Emily doesn't need this job anymore. But one word to my contacts, and your chain—not just your theater, the entire nationwide operation—will never screen a Tristian Lambert film again."

"You can't—"

"David Kellerman is like a father to me. Head of Starlight Studios. Perhaps you've heard of them?" I let that sink in. "I also have the personal numbers for the CEOs of Mountain Studios and Enchanted. Shall I make some calls?"

Adam sputters. "That's—you're threatening me?"

"I'm explaining reality." My accent sharpens, British edges cutting through. "You have a choice. Give Emily her two weeks with pay, or lose access to every major studio's blockbuster releases. Your call."

Emily tugs my sleeve, shaking her head frantically. I ignore her.

"This is highly unprofessional—"

"As is violating ADA regulations." I glance at Emily, who's gone white. "I've seen your theater. The 'accessible' entrance through the kitchen? The bathroom stalls too narrow for wheelchairs? Should I continue?"

Emily's breathing quickens. She mouths *stop*.

But I'm done watching people treat her like she's disposable.

"Mr. Lambert, I don't appreciate—"

"You know what?" Emily snatches the phone back, voice shaking. "I quit!"

She ends the call. Throws the phone on the bed.

Then her hands fly to her chest. "Can't—breathe—"

"Shit." I grab her purse, dumping contents across the mattress. Inhaler. Anxiety medication. I shake out a pill, uncap her water bottle. "Here."

She takes the pill first, swallows. I hold the inhaler to her lips.

"Slow breath in. Hold."

She does, eyes squeezed shut.

"Again."

Three puffs later, her breathing steadies. Mochi presses against her legs, whining.

"I can't believe I did that." Emily stares at her phone like it's a grenade. "I just—I quit. I quit my job."

"You were magnificent."

"I've never—" Her voice cracks. "I've never stood up for myself like that. Ever."

Pride swells in my chest. I cup her face, thumbs stroking her cheeks. "That was incredibly hot, by the way."

She laughs, slightly hysterical. "Hot? I just torched my employment reference and possibly triggered a studio blacklist war."

"You chose yourself." I kiss her forehead. "First time for everything, yeah?"

"I'm unemployed."

"You're a fashion designer with a portfolio that broke Instagram." I gather scattered pill bottles, returning them to her purse. "And you're about to dress a Angoumois political campaign. I think you'll survive."

I carry the last box to Emily's living room, setting it beside the growing tower marked *Fragile - Sewing Supplies*. Through the bedroom door, I hear her muttering about missing thread spools.

Mochi sprawls across the empty couch, paws in the air, pink tongue lolling.

"Oi." I drop beside him, scratching his belly. "Need a word, mate."

His tail thumps against the cushions.

"Your mumma." I glance toward the bedroom, lowering my voice. "She's brilliant, yeah? Gorgeous. Talented. Stronger than she realizes."

Mochi rolls over, cocking his head.

"I want to marry her." The words feel massive, spoken aloud. "Not just dating. Not just moving in together. Proper married. Forever."

He stares at me with those dark eyes, impossibly serious for a dog.

"I know it's fast. Eight months. But Lambert men—we don't do things halfway." I lean forward, elbows on knees. "My grandfather saw Grandmère across a café. Proposed three weeks later. My father met Mum at a dinner party, had the ring ordered before dessert arrived."

Mochi's ears perk up at the word *dinner*.

"Focus." I scratch behind them. "I'm asking permission. Sort of. Since you're the man in her life right now."

He licks my wrist.

"I've got plans. Birthday weekend. Paris. Emerald City reveal at Wonderful World. "Jean's helping me source the stones. Michelle's coordinating with the park."

Mochi sniffs the screen, unimpressed.

"Right. You can't see color properly. My mistake." I swipe to the proposal location photos. "This is where I'll ask. Private balcony overlooking the Emerald City construction. Fairy lights. Her favorite flowers everywhere. Marcus is arranging a photographer to capture it without her knowing."

A crash echoes from the bedroom. "I'm fine! Just knocked over a lamp!"

"You sure?" I call back.

"Yes! Keep packing!"

I turn back to Mochi, voice dropping. "Here's the thing. I need you to trust me with her."

His tail stops wagging.

"I know you're her protector. You sense her anxiety attacks before they happen. Pick up things she drops. Keep her grounded when she spirals." I stroke his soft ears. "But I want to be that for her too. Partner. Husband. Team."

Mochi tilts his head, considering.

"I'm not replacing you. Never." I scratch under his chin. "You're part of the package. Always. I've already ordered you a custom tux for the wedding. Bow tie. Little vest. Very dapper."

His tail resumes thumping.

"So what do you say? Can I marry your mumma? Officially become your dad?" The words catch in my throat. "I'll take good care of you both. Promise. Already renovated the house. Got you the expensive dog food. Even researched the best vet in Los Angeles."

Mochi stands, shakes himself, then plants both front paws on my chest. His tongue swipes across my cheek in one wet, enthusiastic lick.

"I'll take that as yes." I laugh, pushing him back. "Christ, your breath. What did Emily feed you?"

"Mochi, down!" Emily wheels into the room, hair escaping her ponytail, dust smudged on her cheek. "Sorry. He's excited about moving."

"We had a talk. Man to man." I wipe slobber from my face. "He approves of the California weather."

"Good. Because I found seventeen more things that need packing." She surveys the room, overwhelmed. "How did I accumulate this much stuff in four years?"

"Magic." I stand, pressing a kiss to her dusty forehead. "Come on. Let's finish this so we can start our life."

The Gulfstream levels off at cruising altitude, and Emily's already commandeered the entire table. Fabric swatches carpet the surface like confetti, held down by coffee cups and her phone. Her pencil flies across the sketchbook, sketching what looks like a jacket with structured shoulders.

"You've been at this for three hours." I lean over, trying to glimpse her work. "Shouldn't you sleep?"

"Can't." She doesn't look up. "Your mother wants twelve outfits. Complete ensembles. Campaign trail appropriate. Angoumois fashion expectations. Accessible design." Her pencil scratches faster. "That's basically asking me to reinvent adaptive haute couture in three weeks."

"You'll do it."

"Your confidence is adorable and unhelpful." She flips the page, starting a new sketch. "Hand me the navy fabric. The one with the subtle pinstripe."

I pass it over. Mochi snores in his travel crate, completely unbothered by Emily's creative frenzy.

My phone buzzes. Instagram notification. Then another. And another.

I posted forty minutes ago—just a candid shot of Emily working, her face scrunched in concentration, pencil tucked behind her ear. The caption: *My girlfriend's a bloody genius. Watch this space.* Tagged her account.

The likes already hit two hundred thousand.

I scroll through comments, stomach tightening.

She's using him for connections

Gold digger alert

Bet she can't even design

"Christ." I swipe down, reading more.

He could have anyone and chose THAT?

But then:

Her portfolio is incredible you're just jealous

Finally a celebrity dating someone REAL

Michelle's already in the trenches, replying to hate comments with surgical precision. *She graduated summa cum laude and designed her own premiere gown. What have you accomplished?*

Jean posted a story: Emily's graduation photo with the caption *Welcome to the family, Em.*

Marcus went nuclear on someone who called Emily a "charity case." *Say that again. I dare you. My lawyer's bored.*

"You're frowning at your phone." Emily glances up. "What's wrong?"

"Nothing."

"Liar." She sets down her pencil. "Show me."

"Em—"

"Tristian." Her voice carries that stubborn edge. "We're partners, remember? Show me."

I hand over my phone, watching her face as she scrolls. Her expression doesn't change, but her fingers tighten around the device.

She reads silently. One comment. Five. Twenty.

"They spelled 'you're' wrong." She points at the screen. "If you're going to insult someone's intelligence, at least demonstrate your own."

"That's your takeaway?"

"Also, this person's profile picture is a anime girl in a bikini. Hard to feel threatened." She keeps scrolling, eyebrows rising. "Oh. Your family's defending me. Marcus just threatened legal action."

"He does that."

"Michelle called someone a 'malnourished troglodyte with the fashion sense of a bin bag.'" Emily snorts. "I like her."

"She likes you too." I reclaim my phone, pulling up my story. "Ignore them. They're jealous."

"Or they genuinely think I'm not good enough for you." She returns to her sketchbook, but the pencil hovers without moving. "Maybe they're right."

"Absolutely not." I capture her hand. "Look at me."

Those emerald eyes meet mine, uncertain.

"You're brilliant. Talented. You graduated top of your class while managing a disability that would break most people. You design clothes that give people dignity and style." I squeeze her fingers. "Those strangers on Instagram? They don't know you. They don't know *us*."

"They see a movie star dating a girl in a wheelchair. That's all they need to see."

"Then they're idiots."

She huffs a small laugh. "Your family's pretty fierce."

"Wait until they meet you in person."

My phone vibrates against the table. Text from Jean. Then another. And another.

I swipe the screen. Six images flood the group chat—engagement rings from various Grantham Bridge ian jewelers. Emerald-cut diamonds. Round solitaires. Vintage art deco settings.

Jean: *Thoughts? The cushion cut reminds me of her eyes*

Michelle: *Too traditional. She needs something unique*

Marcus: *Get one with poppies engraved or something*

Jean: *That's actually brilliant*

I zoom in on each photo. The cushion cut catches light beautifully, but Michelle's right—Emily deserves extraordinary, not expected. A platinum band with delicate poppy engravings along the sides catches my attention. The center stone sits in a botanical setting, petals forming the prongs.

Tristian: *Second one. But I'll decide at the shop. Need to see them in person*

Jean: *Obviously. When are you proposing?*

Tristian: *Her birthday weekend. At Starlight Studios Paris. In the Wonderful attraction*

Three dots appear. Disappear. Reappear.

Jean: *Perfect. The whole family's already booked for that weekend anyway*

Michelle: *Wait you're proposing at a THEME PARK?*

Tristian: *Not just any theme park. Her favorite musical. The Emerald City. Where Dorothy belongs*

Marcus: *That's actually romantic as hell*

Emily glances up from her sketches. "You're smiling at your phone like Mochi when he sees bacon."

"Just Jean being Jean." I flip the screen face-down. "Planning campaign logistics."

"Tell him not to panic-buy the entire Grantham shopping district."

I laugh, typing quickly.

Tristian: *Emily says don't buy out Grantham's shopping district. Or Amazon. The campaign will go fine*

Jean: *I make no promises*

Levi: *He's already got seventeen tabs open. I can see his screen*

Jean: *STRATEGIC RESEARCH*

Michelle: *You stress-shop like Dad stress-eats chocolate*

Jean: *At least my coping mechanism is productive*

Marcus: *Your credit card company sends you birthday presents*

I grin, pocketing my phone before Emily gets suspicious. Across the cabin, she's returned to her sketches, pencil flying across the page. Her tongue pokes out slightly when she concentrates—unconscious habit that kills me every time.

"What are you designing now?"

"Your mother's debate outfit." She tilts the sketchbook. "Structured blazer, adaptive closures, clean lines. Powerful but approachable. Navy with crimson accents for the Angoumois flag without being literal about it."

"You've been thinking about this."

"Since she asked." Emily flips to another page, showing a full wardrobe board. "Your father needs gravitas. Jean needs modern but respectful of tradition. Michelle can wear anything, but for campaign photos, sophisticated edge. Classic pieces with unexpected details."

"And me?"

"You're not running for office."

"I'm still family. Still doing appearances."

She studies me, eyes narrowing slightly. "Tailored but relaxed. You need to look supportive without overshadowing. Three-piece suits, waistcoats, rolled sleeves for outdoor events. British elegance meets French sophistication."

"You've thought about what I'll wear?"

"I think about you constantly." She says it casually, like commenting on weather. "Occupational hazard of dating a fashion designer."

My chest tightens. Twelve weeks until Paris. Until the ring. Until I ask her to make this permanent.

"We're landing in an hour." I lean back, watching her work. "You should rest."

"Can't. Your family's reputation is riding on this."

"Emily. Breathe."

She sets down her pencil, meeting my eyes. "What if I mess this up?"

"Impossible."

"You don't know that."

"I know you." I capture her hand again, thumb stroking her knuckles. "I know you don't do anything halfway. I know you'll create something extraordinary. And I know my family already loves you, regardless of what you design."

Her shoulders drop slightly. "When did you get so good at pep talks?"

"Eight months of dating you. I've learned things."

She laughs, squeezing my fingers. "Okay. One hour nap. Then back to sketches."

"Deal."

My phone buzzes again. Jean's typing in the group chat like his life depends on it.

Jean: *Speaking of life changes... Levi and I have news*

Michelle: *If he's pregnant I'm going to have questions*

Jean: *Hilarious. No. We're thinking about adoption*

The cabin suddenly feels smaller. I sit up straighter, Emily glancing over at my sudden movement.

Tristian: *Seriously?*

Jean: *After the campaign. We've already started the paperwork*

Levi: *Jean's been reading parenting books for three months*

Michelle: *OH MY GOD FINALLY*

Marcus: *Congrats! Though your kid's going to have the most organized nursery in existence*

Jean: *There's more. Levi's considering leaving Hollywood*

That stops me cold. Levi Williams—A-list actor, three-time Silver Screen nominee—giving up his career?

Tristian: *What?*

Levi: *If Jean wins reelection, I'm moving to Angoumois full-time. Done with LA. Done with the circus*

Jean: *We want to raise our child somewhere real. Somewhere that matters*

Michelle: *But your career—*

Levi: *Is just a job. Jean's my life. Our family is my life. Plus European cinema's calling my name*

I stare at the screen. Levi and I bonded over Hollywood's madness, the constant scrutiny, the exhaustion of performing both on and off camera. Now he's walking away.

Tristian: *You're sure about this?*

Levi: *Never been more sure of anything. Well, except marrying your brother*

Jean: *We want our kid to grow up speaking French and English. Want them running through the château gardens. Want Sunday dinners with the whole family*

Marcus: *This is huge. Michelle's crying*

Michelle: *Am not! Just... emotional about becoming an aunt*

"Everything okay?" Emily's watching me, concern creasing her forehead.

"Jean and Levi are adopting."

Her pencil clatters to the table. "What?"

"After the campaign. And Levi's leaving Hollywood if Jean wins. Moving to Angoumois permanently."

"Oh my God." Her face lights up. "That's wonderful! They'll be amazing parents."

"You think?"

"Jean's the most organized human alive. Levi's got that calm energy kids need. Plus Mochi will have a cousin to play with."

I hadn't considered that. Our future child—because there will be one, multiple ones if Emily agrees—will have cousins close by. Family traditions. The château filled with children's laughter again.

Tristian: *I'm happy for you both. Really*

Jean: *You'll be Uncle Tristian*

Michelle: *Aunt Michelle has a better ring to it*

Marcus: *Uncle Marcus is definitely going to be the fun one*

Jean: *You're all going to spoil this child rotten*

Levi: *Already accepting that reality*

Tristian: *When are you telling Mum and Dad?*

Jean: *After the election. Don't want it to seem like a political move*

Michelle: *Smart. Though Grandmère probably already knows*

Jean: *Grandmère knows everything*

Emily returns to her sketches, but she's smiling now. "Your family's expanding."

"Seems like it."

"Levi's brave, leaving everything behind."

"Or smart. He's choosing what matters."

She glances at me, something unreadable in those green eyes. "Would you ever do that? Leave Hollywood?"

The question hangs between us. Would I? For her? For our future family?

"In a heartbeat."

"Really?"

"Em, I'd leave tomorrow if you asked. Open a restaurant in Grantham Bridge. Cook ratatouille for tourists. Come home to you every night instead of film sets and hotel rooms."

"I would never ask that."

"That's why I'd do it."

She reaches over, fingers finding mine. "Your brothers are lucky to have each other."

"We all are. You included."

"Not officially."

Not yet, I think, feeling the weight of the ring shopping waiting in Grantham Bridge . *But soon.*

Chapter 8: Winkie Vows

The château materializes through morning fog like something from a fairy tale. Stone walls centuries old, ivy climbing the east tower, roses Grandmère planted forty years ago still blooming along the drive. Emily's quiet beside me as we roll through the gates, her hand tight in mine.

"It's enormous," she whispers.

"Wait until you see the inside."

Mochi whines from the backseat, nose pressed to the window. He knows something's different. New territory. New people to charm or protect Emily from.

The car stops at the main entrance. Before I can move, Grandmère appears on the steps, Eighty and elegant in lavender silk. Behind her, Mum hovers, smoothing her dress. And Dad—

Dad stands apart. Dark suit. Arms crossed. That expression I know too well. The one that says he's already calculated the political implications of my choices.

"Ready?" I ask Emily.

"No."

"Perfect. They'll love you anyway."

I round the car, opening Emily's door while the driver retrieves her wheelchair. Mochi bounds out first, immediately investigating the courtyard with enthusiasm bordering on chaos.

"Mon chéri!" Grandmère descends the steps with more grace than people half her age. "Finally."

"Grandmère." I kiss both her cheeks, then turn. "This is Emily."

"The girl who has my grandson texting at all hours." Grandmère bends, taking Emily's hands. "You're as lovely as Tristian claimed. Though he undersold your eyes. Emeralds, truly."

Emily blushes. "It's wonderful to meet you, Mrs. Tribideau."

"Adele, please. We're family now."

Dad's eyebrow twitches at that. Family. Not yet. Not officially.

Mum approaches next, warmer than Dad but cautious. "Emily, bienvenue. Welcome to our home."

"Thank you, Mrs. Lambert. Your home is beautiful."

"Celeste, please." Mum's smile doesn't quite reach her eyes. She's wondering, calculating. How serious is this? How permanent?

Then Dad.

He doesn't move from his position by the door. Just nods. "Mademoiselle Silver."

"Sir." Emily's voice stays steady, but her fingers find mine.

"Your flight was pleasant?"

"Very. Thank you."

Silence stretches. Dad's examining her like a constituent whose vote he hasn't secured. The wheelchair. The service dog now sniffing his roses. The American accent. Every detail filed away, assessed for risk.

"Your accommodations are ready," he says finally. "Tristian's room. The bathroom has been... modified."

Modified. Like she's a problem requiring architectural solutions.

"Thank you," Emily says quietly. "That's very kind."

Dad turns without responding. Disappears into the château like he has more important matters. Which he always does.

"Don't mind Pierre." Grandmère waves her hand. "He's never known what to do with joy. Come. Let me show you the gardens."

"Actually," Mum interrupts gently, "perhaps Emily would like to settle in first? The journey was long."

Code for: *let's assess this situation privately before the guest overhears.*

"I'll get Emily situated," I say. "Then we can do the full tour."

"Perfect." Grandmère winks at Emily. "We'll have tea. I want to hear everything about this boy's terrible movie choices."

The elevator—installed when Grandmère's hip started bothering her three years ago—rises smooth and silent.

Emily's studying the ornate brass panel, the antique mirror on the back wall.

"Your father hates me."

"He doesn't hate you. He doesn't know you."

"Same result."

"Em—"

"It's fine. I'm used to people making judgments."

Mochi leans against her leg. She scratches behind his ears, finding comfort in familiar gestures.

The doors open on the third floor. Our childhood wing. Jean's room to the left, Michelle's to the right, mine straight ahead at the end of the hall.

Nothing's changed. Same paintings of pastoral scenes. Same Persian runner. Same door to my room with the brass number three I used to polish as a kid, thinking it meant something important.

Inside, though—

"Oh," Emily breathes.

They kept my room exactly as I left it. Movie posters. Books stacked haphazardly. The window seat where I'd read scripts and dream about escape. But the bathroom—

The bathroom's transformed. Roll-in shower with built-in bench. Grab bars positioned perfectly. Lowered sink. Everything Emily needs.

"Jean did this," I say. "Had the whole thing renovated."

"Your brother barely knows me."

"You're family. He doesn't need to know you."

She wheels to the window, looking out over Grandmère's gardens. Mochi follows, always vigilant.

"Your father looked at me like I'm a campaign liability."

"Dad looks at everyone like that. Even his own children."

"You don't talk about him much."

I join her at the window, hands on her shoulders. "We respect him. He's brilliant at politics, cares about the constituency. But he was never... present. Not really. His career mattered more than us."

"That's sad."

"It's just how it is."

"Tristian—"

"You're not a liability. You're mine. And if Dad can't see how extraordinary you are, that's his limitation, not yours."

She leans back into me. Mochi curls at her feet, finally settling.

"Three weeks here," she murmurs. "Designing for people who already doubt me."

"Designing for people who will learn to adore you. Because that's what happens. Everyone does, eventually."

"You're biased."

"Completely."

Below, I spot Dad crossing to his study. Shoulders back. Purpose in every step. A man who built a career out of distance.

Let him doubt. Let him calculate. By the time I propose, by the time Emily's his daughter-in-law, he'll realize what Jean and Michelle already know.

The Lamberts just got their best addition yet.

Dinner starts civilized. Crystal glasses. Finest china. Mum's duck confit filling the formal dining room with competing scents.

Dad holds court at the head of the table, Mum at the foot. The rest of us arranged like chess pieces—Jean and Levi to Dad's right, Michelle and Marcus to Mum's left, Emily and I between them. Grandmère positioned perfectly to observe the chaos.

"The working-class vote," Dad says, cutting his duck with surgical precision. "That's where we focus resources. The factories in Ruelle. The agricultural communities."

Jean sets down his fork. "We can't ignore the urban professionals. Tech sector's growing—"

"Growing, yes. Decisive? No." Dad doesn't look up. "You want to win elections, you secure your base first."

"Our base is changing." Jean's voice stays measured. Years of practice. "The demographics—"

"I'm aware of the demographics."

"Are you? Because the projections show—"

"Projections." Dad's knife scrapes porcelain. "I've won six elections without projections."

"Times change, Dad."

"Fundamentals don't."

Emily's hand finds mine under the table. Michelle catches my eye across the arrangement, already tensing.

"Jean's right," I say quietly. "The tech sector's voting bloc is expanding."

Dad finally looks up. At me. Through me. "You've been in Los Angeles how long? Lecturing us on Angoumois politics?"

"I grew up here. I know this region."

"You left."

The words land like verdict. Guilty. Abandoned your duty.

"This isn't about Tristian," Jean cuts in. "The data supports diversifying our approach. Younger voters, urban centers—"

"Younger voters don't show up." Dad's voice rises slightly. First crack in the composure. "You chase demographics that disappear on election day, you lose."

"Not if we engage them properly. Digital outreach, modern messaging—"

"Modern." Dad actually laughs. Sharp. Bitter. "You want to modernize away our principles?"

"I want to win."

"By abandoning the people who've supported this family for generations?"

Jean's chair scrapes back. "I'm not abandoning anyone. I'm expanding our coalition."

"You're chasing trends."

"You're clinging to nostalgia!"

The volume spikes. Dad stands. Jean follows. Across the table, fifty-four years of political calculus meets twenty-seven years of frustrated innovation.

"I have won elections in this region since before you were born—"

"And you'll lose this one if you can't adapt!"

"Adapt?" Dad's voice fills the room. "You think adaptation means pandering to Silicon Valley transplants who don't understand our values?"

"I think it means recognizing our constituency is evolving!"

"Enough!" Mum's fork hits crystal.

Too late.

"You want to lecture me about winning?" Dad's face flushes. "About understanding voters? I've built this party —"

"And Jean's trying to save it," Michelle interrupts. Calm. Cutting. "The numbers don't lie, Dad. Our traditional base is shrinking."

"Michelle—" Mum warns.

"No." Michelle sets down her napkin. "Jean's right. We need comprehensive strategy, not just factory visits and farm photo ops."

Dad's gaze swings to her. To me. The siblings, united. The ones who left. Who chose different paths.

"You tw." His voice drops dangerously low. "You abandoned politics. Abandoned this family's legacy. And now you presume to advise—"

"We didn't abandon anything," I say. "We chose different service."

"Service." The word drips contempt. "Playing dress-up in Hollywood. Parading on runways. That's service?"

Jean slams his palm on the table. Glasses jump. "Stop."

Silence.

"I'm running my campaign," Jean says. Each word deliberate. "Me. Not you. And I will run it my way. With data. With modern strategy. With expanded outreach."

"Then you'll lose."

"Better than winning your way. Clinging to a past that's dying."

Dad's jaw works. Decades of control warring with paternal fury.

"We're done." Jean stands. "Come on."

Michelle rises immediately. I squeeze Emily's hand—*stay here*—and follow my siblings.

Through the dining room. Past Mum's stricken face. Past Grandmère's knowing expression.

Into the gardens where we can breathe.

"Thirty years!" Jean's voice cracks across the manicured hedges. "Thirty bloody years he's controlled every decision, every vote, every goddamn statement!"

The fountain burbles behind us. Moonlight catches the spray.

"Jean—" Michelle starts.

"No!" He spins. Face flushed. Eyes wild. "I've done everything right. Everything he asked. Studied at Sciences Po. Worked his campaigns. Deferred, supported, followed —"

His hands shake. Fists clench, release. Clench again.

"I have ideas. Good ideas. Data-driven strategies that could transform this party. But he won't listen. Won't even *consider* that maybe, maybe his way isn't the only way anymore."

Michelle moves closer. I position myself on Jean's other side.

"The working-class communities he's so protective of? They're struggling because we haven't addressed technological displacement. The agricultural sector needs subsidies for sustainable practices. The urban centers need infrastructure investment." Jean's accent thickens. British bleeding into French. "I know this region. I've spent years analyzing voter behavior, economic trends, demographic shifts. But none of it matters because I'm his *son*, not a serious candidate."

"You are serious," I say quietly.

"Tell him that!" Jean wheels on me. "Tell him I'm not some dilettante playing politician. That I've sacrificed my relationship—Levi moved continents for me. Gave up Hollywood for this. And Dad can't even respect—"

The words break.

Jean's face crumples.

"Merde." He presses his palms against his eyes. "Merde, merde—"

The sobs come. Harsh. Wrenching. Years of controlled composure shattering.

Michelle wraps around him first. I follow, pulling both siblings close. Jean shakes between us, chest heaving, and I feel my own throat tighten.

"I just want..." Jean gasps. "I just want him to see me."

"We see you," Michelle whispers. Her voice wavers.

"I know. I know, but—" He sniffles hard. "He's Dad. And I'm still—God, I'm still the little boy wanting his approval."

My eyes burn. Because I know. We all know.

We left. Michelle to Paris runways. Me to Hollywood soundstages. But Jean stayed. Chose politics. Chose service. Chose to walk Dad's path, and still can't earn his recognition.

"You're brilliant," I say against his shoulder. "Your strategies are innovative. Your understanding of voters—"

"Doesn't matter if he won't implement them." Jean pulls back, swiping at his face. "He'll run his campaign. Lose votes we could've captured. Blame external factors. Never acknowledge that I was right."

The fountain splashes. Somewhere in the chateau, life continues. Mum probably consoling Dad. Grandmère observing. Emily and the others maintaining polite conversation.

"I still want this," Jean says suddenly. Fierce. "That's the worst part. I'm furious with him, but I still want to serve. Still believe in this work."

"Then you will," Michelle says firmly.

"How? If he controls everything—"

"He doesn't." I meet Jean's reddened eyes. "You're your own man. Your own politician. His legacy doesn't define yours."

"Spoken like someone who escaped." But Jean's lip quirks. Almost smiling.

"Escaped implies I'm free." I glance toward the chateau. "We're all still here, aren't we? Still trying to prove something."

"You've proven plenty," Michelle says. "Siver Screen nomination. Box office records—"

"And Dad still calls it playing dress-up."

Silence settles. Three siblings. Three paths. One impossible father.

The garden door opens.

Footsteps on gravel. Multiple sets. Levi's long stride, Marcus's measured pace, the distinct whir of Emily's wheelchair.

Jean straightens, wiping furiously at his face. But Levi's already moving—arms around Jean before my brother can protest.

"Mon coeur," Levi murmurs into Jean's hair.

That's all it takes.

Jean collapses again. Sobbing into Levi's chest. Proper crying now—loud, messy, broken. All the control that survived our sibling huddle completely obliterated by his husband's presence.

Levi holds him. Steady. Unshakable. The way only he can.

Marcus appears beside Michelle, sliding an arm around her waist. She leans into him immediately, exhaustion bleeding through her model composure.

Emily wheels closer to me. Mochi trots beside her chair, vest gleaming in the moonlight.

"He okay?" Her emerald eyes search mine.

"Will be."

Jean's still wrecking himself against Levi. Words tumbling out between gasps—Dad's dismissiveness, years of trying, the campaign strategies being ignored. Everything.

Levi doesn't speak. Just holds on.

Then Mochi decides to help.

The labradoodle bounds toward Jean, launching his considerable fluffy bulk directly into my brother's lap.

"Oof—Mochi!" Jean chokes on a sob-laugh as seventy pounds of dog lands on him. "What—"

Mochi settles across Jean and Levi both, tail wagging wildly. He licks Jean's tear-streaked face with methodical determination, working like he's solving a problem. Service dog mode activated.

"Mochi, down," Emily says automatically. "He's not—"

"No." Jean wraps arms around the dog. Face buried in white curls. "He's perfect."

Mochi's tail thumps faster. Mission accomplished.

Levi meets my eyes over Jean's head. Grateful. Exhausted. They've been navigating this for years—Jean caught between Dad's expectations and his own vision. Levi supporting while sacrificing his own career.

"The duck was excellent, by the way," Marcus offers into the silence. "Before the yelling."

Michelle snorts. "Only you would focus on the food."

"Priorities." Marcus grins. "Life's too short for bad duck and family drama."

"We're drowning in family drama," I point out.

"Yeah, but the duck was *excellent*."

Even Jean laughs. Wet, broken, but real.

Mochi licks his face again for good measure.

"I'm sorry." Jean's voice cracks. "I'm sorry you all had to witness—"

"Stop," Michelle says firmly. "We're family. This is what we do."

"Implode spectacularly at formal dinners?" I ask.

"Support each other after." She squeezes Marcus tighter. "Always after."

Emily's hand finds mine. I thread our fingers together, pulling her closer. Her wheelchair bumps my leg gently.

Jean extracts himself from Mochi enough to breathe properly. The dog remains draped across him like a weighted blanket. Therapy through sheer fluffy mass.

"I don't know how to do this," Jean admits quietly. "Run against his methods while keeping the family intact."

"You don't run against him," Levi says. "You run your way. He'll either adapt or watch you win without him."

"And if I lose?"

"You won't." Levi's confidence radiates. "I've seen your strategies. They're brilliant."

"Levi's right," I add. "Your vision for the campaign— it's what Angoumois needs."

"Dad won't see it that way."

"Dad sees what he wants," Michelle says. "Doesn't make him correct."

Jean's quiet. Processing. Mochi shifts, resting his head on Jean's chest. The dog's dark eyes half-close, completely content.

"Did your service dog just adopt my brother?" I ask Emily.

"Apparently." She smiles softly. "He knows who needs him."

"Smart dog," Marcus observes.

"The smartest," Emily confirms.

Mochi's tail thumps agreement.

I leave the others in the garden and head back inside.

Someone needs to say something. All these years, we've let it slide—Dad's dismissiveness, his constant belittling, the way he treats his children like disappointing campaign props.

Jean's breakdown proved it.

My footsteps echo through the marble entryway. The chateau feels colder now, less home and more museum. Preserving Lambert history while suffocating Lambert futures.

Dad's study door stands open. Light spills across Persian rugs that cost more than most people's houses.

He sits behind his mahogany desk, reading glasses perched on his nose, reviewing debate notes like nothing happened. Like he didn't just eviscerate his eldest son at dinner.

"Dad."

He doesn't look up. "If you've come to lecture me about Jean's feelings—"

"I've come to lecture you about being a shit father."

That gets his attention.

Pierre sets down his papers with deliberate precision. Removes his glasses. Meets my eyes with that politician's stare—calculating, cold, designed to intimidate constituents.

Doesn't work on me anymore.

"Careful, Tristian."

"Or what? You'll be disappointed in me?" I laugh. Sharp. Bitter. "We're long past that."

"Clearly." His gaze drops to my forearms. The tattoos visible beneath rolled sleeves. "Those things on your body prove it."

"These *things* represent my career. Every role I've poured myself into."

"They represent defiance." Pierre stands, commanding presence filling the room. "You marked yourself like a criminal to spite me."

"Not everything's about you."

"No?" His eyebrow arches. "Running to Marseille at nineteen. Becoming an *actor* instead of honoring your family legacy. All coincidentally after our argument about your future."

The argument. Three days of screaming. Dad demanding I join his political office, learn the family business, prepare for inevitable election. Me refusing. Again and again.

Until I couldn't breathe in this house anymore.

"I left because staying was killing me," I say quietly.

"Drama. Always drama with you."

"You wanted me to be someone I'm not."

"I wanted you to be a *Lambert*." Pierre moves around the desk. "To uphold generations of service, of duty—"

"Auguste raised me. And Collette." The words taste like truth finally spoken. "Not you. Not Mum. Your staff. Your employees parented your children while you campaigned and she planned galas."

Pierre's jaw tightens. "We provided everything—"

"Except presence." I step closer. "Jean needed you tonight. Needed his father to listen, to value his perspective. Instead you humiliated him in front of everyone."

"I provided honest feedback—"

"You called his work meaningless. You dismissed years of strategy and planning because it doesn't match your outdated methods."

"Experience matters—"

"So does evolution. Progress. The ability to admit when younger generations might actually know better." My voice rises. "But you can't do that. Can't admit your children might excel at things you don't understand."

"I understand politics—"

"You understand power. Control. Not family."

Silence crashes between us.

Pierre's face reddens. "How dare you—"

"How dare *you*." My British accent sharpens, emotions bleeding through. "Jean followed your footsteps exactly. Became a politician. Dedicated himself to public service. And you *still* treat him like he's insufficient."

"Because he lacks—"

"He lacks nothing except your approval. Which you withhold like it's currency."

Pierre straightens to full height. Trying to tower. "You know nothing about raising children—"

"Because I refuse to repeat your mistakes."

That lands. I watch it hit.

"When I have children," I continue, voice steadying, "they'll know I see them. Actually see who they are, not who I demand they become. They'll know I'm proud of them for being themselves."

"Idealistic nonsense—"

"Emily and I will actually parent our kids. Not outsource it to staff while we chase ambition."

His expression shifts. Calculating again. "Emily. The girl in the wheelchair."

"The woman I'm going to marry."

"A fan." He says it like disease. "Some starstruck girl who followed you—"

"Stop talking."

"Do you understand what this looks like? A Lambert, dating someone from his fanbase? The press will destroy —"

"I don't care about the press."

"You should." Pierre leans forward. "I have an election —"

"There it is." I laugh. Cold. "Your election. Your campaign. Your reputation."

"Which affects the family—"

"We're not props, Dad. Not set dressing for your political theater."

"You're being unreasonable—"

"I'm being honest. Finally." I meet his eyes. "You need to decide what matters more—your campaign image or your actual family."

"That's not—"

"Because if you keep treating us like disappointments, keep dismissing our choices, keep refusing to accept who we actually are?" I move toward the door. "You'll win your election in an empty house. Surrounded by staff and sycophants. No children. No grandchildren. Just legacy and loneliness."

"Tristian—"

"Jean's vision will win him this election. Michelle's modeling career brings joy to millions. My films matter to people. And Emily—" My voice catches. "Emily's the best thing that ever happened to me. You can either accept that or not. Your choice."

I turn.

"Where are you going?"

"To be with people who actually want me around."

"We're not finished—"

"Yes. We are."

I leave him standing in his study, surrounded by debate notes and political strategy, preparing for the wrong battle entirely.

Outside, I find my siblings still in the garden. Emily's hand finds mine immediately.

"Okay?" she whispers.

"Getting there."

Mochi's moved from Jean to Michelle now, spreading therapeutic dog energy democratically.

My family. The one I chose and the ones I'm stuck with.

Maybe it's enough.

The screaming wakes me at 3:17 AM.

I sit up. Find her doubled over the bed, face pale in moonlight.

"Em—"

She vomits. Blood spatters the duvet.

Everything stops.

"*Emily*—"

"Can't—" She gasps. "Hurts—bathroom—"

I lift her. She screams again, body rigid with pain. Mochi follows us, pressed against my legs, nearly tripping me.

The toilet. More blood. Red streaking into water.

"Something's wrong." Her voice breaks. "Tristian, something's—"

"I've got you." My hands shake pulling out my phone. "You're okay. You're—"

Marcus crashes through the doorway first, shirtless, eyes wild. "What happened?"

"Blood. Vomiting blood and—" I gesture helplessly at the toilet.

"Call an ambulance." Marcus kneels beside us. "Now."

"Already—" My fingers won't cooperate with the screen.

Jean appears, takes my phone, makes the call rapidly. Michelle runs for Mum while Levi grabs towels, pressing one against Emily's mouth as she heaves again.

Nothing comes up this time. Just dry retching that makes her whole body convulse.

"Shh." Marcus holds her hair back. "You're okay, baby sister. We've got you."

"It hurts—Marcus it hurts—"

"I know. I know."

I text Ariana with shaking thumbs: *Emily emergency hospital blood call you when I know more*

Mum arrives with a basin just as Emily vomits again. Still blood. Less now, but enough to terrify.

"The ambulance is five minutes out." Jean pockets my phone. "Mum's packing her medications—"

"I'll drive." Dad's voice cuts through the chaos. He stands in the doorway, already dressed. "Faster than waiting."

Nobody argues.

Michelle helps me bundle Emily in blankets while Marcus carries her wheelchair down the elevator. Mochi won't leave her side, whining constantly, pushing his nose against her hand.

"He knows." Emily's voice is barely audible. "He always knows when—"

Another spasm cuts her off.

The drive to Grantham General Hospital takes twelve minutes that feel like twelve hours. Emily in my lap in the back seat, Dad breaking every speed limit, Mum calling ahead to alert emergency services.

Marcus sits on Emily's other side, holding her hand, murmuring things about Austin hospitals and food poisoning he survived once and anything to distract her from the pain.

Jean follows in his car with Michelle, Levi, and Mochi.

We screech into emergency services at 3:43 AM.

Medical staff swarm immediately. A gurney appears. They transfer Emily from my arms to the white sheets and I want to follow, need to follow—

"Only family—" A nurse blocks my path.

"I am family—"

"Sir, you'll have to—"

"She's my fiancée—"

"*Tristian.*" Dad's hand lands on my shoulder. "Let them work."

The gurney moves. Emily reaches for me, eyes terrified.

"Don't leave—please don't—"

"I'm right here—"

"Family only in emergency—" The nurse is insistent.

"He's her person." Marcus steps forward. "He goes."

"I'm sorry, hospital policy—"

"*Please*—" Emily's face contorts with fresh pain.

They're wheeling her away. Toward double doors. Away from me.

Every instinct screams to fight, to force my way through, to stay with her because she needs me and I need to know she's okay and—

"*I love you.*" Emily's voice breaks over the chaos as the doors begin closing. "*Tristian, I love you—*"

"I love you too—Emily—"

The doors slam shut.

Silence crashes.

I stand there, staring at white paint and circular windows, my chest cracking open.

"Come." Mum guides me toward waiting room chairs. "They'll update us soon."

Marcus sinks into the seat beside me, face pale. Michelle and Jean arrive with Mochi, who paces frantically, looking for Emily.

Dad stands near the reception desk, speaking quietly with staff. Still the politician. Still in control.

I'm not in control.

I'm drowning.

Ariana answers on the first ring. Background noise— music, voices, Austin nightlife at whatever ungodly hour it is there.

"What's wrong?"

"Emily—hospital—blood—" The words won't form properly. My accent's gone thick, vowels stretching British, consonants clipping short the way they do when emotion overrides control. "She was sick, violently sick, there was so much blood and they won't let me back there and I don't know—"

"Slow down." Ariana's voice sharpens. "What hospital? What symptoms exactly?"

I force air into my lungs. "Grantham General. Best in Angoumois—hell, all Europe. She woke screaming. Pain in her abdomen. Vomiting blood. Blood in her urine. They took her back twenty minutes ago and nobody's told us anything—"

"Was she fine yesterday?"

"Perfect." The word breaks. "We made love last night. She was laughing, happy, showed me sketches for Mum's campaign wardrobe—"

"Any recent medication changes?"

"No. Nothing. Ari, what if it's—" I can't say it. Can't voice the terror crawling through my chest.

"Don't." She knows anyway. "Don't go there yet."

"Cancer. Kidney failure. Internal bleeding from something we did—"

"*Tristian*." Sharp. Cutting through panic. "Emily's tough. Tougher than any of us. She survived seventeen foster homes and lunatics locking her in closets. She'll survive this."

"But what if—"

"No what-ifs. Just facts. She's at the best hospital with the best doctors and she has you and your entire family waiting. She's not alone."

She's alone behind those doors. Without me. Where I can't protect her or hold her hand or tell her everything's going to be fine even if it's a lie.

"I just found her." My voice cracks completely. "Eight months. That's all I've had. It's not enough. I need—I need decades. I need forever. I can't lose her now—"

"You won't—"

"You don't know that—"

"*Listen to me*." Ariana's voice gentles. "Emily needs you strong when they let you back. So breathe. And wait. And trust that she's fighting right now because she knows you're waiting."

The call ends.

I stare at my phone. At the photo that's been my lock screen since graduation—Emily in her rhinestoned cap, diploma in hand, face radiant with joy.

Four days ago. She was perfect four days ago.

The sob hits without warning. Rips from somewhere deep, somewhere primal that doesn't care about control or image or the hospital staff watching.

Mochi presses against my legs immediately, whining. His weight grounds me for half a second before another wave crashes.

"Come here." Marcus pulls me against his shoulder. "I've got you, brother."

"She can't—I can't—"

"I know." His voice is steady despite the terror I hear underneath. "I've been praying since the car. God's got her. He brought you two together—He's not separating you now."

Jean kneels in front of me, hands gripping mine. "The doctors here are brilliant. If anyone can help her—"

"What if they can't?" The British vowels stretch longer, consonants harsher. "What if we're too late? What if something ruptured while we were asleep and she's bleeding internally and—"

Michelle sits on my other side. "She was conscious. Talking. That's good, Tris. That means—"

"It means nothing." I pull away from them all, standing, pacing. Mochi follows. "It could be anything. A dozen different catastrophic failures that present exactly like this—"

"*Tristian Alexandre*." Mum's voice stops me mid-stride. "Come here."

I turn. She's standing now, arms open.

And suddenly I'm not twenty-seven. Not a Hollywood actor or a man planning proposals or someone capable of handling crisis.

I'm just her son. Terrified. Breaking.

"Mummy—" The word comes out choked, childish, desperate. I collapse into her arms. "Mummy, I can't—she can't—"

"Shh." She holds me tight, one hand in my hair like she used to when nightmares woke me as a boy. "I know, mon cœur. I know."

"She was fine. We made love and she was laughing and now—" Another sob. "Now there's blood and pain and I can't help her—"

"The doctors will help her."

"What if they can't?" I'm repeating myself, spiraling, but can't stop. "What if I lose her? Mummy, I just found her. I need her. I can't—I can't do this without her—"

"You won't have to." She pulls back, cupping my face. "Emily is strong. Stronger than you know. She'll fight."

"But what if fighting isn't enough?"

Mum has no answer for that.

Across the waiting room, Dad sits alone in a corner chair, watching. His face is unreadable. Always the politician. Always controlled.

But his hands shake slightly as they grip the armrests.

A doctor emerges through the double doors at 4:23 AM. White coat, tired eyes, clipboard tucked under one arm.

"Lambert family?"

We all stand simultaneously. Even Dad moves forward from his corner.

"I'm Dr. Rousseau." She glances at her notes. "Emily Silver is stable. She's experiencing severe renal colic—kidney stones. Three of them, actually. One passed naturally, which caused the hematuria—the blood you saw. The other two are still present but small enough they should pass with treatment."

The relief hits so hard my knees buckle. Jean catches my elbow.

"Kidney stones?" Marcus exhales shakily. "That's—that's it?"

"It's quite painful, I assure you." Dr. Rousseau's expression softens. "But yes. Not life-threatening. Common in patients with mobility limitations, especially during warmer months. Dehydration, limited movement—both contribute."

"Can I see her?" My voice comes out hoarse.

"In a moment. We're administering pain medication and fluids. She'll need to stay overnight for observation and hydration therapy." Dr. Rousseau looks directly at Dad. "Assemblyman Lambert, given your family's... prominence, and Mademoiselle Silver's accessibility needs, we'd like to offer a private recovery suite. If she requires future care, we can arrange a permanent room decorated to her preferences."

Dad nods slowly. "Oui. Whatever she needs."

I stare at him. He won't meet my eyes.

"The prevention protocol involves increased hydration —" Dr. Rousseau continues, addressing me now. "At least three liters daily. Dietary modifications—less sodium, limited animal protein. Regular movement when possible. Monitoring for infection. We'll provide complete instructions before discharge."

"I can make sure she—" I start.

"Also." The doctor's mouth quirks slightly. "She's asking for you. Quite insistently."

"I'm going—"

"One visitor at a time in recovery. Hospital policy."

Marcus squeezes my shoulder. "Go. We'll update Ariana."

"Ari—" I'd forgotten she was still on the phone. Michelle holds it up, Ariana's face filling the screen via video now.

"I heard everything." Ariana wipes her eyes. "I'm still flying out. Landing at noon."

"You don't have to—"

"Emily almost died of kidney stones while I'm in Austin partying. I'm coming." She disconnects before I can argue.

Dr. Rousseau leads me through the double doors, down hallways that smell like antiseptic and fear, into a private room where Emily lies small and pale against white sheets.

An IV drips clear fluid into her arm. Monitors beep steadily. Her eyes are closed.

"The morphine's taking effect." Dr. Rousseau checks the IV. "She should rest comfortably now. You can stay until she sleeps."

The door closes softly.

I sink into the chair beside her bed, taking her free hand carefully.

"Tristian?" Her eyes flutter open. Pupils dilated, unfocused.

"Right here, mon cœur."

"I'm not dying?"

"No, love. Kidney stones. You're giving birth to rocks."

A weak laugh. "That's—that's so stupid."

"Very stupid." I kiss her knuckles. "But you're okay. You're going to be okay."

"Hurts."

"I know. The medicine will help."

Her fingers tighten around mine. "Don't leave."

"I'm not—"

"*Promise*."

"Emily—"

"I need—" Her voice breaks. "I need cuddles. I gave birth to rocks and I need you to stay."

"The hospital has rules—"

"Don't care." Tears slip down her temples. "Please. Just —just stay."

I climb onto the narrow bed carefully, gathering her against my chest. She burrows into me immediately, face pressed to my neck.

"Better?" I murmur against her hair.

"Mmm." Already drifting. "Don't go."

"I won't."

"Liar." But she's smiling slightly. "You'll leave once I'm asleep."

She knows me too well.

"Maybe." I stroke her back in slow circles. "But only if you promise to rest. Really rest."

"For you?" The words slur together.

"For you. So you can come home and let me take care of you properly."

Her breathing evens out. Deepens. The monitors continue their steady beeping.

I wait until I'm certain she's fully under before carefully extracting myself. Tucking blankets around her. Pressing one last kiss to her forehead.

"I love you," I whisper. "Even when you're giving birth to geological formations."

Her mouth twitches but doesn't wake.

I slip out at 5:47 AM, dawn breaking pink over Grantham Bridge.

"Star Buzz. Le Angoumois. Even Hollywood Hype picked it up." Michelle scrolls through her tablet at breakfast, accent thick with exhaustion. "Hollywood Star Rushes Girlfriend to Hospital in Dramatic Midnight Dash."

I drain my espresso. "Fantastic."

"They've got photos of Dad driving." Jean sets down his phone, words clipped British-sharp. "Breaking every traffic law in Grantham Bridge. The opposition's already calling it 'Lambert privilege.'"

"Saving Emily's life is privilege?" My cup hits the saucer harder than intended.

"According to them?" Levi passes me croissants. "Absolutely."

Dad enters the breakfast room, suit already immaculate despite the hour. His PR director Margot trails behind, laptop open.

"We need a statement." Dad's accent slides fully British when he's strategizing. "Unified family message. Control the narrative before—"

"Before what?" I interrupt. "Before people realize we're human?"

"Before this becomes ammunition." Dad ignores my tone. "The campaign—"

"Is your problem, not Emily's."

"It's everyone's problem when TMZ runs 'Movie Star's Disabled Girlfriend Hospitalized' for clicks." Margot doesn't look up from typing. "We need to shape this story. Maybe—perhaps we announce an engagement. Show family unity. Give them romance instead of scandal."

The room goes silent.

"You want me to propose for your campaign?" My accent thickens, French vowels bleeding through. "Use Emily's hospital visit as PR?"

"I'm suggesting," Dad says carefully, "that if an engagement is already planned—"

"It is." The words come out harsh. "I was going to do it at Starlight Studios Paris. Weekend of her birthday, end of August. Whole Wonderful Wizard of Oz setup because that's what she loves. Not because some tabloid needs a distraction."

Mum's hand finds Dad's arm. "Pierre—"

"Then we simply..." He pauses. Regroups. "We simply move the timeline. Make it official before the media invents their own story."

"No."

"Tristian—"

"I said no." I stand, chair scraping tile. "Emily nearly died last night because I didn't hydrate her properly. Because I was so focused on making this trip perfect I missed the signs. I'm not turning that into a photo opportunity."

The front door opens. Closes. Ariana appears in the breakfast room doorway, travel bag over her shoulder, face blotchy from crying.

"Where is she?"

Marcus moves immediately. "Still at the hospital. Tristian convinced—"

"You left her?" Ariana rounds on me.

"She made me." I scrub my face. "Said I looked like death. Promised she'd sleep. Texted me every hour to prove she's fine."

"She's not fine. She has kidney stones."

"Which are passing with treatment." Dr. Rousseau said so. But the guilt still twists sharp.

Ariana's shoulders sag. "I need to see her."

"We'll go soon as visiting hours start." I check my watch. "Another hour."

"Then I need coffee." She collapses into an empty chair. "And someone to explain why the internet thinks you're getting engaged to help your dad's campaign."

Dad's jaw tightens.

"Because," Jean says quietly, accent crisp, "Dad's PR team thinks a romantic proposal will distract from Assemblyman Lambert Using Political Connections to Break Traffic Laws."

"That's the stupidest—" Ariana stops. Looks at me. "Wait. You're really planning to propose?"

"End of August. Starlight Studios. Yellow brick road to Emerald City." I glance at Jean, Marcus. "Which means I need to go ring shopping. Soon. Before the media decides Emily's engagement ring should be a campaign prop."

Jean straightens. "I know a jeweler. Private. Discreet."

"I'm in." Marcus grins despite the tension. "Someone needs to make sure you don't buy something too Hollywood."

"What's wrong with Hollywood?" Michelle protests.

"Emily's not Hollywood." Ariana accepts coffee from Mum. "She's vintage Dorothy Gale with modern disability awareness. The ring needs to reflect that."

"Emeralds." I've thought about this. Dreamed about it. "Set in something classic. Maybe art deco? She loves the twenties aesthetic."

"Emeralds like her eyes." Levi smiles. "That's actually perfect."

"We leave in twenty minutes." Jean's already texting. "Jeweler opens early for Lambert family. Perks of generations of political connections."

Dad opens his mouth. Closes it. His accent thickens when he finally speaks, British formality cracking slightly. "The statement still needs addressing."

"Then address it honestly." I meet his eyes. "Tell them Emily had a medical emergency. We responded. End of story. Leave the engagement out of it until I put that ring on her finger."

"And if they demand more details?"

"Tell them," Ariana says coldly, "that Emily Silver's medical information is private. And anyone who uses a disabled woman's health crisis for clicks can go to hell."

Mum actually laughs. "I like this one, Tristian."

"Everyone does." I grab my jacket. "Now let's go find Emily a ring worthy of the woman who criticized my film choices on our first date."

Grantham Bridge's shopping district stretches along Rue Royale, where Georgian storefronts painted cream and sage sit beside French Renaissance townhouses with mansard roofs. National flags hang from iron brackets—that distinctive horizontal split of red-white over white-blue, diagonal crimson stripe cutting through, Angoumois coat of arms centered with its crowned shield. British precision meets French flair in every architectural detail, every shop window display.

"There." Jean points past a patisserie advertising both scones and macarons. "Bijouterie Laurent. Three generations. Grandmère bought her anniversary pieces here."

The shop front barely announces itself—discreet gold lettering on forest green, window displays minimal. A single strand of pearls. Vintage watch. Nothing flashy.

Marcus holds the door. "After you, Romeo."

Inside smells like old money and discretion. Wood paneling. Velvet display cases. A woman emerges from the back room, silver hair swept into a chignon, reading glasses on a chain.

"Monsieur Lambert." Her accent blends British formality with French warmth. "Jean mentioned you'd be visiting. I'm Madame Laurent."

"My brother's getting engaged." Jean grins. "He needs something special."

"Not special." I correct him. "Perfect. The woman—she's..." How do I explain Emily to a stranger? "She's a fashion designer. Loves vintage aesthetics, particularly 1920s. Her eyes are emerald green. She's the kind of person who notices craftsmanship, who appreciates the story behind things."

Madame Laurent's expression softens. "Sounds like someone who deserves more than a standard solitaire."

"Exactly."

"And your budget?"

"Irrelevant." I don't care what it costs. "I want the ring that's meant for her. Price isn't a factor."

Ariana wanders the cases, stopping at art deco pieces. "What about era? You said twenties?"

"She wore a 1925 Christine Daaé costume to our first photo op." The memory makes me smile. "Handmade. Every detail researched, authentic."

"Art deco then." Madame Laurent unlocks a case. "I have several pieces from that period. Most are estate acquisitions. Each with provenance."

She spreads velvet across the counter. Rings appear—geometric platinum settings, sapphire clusters, diamond bands with millegrain edges.

Beautiful. All of them.

None of them *Emily*.

Marcus picks up a square-cut diamond. "This one's classic."

"Too cold." Ariana shakes her head. "Emily's warm. She needs color."

"Emeralds?" I ask Madame Laurent.

"Fewer from that era, but..." She disappears into the back room.

Jean leans against the counter. "You really thought this through. The Emerald City theme, matching her eyes—"

"I've been planning since the night she fell asleep watching Wonderful in my suite." Nine months ago. Feels like yesterday and forever simultaneously. "Knew then I'd marry her."

"Lambert curse strikes again." Marcus laughs. "Remember when I realized about Michelle? Three days. Bought a ring in five."

"Grandpère proposed to Grandmère after one dance." Jean smiles. "Dad asked Mum within the week. We don't do slow."

Madame Laurent returns carrying a small wooden box. "This arrived in an estate sale last autumn. Parisian jeweler, circa 1923. The family couldn't bear to keep it after their daughter..." She pauses delicately. "It needs someone who'll treasure it properly."

She opens the box.

The world stops.

Rose gold band catches the light, warm and vintage and *alive*. The emerald—round-cut, impossibly vivid—sits elevated in delicate prongs that let light flood through. But the details—God, the details Emily would notice—intricate filigree curls along the band like lace, interrupted by tiny diamonds that sparkle without overwhelming. The setting itself is architecture, art deco craftsmanship meeting romantic flourish.

"That's it." Ariana breathes out. "That's Emily's ring."

She's right. It's everything—vintage without being costume, elegant without being pretentious, detailed enough to reward Emily's designer eye. The emerald matches that precise shade of green when she's happy, when her eyes light up discussing fabric construction or Frances Gale's Dorothy.

"I'll take it."

"You haven't asked the price." Madame Laurent smiles.

"Don't care. That ring was made for Emily Silver." I can already see it on her finger, imagine her studying the filigree details, tracing the rose gold warmth. "What size?"

"Six. But we can resize—"

"She's a six." I know her hands like I know my own lines. "Perfect fit."

Jean examines the band. "The craftsmanship is extraordinary. Look at the millegrain edging, the way the diamonds integrate without competing."

Marcus pulls out his phone. "I'm texting Michelle. She'll want photos."

"Non." Madame Laurent's tone sharpens. "No photographs until after the proposal, s'il vous plaît. This ring deserves its moment."

I like her immediately.

"How much?"

She names a figure that makes Marcus wince. I don't blink.

"Done. Can you hold it here? I'm proposing end of August."

"Of course." She returns the ring to its box carefully. "Shall I prepare documentation? Provenance records?"

"Emily would love that." She'd spend hours researching the original owner, imagining their story. "Everything you have."

"Then congratulations, Monsieur Lambert." Madame Laurent extends her hand. "Your Emily is very fortunate."

"I'm the fortunate one." Truth in every syllable. "She chose me back."

The patisserie next door pumps sugar-butter heaven into the street. Ariana stops mid-stride.

"We're getting croissants." Not a question. She's already pushing through the door, bell chiming overhead.

Inside smells like childhood summers in Grantham Bridge before politics consumed everything—warm dough, dark chocolate, that particular French coffee bitterness Mum preferred. Display cases overflow with jewel-bright tarts, éclairs glazed to perfection, pain au chocolat stacked in golden pyramids.

"Quatre chocolat croissants." Jean orders in fluid French that makes the woman behind the counter smile. "Et quatre cafés."

We claim a corner table, wrought iron and marble, windows overlooking the street where morning shoppers drift past carrying baguettes and newspapers. Marcus distributes pastries while Jean handles coffee.

I tear into mine without tasting. Can't taste. My brain's already in Paris, constructing the Emerald City setup at Starlight Studios, imagining every detail that could go wrong. What if she says no? What if I trip carrying her to the yellow brick road? What if Mochi knocks over the fog machines? What if—

"Tristian." Ariana's voice cuts through the spiral. "Breathe."

"I just bought an engagement ring." The words come out strangled. "A ring. For proposing. Marriage."

"Generally how that works, mate." Marcus grins around his croissant.

"But what if—" I set down the pastry, appetite gone. "What if Emily thinks it's too fast? We've only been together nine months. What if her kidney stones made her realize dating me isn't worth the hospital visits and media scrutiny? What if she wakes up and decides she wants someone normal, someone without Dadrazzi camping outside or political families dissecting her medical emergencies?"

Jean's hand lands on my shoulder. "The trip isn't scheduled until the weekend around her birthday. August thirtieth through September fourth. Six weeks away. You have time."

"Time for what? To convince myself she won't run screaming?" My accent thickens, British consonants sharpening with panic. "She vomited blood last night.

Blood, Jean. And instead of focusing on her recovery, I'm planning proposals and buying rings and—"

"And loving her exactly how Lamberts love." Ariana interrupts, stealing my untouched croissant. "All in. No halfway. Emily knows what she signed up for."

"Does she though?" I drag both hands through my hair. "Does she really understand what marrying into this family means? Grandmère already claimed her. Mum's requesting wardrobe designs. Dad's using our relationship for campaign optics. And I'm—I'm ready to tattoo her name above my heart but terrified she'll realize she deserves better."

Marcus leans forward. "Michelle told me once that the scariest part wasn't falling for me. It was trusting I'd fallen just as hard." He pauses, letting that sink in. "Emily's already there, Tristan. She quit her job to come here. She's designing for your family. She told you she'd stay if you asked."

"After watching Wonderful." The memory steadies me slightly. "She said she'd stay too."

"Exactly." Jean sips his coffee. "And you have six weeks to plan every perfect detail. Not six minutes. Weeks. Time to coordinate with Pierre about the studio setup, time to get Emily's ring size officially confirmed, time to rehearse your proposal speech until it's flawless."

"I haven't written a proposal speech."

"Then start." Ariana shoves my croissant back. "Eat. Emily's getting discharged this afternoon. She'll want that chocolate croissant you're currently having an existential crisis over."

She's right. Emily loves chocolate croissants, especially the French ones with dark chocolate that melts bitter-sweet on the tongue.

I take a bite. Force myself to taste it this time.

"Six weeks," I repeat.

"Six weeks," Jean confirms.

Time enough to plan the perfect proposal.

Time enough to panic properly.

Emily's discharge paperwork takes forty minutes. Forty agonizing minutes where I pace the recovery room while Dr. Rousseau explains hydration schedules and medication timing and warning signs that would require immediate return.

"Drink minimum two liters daily," he tells Emily in careful English. "The stones passed, but you remain at risk."

"I will." Emily signs the final form with shaky fingers. Still pale. Still too fragile.

Mochi explodes the moment we clear the hospital doors. His entire body wiggles, tail whipping dangerous arcs while he licks Emily's face like she's returned from war instead of a one-night stay.

"I know, baby. I know." She buries her face in his white curls. "Momma's home."

The chateau greets us with organized chaos.

"Two days." Mum announces from the salon doorway. "The campaign launch is Friday evening. Eight o'clock.

Sixty-seven confirmed guests, all high-ranking party members and donors."

Emily goes rigid in my arms—I'm carrying her up the front steps because the wheelchair's still in the car and I'm not letting go anyway.

"What do they need?" Her voice climbs half an octave. "What haven't I—I lost almost two days, I haven't started anything, I don't even have measurements for—"

"Breathe." I set her carefully on the settee in my old bedroom. "Just breathe."

"Can't breathe. Need to—" She's already pulling out her design tablet, fingers flying across the screen. "Charcoal suits for the men, you said? And red for accents?"

"Charcoal and red." Mum appears with fabric swatches, Grandmère trailing behind with her measuring tape. "Traditional. Elegant. Nothing too modern."

"Red dresses for the women?" Emily's sketching frantically, lines appearing like magic. "What silhouette? A-line? Sheath? How conservative?"

"Sophisticated." Grandmère drapes burgundy silk across Emily's lap. "These women appreciate classic tailoring. Nothing too—how do you say—Hollywood."

I catch the way Emily's hand trembles. "You just got released from hospital."

"I'm fine."

"You're exhausted."

"I'm behind." She doesn't look up from her tablet. "Dad needs charcoal three-piece, right? Classic cut, nothing trendy. Mum's dress—tea length or floor?"

"Floor." Mum settles beside her. "I prefer traditional hemlines for formal events."

The afternoon dissolves into fabric and measurements. Jean strips to his undershirt so Emily can map his shoulders. Michelle models potential dress shapes while Marcus holds swatches against different lighting. Dad even submits to measuring, though he maintains stiff silence throughout.

Ariana appears every thirty minutes like clockwork.

"Drink." She shoves water glasses into Emily's hands. "Doctor's orders."

"I'm working."

"You're dehydrated." Ariana doesn't budge. "Drink or I'm calling Dr. Rousseau."

Emily drinks. Returns to draping red silk across Michelle's frame, pinning and adjusting until the fabric flows like liquid fire.

By evening, my bedroom resembles a design studio. Sketches cover every surface. Fabric swatches create rainbow chaos across the floor. Emily's transferred to my desk chair—better back support—surrounded by the entire Lambert clan offering opinions on lapel widths and hem lengths.

Mochi plants himself at her feet, massive head resting on her footrest. Vigilant. Protective.

"This cut?" Emily shows Dad two nearly identical jacket designs.

He studies them with unexpected focus. "The second. More traditional through the shoulders."

"Perfect." She makes notes. "I can have everything ready by Thursday afternoon. Final fittings Friday morning."

"Emily." I crouch beside her chair. "You need rest."

"I need caffeine and focus." But she leans into my touch when I brush hair from her face. "I lost two days, Tristian. I can't let your family down."

"You could never—"

"Drink." Ariana materializes with another water glass. Emily drinks.

"Up you go." Marcus lifts me from my Parmobil before I fully register what's happening.

"Wait—what are you—"

"Doctor's orders." Ariana wheels a basic manual push chair beside us. Black frame. Standard cushions. Nothing like my custom pink power chair. "You need fresh air and sunlight. Not another twelve hours in Tristian's bedroom turned textile factory."

Marcus deposits me in the unfamiliar chair. "Dr. Rousseau specifically said gentle activity promotes recovery."

"He said hydration and rest—"

"Rest from stress." Ariana positions Mochi's leash across my lap. "Which means a break from campaign panic."

Through the chateau windows, I spot Jean physically blocking the front door. Levi's got his phone out—recording something. Michelle waves cheerfully.

"Tristian's going to kill you."

"I know." Marcus grins, pure mischief lighting his face. "That's what makes it fun. Plus you'll thank me later once you've had possessive Tristian sex. Trust me. Late bloomer he may be, but the curse has hit him the worst since great-great-grandpère."

Heat floods my cheeks. "Marcus!"

"What? I've seen the way he looks at you after you've been apart for thirty seconds." He starts pushing the manual chair down the gravel path. "This'll be good for him. Build character."

Ariana falls into step beside us, Mochi prancing between us like this kidnapping is the best adventure ever. "Besides, you need macarons. Medical fact."

"That's not—"

"Macarons cure everything." Marcus navigates us through the chateau gates. "It's Angoumois law."

Grantham Bridge unfolds like a storybook village. Cobblestone streets wind between buildings that predate electricity. Window boxes overflow with geraniums. The morning market fills the square with voices haggling over cheese and wine and summer vegetables.

My phone buzzes.

Tristian: Where are you?

Tristian: Emily.

Tristian: Jean won't tell me anything except you're "perfectly safe."

Tristian: That's not an answer.

"Oh, he's spiraling." I show Ariana the messages.

She smirks. "Give it two more minutes."

Tristian: Your chair is here. Roger says you left in a MANUAL chair.

Tristian: With MARCUS.

Tristian: Answer your phone.

"British Tristian has entered the chat." Marcus reads over my shoulder. "Time for a little cat and mouse, sis."

"Don't call me—" But warmth blooms in my chest. Sis. Like family already.

I type quickly: *Getting fresh air. Doctor approved.*

Tristian: Which doctor? Rousseau didn't mention outings.

Tristian: Where exactly are you getting this air?

Tristian: EMILY.

The texts arrive rapid-fire. I picture him pacing his bedroom, accent thickening with each unanswered question. That specific blend of French precision and British panic he gets when plans deviate.

Grantham Bridge shopping district. Very public. Very safe.

Tristian: The market? You're at the MARKET?

Tristian: Do you have water? Your medication? What if your back spasms?

Tristian: I'm coming to get you.

Ariana plucks the phone from my hands. She types something I can't see, then shows me:

She's fine. Eat your breakfast. We'll be back in two hours.

Then she turns my phone off.

"Ariana!"

"He needs to learn you won't shatter." She points toward a patisserie with yellow awnings. "Now. Macarons. I'm thinking pistachio."

"Rose," Marcus counters. "Obviously rose for our fashion designer."

"Salted caramel."

"Lemon."

They bicker like siblings while Mochi sniffs every cobblestone. The manual chair handles differently than my power chair—Marcus controls direction and speed, making me acutely aware of my dependence. But also... free. No battery anxiety. No worrying about accessibility.

Just morning sun and flower boxes and the simple pleasure of watching Grantham Bridge wake up.

The patisserie smells like butter and sugar and possibility.

The patisserie counter glitters with rows of macarons—pastel shells sandwiching cream in every shade imaginable. Marcus orders an entire box while Ariana debates between coffee or champagne pairing.

My phone vibrates against my thigh.

I pull it out—Ariana must've turned it back on—and nearly drop it.

Tristian: You think Marcus can protect you from me?

Tristian: When you get back, I'm carrying you straight to our bedroom.

Tristian: That manual chair won't be needed for a while, darling.

Heat crawls up my neck. I glance at Marcus and Ariana, but they're absorbed in macaron selection.

Tristian: I'll start with your neck. Right where you're most sensitive.

Tristian: Then I'll work my way down. Very slowly.

Tristian: By the time I'm finished, you won't remember your own name.

I press my thighs together. This possessive side of Tristian—it reminds me of Nathan Cross in Extinction Protocol. The way he'd marked Maya Reyes as his after that raptor attack scene. Territorial. Claiming. The half-raptor paleontologist protecting his assistant from the pack.

God, I'd watched that movie seventeen times.

And Felix in Wonderful—the prince who'd burn Oz to ash before letting anyone touch Dorothy. Tristian plays possessive beautifully on screen.

Experiencing it directed at me? Different universe entirely.

Another text arrives:

Tristian: I can smell your arousal from here.

No he can't. That's impossible. But my body responds anyway, heat pooling low in my belly.

"Earth to Emily." Ariana waves a pistachio macaron in front of my face. "You're blushing."

"I'm fine."

Marcus peers at my phone. His eyebrows shoot up. "Oh, he's big mad."

"Give me that." Ariana snatches it, reads, and cackles. "Lambert possessive genes strike again. This is gold."

"What's gold?" I reach for my phone.

She holds it out of range. "We're making him worse."

"Why would we—"

"Because it's hilarious." Marcus grins. "Plus Michelle owes me twenty euros if we can get him speaking full Nathan Cross Alabama accent via text."

"That's cruel."

"That's family." Ariana pockets my phone. "Come on. We've got one more stop before he breaks free and hunts you down."

The tattoo parlor sits tucked between a bookshop and a wine merchant. Ink & Iron, the sign reads in Gothic script.

"Absolutely not." I grip my armrests. "I've never even —"

"Exactly." Marcus wheels me through the door. "Time to remedy that."

Inside smells like antiseptic and incense. Flash art covers every wall—skulls, roses, geometric patterns. A woman with purple hair and full sleeve tattoos looks up from her desk.

"Bonjour. I'm Sylvie." Her English carries barely a trace of accent. "You must be Emily. Jean called ahead."

"Jean—of course he did."

"He described exactly what you need." Sylvie pulls out a sketch. "Small. Meaningful. Somewhere your boyfriend loves to kiss."

The design steals my breath.

A raptor pack symbol from Extinction Protocol—the stylized claw marks Nathan Cross's pack used. But inside the three curved lines, Sylvie's added a delicate "T" in script font.

"Between collarbone and left breast," Ariana says. "Right where Tristian always—"

"I know where he kisses." My face burns.

Sylvie smiles. "It's small enough to hide under most necklines. But visible enough that he'll see it. First time getting ink?"

I nod.

"I'll make it gentle. Twenty minutes, tops."

Marcus is already typing on my phone—which he apparently stole from Ariana. "Smile, Emmy."

He snaps a photo of me in the chair, Sylvie's sketch visible on the desk beside me.

"Don't you dare—"

"Too late." He hits send. "Jean wants photographic evidence for the family chat."

My phone explodes with notifications.

Tristian: That better be permanent, darlin'.

The accent. He's typing in Nathan Cross's Alabama drawl.

Michelle: WE BROKE HIM

Jean: Levi won't let him leave the house

Marcus: 🦖 🦖 🦖

Tristian: You're mine, Emily. Every inch.

Tristian: That mark proves it.

Tristian: Get home. Now.

"Full raptor mode activated." Ariana shows me the family chat where Levi's posted a video of Tristian pacing like a caged predator. "This is the best day of my life."

Sylvie preps the tattoo gun. "Your boyfriend is intense, yes?"

"You have no idea."

The needle buzzes to life. I focus on breathing while Sylvie works, the sharp sting almost meditative. Mochi rests his head on my lap, sensing my tension.

My phone won't stop vibrating.

Tristian: I can taste you already

Tristian: Sweet and mine

Tristian: You better run when you see me, baby

"He escaped," Ariana announces, reading over my shoulder. "Levi just texted. Tristian broke through the garden door."

"What?" I try to sit up but Sylvie gently pushes me back.

"Almost done. Don't move."

Marcus checks his watch. "We've got maybe fifteen minutes before he tracks us down. Twenty if Jean slows him."

The tattoo gun stops. Sylvie wipes the area clean, applies ointment, covers it with transparent film. "All set. Keep it clean, no swimming for two weeks."

I barely hear her. Tristian's texts have become pure predator:

Tristian: I know where Ink & Iron is

Tristian: I'm coming for what's mine

"Bathroom," I gasp. "Now."

Ariana helps me transfer, wheels me into the single accessible restroom. Locks the door.

"What's wrong?"

"I need—" Heat floods my face. "Privacy. Thirty seconds."

Understanding dawns. "Oh. OH. Yeah, I'll wait outside."

Alone, I assess the damage. My underwear is soaked through. The arousal, the possessive texts, the Nathan Cross accent—my body betrayed me completely.

Thank God I always carry spares and pads. Foster care taught me to pack for every contingency.

I change quickly, tucking the wet pair into a plastic bag in my purse. Fresh underwear. Pad in place. Slightly more composed.

My phone buzzes.

Tristian: Got your location. Two blocks away.

Tristian: Run.

I open the bathroom door. Ariana takes one look at my face and understands.

"Marcus!" She sprints—actually sprints—back to the main room. "We need to move. NOW."

"Why—"

"He said RUN."

Marcus's eyes widen. He grabs my chair handles. "Where?"

"Park district. Other side of the city."

"That's forty minutes on foot—"

"Train station's six blocks." Ariana's already mapping on her phone. "We can catch the 10:47."

We burst onto the cobblestone street. Mochi barks excitedly, thinking this is a game.

"Is running really—" I start.

"YES." Both of them answer in unison.

Marcus pushes the manual chair faster than I thought possible. We weave between market stalls, Ariana clearing a path through the Saturday crowd. My heart pounds—part fear, mostly anticipation.

Nathan Cross hunted Maya through the jungle for three full scenes in Extinction Protocol. The audience could feel his need through the screen.

Experiencing it firsthand? Terrifying. Exhilarating.

We round a corner toward the train station.

My phone rings. Not text—actual call.

Tristian's name flashes on screen.

"Don't answer it," Marcus pants. "It's a trap."

"He's tracking us anyway—"

"THERE!" Ariana points.

Across the square, maybe a hundred yards away, Tristian emerges from a side street. Dark jeans. White t-shirt. Hair disheveled. Eyes locked on me like a raptor spotting prey.

He starts running.

"GO GO GO!" Marcus shoves my chair toward the station entrance.

The last thing I see before we plunge underground is Tristian's smile—all predator, no pretense—and the absolute certainty in his stride.

He's going to catch me.

And God help me, I want him to.

The train lurches to a stop on the opposite side of Grantham Bridge. Marcus practically launches me out of the manual chair, wheeling through the station at a speed that makes pedestrians jump aside.

"Where now?" he gasps.

Ariana consults her phone. "Piercing studio. Three blocks north."

"Another—Emily, are you trying to kill him?"

"I'm trying—" I grip the armrests as we careen around a corner. "—to be braver."

Because Tristian sees me. All of me. The scars, the wheelchair, the anxiety attacks. He renovated his entire house. Stood up to his father. Chose me over Gabrielle, over his pristine Hollywood image.

The least I can do is choose him back. Permanently.

Mochi trots beside us, tail wagging like this is the best adventure of his life.

The piercing studio—Starlight Body Modification—occupies a narrow shopfront between a pharmacy and a café. Inside, a man with gauged ears and a nose chain looks up from his magazine.

"Bonjour. Walk-ins?"

"Navel piercing." I'm breathless, partly from the run, mostly from anticipation. "Fast as possible."

"Ah." Recognition flickers across his face. "You're Emily. The girlfriend, yes? Jean called."

"Of course he did."

The piercer—Matthieu, according to his name tag—leads us to a private room. Sterile equipment gleams on a metal tray. "Standard titanium barbell to start?"

"No." I pull out my phone, open the photo I saved three days ago. "Custom order. Multiple rings."

The image shows a velvet-lined jewelry box containing six interchangeable belly rings:

"I want a mark for every film he's made." My voice steadies. "His favorite place to kiss."

Matthieu studies the photo. "This is beautiful work. Where did you—"

"I designed them. Emily Silver Adaptive Designs." Pride tingles through me. "Can you do the piercing today? I'll have the custom rings shipped next week."

"Absolument." He preps the area with professional efficiency. "This will pinch."

Ariana grabs my hand. "You're sure?"

"Positive."

Because I'm not that terrified girl in the group home anymore. I'm not the wheelchair user apologizing for taking up space. I'm Emily Dorothy Silver—fashion designer, college graduate, woman who walked away from toxic jobs and abusive systems.

Woman loved by Tristian Alexandre Lambert.

The needle slides through. Sharp sting, then pressure, then the cool weight of titanium settling against my skin.

Matthieu steps back. "Done. Standard aftercare applies —"

Ariana's already typing. "Sending photo evidence in three... two..."

"Wait—" But my protest comes too late.

My phone explodes.

Tristian: Your navel

Tristian: Jesus Christ, Emily

Tristian: That's MINE

Tristian: Every ring. Every film. Marking yourself for me.

Tristian: I'm gonna worship that piercing until you forget your own name

The accent's gone full Alabama drawl. Nathan Cross in hunting mode.

Marcus reads over my shoulder and whistles. "You broke him in a completely different way."

Tristian: Where are you RIGHT NOW

I type quickly: *For the record, going out was Ari's idea.*

Tristian: I don't care whose idea it was, darlin'

Tristian: You're the one who got my name permanently inked

Tristian: The one who pierced the spot I kiss every night

Tristian: You belong to me

Tristian: And I'm coming to collect

Heat pools low in my belly. The piercing throbs—not painfully, just... present. A constant reminder.

What happened to sweet Tristian? I text back.

Tristian: Sweet Tristian left when his girl started running

Tristian: Nathan's driving this bus now, baby

Tristian: And he don't take prisoners

"Oh my God." Ariana shows me the family group chat. Jean's posted a video of Tristian commandeering someone's bicycle, pedaling through Grantham Bridge like a man possessed. "He's tracking your phone."

"Of course he is."

Matthieu hands me aftercare instructions. "Keep it clean. No swimming. And maybe... warn your boyfriend to be gentle?"

My face burns. "Yeah. I'll mention it."

We burst back onto the street. Sunlight glints off old stone buildings, off the river winding through the park district.

"Where to?" Marcus positions behind my chair.

I check my phone. Tristian's location marker moves steadily closer. Maybe fifteen minutes out.

"Run again?" Ariana grins.

"Duh."

We head toward the park—sprawling green space with winding paths and hidden alcoves. Mochi barks happily, sensing the game.

My phone buzzes with one final message:

Tristian: I can smell you from here, sweetheart

Tristian: Running just makes it better when I catch you

Tristian: And I always catch my prey

Marcus pushes faster. Ariana scouts ahead. My heart pounds against my ribs, the new piercing a sweet ache, the tattoo burning beneath its protective film.

No more sweet little girl.

Just Emily. Marked. Claimed. Running through a Angoumois park with her boyfriend in full predator mode somewhere behind us.

And absolutely, completely his.

Marcus wheels me out of the park at a speed that makes my teeth rattle. We burst onto a side street, lungs burning, Mochi panting beside us.

"Where to now, genius?" I gasp.

Ariana's already pulling up maps. "The winter house. Chaudeaux—mountain town, thermal springs. Nobody's there this time of year."

"How far?"

"Forty-five minutes by train. Maybe thirty by car."

A bicycle bell rings behind us. Close. Too close.

I twist in the manual chair just as Tristian rounds the corner three blocks back, pedaling like his life depends on it. His eyes lock onto mine.

"GO!" I shriek.

Marcus abandons all pretense of caution, running full-out toward the train station. Ariana sprints ahead, clearing pedestrians with shouted warnings in broken French.

"He's gaining!" Marcus pants.

Because of course he is. Tristian's got the raw athleticism of someone who does his own stunts. We've got gravity working against us on the uphill street.

The train station appears ahead. Ariana's already at the ticket counter, credit card out, speaking rapid-fire to the agent.

"Platform seven!" She waves us through. "Train leaves in four minutes!"

We careen through the turnstile. The elevator's too slow—Marcus hauls the manual chair and me down a ramp designed for luggage carts, wheels bouncing over uneven concrete.

Tristian's voice echoes through the station. "EMILY!"

Full Nathan Cross drawl. My thighs clench.

"There!" Ariana points to a blue regional train, doors still open.

But there's stairs. Six of them leading up to the platform.

"Leave the chair," I decide. Heart hammering. "Help me walk."

Marcus hesitates. "Emily—"

"I can do short distances. You know that." I grab his arm, Ariana taking my other side. "Go."

They haul me upright. My legs shake but hold. We stumble-walk toward the platform stairs, Mochi pressed against my hip for balance.

Behind us, Tristian's bicycle crashes against something metal.

"Don't look back," Ariana commands.

We climb. One step. Two. My quads scream. Three. Four.

"Platform seven, final boarding!" The conductor's voice crackles over speakers.

Five steps. Six. We're up.

"Wait!" I twist free, turning back to the ramp where Marcus abandoned the manual chair.

My wet panties from earlier—still in my purse. I pull them out, throw them across the seat like a flag of surrender.

Or a promise.

"Emily, what—"

"He'll bring the chair." I'm already moving again, supported between my best friends. "And he'll know exactly what those mean."

We collapse into train seats just as the doors beep their warning. Through the window, I spot Tristian taking the platform stairs three at a time.

He's going to make it.

He's going to catch me.

The train lurches—

No. Wait.

Tristian reaches the platform. Our eyes meet through glass. He's breathing hard, hair wild, still wearing that predator smile.

But the doors are closing.

Something shifts inside me. Braver than I've ever been. More certain than I've ever felt.

This is just like the wedding scene in *Wonderful*. Dorothy running through the Winkie grasslands, Felix chasing her, proving himself worthy before witnesses.

Singing their vows.

I press my palm against the window. Start singing, voice shaking at first, then stronger:

Tristian's face transforms. Recognition, shock, pure joy.

He presses his palm to match mine, separated only by glass. Sings back in an accent I've never heard from him— younger than Nathan's drawl, higher, definitely Midwestern.

Felix. He's singing as Felix, heir to the Emerald Throne.

My heart stops.

People on the platform turn to watch. Passengers around us pull out phones.

We harmonize the chorus, his tenor blending with my mezzo through the barrier:

The train starts moving. Slowly at first.

Tristian walks alongside, hand still pressed to glass, never breaking eye contact or missing a note:

Together now, voices rising.

The train picks up speed. Tristian jogs, then runs.

He's sprinting now, full-out, keeping pace.

Our voices crack on the same word. The train pulls ahead.

Tristian stops running. Throws his head back.

And roars.

Not human. Pure raptor—the territorial claiming sound from *Extinction Protocol*. The noise Nathan Cross's pack made when marking their mate.

Mine.

I learned raptor-speak for him. Spent hours studying *Extinction Protocol* lore, the pack dynamics, the claiming rituals.

He learned Winkie tradition for me. All of Oz mythology. The marriage customs from Jeremy Corbyn's *Wonderful: The Life and Times of Dorothy Mae Gale*—the book that inspired the musical, that only die-hard fans read.

The bride chase. Singing vows before witnesses.

We just married each other.

My phone rings before the train even clears the platform.

"You clever, beautiful, brilliant woman." Tristian's breathing hard. "Winkie law says we're married."

"I know."

"And raptor law follows tonight when I catch you at Chaudeaux."

Heat floods through me. "I'm counting on it."

"I'm going home for supplies. Telling the family and staff. You good with that?"

"Tell them Mrs. Lambert is waiting for her husband."

Silence. Then: "Say that again."

"Mrs. Lambert." Warmth spreads through my chest. "I like how it sounds."

"Emily Dorothy Lambert." His voice breaks. "God, I love you."

"I love you too. Now drive fast, husband."

"Already moving, wife."

The call ends. I slump against Ariana, who's filming everything on her phone with tears streaming down her face.

"That," she whispers, "was the most romantic thing I've ever witnessed."

Marcus just shakes his head, grinning. "The Lambert curse strikes again."

Outside the window, the Angoumois countryside blurs past. Forty-five minutes to Chaudeaux.

Thirty if Tristian drives.

I press my fingers to the new piercing beneath my shirt. To the tattoo still healing over my heart.

Marked. Married. His.

And absolutely, completely ready for whatever comes next.

The train sways through rolling hills, and I can't stop replaying it. The singing. The raptor roar. The way Tristian's palm pressed against mine through glass like we could merge molecules.

"Okay, but legally speaking—" Marcus shifts in his seat across from me, grinning. "How binding is a fictional double-lore wedding?"

Ariana's reviewing footage on her phone, wiping tears. "She sang Winkie vows. He answered as Felix. That's legally binding in Oz mythology according to Jeremy Corbyn's extended universe."

"But we're not in Oz—"

"And the raptor claim?" I interrupt, heat crawling up my neck. "Nathan Cross marked Maya with that exact roar in chapter seventeen of the novelization."

"Which makes you..." Ariana's eyes go wide. "Pack mate. Wife. Claimed."

My phone buzzes. The Lambert family group chat explodes with notifications.

Tristian: Team - effective immediately, Emily is to be addressed as Mrs. Lambert

Tristian: Alfred, Collette - I need the winter house prepared for tonight

Tristian: Full romantic setup. You know what I like

Alfred Dupont: Already there, Master Tristian. Everything is prepared.

Jean: How are you ALREADY THERE

Alfred Dupont: A good butler anticipates needs.

Collette Dupont: Fresh linens on the bed. Champagne chilling. Dinner for two at seven.

Michelle: They're psychic. I've been saying this for years.

Tristian: Emily arrives at 4:47pm. I'll be there by 5:15.

Jean: You just married her via LORE WEDDING

Jean: In a TRAIN STATION

Tristian: Best decision I ever made

Levi: Jean's spiraling. Says you've completely lost it.

Tristian: Tell him I found it, actually

My heart does something complicated. Tristian's already telling everyone. His team, his family, the staff who raised him. No hesitation. No second-guessing.

Mrs. Lambert.

Another message pops up—Tristian directly to me:

Tristian: Roger's already drafting the press release

Tristian: Simone's beside herself (happy tears)

Tristian: Alfred says he knew the moment he met you

Tristian: I'm driving like a madman, darling

Tristian: Can't wait to make this official

His accent bleeds through even in text. The British precision melting into French enthusiasm, all wrapped around that Alabama drawl still lingering from Nathan mode.

Heat pools low in my belly. The piercing throbs—a sweet ache.

Then my hip joins in.

No.

Not now.

The familiar deep throb starts in my left hip joint, radiating down my thigh. The kind that signals my muscles are done playing nice.

I shift positions. The manual chair's basic cushion offers zero support compared to my custom Parmobil. Forty-five minutes of sitting wrong, plus the running, the stairs—

"Emmy?" Ariana leans forward. "What's wrong?"

"Nothing." I force a smile.

"Your face just went pale."

Marcus sets down his phone. "Emily."

The throb intensifies. My arthritis screaming. I left my medication at the chateau—the prescription anti-inflammatories that actually work. All I've got is the acetaminophen in my purse.

Which will barely touch this.

"Just tired." I dig through my bag, pop two pills dry. "Long day."

"That's not your tired face." Ariana knows me too well. "That's your pain face."

"I'm fine—"

"You forgot your meds." Not a question.

Marcus curses softly. "Can we turn back?"

"No." The word comes out sharper than intended. "Absolutely not."

"Emily—"

"It's my wedding night." Heat floods my face. "Tristian's driving ninety miles an hour to get to me. The

Duponts have prepared everything. I am not ruining this because my hip hurts."

The pain ratchets up another notch. I breathe through it, the way physical therapy taught me. In for four, hold for four, out for six.

"How bad?" Ariana's voice goes soft.

"Manageable." Lie. "The acetaminophen will take the edge off."

Marcus and Ariana exchange one of those looks—the kind that says they're communicating telepathically about how stubborn I'm being.

"Don't," I warn. "Don't you dare text him."

"We should—"

"Promise me." I grip Ariana's wrist. "Both of you. Promise you won't tell Tristian."

"Emmy, if you're in pain—"

"He'll postpone everything. Cancel the romance. Turn it into a medical emergency." My voice cracks. "I want one night where I'm just his wife. Not his patient."

The train rocks. My hip screams. I don't let it show.

"Please," I whisper. "Let me have this."

Ariana's jaw tightens, but she nods. Marcus looks away, conflicted.

"We won't tell," Ariana finally says. "But if it gets worse—"

"It won't." Another lie.

My phone buzzes.

Tristian: At the chateau, Mrs. Lambert

Tristian: Can't stop thinking about you

Tristian: About tonight

Tristian: About making you mine in every way that matters

I type back with shaking hands: *Drive safe, husband. I'll be waiting.*

The acetaminophen hasn't kicked in yet. Won't for another thirty minutes. And even then, it'll only dull the worst of it.

But Tristian sang Winkie vows through train station glass.

Claimed me with a raptor roar.

Called me Mrs. Lambert to his entire team.

I can handle one night of pain.

For him.

For us.

For whatever comes next.

The curse hits different when it's yours.

I stand in my childhood bedroom at the winter house, shoving supplies into a leather duffel with hands that won't stop shaking. My accent's gone thick—proper British vowels dissolving into French desperation with that Alabama drawl still clinging from Nathan mode.

"You've lost your bloody mind." Jean leans against the doorframe, arms crossed.

"Haven't." I grab the *Ozomopolitan: The Wonderful Companion* from my nightstand—the comprehensive guide explaining L. Frank Baum's original 1900 novel, Jeremy Corbyn's 1994 adaptation *Wonderful: The Life and Times of Dorothy Mae Gale*, and the 2005 musical. "It's legitimate. Page two hundred seventeen."

I flip to the section on Winkie marriage traditions, shoving the book at Jean's face.

"See? 'Winkie vows exchanged through glass or distance are considered binding when witnessed by the land itself. The couple is married in the eyes of Oz, though formal ceremonies typically follow.'" My accent twists tighter. "'Felix himself underwent both Emerald City and Winkie ceremonies—'"

"Felix is fictional—"

"He married Dorothy in the Emerald Cathedral while still a scarecrow. The Wizard witnessed. Nick and Roar witnessed. Then Agnar insisted on a proper Winkie ceremony because Dorothy was his adopted daughter." I'm pacing now, can't stop moving. "We followed the lore exactly. Train station glass. Witnesses. The land acknowledged us."

Michelle appears with her phone, filming. "This is incredible content."

"Stop recording my crisis."

"This isn't crisis. This is the Lambert curse hitting you like Great-Great-Grandpère." She zooms in on my face.

"The curse," Jean says flatly, "made me drag Levi to Vegas three weeks after meeting him. We got married by an Elvis impersonator at two AM."

"Exactly!" I grab *Extinction Protocol: Guide to Paradise* from my shelf—the companion guide covering all eight films, including detailed species lore. "It's not just Lambert. It's raptor biology. Look."

I flip to the section on raptor mating behaviors. "'Raptors are dominant, possessive creatures who claim their mates through scent-marking, territorial displays, and breeding. They desire large clutches—twins or triplets are common. Once a raptor identifies their mate, they become single-mindedly focused on—'"

My phone buzzes. Marcus.

I answer. "What—"

"She's in pain." Marcus's voice comes low, urgent. "Bad. Her hip. She forgot her meds and she's been hiding it because she doesn't want to ruin tonight."

Everything stops.

"How bad."

"Ariana says it's her arthritis. The running, the stairs, the cheap chair—she's been masking for the last hour. Took acetaminophen but it's not touching it."

The Nathan Cross part of me—the half-raptor shifter who marked Maya with his teeth—goes absolutely still. Predator-calm.

"Where is she now."

"Collette already has her in an Epsom salt bath. Hot spring water. Master bathroom."

I'm moving before conscious thought. Dumping the duffel, repacking.

"What are you doing?" Jean follows me down the hall.

"Different night." I grab Emily's favorite nightgown from the guest room where Collette unpacked her things—silk with Dorothy and Toto embroidered on the pockets. Matching silk robe. The massage oil from my bathroom. Not for sex. For actual massage.

My faded *Extinction Protocol* shirt and boxers. Clothes for tomorrow. Extra clothes for Marcus and Ariana because they're staying too.

"Tris—"

"She's in pain." My accent goes razor-sharp. "My wife is hurting and she hid it because she thought I'd choose romance over her comfort."

Michelle's still filming. "That's actually really sweet—"

"Stop. Recording."

She lowers the phone.

I check my watch. Five-oh-seven. The jeweler closes at six.

"I need twenty minutes."

"For what?" Jean asks.

"Winkie tradition." I'm halfway down the stairs. "The groom gifts the bride body jewelry. A stone representing him. Rose gold to match her ring."

"She already has the navel piercing—"

"With placeholder jewelry." I grab my keys from the hall table. "I'm getting her an emerald. Proper one."

"The shops—"

"Bijou stays open for Lamberts."

I'm out the door before Jean can argue.

Bijouterie Laurent sits tucked between the patisserie and a bookshop on Rue Principale. Monsieur Laurent himself greets me at the door.

"Master Tristian. Twice in one week?"

"Need an emerald." I'm breathless, accent mangled. "For a navel piercing. Rose gold setting to match the engagement ring I bought."

His eyebrows rise. "You proposed—"

"We married via Winkie vows at the train station." I pull out my phone, show him the video Michelle definitely sent to the family chat. "Need the body jewelry tonight. It's tradition. Groom's claim."

Understanding dawns. "Ah. The Oz ways."

"Every piece of lore." I'm pacing his shop. "Quadling, Emerald City, Gillikin, Munchkin, Winkie—I learned it all. She knows every detail. This matters."

He disappears into the back, returns with a tray of emeralds.

"Round-cut to match the ring?" He selects one, holds it to the light. "Bezel setting for comfort?"

"Perfect."

He names a price that would make normal people flinch. I don't blink.

"Need it in thirty minutes."

The winter château glows warm against the Angoumois dusk as I pull through the gates. Marcus appears on the front steps before I've even killed the engine.

"Please tell me you brought her muscle relaxers and pain meds!"

I grab the pharmacy bag from the passenger seat. "Everything Dr. Moreau prescribed. Plus the good heating pad."

"Thank God." He deflates. "She's upstairs. Master bath."

Mochi meets me at the door, whimpering, pacing tight circles around my legs. I kneel, let him nose my face.

"I know, buddy. I know. Daddy's here. We'll fix Mumma, yeah?"

He leads me up the stairs, claws clicking on marble. The master suite door stands open.

Emily lies in the massive copper tub, water cloudy with Epsom salts. Ariana kneels beside her, whispering something low. Collette Dupont perches on the counter, wringing a cool cloth that she presses to Emily's forehead.

"Here you are, my li'l rebel."

Emily's eyes find mine. Red-rimmed, exhausted. "I'm sorry—"

"No. Shhhh." I set everything down, cross to the tub. "None of that."

Ariana stands, gives me space. "Her hip seized about forty minutes ago. The running to catch the train, the stairs at the station, that cheap-ass chair on the ride—"

"I've got her." I stroke wet hair back from Emily's face. "Thank you."

Collette hands me the cloth. "Monsieur Alfred is preparing dinner in bed for the newlyweds. Cassoulet and fresh bread."

"Perfect."

They file out, leaving us alone except for Mochi, who plants himself beside the tub.

I help Emily from the water, wrap her in heated towels. She's trembling, muscles locked.

"Let's get you dry, yeah? Then meds, then we'll cleanse the piercing."

"You still want to—"

"'Course I do." I towel her legs gently. "My wife deserves her proper claim."

That earns a watery smile.

She's propped against pillows when I return with the Bijouterie Laurent box. The muscle relaxer's already softening the lines around her mouth.

"Close your eyes."

"Tristian—"

"Trust me."

She does.

I unwrap the emerald carefully, use the antiseptic wipes to clean her navel, then her temporary stud. The new jewelry catches the lamplight—rose gold curved barbell, emerald glinting at the bottom.

"This is gonna be cold."

I work quickly, professionally. The emerald settles perfect against her skin, the rose gold warm against her fairness.

"Okay. Look."

Emily glances down, breath catching.

"My darlin' wife." Nathan's Alabama drawl slips out unbidden, rough and possessive. "Proper Winkie claim. And raptor tradition—males gift their mates shiny rocks."

I can't help the grin. "Maya got fossilized amber in film seven. Nathan hunted three weeks for it."

"I remember." Emily traces the emerald with one finger. "Husband."

The word hits different this time. Fuller.

Then she switches languages entirely. "*Ka-reek*."

Raptor. She learned raptor.

My entire body goes still.

"*Griss-aak ch'kkt*." Her pronunciation's perfect. *Bite me, claim me*.

I groan, forehead dropping to her shoulder. "Darlin'. *Later*. You're hurtin'—"

"I'm serious." She tugs my hair until I look at her. "*Ka-reek*. When I'm better. Claws on my thighs. Teeth on my shoulder. The whole claiming."

Christ.

"I'll get the prosthetics from makeup," I manage. "Raptor nails and fangs. Mark you proper."

"Promise?"

"*Aak'tch*." *Promise*.

The nightgown slides over her head easy—silk, Dorothy and Toto dancing across cream fabric. I settle her against the pillows, make sure her hip's supported.

"Comfy?"

"Yeah."

I change quick—my oldest *Extinction Protocol* shirt, soft from a hundred washes, boxers. Mochi claims his spot at the foot of the bed.

"Movie?" I grab the remote.

"Which one?"

"Thought we'd start where I did. First one. I was seven when it came out." I queue it up on the mounted screen. "Fell in love with the raptors immediately. The intelligence. The pack dynamics."

"And now you are one."

"Half." I slide in beside her, careful of her hip. "Nathan Cross, paleontologist-turned-pack-leader."

The familiar score fills the room— voice narrating the wonder of resurrection. Emily nestles against my chest, warm and solid.

"Tristian?"

"Mm?"

"This is better than seduction."

I kiss her hair. "Good. 'Cause you're stuck with approximately seventy-three hours of dinosaur content."

"Best honeymoon ever."

Mochi sighs, content.

My wife. My *ka-reeka*. Safe, claimed, home.

The Lambert curse never felt so right.

My phone vibrates at 2:13 AM, pulls me from half-sleep. Emily's dead weight against my chest, mouth parted, the muscle relaxers doing their job. Mochi lifts his head, ears perked.

I check the screen. Thirty-seven notifications. Forty-two. Fifty-nine.

"Christ."

Instagram. Twitter. Every platform explodes simultaneously.

Ariana's posted the whole bloody adventure—Emily getting her tattoo, the piercing, Marcus filming them sprint through Grantham Bridge station. Then the video that makes my heart stop: Emily and me through the train window, voices carrying as we sing. Her face radiant, mine desperate, both of us completely gone.

@AriTattooQueen: *When your bestie gets Winkie married to a movie star at a train station* 🤍🦖💍 *#WinkieWedding #RaptorClaim #TriEmily*

The ship name trends within minutes.

Then Michelle's video loads. Me in my bedroom at the chateau, throwing things into a suitcase, ranting in three languages about Winkie marriage laws and *Ozmapolitan: The Wonderful Companion* while Jean tries reasoning with me.

"—it's REAL, Jean! Witnessed union, she RESPONDED to the claiming song, she's my WIFE—"

@MichelleLambert: *My brother has officially lost his entire mind and I'm here for it* 😂🤍 *Welcome to the family @EmilySilverDesigns #LambertCurse #TristianWedding*

Comments flood in. The Grantham Bridge Metro witnesses post their own footage—better angles, clear audio. Someone's already made a compilation with the original Broadway recording layered underneath.

My publicist texts at 2:47.

Simone: *We need to get ahead of this. Statement in 30 minutes.*

I type one-handed, careful not to wake Emily.

Me: *Make it clear—Winkie zheli/Raptor Ka-reek and zhara/Ka-reeka. Husband and wife spiritually. Legal ceremony to follow.*

Simone: *On it.*

The statement goes live at 3:15 AM Eastern:

"Tristian Alexandre Lambert and Emily Dorothy Silver are honored to announce their spiritual union following Winkie and Raptor traditions. While not legally binding outside Oz and Prehistoric Paradise, they consider themselves husband (Winkie: zheli, Raptor: Ka-reek) and wife (Winkie: zhara, Raptor: Ka-reeka) in every way that matters. A legal ceremony will follow in the coming months. The couple requests privacy during this special time."

The internet loses its collective mind.

Emily's Utah theater friends—the ones who actually showed up,post congratulations mixed with shock. Someone digs up footage of her in a Draper community theater production, barely eighteen, still learning to navigate her chair on stage.

The *Wonderful* fans embrace her immediately. Fan art appears within the hour—Emily as Dorothy, me as Felix, emerald-tinted and perfect.

Then David calls.

David bloody Kellerman, Starlight Studios' head, surrogate father since he signed me after *Dans l'Ombre*. The man who treats every actor under contract like his kid, who vetted and hated every single one of my exes.

"You magnificent idiot."

I slip from bed, pad to the window. "It's three in the morning, David."

"And you got Winkie married at a train station." His laugh rumbles through the speaker. "I love her already."

"You haven't met her."

"Saw the hospital reports. Read Ariana's protective interview. Watched her defend adaptive design in her valedictorian speech." He pauses. "She's real, Tris. First person you've dated who sees *you*."

My throat tightens. "Yeah."

"Which is why I'm calling. I need you both in LA next Thursday. *Wonderful* auditions."

Everything stops.

"David—"

"Felix audition for you, obviously. But I want Emily for Dorothy." He speaks over my sputtering. "She'll audition properly—fair's fair—but Tris, I've watched her clips. That Draper production, the graduation speech. She's got something."

"It's her dream role," I whisper. "Dream *period*. But she's shy. Community theater only, special needs productions—"

"Then you'll convince her." David's voice gentles. "Thursday, ten AM. I'm sending Nathan's prosthetics over too. Heard through the grapevine about raptor claiming traditions."

Heat floods my face. "Christ, does everyone know—"

"Your sister posts everything, kid. Welcome to family oversharing." He chuckles. "Claws and fangs are being couriered tomorrow. Don't traumatize your wife."

"She *asked* for it. In raptor."

"I'm hanging up before I need details." But I hear his grin. "Thursday, Tris. Both of you. Don't make me send Roger."

The line goes dead.

I stand there, phone slack in my hand, watching moonlight paint the winter garden silver.

Emily. My zhara. My Ka-reeka.

Dorothy in *Wonderful*.

I check social media one last time. The fans—my fans, our fans now—rally around her. Disability advocates celebrate representation. Theater communities share her work.

I return to bed, curl around my sleeping wife. She mumbles something, burrows closer.

I shake her shoulder gently. "Zhara. Wake up."

"Mmm. No." She burrows deeper into the duvet, face pressed against my chest.

"Emily." I kiss her temple, her cheekbone. "Raa-ka, wake up."

Her eyes flutter open, unfocused from muscle relaxers. "S'wrong?"

"David Kellerman just called."

She blinks slow, processing. "Your... your studio head? At three AM?"

"He wants us in Los Angeles Thursday. Ten AM." I brush blonde hair from her face, watch comprehension dawn. "For *Wonderful* auditions."

Nothing.

Then she laughs. Broken, disbelieving sound that cracks something in my chest.

"Don't." Her voice comes out strangled. "Please don't joke about Dorothy. Not—not that. Anything else, but—"

"I'm not joking."

"Tristian." She pushes at my chest, tears already streaming. "Stop it. You're being cruel, and you're never cruel, so just—"

I catch her face between my palms, force her to meet my eyes. "Felix audition for me. Dorothy for you. David's exact words: 'She's got something.'"

Her breath hitches. Stops entirely.

"There's no way," she whispers. "The head of Starlight Studios doesn't want *me*. Some disabled girl from foster care who did community theater in Draper. I'm not—I can't —"

The sobs come then, wracking her whole frame. I pull her against me, feel her shake apart.

"Kraa-ta, raa-ka." The raptor purr rumbles from somewhere primal. *Breathe, beloved.* "Kraa-ta."

"It's not real." She clutches my sleep shirt, face buried in my neck. "Dreams don't come true for people like me. They just—they don't—"

"This one does."

"You don't understand." Her words muffle against my skin. "Every caseworker, every teacher, every director who said I was too complicated. Too much work. That wheelchairs don't belong on real stages—"

"*Kraa-shaa.*" The growl cuts through her spiral. *Enough.* "Those people were fools. David Kellerman is not."

I tip her chin up, wipe tears with my thumbs.

"He watched your Draper clips. Your graduation speech. Said you're the first person I've dated who's *real*." I kiss her forehead, her nose. "Thursday, ten AM. You'll audition properly—fair's fair—but he wants you there."

"I'll mess it up." Fresh tears spill over. "I always mess up when it matters."

"You won't."

"How do you know?"

"Because you're brilliant." I shift her carefully, mindful of her hip. "Because you understand Dorothy's vulnerability and strength aren't opposites. Because you've lived in that gray space between hope and survival."

She hiccups, searching my face. "What if I'm not good enough?"

"Then we'll try again next time." I press our foreheads together. "But you *are,* raa-ka. You always have been."

A soft knock interrupts. Collette enters with chamomile tea, takes one look at Emily's tear-stained face, and makes a sympathetic sound.

"*Pauvre petite.*" She sets the tray on the nightstand, pours with practiced efficiency. "Good tears or bad tears?"

"Both," Emily manages. "David Kellerman wants me to audition for Dorothy."

Collette's face transforms. "*Magnifique!* Of course he does. I have been saying since you arrived—this girl has something special."

She hands Emily the cup, strokes her hair once.

"Drink. Rest. You will need your strength for the campaign launch tonight." She eyes me knowingly. "And for Los Angeles Thursday, *oui?*"

"*Oui, Madame.*"

When she leaves, Emily sips tea with shaking hands. I steady the cup, guide it to her lips.

"We'll practice after the campaign launch," I tell her. "Start with the audition sides David sends. Work on blocking that accommodates your chair—"

"What if they don't want wheelchair Dorothy?"

"Then they're idiots who don't deserve your talent." I kiss her knuckles. "But David's not an idiot. He knows exactly what he's asking for."

She sets the empty cup aside, curls into me. "When do we leave for the château?"

"Nine AM. Gives you time to finish the campaign party clothes." I pull the duvet over us both.

I study Emily's face in the moonlight, trace the delicate line of her jaw. "You'll have specialists wherever we go. Here, LA, London. Everywhere."

"Tristian—"

"General practitioner, physical therapy, occupational therapy. Gastro, neuro, urologist." I tick them off on my fingers. "Gynecologist. Nutritionist. Wherever I go, you go. *Especially* if we get married."

The word slips out casual, deliberate. I watch her eyes widen.

"That's—that's a lot of doctors," she whispers.

"You're my wife in every way that matters." I kiss her forehead. "To both of us. Which means you get proper care. No more suffering through pain because you don't want to be a bother."

She goes very still.

"Emily."

"I have diverticulitis." The words rush out. "Since I was sixteen. It's triggered by tomatoes and too much popcorn—more than a cup or so. Raw onions, anything with high gluten content. Jury's still out on corn." She won't meet my eyes. "I'm lactose intolerant too. Ice cream makes me cough, but there's this chocolate one made of rice milk I'm obsessed with—"

"Stop." I grip her chin, force her to look at me. "The ratatouille. You ate it anyway."

"It was delicious! I didn't want to be rude, and you worked so hard—"

"Bloody hell, woman." The words come out sharp. She flinches.

"*Kraa-ta, raa-ka.*" I gentle my voice, run my thumb across her lower lip. "I'm not mad at you. But we'll find modified versions. Hide anything from me again, naughty girl, and you'll get punished."

The possessive edge slips through—Winkie husband, raptor male, Lambert intensity all tangled together.

"Clear?"

"Yes, zheli."

I shift her onto her back, press my palm to her belly. Slightly distended. Christ, how did I miss it?

"You're still bloated from the welcome dinner." My hand moves in slow circles. "Three nights ago, before the hospital."

She nods, miserable.

I check her forehead. No fever. Small mercy.

"What are your symptoms? All of them."

"Diarrhea, cramping, nausea, bloating. Sometimes fever." She bites her lip. "Hot peppers too—the ones high in capsaicin. They make my geographic tongue swell and hurt."

"Geographic tongue?"

"It's a thing. Looks weird, feels worse when I eat certain foods."

I keep massaging, feel her start to relax. "The metformin—does it cause problems?"

"If I eat too much sugar. Nausea, diarrhea." She winces. "Why do you think I'm careful with desserts?"

"Because you're trying not to burden anyone." The frustration bleeds through again. "Even your husband."

She touches my face. "I'm sorry."

"Don't apologize. Just don't hide things." I lean down, kiss her softly. "Dad has to punish Mum sometimes. Last month he took her credit cards. Jean punishes Levi. Michelle's more like Mum—needs Marcus's guidance instead of giving it, though she's just as possessive as Jean and me."

Understanding dawns in her eyes. "The Lambert curse extends to discipline?"

"We're protective. Possessive. When our people endanger themselves—even unintentionally—consequences follow." My hand stills on her belly. "Understood?"

"Yes, Ka-reek."

The raptor title sends heat through me. I resume the massage, gentler now.

She sighs, melts into the mattress. "There's more."

"Tell me."

"Pinched nerve or tendinitis in my left wrist. Doctors couldn't tell which. Flares up if I sew too much. I have a brace that steadies it."

I make a mental note—occupational therapist, top of the list.

"And—" Her voice drops. "I want kids. I want to birth them. But the schizencephaly makes vaginal delivery difficult. C-section's almost guaranteed."

"I know." I press a kiss to her palm. "I researched after our first time. The PCOS makes conception difficult too. About twenty percent chance."

"You researched—" Her breath catches. "Of course you did."

"You want children. So do I." I meet her gaze, steady. "We'll do IVF if needed. However many rounds it takes. And when you're ready for delivery, you'll have the best surgical team money can buy."

Tears slip down her temples into her hair.

"Zheli—"

"*Kraa-ta.*" I wipe them away. "No more crying tonight. Just rest."

She opens her mouth to respond, then gasps. "Bathroom!"

I lift her immediately. "Now?"

"*Now!*"

I carry her to the ensuite, get her settled on the toilet. The winter château has the best bidets money can buy—heated, adjustable pressure, every luxury. I installed them in all Lambert properties after the first time I traveled to Japan.

The diarrhea hits fast and brutal. Emily makes a wounded sound.

"I've got you, raa-ka." I kneel beside her, stroke her hair back. "In sickness and in health."

"We're not legally married yet," she manages between cramps.

"Doesn't matter. You're mine. I'm yours." I kiss her temple. "Let it pass."

It takes maybe ten minutes. When her breathing finally evens out, I help her clean up with the bidet, support her weight as she washes her hands.

"Feel better?"

"Empty. Drained." She leans against me. "But no pain. No bloating. Just relief."

I carry her back to bed. Peppermint tea waits on the nightstand—Collette's work again, somehow anticipating Emily's needs. A dose of stomach medicine sits beside it.

"For any residual pain or gas," I tell her, helping her sit up enough to swallow the medicine.

She sips the tea slowly. "How does Collette always know?"

"The Duponts—both her and Alfred—are magic." I settle beside her, pull her against my chest. "And fiercely protective of family."

While Emily drinks, I text Alfred and Collette Dupont.

Me: *Emily has diverticulitis. Triggers: tomatoes, raw onions, high gluten, possibly corn, ice cream (except chocolate rice milk kind—low sugar). Hot peppers with capsaicin. Ban these from all Lambert properties immediately. Stock her brand of rice milk ice cream.*

Auguste responds within seconds.

Alfred: *Considered done, sir. I will coordinate with LA, London, and New York properties. Does Madame have other dietary preferences I should note?*

Me: *She's lactose intolerant. Metformin sensitive to high sugar. I'll send complete list tomorrow.*

Alfred: *Very good, sir. Give Madame our love.*

Emily finishes her tea, sets the cup aside. "You texted them."

"Banned your triggers from every Lambert property. Alfred's coordinating with LA, London, New York." I brush a kiss across her knuckles. "You'll never have to worry about hidden tomatoes again."

"That's—" Her voice breaks. "Thank you."

"Don't thank me for taking care of my wife." I pull the duvet over us both, tuck her against me. "Now sleep. Campaign launch in six hours, then we start Dorothy prep."

She burrows into my chest, one hand pressed over my heart. "Love you, zheli."

"Love you too, zhara. *Kraa-keet.*" *Forever.*

Within minutes, her breathing evens out. I lie awake, cataloging everything she told me. The medical team I'm assembling mentally grows—gastroenterologist who specializes in diverticulitis, nutritionist familiar with PCOS and chronic conditions, wrist specialist.

My phone buzzes. Michelle.

Jean: *Saw the texts to Alfred. Em ok?*

Me: *Diverticulitis flare. She's been hiding dietary triggers.*

Jean: *Of course she has. Welcome to the "my partner endangers themselves" club.*

Me: *How do you deal with it?*

Jean: *Clear consequences. Consistent follow-through. And reminding them they're worth protecting—even from themselves.*

I glance at Emily, sleeping peaceful now. No pain. No bloating. Just my wife, safe in my arms.

Me: *Got it. Thanks, bro.*

Jean: *That's what family's for. Now sleep. You've got a campaign launch and a Dorothy to prepare.* 🤍

I set my phone aside, wrap both arms around Emily. Mochi shifts at the foot of the bed, his warm weight a comforting presence.

Thursday. Los Angeles. *Wonderful* auditions.

My zhara, my raa-ka, finally getting her dream.

And nobody—not directors, not studios, not her own self-doubt—will stand in her way.

Not while I'm breathing.

I wake at seven, Emily's soft breathing against my throat. Her hand rests over my heart, fingers twitching in her sleep.

"*Ka-reeka,*" I whisper against her ear, switching to raptor. "*Raa-ka.*"

Her eyes flutter open, emerald meeting mine. "Zheli."

"Good morning, wife."

She stretches, winces slightly—hip still tender from yesterday. "Kiss me, zheli."

I oblige, slow and thorough. Her fingers thread through my hair, pulling me closer.

"Zheli, touch me. Please." The whine in her voice shoots straight through me.

"Later, *ka-reeka*. I swear." I kiss her forehead, her nose, her mouth. "It'll be your reward when you finish the clothes. But you'll have to be quiet when I do—can't strain that pretty voice."

She pouts. Actually pouts.

"Thursday," I remind her. "Kellerman wants you perfect for Dorothy. That means vocal rest starting today."

"But—"

"Lavender tea with honey. Singer's diet until the audition." I brush my thumb across her lower lip. "I'm hiring the best vocal coach in Europe. Your dream *will* come true."

Her eyes shine. "You really think—"

"I *know*." I kiss her again, gentler this time. "You're already Dorothy. The audition's just a formality."

By 8:30, we're dressed—Emily in a pale silk dress that flows over her wheelchair, me in a vintage band tee and open button-up with jeans. Marcus appears in the hallway..

Ariana emerges next, looking far too awake for someone who witnessed a raptor-Winkie marriage ceremony last night. "Morning, newlyweds."

Emily blushes. I grin.

"Car's ready," Marcus says. "Mochi's already claimed shotgun."

Indeed, when we reach the gravel drive, my labradoodle son sits in the front passenger seat, tongue lolling.

"Manual chair's in the trunk," I tell Emily as I lift her into the back seat. "I'll grab it when we arrive."

She settles against the leather, looking radiant despite yesterday's drama. "Collette and Alfred already left?"

"For Grantham Bridge. Setting up the venue." I slide in beside her, pull her close. "Everything's ready. You just need to finish the outfits."

Marcus drives. Ariana navigates. Mochi supervises.

My phone buzzes—notification after notification. Our Winkie marriage has exploded across every celebrity news site. *People*, *E! News*, *Entertainment Weekly*, even French and British tabloids.

TRISTIAN LAMBERT MARRIES GIRLFRIEND IN TRADITIONAL OZ CEREMONY

EXTINCTION PROTOCOL STAR CLAIMS FASHION STUDENT AS WIFE

WINKIE WEDDING: INSIDE TRISTIAN & EMILY'S SPIRITUAL UNION

I scroll through headlines, satisfaction warm in my chest. Let the whole world know she's mine.

Then I see Bethany Morrison's Instagram story.

The theater girl from Utah—Emily mentioned her once. Pretty in a generic way, always desperate for attention. She's posted a screenshot of our marriage announcement with a long caption.

can't believe emily would manipulate tristian like this. she's obviously using him for fame and money. i've known her for years and she's ALWAYS been obsessed with celebrities. this is so calculated it makes me sick. tristian deserves someone who loves him for who he is, not what he can do for her career. #SaveTristian #GoldDigger #FakeMarriage

Rage floods hot and sharp.

"What's wrong?" Emily asks, noticing my expression.

I turn the phone face-down. "Nothing, *raa-ka*. Just tabloid nonsense."

But Marcus catches my eye in the rearview mirror. I text him the screenshot.

Me: *Handle this. Quietly.*

Marcus: *On it.*

We arrive at the château at 9:47. I pop the trunk, retrieve Emily's lightweight manual chair—the one she uses for shorter distances when the power chair's charging.

"Bathroom first?" I ask, already knowing the answer.

"Please."

I carry her inside, past the grand salon where garment bags hang like art installations. In the ensuite, I help her pull down her panties, settle her on the toilet.

"I've got the chair," I tell her. "Be right back."

When I return with the manual wheelchair, she's washing her hands at the accessible sink. I lift her into the chair, push her toward the salon.

The unfinished garments wait—Michelle's campaign blazer needs final hemming, Jean's shirt requires cufflinks sewn, Mum's dress needs one more fitting.

"Six hours," Emily murmurs, already reaching for her sewing kit.

"Alfred will have breakfast ready when you need it." I kiss her temple. "Lavender tea. Honey. Toast with butter."

"Singer's diet," she repeats, looking up at me with those devastating green eyes. "Really?"

"Really." I crouch beside her chair. "You *will* be Dorothy. I'm making sure of it."

She touches my face, tender. "What did I do to deserve you?"

"Existed." I turn my head, kiss her palm. "Now work. I'll keep you company."

Chapter 9: Sequins, Strength, and Surrender

The elevator hums softly as I wait in the grand foyer, adjusting my maroon tie for the third time. The deep charcoal suit fits perfectly—Emily's work, naturally. Every seam tells the story of her hands moving across fabric, measuring, pinning, creating.

Jean stands beside me in an identical suit, Levi on his other side. Marcus keeps checking his phone, nervous energy crackling off him. Even Dad looks sharp, though he hasn't said much since we gathered.

The elevator door slides open.

Emily emerges first, and my breath catches.

Deep crimson sequins catch the chandelier light, transforming her into living flame. The v-neckline plunges just enough to make my fingers itch to trace the exposed skin. Sleeveless, showing off her arms—the tattoo on her collarbone still healing beneath transparent medical tape, my initial wrapped in her raptor symbol.

The mermaid silhouette hugs every curve before flaring into flowing tulle that sparkles with smaller beads. She's positioned herself in the chair with the skirt arranged just so, one hand resting on the armrest.

Mine. My wife. My *raa-ka*.

I cross to her immediately, crouch beside the pink wheelchair. "You're devastating."

"You're not so bad yourself." She touches my tie, straightens it even though it doesn't need straightening. Her belly ring catches light beneath the fabric—the emerald I gave her, my claim, my mark.

Possessiveness flares hot and territorial. Every man at that party will see her and want her. They'll look at my wife and imagine—

"Tristian." Emily's voice cuts through the spiral. "Breathe."

I press my forehead to hers. "*Raa-ka.*"

"*Kesh-a.*" Her fingers thread through my hair. "I'm yours. The whole world knows it."

Michelle descends next in a one-shoulder gown that flows like water, high slit revealing leg with each step. Marcus immediately moves to her side, hand possessive at her waist.

"Don't even look at the slit," Michelle warns him.

"Too late." Marcus's voice drops into that protective growl he gets. "You're staying within arm's reach all night."

Jean watches Levi help Mum down the stairs—she's radiant in ruby sequins, puff sleeves romantic against the sweetheart neckline. Dad offers his arm, and for once, they look like a united front.

Grandmère Adele appears in elegant crimson, Ariana beside her in a simpler red dress that still manages to look stunning.

Even Mochi sports a sparkly red bowtie, sitting at attention near Emily's chair.

"The Lambert family," Dad announces, voice carrying that political weight. "Together."

Jean's jaw tightens. Levi's hand finds his immediately, squeezing. I recognize that look—the same possessive fury that burns in my own chest when anyone threatens what's mine.

"Easy," Levi murmurs to Jean. "He's trying."

"Trying isn't good enough," Jean mutters back.

Michelle catches my eye, and I see it there too—that Lambert intensity. Marcus has moved fully behind her now, hand spanning her waist, chin nearly resting on her shoulder. Claiming posture. The same instinct that makes me want to lift Emily from her chair and carry her through the party so no one forgets she belongs to me.

"We should go," Celeste says gently, breaking the tension. "The car's waiting."

I stand, position myself behind Emily's chair. "Ready, *raa-ka*?"

She tilts her head back, looks up at me. "With you? Always."

The possessiveness settles into something warmer. Not just territorial—protective. This woman trusted me enough to marry me in a train station, to move to Angoumois, to let me see her at her most vulnerable.

I lean down, kiss her upside-down. "Let's show Grantham Bridge what a real Lambert looks like."

Her laugh makes everything worth it.

The Grande Salle glitters with crystal and ambition. Chandeliers cast golden light across Angoumois's elite—surnames that carry weight on both sides of the Channel. Dubois. Sheffield. Moreau. Wellington-Price.

Jean works the room like he was born to it. Which, I suppose, he was.

"Monsieur Ashford." Jean's handshake is firm, smile genuine. "Your daughter's initiative on sustainable agriculture—brilliant. We should discuss incorporating those strategies into our rural development platform."

Thomas Ashford lights up. "You've actually read Penelope's proposal?"

"Twice." Jean gestures to Levi. "My husband pointed out the water conservation metrics align perfectly with our environmental goals."

I guide Emily's chair through the crowd, one hand possessive on the handle. "Lord Beaumont. May I present my wife, Emily Lambert."

Wife. The word tastes like victory.

Beaumont's eyebrows rise—surprise, calculation, curiosity. "Mrs. Lambert. Your gown is extraordinary."

"Thank you." Emily's smile could charm kings. "I designed it myself."

"She's a fashion designer," I add, unable to keep pride from my voice. "Graduating valedictorian from Utah State. She's revolutionizing adaptive couture."

Mochi sits perfectly at Emily's side, red bowtie gleaming. Several guests have already asked about him, delighted when Emily explains his service dog status.

Lady Pemberton crouches to pet him. "What a magnificent creature."

"He's certified for anxiety and mobility assistance," Emily explains. "Also exceptional at stealing bacon."

The laughter is genuine. These people—they're seeing her. Not the wheelchair, not the disability. Her.

Mine.

I move us toward the next cluster. "Marguerite Fontaine, enchantée." I kiss her hand. "Your coverage of Dad's last campaign was brilliant. Tough but fair."

"Monsieur Lambert." Marguerite's eyes sparkle. "Flattery?"

"Truth." I pull Emily closer. "My wife, Emily. And I believe you know my brother Jean—his data-driven approach to this campaign is going to transform Angoumois politics."

Jean appears as if summoned, Levi attached to his hip. "Marguerite. I've been hoping to discuss your editorial on urban development."

Across the room, Ariana laughs at something a dark-haired man says. He's maybe thirty, clean-cut, wearing his suit like armor.

"Philippe Moreau," Emily murmurs. "Deputy Minister's son. Legal counsel for the Assemblée."

"How do you—"

"I've been studying." She taps her temple. "You're not the only one who can research."

Possessiveness flares hot. My brilliant wife.

Alfred materializes beside us with a tray. Not champagne—blue raspberry sparkling water, condensation beading the glass.

"Mrs. Lambert." Alfred's British accent is crisp, professional. "Your preferred refreshment."

Emily takes it gratefully. "You're a lifesaver."

"Forty years with the Lamberts teaches one to anticipate needs." He nods to me. "Sir."

I watch Emily drink, remember her confession about diverticulitis, about hiding her triggers. Alfred already knows she hates plain water, already has her favorite stocked.

"Thank you, Alfred."

"Of course, sir." He melts back into the crowd.

Marcus appears with Michelle, both looking slightly overwhelmed. "Is it always like this?"

"Campaign season." I steer Emily toward the buffet. "Jean's in his element. Watch."

Jean stands with Dad now, both deep in conversation with Henri Blackwood—old money, older influence. Jean's gesturing, animated, while Dad listens with actual attention.

"Your son makes excellent points about infrastructure," Blackwood says. "The northern districts need investment."

Dad nods. "Jean's research is comprehensive."

Jean's expression flickers—surprise, pleasure, hope.

Levi's hand finds his back, steadying.

"I didn't know Jean could work a room like that," Emily whispers.

"Lambert blood." I kiss her temple. "Politics or performance, we commit completely."

"Obsessive, you mean."

"*Raa-ka*, you married me in a train station after nine months. You don't get to call me obsessive."

Her laugh draws eyes. I meet each gaze with possession clear in my own.

Look all you want. She's mine.

The party finally ends near midnight. Emily's practically asleep in her chair by the time I carry her upstairs, Mochi trailing behind us.

"Don't wanna miss anything," she mumbles against my chest.

"You won't. I promise." I settle her on the bed, help her out of that devastating gown. "But you need rest. Audition Thursday, remember?"

"Mmm. Dorothy." Her eyes drift shut. "Your fault if I mess up."

"How is it my fault?"

"Too handsome. Distracting."

I kiss her forehead, pull the duvet up. "Sleep, *raa-ka*."

Mochi circles twice before curling at the foot of the bed. I watch them both—my wife, her guardian—until Emily's breathing evens out.

Downstairs, I grab a glass of water, needing air. The château feels too small suddenly, too full of expectations and political calculations.

The garden is quiet. Cool. Moonlight silvers the hedges Grandmère has spent decades cultivating.

I'm not alone.

Marcus kneels on the grass near the fountain, hands clasped, head bowed. His lips move silently—prayer, I realize. Real prayer, not the performative kind Dad does before campaign events.

I should leave. Give him privacy. But something holds me there, watching my future brother-in-law thank God in a Angoumois garden at midnight.

"—for my new sisters." Marcus's voice carries soft through the darkness. "Ari and Emily. Lord, you know I never had sisters growing up. But these women—"

He stops, swallows hard.

"Watch over Emily especially. Her body's been through so much. Those kidneys, the diverticulitis, the pain she hides. Give her strength. Keep her safe. And Ari—she's fierce, Lord, but she's got her own battles. Guard them both."

I shift, gravel crunching under my shoe.

Marcus doesn't startle, just glances over his shoulder. "Hey, Tris."

"Sorry. Didn't mean to interrupt."

"You're not." He stands, brushes grass from his knees. "Just talking to the big guy about family."

I join him by the fountain. "New sisters?"

"Yeah." His smile is genuine, warm. "Back in Louisiana, we Butlers keep records. Family Bible stuff—births, deaths, marriages. Official registry stopped ages ago, but we maintain it ourselves. Tradition."

"Like the Lamberts and our obsessive genealogy charts."

"Exactly." Marcus runs his hand over the fountain's edge. "I'm thinking of adding Emily. As my sister, not just Michelle's sister-in-law. Feels right, you know?"

Something tightens in my chest. "You'd do that?"

"God brought you two together, man. You—this nerdy extinction protocol obsessed actor. Her—this Oz-loving fashion genius. Both of you complete geeks about completely different things, but somehow..." He shakes his head. "That's divine intervention. Can't convince me otherwise."

"We met at FanCon."

"Yeah, because God knew exactly where to put you both." Marcus's Louisiana drawl thickens with conviction. "You think that was random? Emily in her Alice costume, you signing autographs? Nah. That was orchestrated."

I picture it—Emily in periwinkle and white, those emerald eyes meeting mine across the crowd.

"*Bonjour.*"

One word. That's all it took.

"The Lambert curse," I murmur.

"Butler blessing." Marcus grins. "Same thing, different name. Point is—Emily's family now. Not just because she married you, but because she's *supposed* to be family. So yeah, I'm adding her to the registry. Emily Dorothy Silver Lambert. Sister."

"She'll cry when you tell her."

"Good tears though, right?"

"The best kind."

We stand there, two men from completely different worlds—Hollywood and Louisiana, fame and faith—united by the women we love.

"Thanks," I say finally. "For praying for her."

"Always will." Marcus claps my shoulder. "That's what brothers do."

The scream tears through the château's stone walls.

Marcus and I sprint inside, taking stairs three at a time. My heart hammers against my ribs—that sound, God, that *sound*—

Emily.

I burst into the bedroom. She's tangled in sheets, thrashing, sobbing. Mochi paces beside the bed, whining, unable to reach her.

"No, please, Martha, I'll be quiet—I promise—don't lock me in—"

Martha Hendricks. The Provo foster mother. The one who left scars on Emily's arms, who locked her in closets for *hours*.

I'm on the bed, gathering her against my chest. "Emily. *Raa-ka*, you're safe. You're with me."

"Dark—it's so dark—can't breathe—"

"You're in Angoumois. In our bedroom. The lights are on, love. Look at me."

Her eyes snap open, unfocused. Terrified.

"Can't—wet the bed—she'll—"

I feel it then. The dampness. Her nightly diaper did its job, catching most of it, but her shame radiates like heat.

"Hey, no." I tip her chin up, force her to meet my gaze. My accent shifts hard British, the way it does when emotions run high. "You haven't done anything wrong. D'you hear me? Nothing."

Marcus stands in the doorway, fists clenched. "Who the hell is Martha Hendricks?"

"Foster mother." The words taste like poison. "Provo. She—"

"Locked her in closets," Emily whispers. "Hours. Sometimes overnight. If I wet myself, she'd leave me in it. As punishment."

I want to find Martha Hendricks. I want to hurt her the way she hurt Emily.

Mochi growls low in his throat, hackles raised. He understands violence, this dog. He wants to bite.

So do I.

"Right." I stand, Emily in my arms. "We're sorting this. Marcus, grab the swim bottoms and sports bra from the wardrobe. Black set, middle drawer."

He moves without question.

I carry Emily to the bathroom, set her on the counter. Her hands shake as I help her out of the wet diaper, gentle as I can manage.

"I'm sorry—"

"Stop." I cup her face. "You had a nightmare about a monster who tortured you. Your body reacted. That's not your fault, *ka-reeka*."

Marcus returns with the swimwear. Between us, we get Emily changed while she cries silently.

"Indoor pool," I decide. "Hot tub. You need to relax."

"It's midnight—"

"Don't care."

The hot tub bubbles warm and soothing. I settle Emily on my lap in the water, her head against my shoulder. Marcus sits across from us in his boxers, still looking like he wants to murder someone.

Mochi paces the pool deck, refusing to settle.

Footsteps echo. Jean appears first, then Levi, Michelle, Ariana. All in various states of sleepwear and concern.

"Heard screaming," Jean says quietly.

"Nightmare." I keep stroking Emily's hair. "Bad one."

Ariana's eyes go hard. She knows. She was there for the aftermath of Martha Hendricks, helped Emily through panic attacks in their dorm room.

Without a word, my siblings and their partners slip into the hot tub. Creating a circle. A barrier of family around Emily.

"Want to talk about it?" Michelle asks softly.

Emily shakes her head against my chest.

"Don't have to." Levi's voice carries surprising gentleness. "We're just here."

Alfred appears at the pool deck with a silver tray. No uniform—just pajamas and a robe, like he's been awake for hours rather than seconds. He probably has been. The man has an uncanny ability to sense when this household needs him.

"Young Madame." His formal tone softens. "Your anxiety medication, chamomile tea with honey, and lavender biscuits. The kind you favor."

Emily lifts her head from my chest. "Alfred, you didn't have to—"

"Nonsense." He sets the tray on the table beside the hot tub. "Madame Collette is handling the linens personally. She insists."

My throat tightens. Collette raised us—changed our nappies, kissed our scraped knees, taught us manners Dad was too busy to enforce. Of course she's washing Emily's sheets herself. Not delegating to staff, not making a production of it.

Just loving her the way she loved us.

"Thank you," Emily whispers.

Alfred's weathered face creases with something fierce and protective. "You are family, Madame Emily. We care for our own."

He disappears as silently as he arrived.

I reach for the medication, shake out the proper dosage. Emily takes it with trembling fingers, chases it with chamomile tea that steams in the cool night air.

"Collette's washing my sheets," she says to no one in particular. "Like I'm..."

"One of her babies." Michelle smiles. "She did the same for me when I got food poisoning at fourteen. Mum offered, but Collette refused. Said it was her job to take care of us."

"She held my hair back when I puked," Jean adds. "For hours."

"Sang me French lullabies when Dad made me cry," I murmur against Emily's temple. "Every single time."

Emily's shoulders shake. Not with fear this time. With something else.

"Sibling sleepover," Ariana announces suddenly. "Right now. All of us."

Levi raises an eyebrow. "Where exactly?"

"Small salon," Marcus suggests. "Like a proper slumber party."

"With junk food," Michelle adds.

"And terrible movies," Jean grins.

Emily's crying turns to watery laughter. "You're all ridiculous."

"You married into ridiculous, *raa-ka*." I kiss her hair. "No returns."

The small salon has been transformed.

Collette's magic again—blankets draped across furniture, pillows everywhere, the fireplace crackling warm. A spread of food covers the low table: crisps, chocolates, the lavender biscuits Emily loves, cheese, fruit.

Alfred's laid out pajamas for everyone who needs them. Including Emily's Wonderful set—the one with Dorothy on the shirt, silver slippers on the pants.

"How did they know?" Emily stares at the layout.

"They always know," I tell her. "It's unsettling."

Collette herself appears, silver hair in a braid, Emily's freshly laundered sheets folded in her arms. "Bedroom is ready when you need it, *ma chérie*. But enjoy your family first."

She cups Emily's face with hands that raised three wild Lambert children. "You are precious to us. Never forget."

Emily dissolves again. Collette holds her, rocking slightly, murmuring in French.

When she finally releases Emily, I help my wife into her Oz pajamas while the others change. Then I settle her on the pile of pillows, grab the brush from the kit Alfred's provided.

"Turn around, *ka-reeka*."

Emily shifts, presenting her back. Her hair—still damp from the hot tub—cascades down in golden waves.

I begin brushing. Slow, methodical. Base to tips, section by section. The way Ozian husbands do for their wives every night. The way I've done since we started this.

The room quiets. Everyone watching this small intimacy.

"Does it feel different?" Michelle asks softly. "Now that it's real?"

"Feels the same," Emily murmurs, eyes drifting closed. "Safe."

I work through a tangle, gentle. "Always safe with me."

Mochi sprawls across Emily's lap. Jean queues up some godawful comedy on the television. Marcus raids the chocolate stash.

And we settle in—siblings, spouses, chosen family—wrapped in blankets and love while Emily's breathing finally evens out.

The dining room gleams with morning light. Crystal catches sun through floor-to-ceiling windows, throws rainbows across white linens. Alfred's outdone himself—the table groans with singer-appropriate breakfast. Poached eggs, plain oatmeal with honey, whole grain toast, fruit plates arranged like art. Lavender tea steaming in delicate cups.

Emily sits beside me in her chair, hair still damp from our shared shower. She wears one of my hoodies—oversized, sleeves covering her hands. Looks young and soft and mine.

"Four days," Jean reminds us, spreading jam on toast. "Thursday's the biggest audition of your lives."

"No pressure," Michelle adds, grinning.

I reach for Emily's hand under the table. Squeeze. "We'll be brilliant."

"You'll be brilliant," she corrects. "I'll probably trip over my own feet."

"You're playing Dorothy in a wheelchair, *ka-reeka*." I lift her knuckles to my lips. "You can't trip."

Mochi's head pops up from beneath the table. Sniffs hopefully at Marcus's plate.

"Absolutely not, boy." Marcus scratches behind his ears. "You get your fancy dog food."

Ariana laughs. "He's spoiled rotten."

"He's earned it." Emily smiles, reaches down to pet him.

Her phone buzzes. She glances at the screen, goes pale.

"What?" I lean closer.

"Bethany." Emily's voice drops. "From the theater."

The name tastes wrong in my mouth. The one who commented on our Metro marriage announcement—all passive-aggressive concern, thinly veiled jealousy dripping from every word.

"Don't answer it," Ariana says immediately.

Emily's thumb hovers over the screen. "She might need something."

"She needs to back off," Ariana mutters.

But Emily's already answering. "Hello?"

Even from here, I hear Bethany's voice—sugary sweet, poisoned underneath. "Em! Oh my god, I've been so worried about you."

Emily straightens slightly. "I'm fine, Beth."

"Are you though?" A pause, calculated. "I saw the videos. The train station thing? Em, honey, that's not a real marriage."

My jaw clenches. Under the table, my free hand fists against my thigh.

"It is real," Emily says quietly. "In Oz—"

"In a fictional universe from a musical." Bethany's laugh cuts sharp. "Come on. You're smarter than this. He's an actor, Em. They pretend for a living."

Emily's breathing quickens. I feel it in the way her hand trembles in mine.

"Bethany—"

"Look, I get it." Condescension drips from every syllable. "He's gorgeous, he's famous, he paid attention to you. But this fantasy will end, and you'll be left looking foolish. Come home before you embarrass yourself further."

"I'm not—" Emily gasps. "I can't—"

The wheeze hits. Sharp, desperate. Her inhaler's in her bag across the room.

I'm moving before conscious thought kicks in. Scoop her from her chair, cradle her against my chest. Long strides across marble while she fights for air.

"Breathe, *zhara*." My voice drops into something primal. "I've got you."

Ariana's already there with the inhaler. Emily takes two puffs, chest heaving.

Bethany's voice still squawks from the phone on the table. "Em? Emily, are you there? What's happening?"

I keep walking. Tight circles around the dining room. One hand stroking Emily's hair, the other supporting her back. My accent thickens—British bleeding through French, Nathan Cross's possessive growl underneath.

"*Zheli*." Emily's face burrows into my neck. Tears hot against my skin. "*Zheli, zheli*."

Husband. Fierce protector. The Winkie word for everything I am to her.

"Here, *zhara*." I press my lips to her temple. "Always here."

Her breathing evens slightly. Still crying though. Still shaking.

Bethany's oblivious rambling continues. "—just think about what I said, okay? You deserve someone who—"

Something snaps. The careful control I've maintained since childhood—the polished actor, the diplomat's son— shatters.

I stride to the table. Snatch up Emily's phone.

And roar.

Not words. Not English or French or Winkie. Pure raptor—the territorial challenge Nathan Cross uses when another male threatens his mate. Guttural, fierce, absolutely feral.

Bethany's shocked silence stretches.

"You listen." My voice drops dangerous. British accent clipped, precise. "Emily is my wife. My *zhara*. My *ka-reeka*. You will never speak to her again. You will delete her number. You will forget she exists."

"Who the hell—"

"Her *zheli*." The word comes out lethal. "Her husband. Her fierce protector. And if you ever make her cry again, I will ensure your life becomes spectacularly difficult. Are we clear?"

Another beat of silence.

Then Marcus is there, plucking the phone from my hand. "Hey Bethany. Marcus Butler. Yeah, the tabloid journalist. The one with connections in every newsroom from here to Austin."

His drawl sharpens into something dangerous. Michelle calls it his investigative voice—the one that makes sources squirm.

"See, Emily's my honorary baby sister. I'm real protective of family. And I'm real good at digging up dirt. Social media posts, employment history, that DUI you got expunged..."

Ariana leans over his shoulder. "Oh, and I'm the best friend who's hated your fake-ass since freshman year. Keep

Emily's name out of your mouth before I make you regret every petty thing you've ever done."

"She's done," Marcus promises into the phone. "Trust me."

He ends the call. Blocks the number. Hands the phone back to me.

Emily's still crying against my chest. Still whispering *zheli* like a prayer.

I resume pacing. Stroking her hair, her back. Letting my heartbeat calm hers.

"That's my girl." I kiss her forehead. "My brave *zhara*."

"I tried," she hiccups. "Tried to tell her no."

"You did beautifully." Another kiss. "So proud of you."

Gradually, her tears slow. She pulls back enough to look at me with red-rimmed eyes.

"I'm hungry, *zheli*."

Relief floods through me. "Yeah?"

A tiny nod. "Brunch got interrupted."

I carry her back to the table. Settle in my chair with her in my lap instead of her own seat. Let her curl against me while I feed her bites of scrambled eggs, toast with honey, strawberries.

Mochi rests his head on my knee. Protective, watchful.

"After brunch," Marcus says casually, "want to meet your horse?"

Emily's head snaps up. "My what?"

"Horse." Marcus grins. "Palomino mare. Gentle as they come. I've been teaching you to ride, remember? Honorary baby sisters need horses."

"Marcus." Emily's voice cracks. "You bought me a horse?"

"Family does what family does." He shrugs. "Figured you'd want to name her yourself though."

Emily looks at me. Wonder replacing the last traces of fear.

"We'll meet her after you eat." I brush hair from her face. "Your *zheli* wants you fed and happy first."

She leans up. Kisses me soft and sweet. "Love you."

"Love you, *zhara*." I tuck her back against my chest. "Now eat. Singer's diet. Four days until we show David Kellerman what Dorothy and Felix really are."

Jean raises his teacup. "To Thursday."

"To family," Michelle adds.

"To telling Bethany where to shove it," Ariana mutters.

We all drink to that.

Chapter 10: Dorothy

The stables smell like hay and sunshine. Emily's eyes widen as we approach the paddock where a stunning palomino mare grazes peacefully beside my stallion.

"*Zheli*." Emily grips my hand. "*Zheli*, she's perfect."

The mare lifts her head. Cream-colored coat gleaming, white mane catching the breeze. She moves toward us with the careful, deliberate gait of a horse trained for therapy work.

"Meet your girl," Marcus says. "Raised from foalhood for adaptive riding. Steady as they come."

I help Emily transfer from her chair to the fence rail, supporting her as she reaches out. The mare nuzzles her palm immediately.

"Emerald," Emily whispers. "Like the city."

The name fits. Beautiful, magical, everything Emily dreams of.

My black stallion Phantom—usually territorial and standoffish with everyone except me—suddenly perks up. His ears swivel forward. Nostrils flare.

Then he moves.

Not his usual proud strut. This is different. Purposeful. Interested.

He approaches Emerald with the same possessive determination I recognize from my own mirror.

Oh bloody hell.

Phantom touches his nose to Emerald's. She doesn't shy away. Just returns the greeting with calm acceptance.

Then my horse—my notoriously difficult, refuses-to-tolerate-anyone-but-me horse—turns to Emily. Nuzzles her shoulder with the gentleness he usually reserves for me after long shoots.

He *knows*.

Knows she's mine. Knows she's his human's mate. Knows she's family now.

"Well," Marcus drawls. "That's new."

"He hates everyone," Michelle breathes.

But Phantom's already nuzzling Emily again. Huffing soft breath against her hair. Then he returns to Emerald, circling her, body language screaming *mine mine mine*.

Mochi trots over, tail wagging. Sniffs both horses. Phantom tolerates this—barely—because Mochi is Emily's and therefore acceptable.

Within minutes, Mochi's play-bowing at Phantom's hooves. Emerald lowers her head to let the labradoodle lick her nose.

"Think they've adopted him," Emily murmurs.

Phantom suddenly rears. Not aggressive—triumphant. Then paws the ground, looking straight at me.

I know that expression. Raised him from a foal, taught him everything. Can read his body language like words.

Mate. Want babies. NOW.

"Not yet, bud."

Phantom tosses his mane. Stamps. The equine equivalent of *but WHY?*

"Because you're courting her properly first. Like I did with your mother."

Emily laughs. "Did you just call me his mother?"

"Apparently." I kiss her temple. "And he's demanding siblings."

Phantom huffs. Circles Emerald again. Nuzzles her neck, her flank. Pure possession.

The look he shoots me is absolutely accusing. *You'd have Mum pregnant right now if you could! Why can't I?*

Heat floods my face. Because he's not wrong. If Emily's body could handle it immediately, if doctors weren't insisting we wait—

"Tristian Alexandre Lambert." Emily's grinning. "Are you blushing?"

"My horse is judging my restraint."

"*Our* horse." She strokes Phantom's nose. "And he makes excellent points."

Marcus chokes. "I'm uncomfortable with where this conversation's going."

Phantom paws the ground again. More insistent. Then deliberately positions himself between Emerald and the other horses in the far paddock.

MINE, his body screams. *My mate. My family. Touch her and die.*

"Christ, he's me." The realization hits. "He's literally me as a horse."

"Possessive, dramatic, and absolutely devoted?" Emily touches my cheek. "Yeah, *zheli*. He's you."

Phantom returns to his circling. Emerald tolerates this with remarkable patience, occasionally nuzzling him back.

Mochi flops between them, tongue lolling. Happy to be part of this new herd.

"They're perfect," Emily whispers.

I watch Phantom finally settle beside Emerald. Still touching, still possessive, but calmer now. Accepting that courtship takes time.

"Proper courtship first," I tell him firmly. "Demonstrate you can provide. Prove you're worthy. Romance before babies."

He snorts. But stays put.

"Good lad." I stroke his neck. "That's how Lamberts do it."

Emily laughs against my shoulder. "We got married on a train platform after known each other nine months."

"Proper *Winkie* courtship," I correct. "Very traditional."

"Sure, *zheli*."

Phantom nuzzles Emerald again. Patient now. Devoted. Learning from his human.

Just like I learned from mine.

We're halfway across the courtyard when Emily gasps. Her hands fly to her abdomen.

"*Mon cœur*?" I kneel beside her chair.

"Just—" She breathes through it. "First one. I'm fine."

I'm already mentally cataloging symptoms. Cramping. Pale. Breathing shallow. "Right, back to bed. Heat pad. Medication—"

"Tristian." Marcus touches my shoulder. "Brother, you're hovering."

"She needs—"

"Space." Michelle appears with Ariana. "We've got this."

But Emily's doubled over now, face tight with pain. My chest constricts.

"Heating pad," I tell Michelle. "And her prescription bottle, left nightstand. Blue raspberry water, not regular—"

"*Tris*." Ariana rolls her eyes. "We're not idiots."

"The red pills, not the white ones—"

"Out." Michelle physically pushes me toward the stables. "Go stress somewhere else."

"But—"

Emily reaches for my hand. Squeezes. "I love you. But you're making it worse."

That stops me cold.

"She's right, mate." Marcus steers me away. "When Michelle gets hers, I become completely useless. End up pacing holes in the carpet."

I watch them wheel Emily inside. Michelle already texting—probably ordering proper supplies since we weren't expecting this for another week.

My hands shake.

"She's fine," Marcus says quietly. "Women do this monthly. It's normal."

"I know." But my throat's tight. "I just—"

"Want to fix it. Yeah." He squeezes my shoulder. "Can't fix biology, brother. But you can give her space to deal without your panic feeding hers."

Right. Space.

I turn toward the stables instead. "Ride?"

"Nah. This is your thing." Marcus grins. "Besides, someone needs to supervise Jean's coffee intake before he rewrites Dad's entire platform."

Phantom's already saddled when I arrive—Auguste apparently anticipated my need to escape. The stallion tosses his head eagerly as I approach.

But he doesn't move toward the gate.

Instead, he circles back to Emerald's stall. Nickers softly. The mare appears, poking her head over the half-door.

Then Phantom *prances*.

Literally. High-stepping like he's in a bloody dressage competition. Neck arched, tail flagged, every muscle displayed.

Showing off.

"Christ, you're worse than I am."

He ignores me. Too busy performing for his lady. Rears slightly—controlled, graceful. The equine version of flexing.

Emerald watches with what can only be described as feminine amusement. Her ears forward, eyes soft.

She's into it.

"At least someone's love life is progressing smoothly," I mutter, swinging into the saddle.

Phantom settles immediately once I'm mounted. But throws one last look at Emerald. A soft whicker that sounds suspiciously like a promise.

Wait for me.

Then we're moving. Through the formal gardens, past the reflecting pool, toward the forest path that borders the eastern property line.

The moment we hit the tree line, Phantom surges forward. Not quite a gallop—the path's too winding—but faster than a canter. Burning off the same restless energy coursing through me.

Branches blur past. Sunlight dapples through ancient oaks. The rhythm of hoofbeats matches my pulse.

Emily's fine. Michelle and Ariana know what they're doing. This is normal. Natural.

But the image of her face—tight with pain—won't leave.

Phantom seems to sense my mood. He stretches into a full gallop where the path widens, giving us both the speed we need. Wind whips my face. The world narrows to movement and breath and the thunder of hooves against packed earth.

This. This I can control.

We round the bend toward the old hunting lodge, Phantom's breathing hard but steady. Still powerful. Still mine.

Still showing off, probably, hoping Emerald somehow witnesses his magnificence from kilometers away.

"She's already yours, mate," I tell him.

He snorts.

Fair point. Emily's already mine too.

Doesn't stop either of us from wanting to prove we're worthy.

We reach the clearing near the old stone fountain— mostly rubble now, but the water still flows. Phantom slows without prompting, sides heaving. I dismount, let him drink while I lean against the crumbling wall.

My phone buzzes. Michelle: *She's asleep. Heating pad. Meds kicked in. Stop freaking out.*

I exhale properly for the first time since the courtyard.

Phantom finishes drinking, then comes to stand beside me. Nudges my shoulder with his nose. Not demanding—checking in.

"I know." I stroke his neck. "I'm being ridiculous."

He huffs agreement.

"She was bleeding. In the hospital. Before you met her." The words spill out before I can stop them. "Screaming. And I couldn't—they wouldn't let me go with her. Just took her away while she begged me to stay."

Phantom goes still. Listening.

"Kidney stones, turned out. Not life-threatening. But for two hours, I thought—" My throat closes. "Thought I'd lose her before I could even propose properly."

The stallion presses his forehead against my chest. Solid. Steady.

"Then there's the diverticulitis she hid from me. The hip pain. The spasms." I scratch behind his ears. "Every time she hurts, I want to fix it. But I can't. Can't make her body stop betraying her. Can't take the pain myself."

Phantom nickers softly.

"So yeah, maybe I hover. Maybe I catalog symptoms and memorize medication schedules and renovate entire bloody houses just so she has one place where nothing's difficult." I meet his dark eyes. "But what else am I supposed to do? Stand back and watch?"

He pulls away. Walks to the fountain. Takes another long drink.

Then turns and gives me a look.

That look.

The same one he shot me in the paddock when I told him to wait on Emerald. Pure accusation mixed with understanding.

You'd have your mate pregnant right now if biology allowed it. Don't lecture me about patience.

"That's different."

Phantom tosses his mane. *Is it?*

"I'm protecting her. Making sure she's comfortable and safe and—"

He paws the ground. Deliberately. The way he does when I'm being particularly dense during training.

"Don't give me that look." But heat creeps up my neck. "You're in love too."

Another huff. This one sounds smug.

Because he's right, the bastard. We're the same—both of us desperate to prove ourselves worthy, to provide, to make our mates' lives easier. Both of us struggling with the reality that sometimes love means stepping back instead of charging forward.

Phantom demonstrated it perfectly in the paddock. That shift from demanding to patient. From *want babies NOW* to accepting the courtship process.

While I'm still hovering over Emily's every symptom.

"She told me I was making it worse," I admit quietly.

Phantom walks back over. Rests his chin on my shoulder.

Yes. But you'll learn.

"When did you get so bloody wise?"

He snorts directly into my ear.

I push his massive head away, laughing despite myself. "Right then. Lesson received. Give her space to handle what she can handle. Stop catastrophizing every cramp."

Phantom seems satisfied with this. He turns toward the path home, ready to return to Emerald.

To demonstrate proper devotion through presence rather than panic.

"One more thing," I tell him, swinging back into the saddle. "When we get back, you're going to calmly graze near her stall. Not perform. Not demand attention. Just... be there."

He tosses his head but starts walking.

"And I'm going to check on Emily without turning it into a medical examination."

Another snort. This one distinctly skeptical.

"I can do it."

Phantom breaks into a trot, clearly unconvinced.

Fair enough. We're both works in progress.

Phantom deposits me at the side entrance with significantly less grace than usual. He's practically dancing in place, ears swiveling toward the château.

Then Emily's scream cuts through the afternoon air.

The stallion rears. I'm already running.

Through the servants' corridor, past Auguste who points wordlessly toward the east wing. My boots thunder against marble. Another scream—raw, desperate.

I burst through the bedroom door.

Emily's curled on her side, face buried in pillows. Mochi paces frantically beside the bed, whining. Michelle and Ariana hover uselessly near the window.

"Out." The word comes harsh. They scatter.

I'm beside her in seconds. "Mon cœur—"

"Don't." She gasps. "Don't be nice. Can't handle nice right now."

Her hand finds mine. Crushing grip. Another wave hits and she keens against it.

Right. The hydrocodone. I grab the bottle from the nightstand.

"No." Emily shakes her head. "Makes me fuzzy. Nauseous."

"Don't care." I shake out two pills. "Open."

"Tristian—"

"*Zhara.*" The Winkie term drops my voice lower. Command, not request. "You're in agony. Take the bloody pills."

Her eyes flash. "That's not—"

"Your *zheli* is telling you to open your mouth." I cup her jaw. Firm. "Now."

The pills sit in my palm. She glares at me.

But doesn't open.

Stubborn woman.

Fine. Different tactic.

"*Za-reeka.*" The raptor growl rumbles from my chest. Possessive. Demanding. "*Ree-ka*, you will take these pills for your *za-reek*. Let me take care of you."

Her breath hitches. Not from pain this time.

"That's cheating," she whispers.

"Don't care about fair. Care about you not suffering." I press closer. "Open. Let me help you."

Another cramp hits. She whimpers.

"Now, *za-reeka*."

Her mouth finally parts. I slip the pills onto her tongue, hold the water glass to her lips. She swallows, grimacing.

"No fair." Emily burrows into my chest. "Your fault if I puke on you."

"Accepted." I gather her close, one hand finding her lower abdomen. Apply gentle pressure where she guides me. "Worth it."

She trembles through another wave. I'm reaching for my phone when she catches my wrist.

"The book," she gasps. "Need the book."

Right. The audiobook of *The Wonderful Wizard of Oz*—her comfort measure for severe pain and PCOS insomnia. I grab my tablet, pull up the familiar file.

"Dorothy lived in the midst of the great Kansas prairies..."

Emily's breathing shifts almost immediately. Still tight with pain, but focusing on the words instead of the cramping.

A sharp whinny cuts through the narration.

I look up. Phantom's at the window, somehow balancing on the narrow ledge of the formal garden wall. His mouth is stuffed full of red poppies.

Wild ones, from the looks of it. Growing in the forest where we just rode.

He knows they're Emily's favorites.

My throat tightens. "She's fine, bud." I cross to the window. "Hand those to Alfred and he'll bring them to Mum. Then go see Emerald."

Phantom snorts around his mouthful of flowers but carefully deposits them on the stone ledge. Tosses his head once—checking that I'm serious about Emily being alright—then trots toward the stables.

Moments later, Alfred appears at the door with impeccable timing. The poppies in a crystal vase. Ginger tea steaming. Candied ginger on a small plate.

And a bucket.

"Just in time," I tell him.

Emily lurches upright. I grab the bucket, hold her hair back as she retches. Nothing comes up—she hasn't eaten since brunch—but the hydrocodone and empty stomach aren't mixing well.

"Told you," she gasps between heaves.

"Still worth it." I wipe her mouth with a cool cloth Alfred silently provides. "Pain will ease soon."

The audiobook continues. *"...a cyclone cellar in the middle of the floor..."*

Emily collapses back against pillows. I settle beside her, one hand still applying pressure to her abdomen. The other threads through her hair.

"Hate this," she whispers.

"I know."

"Hate that you have to see me like this."

"*Za-reeka.*" I kiss her temple. "In sickness and health. We already said the vows, remember?"

"On a train platform. Doesn't count."

"Counted enough for Phantom to claim Emerald." I gesture to the poppies now displayed on her nightstand. "He's already treating you like his mum. Brought you flowers while his lady waits."

A weak laugh. "He's sweet."

"He's smitten. Like his human."

The medication's starting to work. Her breathing evens out, though her face stays pinched. Another cramp makes her whimper, but it's not the sharp scream from before.

"Tomorrow," I murmur against her hair. "Tomorrow ibuprofen will probably handle it. First day's always worst."

"Promise you'll still love me when I'm a pain-riddled disaster?"

"*Zhara*." I tilt her face toward mine. "I'll love you through every cramp, every flare, every nightmare. That's what *zheli* do."

Her eyes are already glazing from the hydrocodone. But she manages to cup my cheek.

"Lucky me."

"Lucky us."

Dorothy's journey continues. Emily's breathing shifts into the deeper rhythm of approaching sleep. Her hand stays against my face even as consciousness fades.

Mochi finally settles at the foot of the bed. Still watchful, but calmer now that Emily's pain is managed.

I reach for the ginger tea. Cool enough now. When the next dose is due in four hours, maybe the candied ginger will help settle her stomach first.

Through the window, I can just see Phantom in the paddock. Standing beside Emerald, neck curved protectively over hers.

Learning patience. Demonstrating devotion.

Both of us trying to be worthy of our miracles.

The private plane climbs toward cruising altitude. Emily sits beside me, script balanced on her lap, fingers tapping the armrest. Mochi sprawls across both our feet, already snoring.

"I'm going to ruin it." Her voice barely registers above the engine noise. "Community theater isn't Hollywood. I don't—I can't—"

I close my laptop, turn fully toward her. "Read the Felix scene again. With me."

"Tristian—"

"Humor your husband."

That gets a ghost of a smile. She opens to the marked page, the one where Dorothy first encounters Felix stuck on his pole. We've run through it seventeen times since leaving Angoumois, but her hands still shake.

I stand, stretch into character. Let my posture go loose, head tilting at an unnatural angle. Channel the disorientation of a man who doesn't know himself.

"Manners require a brain to remember them," I say in Felix's lighter register. "And I'm afraid I haven't got one."

Emily straightens in her chair. When she speaks, Dorothy emerges—practical, sharp, but with loneliness bleeding through every syllable.

"You can talk but you can't remember manners? That seems rather backward."

We fall into the rhythm. Her Dorothy grows bolder with each exchange, matching Felix's absurdity with Kansas pragmatism. When we reach the proposal—that ridiculous, perfect moment where he asks purely because she mentioned a terrible fiancé—Emily's laugh sounds genuine.

"You have a cornfield, not a house."

I drop character, kneel beside her wheelchair. "That. Right there. That's what Marianne wants."

"What, disbelief that a scarecrow proposed marriage?"

"Truth." I catch her hand. "You don't perform Dorothy. You *are* her. You understand what it means to survive places that tried to break you, to find family in unexpected places."

Her thumb traces my knuckles. "Community theater in Logan isn't exactly—"

"Richard saw your graduation speech. Watched you stand despite the pain because the message mattered more. He knows you can carry this."

"You told him to offer me the audition."

"I suggested he watch your speech. He made the call himself." I kiss her palm. "David's known me since I was nineteen. He doesn't waste time on charity cases. If you weren't right for this, he wouldn't have flown you to LA."

Mochi lifts his head, noses Emily's free hand. She scratches behind his ears, breathing evening out.

"What if I freeze?"

"You won't."

"What if my hip seizes during the read?"

"We've arranged breaks every thirty minutes. Marianne knows your medical needs."

"What if—"

I silence her with a kiss. Gentle, grounding. When I pull back, her eyes are clearer.

"The script says Dorothy chooses courage even when she's terrified," I murmur. "Show them that."

The audition room at Starlight Studios feels deliberately designed to intimidate. Massive windows overlook the lot. A table seats seven people, all holding scripts, all watching as I wheel Emily inside with Mochi trotting beside us.

David Kellerman stands immediately. Sixty-three, silver-haired, wearing his signature navy suit. He crosses to Emily, hand extended.

"Miss Silver. Thank you for coming."

Emily shakes his hand, and I watch her theater training kick in. Shoulders back, smile genuine but composed. "Mr. Kellerman. I appreciate the opportunity."

"David, please." He gestures to the woman beside him —Marianne Parks, fifty-something with sharp eyes and graying auburn hair pulled into a low bun. "This is our director. And you know Tristian, obviously."

Polite laughter ripples through the room. I take my seat at the table, trying to telegraph calm confidence toward Emily while every protective instinct screams to stay beside her.

Marianne doesn't waste time on pleasantries. "We'll start with the chemistry read. Felix and Dorothy's first meeting. You've reviewed the sides?"

"Yes, ma'am." Emily's voice stays steady.

"Mochi will play Toto for blocking purposes." Marianne nods to the yellow brick road set piece already positioned. "Whenever you're ready."

I move to the pole positioned center-stage—an actual wooden post with rope coiled nearby. Emily wheels to her mark, Mochi settling beside her chair.

The production assistant calls action.

Emily's entire bearing shifts. Her face loses its careful composure, replaced by exhaustion and wonder. She looks around at the blue cornfield backdrop like she's genuinely seeing Oz for the first time.

Then she spots me on the pole.

I wink.

Her double-take is perfect—skeptical, practical Kansas girl confronting impossible magic. When she speaks, it's not performed. It's *lived*.

"Well. Either I'm losing my mind, or scarecrows in Oz have terrible manners."

I let Felix emerge. Not the princely underneath—Dorothy doesn't know that yet—but the confused, charming creature who can't remember anything before waking on this pole.

"Manners require a brain to remember them, and I'm afraid I haven't got one."

We volley lines back and forth. Emily's Dorothy matches Felix's absurdity with dry observations, but underneath runs genuine loneliness. This girl who's been beaten and starved, who conjured a cyclone to escape assault, who has nothing waiting in Kansas except more abuse.

When I propose—sudden and ridiculous after she mentions her awful fiancé—Emily's laugh bubbles up authentic and surprised.

"Why not? You're already better company than Hiram."

I lean forward for the kiss. Just a brush of lips, but Emily's sharp inhale registers real. Her hand comes up, fingers ghosting over her mouth.

"That was hardly a proper kiss."

The undercurrent shifts. Felix's playful possessiveness threading through. "Best I could manage under the circumstances." I offer my arm, voice dropping into something more serious. "Well then, love, now that you have a home with me, what will you ask the Wizard for?"

Emily looks around the imaginary cornfield, expression caught between hope and disbelief. "You have a cornfield, not a house."

"Details."

Silence holds for three heartbeats.

"Cut." Marianne's voice breaks the spell. She exchanges looks with David, with the casting director, with the producers flanking them.

Emily's theatrical mask cracks. Uncertainty floods back.

David leans forward, pen tapping against his script. "Emily. Have you ever done film work?"

"No, sir. Just community theater."

"Hmm." He makes a note. Looks to Marianne.

She's smiling. Actually smiling.

Marianne dismisses me with a look. "Tristian, back to the table."

I return to my seat, but keep my eyes on Emily. She sits straighter, preparing.

David addresses her directly. "For this next piece, we want Dorothy's first moment alone on the yellow brick road. You've just met Maxime—the Witch of the North—and he's sent you toward the Emerald City. He's sensed something in you. Possible magic. The Wizard is your only way back to Kansas."

Emily nods, absorbing the context.

"We'd like you to sing for us." Marianne gestures to the producer on her right—Helena, mid-forties with kind eyes. "Helena will read Maxime's lines to set up your moment. You received the sheet music?"

"Yes, ma'am."

"You're welcome to adapt lyrics as feels authentic to your Dorothy." Marianne's expression softens. "This is her hope song. Her belief that maybe, finally, someone will see her value."

Emily's hand finds Mochi's head. The dog leans into her touch.

Helena reads from her script, voice taking on an otherworldly quality. "The Wizard is very wise, child. If anyone can unlock what's dormant in your blood and send you home, it's him. Follow the yellow brick road. Don't stray from the path."

Emily looks down at the painted yellow bricks on the floor. When she lifts her head, tears already glisten in her eyes.

She begins without accompaniment. Just her voice, raw and clear.

The room goes still. Emily's not performing anymore—she's confessing.

Her voice builds, stronger with each line. I watch the casting director lean forward. David's pen hovers motionless above his notes.

Emily's hands grip her wheelchair rims, knuckles white.

The melody shifts, Dorothy's desperate hope bleeding through every note.

My throat tightens. She changed it. Made it hers.

Her voice cracks on the word, but she pushes through.

Emily closes her eyes, and I know exactly where she's gone. Back to those group homes. Those closets. Every person who looked at her wheelchair and decided she was less.

A tear slides down her cheek. She doesn't wipe it away.

The producers are crying. Helena presses fingers to her lips. Even David's eyes look suspiciously bright.

Emily's voice breaks completely. She's sobbing now, singing through tears.

She opens her eyes, looking directly at me.

The final note hangs in the air. Silence stretches, broken only by Emily's ragged breathing.

I'm out of my chair before conscious thought takes over. Cross the space between us in four strides, drop to my knees beside her wheelchair, and kiss her. Deep and claiming, tasting salt from her tears, pouring every ounce of pride and love into the contact.

"You're perfect," I whisper against her mouth. "Absolutely perfect."

Marianne flips through her notes. "Tristian, we need Felix's introduction. Before Dorothy. His solo."

I nod, standing. Move back to the center of the stage where the pole waits.

David clarifies for others' benefit. "Felix Ozian Oz the Third. Crown Prince of the Emerald City before the coup. Before the Wizard's rise twenty years ago."

I let my posture shift—shoulders loose, weight balanced on my heels. The prince who never took anything seriously because nothing ever had consequences. Not yet.

The music director cues the track. Bright, infectious. I spin away from the pole, movements sharp and careless.

My voice comes out smoother than Felix post-transformation. This is before the burlap, before the memory loss. This is privilege incarnate.

I dance across the stage, each gesture deliberately cavalier. Point at imaginary courtiers, spin past them like they're furniture.

The choreography flows from muscle memory—weeks of rehearsal making it second nature. I leap onto a platform, gesture grandly at nothing.

My midwestern accent bleeds through stronger now, the way it does when I slip into old patterns. Felix's royal arrogance, his complete disconnect from reality beyond palace walls.

I drop into a chair positioned stage-left, drape myself across it like a bored cat.

The tempo shifts. Darker undertones creeping into the melody. I stand, movements losing their fluid grace. Stiffening.

"Until they're not."

The music cuts. Silence fills the soundstage.

When it returns, it's slower. Haunting. I move differently now—testing each step like I'm learning to walk. Like I'm trapped in burlap and straw, consciousness flickering in the dark, tied to a pole.

"Twenty years of nothing,
Twenty years of corn and sky,
No name, no past, no future,
Just wondering why.
Did I deserve this?
Must have, somehow.
Because the Wizard's always right,
And I'm just the Scarecrow now."

I sink against the pole, sliding down until I'm crumpled at its base. Head tilted at that unnatural angle—the position Dorothy finds me in.

The final note dies.

I stay there, letting Felix's broken confusion settle into my bones. Twenty years of darkness. Twenty years of stolen identity.

Then I look up.

Emily's crying again. But she's smiling through the tears, hand pressed over her heart.

One week later, I'm pacing our bedroom at the château. Emily sits propped against pillows, laptop balanced on a bed tray across her legs. Mochi sprawls beside her, taking up more than his fair share of space.

My phone buzzes with the incoming video call at precisely three o'clock California time. David's face fills the screen—he's at his desk, Marianne visible in the background.

"Afternoon, you two." David's expression gives nothing away. "Thank you for making time."

"Of course." My accent thickens, slipping British around the edges. I settle beside Emily, angling the phone so we're both visible.

David glances at something off-screen. "I'll get straight to it. We've finished casting decisions for *Wonderful*."

Emily's hand finds mine. Her palm is damp.

"Emily." David's face softens in that particular way he reserves for actors he's genuinely proud of. "Welcome to Oz. You're our Dorothy."

The scream that tears from Emily's throat could shatter glass. Mochi jumps, barking, tail whipping my face. Emily's shaking, tears already streaming, hands pressed over her mouth.

"You—I—really?" She can't form complete sentences.

Marianne leans into frame, grinning. "Really. You gave us something raw and true. That's what Dorothy needs."

"And Tristian." David turns his attention to me. "Obviously you're Felix. But I suspect you already knew that."

I did, but hearing it officially still sends relief flooding through my chest. "Thank you, David."

"There's more." David shuffles papers. "Mochi will be playing Toto. We'll have trainers work with him, but Emily, if you're comfortable handling most of his scenes yourself, we'd prefer that for authenticity."

Emily nods frantically, scratching Mochi's ears. The dog preens under the attention.

Marianne takes over. "The composer—Ethan Morris— loved what you did. He wants to incorporate your lyric changes into the final version. He's also writing a new song for you."

"A new—what?" Emily's voice comes out strangled.

"It'll play during the cyclone sequence. Dorothy in Kansas, Hiram and Aunt Em and Uncle Henry tearing her down, how she's learned to just float above it all." Marianne's eyes gleam with creative excitement. "Your audition inspired it. That moment where you made the song about survival, not fantasy."

Emily's crying properly now. I pull her against my chest, phone angled to keep David and Marianne in view.

"Rehearsals begin October third on the Burbank lot," David continues, "but the cast is welcome to rehearse anywhere beforehand. We'll send scripts, sheet music, and blocking notes by next week."

"Emily." He pauses, and something in his tone makes my protective instincts flare. "I'd like you to collaborate with our costume designer. Your understanding of adaptive fashion and period silhouettes—we need that perspective.

Dorothy's costumes should reflect both her disability and her practicality."

Emily lifts her head from my shoulder. "My favorite musical. Becoming a movie. And you want me to help design it?"

"Yes."

"Yes. Yes, absolutely, yes—"

I kiss her temple, grinning so hard my face hurts.

David chuckles. "I'll take that as acceptance. Contracts will arrive this week. Welcome to the family, Emily. Officially."

The call ends. Emily stares at the blank screen, chest heaving.

"*Zheli*, I think I'm going to faint."

"Easy, *Ka-reeka*." I guide her head between her knees, rubbing circles on her back. My accent's gone full Grantham Bridge now, British inflection thick as honey. "Breathe. In through your nose, out through your mouth."

Mochi whines, licking Emily's face. She laughs—high and slightly hysterical—and sits up too fast.

"We got it. We actually got it. I'm going to be Dorothy. Your Dorothy. In *Wonderful*. On film. With you as Felix, and Mochi as Toto, and Ethan Morris writing me a song—"

She's spiraling. I recognize the pattern. Joy bleeding into panic, her brain cataloging every way this could go wrong.

"EVERYONE GET UP HERE!" I bellow toward the door. "NOW!"

Footsteps thunder up the stairs. Jean arrives first, Levi right behind him. Michelle and Marcus appear seconds later, followed by Mum and Dad. Even Grandmère makes the climb, leaning on Alfred's arm. Ariana rounds out the group, breathless.

"What happened?" Jean's already scanning for threats. "Is Emily hurt?"

"She got Dorothy!" The words burst out of me. "David cast her. And Mochi's Toto. And they want her designing costumes."

Chaos erupts.

Michelle screams, launching herself at Emily for a hug. Marcus whoops, fist-pumping the air. Mum clasps her hands together, eyes shining. Even Dad cracks a genuine smile.

"*Ma petite-fille*," Grandmère murmurs, taking Emily's face in her weathered hands. "You will be magnificent."

Ariana's crying, make-up already running. "You're going to be Dorothy. You're actually going to be Dorothy."

Jean pulls me aside while the women cluster around Emily. "David Kellerman doesn't take chances. If he cast her—"

"She earned it." My voice comes out fierce. "You should've seen her audition, Jean. She destroyed everyone in that room."

"I don't doubt it." He grips my shoulder. "But you realize what this means? She's his new favorite. You've been replaced."

I glance at Emily—surrounded by family, glowing with joy despite the tears. David's always treated his actors like children, guided and protected us. For eight years, I've been his golden boy.

Watching him hand that mantle to Emily feels right.

"Good," I say simply. "She deserves it."

Emily's laughter echoes through our bedroom, champagne bubbles tickling her nose. She's giddy, eyes sparkling brighter than any emerald. "To Dorothy and Felix," she toasts, clinking her mug against mine. Hot cocoa sloshes onto her fingers, but she doesn't notice or care.

I take a sip, the sweetness coating my tongue. "To my *Zhara*," I murmur, setting aside my drink. Her breath hitches at the Winkie endearment.

Her cheeks flush pink. "And to my *Zheli*."

The word from her lips sends heat coursing through me. I take her mug, place it on the nightstand. She watches me, chest rising and falling rapidly.

"You're mine now, Zhara." I let my voice drop into Felix's register—thick, Midwestern, commanding. "Mine to care for. Mine to protect."

Her eyes darken, pupils dilating. I run a hand up her calf, over her knee, squeezing gently. She gasps, hips lifting slightly.

"These won't work much longer," I say, tracing patterns on her thigh. "Legs all stiff and sore. But that's alright, *Zhara*. I'll carry you. Bathe you. Feed you."

I lean down, press a kiss to her inner thigh. She shivers.

"Brush your hair each night." I move higher, nuzzling the crease where leg meets hip. "Dress you."

A soft moan escapes her. I smile against her skin.

"Pleasure you."

Her fingers find my hair, gripping tight. I look up, hold her gaze.

"*Zheli*," she whispers. A plea. A promise.

I stand, strip off my shirt. Her eyes roam over me, hungry. I let her look, preen under her admiration. Then I kneel before her, take her foot in my hands.

She sucks in a breath as I massage her sole, thumbs digging into tender spots. I work slowly, thoroughly, until she's squirming, trying to pull away.

"Too much?" I ask, grinning.

"It tickles," she pants.

I hold her calf firmly, keep rubbing. "You'll take what I give you, *Zhara*."

Her mouth opens, closes. She nods, surrendering.

Good girl.

I spend almost an hour on her feet, until she's boneless, melting into the mattress. Then I move up, stroking her calves, kneading her thighs. She whimpers when I hit a particularly tight muscle.

"Hurt, *Deshtari*?" I murmur.

She shakes her head. "More."

I give her more. More pressure, more touch, more possession. Her body is mine tonight. Mine to worship. Mine to claim.

When she's loose and pliant, I strip off her pants, her underwear. She watches me, eyes heavy-lidded, trusting. I lift her gently, settling her higher on the bed. Grab a pillow, prop it under her hips.

"Comfortable?" I ask.

She nods.

I strip off her top, her bra. She's naked now, laid out like a feast. I crawl over her, caging her with my arms.

"You're beautiful, *Zhara*," I murmur. "Every inch of you. Every scar. Every perfect imperfection."

Tears well in her eyes. I kiss them away, trailing kisses down her cheek, her neck, her collarbone. I linger at her breasts, lavishing attention on each one until she's arching into me, begging for more.

I move lower, kissing her stomach, her hips, the tops of her thighs. She tenses, anticipating. I grin, blowing cool air over her heated flesh.

"Please," she whispers.

"Please what, *Zhara*?" I tease. "Tell me what you want."

"You," she gasps. "I want you."

I chuckle, low and dirty. "You've got me, sweet one. All of me."

I dip my head, taste her. She cries out, hips bucking. I grip them tightly, holding her still as I explore her folds, learning what makes her gasp, what makes her scream.

Her orgasm builds slowly, inexorably. I can feel it in the tension of her muscles, the hitch of her breath. I back off, deny her the release. She sobs, frustrated.

"Not yet, *Deshtari*," I croon. "Not until I'm inside you."

She moans, head thrashing. I climb up her body, capture her mouth in a searing kiss. She can taste herself on my lips, my tongue. It drives her wild.

I break away, flip her onto her stomach. She gasps, surprised. I arrange her carefully, slipping the pillow under her hips again.

"*Zheli*?" she asks, uncertain.

"Trust me, sweet one." I run a hand down her spine, soothing. "I won't hurt you."

She relaxes, melting into the mattress. I straddle her thighs, lean forward to murmur in her ear.

"Winkies don't use birth control, *Zhara*." I nip her earlobe, grin when she shivers. "We breed our wives. Fill them with our seed. Watch their bellies swell with our children."

She moans, low and deep. I rock against her, let her feel my hardness.

"You want that, don't you?" I growl. "Want me to fill you up. Make you mine completely."

"Yes," she whimpers. "Please, *Zheli*. Please."

I sit back, grip her hips. Position myself at her entrance. She's dripping wet, ready for me. I push in slowly, gently, mindful of her limitations.

She gasps, fingers clutching the sheets. I pause, giving her time to adjust. When she nods, I slide deeper. Inch by inch, until I'm fully seated inside her.

We both groan, overwhelmed by the sensation. I lean forward, bracing myself on my arms. Kiss her shoulder, her neck, her cheek.

"You feel incredible, *Zhara*," I murmur. "So hot. So tight."

She turns her head, captures my lips in a fierce kiss. I start to move, slow and steady. Building speed, building force. She meets each thrust, pushing back against me.

Sweat beads on my forehead, drips onto her back. I lick it away, savoring the salt of her skin. She's mine. All mine.

Her body tenses, muscles clenching around me. I can feel her orgasm building again. This time, I won't deny her.

I reach around, find her clit. Rub gentle circles until she's crying out, begging for release. I thrust deeper, harder, chasing my own climax.

"Come for me, *Zhara*," I growl. "Come on my cock."

She does, screaming my name. Her body convulses, milking me, pulling me over the edge with her. I roar, filling her with my seed. Claiming her completely.

We collapse together, panting, slick with sweat. I roll off her carefully, gather her in my arms. She snuggles against my chest, sighing contentedly.

"I love you, *Zheli*," she murmurs.

I kiss her forehead, smooth her hair back from her face. "And I love you, *Zhara*. Forever."

We lie there, basking in the afterglow. When our breathing evens out, I slip from the bed, pad to the bathroom. Run a warm bath, pouring in her favorite lavender soap.

She's dozing when I return, eyelashes fluttering against her cheeks. I scoop her up gently, carry her to the bathroom. Lower her into the water.

She sighs, leaning back against the tub. I climb in behind her, pull her against my chest. We soak in silence, her fingers tracing patterns on my thighs.

When the water cools, I help her out, dry her off. Carry her back to bed. She's already half-asleep, eyes heavy. I tuck her in, kiss her softly.

"Sleep, *Deshtari*," I whisper. "I'll be here when you wake."

She smiles, rolls onto her side. I climb in beside her, molding my body to hers. Wrapping her in my arms, my protection, my love.

Tomorrow, we'll start our journey down the yellow brick road. Together. As husband and wife. As *Zheli* and *Zhara*.

But tonight, we sleep. Dreaming of Oz, of home, of forever.

I trace lazy patterns across Emily's bare shoulder, both of us still catching our breath. She's draped across my chest, one leg hooked over mine, emerald belly ring catching the afternoon light streaming through the bedroom windows.

My phone buzzes on the nightstand. Once. Twice. Then it doesn't stop.

"What the—" I reach for it, Emily grumbling protests as she shifts to let me see the screen.

The Starlight Studios logo fills my notifications. I tap the Instagram post, and my entire body goes rigid.

The *Wonderful* title card gleams in emerald and gold Art Deco lettering. Below it, character portraits rotate in slow motion—digital paintings based on costume sketches I've never seen.

Dorothy appears first. Emily's design, unmistakably. Blue gingham dress, one thick braid tied with straw—*my* straw, Felix's claiming gift. Silver slippers that look like liquid moonlight trapped in metal and diamonds, their twisted heels spiraling upward. In Dorothy's hand, a wand crystallizes from nothing—clear with light blue accents, snowflake crystals radiating from a sapphire center. As the wand materializes, tiny blue diamonds bloom across the slippers' surface like frost.

The name beneath reads: **Emily Lambert as Dorothy Gale**.

Not Emily Silver. Not Emily Dorothy Silver.

Emily Lambert.

My wife's name. The name she took in our Winkie ceremony. The name that legally means nothing in California or Angoumois, but means *everything* to us.

"*Zhara.*" My voice comes out strangled. "Look."

She props herself up on one elbow, squinting at the screen. Then she freezes. Her hand flies to her mouth.

"I told David I wanted to use Lambert," she whispers. "I filled out the contract paperwork that way. But I didn't think—I didn't know if he'd actually—"

The portrait shifts to Felix. Two versions layer over each other—princely emerald jacket with gold epaulettes and cross-body strap, ornate medallion hanging from gold cord, pleated skirt over tailored trousers, sturdy black boots. Then it transitions to the Scarecrow: weathered burlap, straw spilling from seams, the same boots worn and scuffed.

Tristian Lambert as Felix Ozian Oz III / The Scarecrow

"*Zheli*." Emily traces the screen with trembling fingers. "Your costume. The detail on the epaulettes alone—"

"*You* designed this?" I sit up fully, pulling her with me. "This is your preliminary work?"

She nods, cheeks flushing. "Marianne wanted early concepts. I sent sketches last week. I didn't realize they'd use them for the announcement."

I kiss her. Deep and claiming, tasting triumph and joy and *mine*. "You're brilliant. Absolutely brilliant."

More portraits rotate through. A Black woman with purple robes and a witch's hat, one eye clouded white, frame painfully thin. **Zara Washington as Noelle "Ellie" Ryder, Wicked Witch of the West.** Beside her, a broad-shouldered man in yellow Winkie regalia. **Michael Washington as Agnar Ryder, Winkie King.**

A warrior woman in red with a staff, dark hair braided intricately. **Sophia Martinez as Glinda Guerra.** Her counterpart in matching Quadling crimson. **Dante Ruiz as Darius Guerra.**

An older gentleman in elaborate robes, green and intimidating. **Daniel Brooks as The Wizard.**

A man in metallic armor. **Braden Michaels as Nick Chopper.**

A lion's face, massive and golden. **Carlos Rivera voices Roar.**

My phone explodes with notifications. The post already has three million likes. Comments scroll faster than I can read them.

EMILY LAMBERT???? ARE THEY MARRIED????

She took his name omg I'm crying

That Dorothy costume is PERFECTION

The silver slippers>>>

DOROTHY IS DISABLED THIS IS EVERYTHING

Then the uglier ones start appearing.

She can't even walk how is she supposed to dance

Diversity hire much?

Tristian could do so much better

Emily's breathing changes. Short, sharp gasps. She reaches for her phone, opens Twitter.

"Don't." I try to take it from her. "Don't read that garbage."

But she's already scrolling. Her face goes white.

Bethany's tweet sits pinned at the top of the trending topics.

@BethanyActress: So I guess wheelchair girls get leading roles now? Must be nice sleeping your way to the top. #Wonderful #NotMyDorothy

The replies are vicious. Some defending Emily, more piling on. Bethany's quote-tweeted herself four times, each one nastier.

She can't sing. I've heard her. Community theater quality at best.

Tristian's just using her for PR. Watch them "break up" after filming.

Emily's chest heaves. She fumbles for her nightstand drawer, hands shaking too badly to open it.

"Inhaler." The word comes out strangled.

I grab it, press it into her palm. She takes two puffs, eyes squeezed shut. Mochi appears from nowhere, nosing her leg, whining.

"Breathe, *Zhara*." I pull her against my chest. "In through your nose. Out through your mouth."

"They're right." Her voice breaks. "I'm not—I can't—"

"They're *wrong*." I grip her shoulders, force her to look at me. "David Kellerman doesn't do charity casting. Marianne Parks doesn't waste time on bad actresses. You *earned* this role."

My phone rings. Video call. I answer without checking the caller ID.

Zara Washington's face fills the screen. Late thirties, gorgeous, eyes fierce with protective fury.

"Emily Lambert, you listen to me right now."

Emily startles, wiping tears. "Ms. Washington—"

"Zara. We're family now. Ellie's adopting Dorothy, which means *I'm* adopting *you*." Her voice brooks no argument. "I've been watching this Twitter garbage for the last twenty minutes. Michael's about to drive to Utah and handle Bethany personally."

A deep voice rumbles off-screen. "I'll bring Dante. Make it a group activity."

"That's my husband," Zara says fondly. "Now, Emily. You've got the voice of an angel and the talent to back it up. David showed me your audition tape. I *cried*. Actual tears. You made me believe in Dorothy's pain."

Emily's breathing evens slightly. Mochi licks her hand.

"Bethany's jealous." Another voice—Sophia Martinez—squeezes into frame beside Zara. "She's been auditioning for leads for eight years. Never booked one. Meanwhile, you waltz in and nail Dorothy on your first try."

"Sophia's right." Dante appears, grinning. "Also, your costume designs are *insane*. The detail on Glinda's staff alone—I showed it to my costume designer friends. They're losing their minds."

Emily laughs wetly. "You like them?"

"Like them?" Zara waves a hand. "Baby girl, you're revolutionizing adaptive costume design. Every disabled actor in Hollywood is about to worship you."

"Bethany who?" Sophia adds. "Never heard of her. Must not be important."

That pulls a genuine smile from Emily. I kiss her temple, relief flooding through me.

"Thank you," Emily whispers. "All of you."

"We protect our own." Zara's expression softens. "Dorothy calls Ellie 'Ma' in the script. That makes you my daughter now. Anyone comes for you, they deal with me."

"And me," Michael calls.

"And us," Sophia and Dante chorus.

The call ends. Emily sags against me, trembling.

"You designed my costume," I murmur into her hair. "The epaulettes. The medallion. The boots."

"You like them, *Zheli*?"

"Like them?" I pull back, cup her face. "I can't wait to wear them. To see you bring Dorothy to life in that blue gingham. To watch you conjure that wand.My *Zhara* designed them." I kiss her softly. "I love them."

She smiles, fragile but real. "I love you."

"And I love you, Emily Lambert." I taste her married name, let it settle warm and right in my chest. "My wife. My Dorothy. My everything."

The news broadcast plays on the bedroom television. I'm half-watching, more focused on the warmth of Emily curled against my side, when Martha Hendricks's face fills the screen.

My entire body goes rigid.

"That woman stole from me." Martha's voice drips false sweetness, sitting in some cheap studio with crocodile tears streaming down her face. "Irreplaceable family heirlooms. A first edition *Wonderful Wizard of Oz* book that belonged to my grandmother. A vintage poppy brooch. Silver jewelry passed down through generations."

The interviewer leans forward, all sympathy. "And Emily Silver—sorry, Emily *Lambert*—took these items?"

"She was always sneaking around. I gave that girl a home when nobody else would." Martha dabs at her eyes with a tissue. "This is how she repays me? By stealing what's rightfully mine and then becoming famous?"

Emily makes a sound like a wounded animal. Her fingers claw at the sheets, chest heaving.

"Those were *mine*." Her voice comes out strangled. "My mother's things. The social worker gave them to me. Martha—she—"

"Breathe, *Zhara*." I grab her inhaler, press it into her shaking hands. "She's lying. We'll prove it."

"She pawned them." Emily's crying now, gulping air between sobs. "After the closet. After she—I asked where my mother's necklace went. The silver slipper. She said I'd lost it. But I *never* took it off. She *sold* it."

Mochi jumps onto the bed, whining, licking Emily's face. She's spiraling, hyperventilating, and I can't—

My phone explodes. Text after text flooding in.

Jean: *Dad's calling his lawyers. Now.*

Michelle: *I'm booking a flight to Utah. Going to handle this bitch personally.*

Ariana: *I WILL DESTROY HER*

Marcus: *Already tracking down pawn records. Give me an hour.*

Then the video call comes through. Not one contact. A group call. Zara, Michael, Sophia, Dante—all their faces crammed into the screen.

"Answer it," I tell Emily, holding the phone where she can see.

Her hand shakes as she taps accept.

"EMILY!" Sophia's voice comes through first. "We're ten minutes out. West End show wrapped early. We're coming to you."

"You're—what?" Emily blinks through tears.

"Already landed in Grantham Bridge." Zara's face fills more of the screen. "Hired a car. Michael's driving like a maniac. We'll be there in eight minutes now."

"Make that six," Michael calls from off-screen. "These Angoumois roads are tiny."

Emily dissolves into fresh sobs. "Ma. *Ma*."

"I'm coming, baby girl." Zara's voice gentles. "Your Pa and I both. Nobody messes with our daughter."

"We've got backup," Dante adds, grinning fiercely. "Sophia found Martha's pawn records. Posted them twenty minutes ago. She pawned a first edition Baum for three hundred dollars."

"And a sterling silver Wonderful Wizard of Oz necklace for fifty," Sophia spits. "Fifty! The chain alone was worth more than that."

Emily's breathing hitches. "The slipper necklace. My mother's—"

"We know, baby." Zara's expression hardens. "Michael's already got legal working on recovering everything. Your *actual* family heirlooms. Not hers."

Car doors slam through the phone speaker. Footsteps pound across gravel.

"We're here!" Sophia announces.

I'm already moving, pulling on pants, lifting Emily into my arms. She clings to me, face buried against my neck. Mochi trots beside us as I carry her downstairs.

The château's front entrance bursts open. Zara enters first—commanding presence, purple dress swirling, Michael right behind her in yellow Winkie-inspired formal wear. Sophia and Dante follow in matching red, clearly coming straight from their West End performance.

Emily reaches for them like a child. "Ma! *Ma!* Pa! Pa!"

Zara crosses the foyer in seconds, gathering Emily from my arms into a fierce embrace. Michael wraps around them both, this protective wall of fury and love.

"We've got you," Zara murmurs. "Nobody hurts our girl. *Nobody.*"

Sophia joins the embrace, then Dante. They surround Emily, this chosen family forming an impenetrable shield.

My own family appears—Mum, Dad, Jean, Michelle, Grandmère. Even Ariana emerges from somewhere, eyes blazing.

"The necklace." Marcus's voice cuts through as he strides through the door, phone pressed to his ear. "Found it. Bijoux Anciens on Main Street, Salt Lake City. Sterling silver, slipper pendant. Owner confirmed Martha Hendricks pawned it July fourteenth, 2019."

Emily's head snaps up. "That's—that's three days after—"

"After she locked you in the closet." Ariana's voice could cut glass. "I remember. You asked about it at school."

Dad steps forward, phone already dialing. "I'll have it purchased and shipped within the hour. Along with everything else that woman stole."

Emily's crying again, but different now. Relieved. Overwhelmed.

Zara rocks her gently. "You're ours now, Emmy. And we protect what's ours."

Zara hasn't released Emily in four hours. She's positioned in the grand salon's most comfortable chair, Emily cradled against her chest like a child, rocking gently while humming the lullaby from the script—the one Ellie sings when Dorothy's first magical period arrives and she's convinced she's dying.

Michael takes over at the hour mark, strong arms lifting Emily with practiced ease. He walks the perimeter of the room, bouncing slightly, voice low and soothing in Winkie. Emily's stopped forming complete sentences. Just "Ma" and "Pa" and occasionally "*Zheli*" when she reaches for me.

When Michael passes her to me, she's boneless, exhausted from crying. I settle into the chair Zara vacated, pulling Emily tight against my chest. Her head fits perfectly beneath my chin.

"*Zheli*," she whispers. Just that. Like she needs to confirm I'm real.

"I'm here, *Zhara*." I press my lips to her hair. "Always."

The front door opens again. Daniel Brooks enters carrying a cardboard box, expression thunderous. He's seventy-two, distinguished, and currently radiating protective grandfather energy so fierce it fills the room.

"Found everything." His voice could freeze fire. "Every piece that woman pawned. Some items required negotiation."

Emily lifts her head, eyes red and swollen. "Daniel?"

"Granddad," he corrects gently, setting the box on the coffee table. "The Wizard's Dorothy's maternal grandfather. Which makes you my granddaughter. And nobody hurts my Emmy."

She dissolves again. I hold her tighter while Daniel unpacks his treasures.

The silver slipper necklace emerges first. Tarnished, chain broken in two places, but unmistakably the same piece from Emily's childhood photos. Her mother wore it in every picture—simple sterling silver, one tiny slipper dangling from delicate links.

"Ma wanted diamonds," Emily chokes out. "On the slipper. But we couldn't—foster care doesn't—"

"Consider it done." I'm already texting my jeweler in Grantham Bridge. "We'll have it restored. Proper diamonds. Exactly how your mother envisioned it."

Daniel lifts out a music box next. Wooden, painted with yellow brick roads and emerald spires. The mechanism's broken, but I can see the two figures inside—a girl in gingham and a scarecrow in a cornfield.

"Does it play?" Emily asks, voice small.

Daniel winds the key. Nothing happens. He tries again, and a single broken note wheezes out before dying.

"I'll fix it," I promise. "*Zhara*, what song does it play?"

"The marriage song." Fresh tears stream down her face. "The one we sang. At the Metro. Ma loved *Wonderful*. She wanted to see the original Broadway run. Saved for months. Then the car accident—"

She can't finish. Zara's there instantly, taking Emily from my arms, resuming that gentle rocking.

"Your mama loved Oz," Zara murmurs. "Named you Dorothy because she believed in magic. In finding home. In yellow brick roads leading somewhere better."

"She never saw Wonderful close," Emily sobs. "Never knew if Dorothy and Felix got their happy ending. She died before—"

"Then we'll make sure she sees it now." Daniel's voice breaks slightly. "Through you. You'll *be* Dorothy. You'll give her that ending."

I take the music box, turn it over in my hands. The craftsmanship is delicate, clearly expensive once. Martha pawned it for what—two hundred dollars? Maybe less?

My jeweler texts back within minutes. *Send everything. I'll restore it properly. Diamonds, repairs, the works. Two weeks.*

"Daniel." I meet his eyes. "How much for all of it?"

"Seventeen hundred dollars." His jaw tightens. "Total. For items worth at least twenty thousand."

The room goes silent. Michelle makes a sound like she's been punched. Dad's face darkens dangerously.

"She stole from a child." Mum's voice shakes with fury. "Sold her dead mother's treasures for—"

"For drug money," Marcus cuts in, phone still pressed to his ear. "Found Martha's arrest records. Multiple possession charges. She pawned Emily's things to buy meth."

Emily screams. Not words—just raw, broken sound. Zara holds her through it, Michael joining them, Sophia and Dante wrapping around the outside. This chosen family cocooning their daughter against truths too horrible to bear.

I watch them, these people who've known Emily for barely a month but love her like she's always been theirs. Daniel carefully repacking the box with reverent hands. Marcus already coordinating legal action. My own family mobilizing resources.

Emily Silver survived thirteen years of hell. Emerged with music boxes and necklaces somehow intact. Learned to sing through closet darkness.

Now Emily Lambert will have everything restored. Every stolen treasure returned. Every diamond her mother dreamed of placed exactly where it belongs.

"Two weeks," I tell Zara quietly. "The necklace and music box will be perfect. I promise."

Emily turns her head, finds my eyes. "Thank you, *Zheli*."

"Anything for you, *Zhara*. Anything."

Chapter 11: A Wonderful Way to Say "Will You?"

August 23rd. Seven days until the Emerald City proposal. My phone buzzes with the sixteenth notification this hour—the men's cast chat this time.

Carlos: *Just watched Emily's vocal warm-up videos. She's going to destroy us all.*

Braden: *In the best way. Nick Chopper's crying already and we haven't even started filming.*

Daniel: *Told you she was Dorothy. Knew it the moment I met her.*

I scroll up through forty-seven messages. Michael started the group three weeks ago after our first table read, declaring we needed "Wonderful brotherhood" before cameras rolled in October. Now it's descended into Carlos sending lion memes at 3 AM and Dante sharing Quadling warrior training videos that make me question my life choices.

Michael: *Tristian. You're suspiciously quiet. Emily's not pregnant yet, is she?*

Tristian: *We're WORKING on it.*

Carlos: *TMI, King Raptor. TMI.*

Dante: *Let the man claim his wife properly. Winkie traditions matter.*

The notifications shift to the main cast chat—all fifteen of us, including crew. Sophia's posted another behind-the-scenes photo from yesterday's costume fitting. Emily in her Dorothy dress, standing with parallel bars, grinning at something off-camera. My stomach flips every time I see that smile.

Sophia: *Our girl's been working so hard. Physical therapy every morning, vocal coaching every afternoon. When does she REST?*

Zara: *She doesn't. I've tried. Woman's possessed.*

Emily: *I'm literally right here in this chat.*

Sophia: *We know, darling. We're staging an intervention. You need a spa day.*

I switch back to my texts with Jean. His latest message includes polling data—Dad's campaign surging in urban districts after Jean implemented his tech-sector outreach strategy. The numbers don't lie. Jean's vision works.

Jean: *Dad actually thanked me today. In front of Henri Blackwood. I almost fainted.*

Tristian: *Proud of you, brother. President Lambert has a nice ring.*

Jean: *In ten years maybe. One campaign at a time.*

Jean: *How's Operation Emerald City?*

Tristian: *Starlight Studios confirmed setup for the 31st. Roger's coordinating with David Kellerman personally.*

Emily's laughter drifts from the bedroom. She's FaceTiming with Sophia and Zara—their group chat evolved into daily video calls where they discuss everything from costume design to period cramps. I've walked in on conversations that made me reconsider eavesdropping.

I find her propped against pillows, phone balanced on her knees, fingers tracing the silver slipper at her throat. She hasn't removed the necklace since Daniel gave it back. The chain's been repaired, five tiny diamonds now glittering on the slipper itself. Exactly how her mother imagined.

The music box sits on the nightstand. Restored, repainted, mechanism perfect. I wind it every night while Emily gets ready for bed. Those haunting notes—our wedding song—fill the room as she brushes her teeth, takes medication, settles under covers.

Tonight's no different. I reach for the key, twist three full rotations. The melody begins, dancers spinning on their emerald platform. She throws a pillow. I catch it, grinning.

She pats the bed beside her. "Get over here. Marcus sent me the final campaign photos and you look criminally attractive in that suit."

I climb in, pull her against my chest. The music box plays its final notes, dancers slowing to stillness. Outside, Grantham Bridge settles into summer twilight. My phone buzzes again—Marcus sending photos of Emerald and Phantom in the stables, Mochi sprawled between them.

This family we've built. Blood and chosen, human and animal, stretching across continents. Richard Kellerman's directive makes sense now. *Be family before filming starts.*

We already are. Have been since Emily walked into my FanCon signing nine months ago.

Seven more days. Then I make it permanent with rings and vows and whatever elaborate Oz spectacle Roger's arranged.

"Love you, *Zhara*."

She kisses my jaw. "Love you more, *Zheli*."

The music box sits silent on the nightstand, waiting for tomorrow night's winding. Waiting for the proposal that'll make Emily Lambert my wife in every tradition that matters.

The brownstone smells like fresh paint and sawdust. Dante's been renovating the third floor for months, converting what used to be storage into a proper studio for Sophia's dance work. I knock twice before pushing through the heavy oak door, finding controlled chaos.

Zara stands center stage—well, center living room—script clutched in one hand, the other gesturing wildly. Sophia mirrors her across the makeshift rehearsal space, both women barefoot on hardwood, hair pulled back, completely lost in their characters.

"You were my sister." Zara's voice cracks. "Before the Wizard, before the curse, before everything went to hell. My *sister*, Glinda."

"And you were mine." Sophia's composure shatters. "Do you think I wanted this? That I chose power over family?"

Michael watches from the piano bench, fingers tracing silent chords. Dante's sprawled in the armchair, notebook balanced on his knee, scribbling blocking notes. Neither notices me slip inside.

Upstairs, children's laughter echoes. Emily's voice rises above the chaos. "Mochi, give that back. Oliver, no climbing on furniture. Yes, sweetheart, you can have more juice."

Fifteen kids total. Our entire Oz family's offspring crammed into Sophia and Dante's brownstone for what they're calling "character bonding." Really it's supervised mayhem while the adults rehearse.

"From the top." Michael plays the intro. "Remember, this is twenty years of regret."

They begin again. The dialogue transforms, becomes something raw. Zara's Ellie radiates exhaustion—two decades fighting a tyrant, raising six boys alone, never stopping. Sophia's Glinda carries shame like armor, every word careful, measured, desperate.

The reconciliation builds. Forgiveness earned through sacrifice, through Glinda finally choosing family over the

Wizard's empty promises. Through Dorothy—her niece, their hope—rescuing everyone from the Quadling palace.

I lean against the doorframe, watching my co-stars become sisters. Watching them create the emotional foundation our film needs.

"That's it." Dante stands, crosses to them. "Right there. That vulnerability. Don't lose it."

Michael's hands still on the keys. "Tristian. When'd you sneak in?"

"Five minutes ago." I straighten. "Didn't want to interrupt."

Sophia grabs a water bottle, tosses one to Zara. "Emily's upstairs mediating World War Three. Your nieces and nephews decided building an Emerald City fort required every pillow in the house."

"And Mochi's apparently the Cowardly Lion now." Zara grins. "The kids cast him. He's very committed to the role."

"Speaking of roles." My throat tightens. "I need to ask you something."

Michael and Dante exchange glances. Sophia sets down her water.

"The proposal." She doesn't phrase it as a question.

"How did you—"

"Please." Zara laughs. "You've been asking about Emily's ring size for three weeks. Also, Jean can't keep secrets."

I drag a hand through my hair. "Right. So you know."

"That you're planning some elaborate Oz spectacle?" Dante stands, crosses his arms. "That you're proposing during the Wonderful World show finale? That Roger's been coordinating with park management since July?"

"Marcus told you."

"Marcus tells Michelle everything. Michelle tells everyone." Sophia moves closer. "You want our blessing."

Not a question. A statement.

"Emily talks about you like family." The words come easier now. "Calls you her Oz sisters. Says working with you feels like coming home." I meet Zara's eyes, then Sophia's. "You were there before me. Before any of this. You matter to her."

"You matter to her more." Zara's voice softens. "Should see how she lights up when you text. How she defends you in interviews. How she fights through pain just to be ready for rehearsals because she won't let you down."

"That's what worries me." My hands clench. "What if she's pushing too hard? What if this—the film, the proposal, all of it—is too much?"

Michael joins us. "Emily's stronger than you think. Stronger than she thinks."

"She survived Martha." Sophia's jaw tightens. "Survived foster care, abuse, years of being told she wasn't enough. You think a proposal's going to break her?"

"No, but—"

"You're terrified she'll say no." Dante's bluntness cuts through my spiraling. "That's what this is. You're scared."

The accusation hangs there. True and horrible.

"We got married on a Metro train platform." The confession spills out. "Sang Winkie vows through windows while Marcus filmed and half of Grantham Bridge watched. She wears my emerald, my tattoo's on her skin, we've built this entire life together and I *still* think she might realize she deserves better."

Silence.

Then Zara laughs. Actually laughs.

"Oh, Tristian. You beautiful, ridiculous man." She crosses to me, takes my hands. "Emily Dorothy Silver—*Lambert* now, thank you—chose you when she had nothing. When dating you meant tabloid scrutiny and online harassment and people calling her a gold digger."

"She quit her job for you." Sophia joins us. "Moved across the world. Let you renovate your entire house. Married you in the most public way possible."

"She's upstairs right now." Michael gestures toward the ceiling. "Babysitting fifteen children who call her Aunt Emmy. Practicing Dorothy's mannerisms. Learning our family dynamics. Becoming part of this world because she loves you."

Dante claps my shoulder. "So yes. You have our blessing. All of us. Propose during the finale, make it spectacular, give her the fairy tale she deserves."

My eyes burn. "Thank you."

"But Tristian?" Sophia's expression turns serious. "When she says yes—and she will—you better take care of her. Physical therapy, medications, bad days, all of it."

"I will. I am. I—"

"We know." Zara squeezes my hands. "That's why we're saying yes. Because you see all of her. Not just Dorothy, not just the talented designer, not just the beautiful woman. You see Emily. Completely."

Upstairs, something crashes. Emily yelps. Children scatter.

Michael grins. "Better go rescue your wife."

I take the stairs two at a time, finding absolute chaos. Pillows everywhere, blankets draped over furniture, Mochi wearing a makeshift mane of yellow yarn. Emily sits in her wheelchair at the center of the fort, laughing so hard tears stream down her face.

"Uncle Tris!" Oliver launches himself at me. "We built Emerald City! Aunt Emmy helped!"

"I see that." I catch him, ruffle his hair. "Very impressive."

Emily wipes her eyes. "They're creative. I'll give them that."

Our nieces and nephews swarm around us. Fifteen kids who already call us family. Who'll be in our wedding photos, our future family gatherings, our lives.

Seven days until I make it official.

Seven days until Emily Lambert becomes my fiancée in every tradition that matters.

August 30th arrives too fast and too slow simultaneously. I've counted every hour since buying that ring—1,008 total—and now we're down to the final eighteen before I propose.

The chartered bus idles outside Dad's château, exhaust curling into morning air. Our entire family's packed for a weekend at the Starlight Studios Paris resort hotel. Michelle's already claimed window seats for her and Marcus. Jean and Levi coordinate luggage with military precision. Grandmère supervises from the steps, Alfred hovering with last-minute supplies.

Emily emerges in denim shorts and my Extinction Protocol hoodie—the one from our first night together, sleeves rolled to her elbows, collar sliding off one shoulder. My tattoo peeks from beneath the fabric. The emerald at her navel glints when she stretches.

Six weeks of marriage. Six weeks of learning her body's rhythms, discovering what makes her gasp, memorizing every sound she makes when I—

"Tristian." Ariana snaps fingers in front of my face. "Stop mentally undressing your wife and help me with Mochi's travel crate."

"I'm allowed to mentally undress my wife." I grab the crate anyway. "It's in our vows."

"The Winkie vows you made up?"

"We didn't make them up. *Ozmapolitan* clearly states —"

"You're impossible." But she's grinning.

I load Mochi's crate, then wheel Emily's pink chair up the bus ramp. She's already settling into the accessible seating area, phone out, texting the Wonderful cast group.

I slide into the seat beside Emily, hand immediately finding her thigh. She doesn't look up from her phone, but her leg shifts, pressing into my palm.

"Behave." Her voice stays steady. "Your grandmother's watching."

"Grandmère thinks we should have three children minimum. Pretty sure she approves of my hands on you."

"Three?" She finally meets my eyes. "We haven't discussed—"

"Later." I lean closer, breath against her ear. "Right now I'm thinking about tonight. Hotel room. King bed. No family interruptions."

Her cheeks flush that perfect pink I've catalogued. "Tristian Alexandre Lambert, we are on a family trip."

"Doesn't mean I can't touch my wife." My thumb traces circles on her inner thigh. "Or remind her exactly what happens when we're alone."

The bus lurches forward. Michelle wolf-whistles from three rows back.

"Get a room!"

"We have one!" I call back. "Booked the honeymoon suite!"

Jean throws a granola bar at my head. I catch it one-handed, grinning.

Emily tries glaring. Fails spectacularly. Her hand covers mine, squeezes.

"Six weeks," she whispers. "Feels like forever and yesterday."

"Tomorrow's forever." The words slip out before I can stop them. "Tomorrow I—"

Her phone buzzes. Marcus sending photos of the resort's Emerald City section, all green glass and soaring towers. Emily gasps, starts typing responses.

I watch her instead of the screen. Watch excitement transform her face, watch her hands dance across the keyboard, watch her belong completely in this moment.

Tomorrow I give her the ring. Tomorrow she becomes my fiancée officially. Tomorrow the Lambert curse claims another.

But today? Today I get to touch her thigh on a charter bus while our entire family sings off-key songs. Get to plan exactly how I'll worship her tonight in that honeymoon suite. Get to count down the final hours until Emerald City and yellow brick roads and the beginning of our actual forever.

My hand slides higher. She swats it away, laughing.

"Behave."

"Never."

The Starlight Studios Paris gates shimmer in afternoon sun—exact replicas of the Hollywood originals, but bigger, bolder, more European in their grandeur. Our bus pulls through VIP access, bypassing regular guest security.

Emily presses against the window, breath fogging glass. "It's real. It's actually real."

"Welcome to my second home." I kiss her temple. "Our second home now."

The resort sprawls before us like a fever dream made concrete and steel. Wonderful World rises to our left, all emerald spires and yellow brick pathways. Prehistoric Paradise's volcanic peaks steam in the distance. Erik's Opera House—my Opera House, technically—lurks at the far edge, gothic and beautiful and barely visible from this angle.

"Monsieur Lambert!" A concierge in pristine uniform greets our bus. "Your suite is ready."

"Suite?" Emily turns to me. "You said room."

"I lied."

Jean snorts behind us. "He's been lying for weeks."

The concierge leads us through crystal revolving doors into a lobby that makes Dad's château look modest. Chandeliers cascade from cathedral ceilings. Marble floors reflect emerald and gold lighting. A massive mural depicts Dorothy's journey—my wife's journey now—across one entire wall.

"The Wonderful Signature Suite," the concierge announces at the penthouse elevator. "Mr. Kellerman insisted."

Emily grips my hand. "Tristian, how much did this—"

"David said we can use it whenever we want. No charge." I squeeze back. "Perks of being his favorite children."

The elevator opens directly into our suite.

Emily goes silent.

Floor-to-ceiling windows overlook the entire park. Wonderful World glitters directly below—we're high enough to see the Emerald Palace, the Yellow Brick Road winding through munchkin villages, the poppy fields that'll make her cry during filming. Prehistoric Paradise stretches beyond, its waterfalls and caves miniature from this height. Erik's Opera House sits at the horizon like a dark jewel.

"Tristian." She whispers my name like prayer.

The living room could fit her entire Logan apartment. Cream leather sofas. Glass coffee tables. Abstract art I recognize from the film's concept designs. And in the corner—a massive dog bed with Mochi's name embroidered in gold thread, matching food and water bowls already filled.

Mochi whines, tail wagging.

"Go ahead, boy." Emily releases his harness.

He bounds to the bed, circles three times, collapses with a satisfied huff.

"The bedroom's through here." The concierge gestures to double doors. "Mr. Kellerman had it specially designed."

I wheel Emily forward. She gasps.

The bed dominates the space—an exact replica of Felix's bed from the coronation scene. The headboard curves in art deco patterns, real emeralds embedded in rose gold filigree. But the comforter steals my breath. Sunflower yellow, soft as clouds, identical to the one from Ellie's castle where Dorothy and Felix make love for the first time.

"The original was too fragile for your, shall we say, enthusiastic style." The concierge doesn't quite smile. "This one's been reinforced. Winkie construction standards, per your request."

Emily's face flames crimson. "You didn't."

"I absolutely did." I dismiss the concierge with a nod, wait until the elevator closes. "Winkies are sexually adventurous. It's in the lore."

"The lore you keep inventing—"

"Chapter seven. Dorothy discovers the Winkie culture values creativity in all things, especially—"

She covers my mouth. Laughing. Mortified. Beautiful.

I kiss her palm. "Saturday night we're sleeping in Nathan and Maya's cave. Full Prehistoric Paradise experience."

"The one from Extinction Protocol Singularity?"

"David had it built to exact film specifications. Climate controlled, completely private, and—" I pull the velvet box from my pocket, show her what's inside. "He sent these."

Nathan's raptor claws rest on black silk. The actual props from filming, modified for human hands, edges dulled but still dangerous-looking. The fangs nestle beside them—perfectly crafted, able to leave claiming marks without breaking skin.

"For proper raptor bonding." I snap the box closed before she can process fully. "We have permanent access. David said the cave's ours whenever we want it."

"He knows?" Her voice cracks. "About the claiming?"

"He knows I'm obsessed with you. The rest he can guess." I set the box on the nightstand. "Tomorrow's your birthday. Tomorrow we explore the park, ride every attraction, eat too much themed food. Tomorrow night I show you Emerald City after dark when all the crystals light up."

"And Saturday?"

"Saturday you become my prey." The words come out rough. Possessive. Nathan bleeding through. "Saturday I hunt you through Prehistoric Paradise until you can't run anymore, until you surrender completely, until everyone who sees those marks knows exactly who you belong to."

She shivers. Not from fear.

"But tonight?" I lift her from the wheelchair, carry her to that reinforced Winkie bed. "Tonight I make love to my wife in the bed where our characters become king and queen. Tonight I show you exactly why this comforter needed reinforcements."

Her arms circle my neck. "The family's right downstairs."

"In their own suites. With excellent soundproofing." I lay her down on sunflower yellow. "Happy early birthday, Mrs. Lambert."

She pulls me down, kisses me hard enough to bruise.

Through the windows, Emerald City glows green against darkening sky.

Tomorrow I propose. Tomorrow she says yes. Tomorrow our forever officially begins.

Madame Sucre's Chocolate Factory & Grille rises three stories above the Boardwalk, all brass gears and candy-colored glass. Steam billows from copper pipes. Animatronic chocolate makers wave from windows.

"This is obscene." Emily stares up at the revolving chocolate fountain that crowns the building. "I love it."

Jean holds the door while Levi guides Emily inside. The hostess—dressed like a Victorian factory worker—leads us past bubbling vats of melted chocolate, through rooms where mechanical arms dip strawberries and pretzels, up to a private dining room overlooking the Boardwalk.

"The birthday menu." She presents Emily with a leather-bound book. Gold foil spells out *Indulgence*.

"My birthday's tomorrow—"

"Close enough." Michelle slides into the booth beside Marcus. "Order everything."

Emily's eyes scan the options. Widen. "They have a chocolate bacon jam burger."

"That sounds like a heart attack." I sit beside her, studying the menu over her shoulder. "A delicious heart attack."

"With cocoa-dusted fries." She points to the description. Practically vibrating. "Tristian, they put chocolate in everything."

"Including the vodka." Dad examines the cocktail list with academic interest. "Remarkable."

Mum orders alcahol-free champagne for the table. The server arrives—dressed as a chocolate engineer—with a tray of samples. Dark chocolate ganache. Milk chocolate caramel. White chocolate raspberry.

Emily tastes each one. Moans. "This is better than sex."

"Excuse me?" The Nathan voice surfaces. Low. Possessive.

She pats my hand. "You're tied with the dark chocolate."

Jean snorts into his water glass.

"I'll have the chocolate bacon jam burger." Emily closes her menu with finality. "Cocoa fries. And—" She points to the dessert section. "The Six Times Chocolate Milkshake. In the souvenir glass."

"That's two thousand calories of chocolate." I try keeping my voice reasonable. "Before dessert."

"It's my birthday trip." She uses the voice that always wins arguments. Sweet. Stubborn. "I'm Dorothy. I deserve chocolate."

"That shake has six kinds of chocolate layered in it." The server confirms. "White chocolate base, milk chocolate syrup, dark chocolate chips, cocoa powder rim, chocolate whipped cream, and a chocolate-dipped spoon."

"Perfect."

I recognize defeat. "I'll have the steak. No chocolate."

The food arrives forty minutes later. Emily's burger towers impossibly high—bacon glazed with chocolate jam, cheese that somehow incorporates cocoa, a brioche bun dusted with dark chocolate powder. The fries arrive in a basket, salted with cocoa crystals that sparkle under the lights.

She bites into the burger. Closes her eyes. Makes sounds that should be illegal in public.

"Ma chérie." I keep my voice low. Warning. "Everyone can hear you."

"Don't care." She takes another bite. "This is heaven."

The shake arrives in a glass the size of Mochi's head, so thick the straw stands vertical. Emily attacks it with enthusiasm that would impress the raptors.

Halfway through the fries, she slows. Three-quarters through the shake, she sets the glass down.

"You good?" Marcus raises an eyebrow.

"Perfect." But her voice lacks conviction. "Just... pacing myself."

"Emily." I recognize the signs. Flushed cheeks. Slightly glazed eyes. "Put down the chocolate."

"It's my birthday trip—"

"It's sugar overload." Mum signals the server. "Some water, please."

Emily manages two more bites of burger before surrendering. She stares at the remaining food like it personally betrayed her.

"No regrets?" Michelle grins.

"So many regrets." Emily slumps against my shoulder. "Why didn't you stop me?"

"I tried. You played the Dorothy card."

"Revoke my Dorothy privileges." She groans. "I never want to see chocolate again."

"You have ten hours." I check my watch. "Then we're having chocolate croissants for breakfast."

"Monster."

But she's smiling when I kiss her temple, even if her lips taste like cocoa overload.

Emily's laid out on the bed, a vision in blue silk and lace. The Dorothy-themed lingerie hugs her curves, sparkling like a Kansas sky. She's propped against plush pillows, her blonde waves cascading down her shoulders. Her emerald eyes, bold and inviting, meet mine as I stand in the doorway, towel slung low around my hips.

"Come to me, my Scarecrow," she whispers, hand outstretched. "My Felix."

I don't need more invitation. I'm across the room in three strides, kneeling on the bed beside her. Her fingers trace the tattoos across my torso, each character a stepping stone to this moment.

"You're overdressed, Zhara." My voice already slips into Felix's midwestern drawl. I tug at the silk ribbon holding her top together, watching as the bow unravels. Her breath hitches, eyes never leaving mine.

"Help me, Zheli?" She lifts her arms, wrists together, offering herself to me. I slide the top off, revealing inches of soft skin, flushed pink. Her breasts are perfect, nipples already tightening from the cool air and anticipation.

"You had your fun at dinner." I lean down, capturing one bud between my lips. Her back arches, just a little. "Now it's my turn to indulge."

I take my time, tasting every inch of her. The valley between her breasts, the curve of her waist, the smooth expanse of her belly. She giggles when I dip my tongue into her navel, twirling around the emerald piercing. Her hands find my hair, gripping tight.

"Felix," she gasps, as I hook my fingers into her panties, drawing them down her legs. I press kisses to her inner thighs, her knees, her calves. Each touch is careful, mindful of her limits. She can't move much, but her body responds to me, trembling under my hands and mouth.

"Tell me what you want, Dorothy." I look up at her, chin resting on her thigh. Her cheeks are flushed, eyes dark with desire.

"I want you, Felix." Her voice is barely a whisper. "All of you."

I crawl back up her body, caging her with my arms. Her legs wrap around my waist, as much as they can. I can feel her heat, her need. But I don't rush. Not tonight. Tonight, we savor.

"You're mine, Dorothy." I murmur against her lips. "My deshtari. My beloved."

Her eyes flutter closed as I kiss her, deep and slow. Her arms loop around my neck, holding me close. I can feel her heartbeat, steady and strong against my chest.

I break away, just enough to whisper in her ear. "And tonight, I'm going to make you feel every inch of Oz."

Her breath hitches again, ending on a soft moan. I trail kisses down her neck, her collarbone, her sternum. Each touch is deliberate, designed to ignite. And she burns, oh, she burns so beautifully for me.

When I finally sink into her, it's like coming home. Her body welcomes me, grips me tight. I keep my movements slow, gentle. She can't thrust back, can't match my rhythm, but she doesn't need to. This is our dance, our song. And we move together, perfectly in sync.

Her hands roam my back, my shoulders, my arms. She touches each character, each story etched into my skin. Claiming them. Claiming me.

"Felix," she whispers, her voice ragged. "My Felix."

"Yours," I growl, my forehead pressed to hers. "Always, Zhara. Always."

Her body tenses, her breath comes in short gasps. She's close. So am I. But I hold back, waiting for her. Always waiting for her.

"Come for me, Dorothy." I whisper, my voice hoarse. "Let me see you fly."

And she does. Her body convulses around me, her cry of release echoing through the room. It's enough to send me over the edge, spilling into her with a groan.

We stay like that, tangled together, as our breathing slows. Her fingers trace lazy patterns on my back. I press soft kisses to her shoulder, her neck, her cheek.

As she begins to drift, I sing to her. Softly, barely a whisper. Her lips curve into a smile, her eyes flutter closed.

I rub her tummy gently, checking for any distention, any sign of discomfort. But she's fine. More than fine. She's perfect.

Tomorrow is the day. The day I make her mine forever. But for now, I hold her close, singing her into dreams.

Morning light filters through the curtains, painting Emily's sleeping face in soft gold. I brush my lips against hers, gentle enough to wake her without startling.

"*Deshtari*," I murmur in Winkie, watching her eyelashes flutter. "Happy birthday."

Her emerald eyes open, focusing on me with that sleepy smile that makes my chest ache. "Felix?"

"Still me." I kiss her again, deeper this time. "Ready for your birthday adventure?"

She stretches, wincing slightly as her muscles protest. I help her sit up, already cataloging her movements for signs of pain. Today has to be perfect. Everything depends on it.

"Starlight Studios awaits, Dorothy." I wheel her chair closer to the bed. "And I have a surprise for you."

"Another one?" She laughs as I lift her into the chair. "You've already given me everything."

Not yet. The ring burns a hole in my consciousness, hidden deep in my Felix backpack where she won't accidentally find it. I spent an hour last night positioning it in the inner pocket, beneath the water bottle and emergency supplies.

In the bathroom, I help Emily into her blue gingham sundress—the perfect Dorothy costume without being costume-y. The fabric flows around her legs, the bodice fitted enough to show her curves. When she leans forward to brush her teeth, I catch sight of the emerald at her navel and have to grip the counter.

"Behave," she warns, meeting my eyes in the mirror.

"I'm trying." My accent thickens, slipping into Felix's midwest cadence. "You make it difficult, Zhara."

I braid her hair—one long plait that falls over her shoulder. She ties it with a piece of straw-colored ribbon, and I add a silver glitter bow at the end. Her high-top sneakers are silver glitter too, catching the light with every movement.

My own outfit is simpler. Green shirt, jeans, the Felix pin I had made last week with his scarcrow symbol. I catch my reflection and barely recognize myself—not the Hollywood star, not the Lambert heir, just a man in love planning to propose to his wife.

"Wait." Emily's voice stops me at the door. "What's that box?"

The package from Kellerman sits on the table, delivered while we slept. I retrieve it, heart pounding. Inside, nestled in velvet, are two pieces of jewelry that make Emily gasp.

The tiara is breathtaking—silver metal worked into swirling patterns and starbursts, studded with emeralds of varying sizes. It's Dorothy's crown from the film's final scene, when she and Felix rule Oz together. The emeralds catch the light, throwing green fire across the walls.

My crown is simpler but no less stunning. Silver with emeralds set into the band, the Ozian family crest etched into the front—a Z inside an O, Felix's birthright as son of the late Queen Ozma.

"He sent replicas." Emily's fingers hover over the tiara, not quite touching. "For my birthday?"

"For Dorothy." I settle the crown on her head, adjusting it until it sits perfectly. "And Felix."

I put on my own crown, feeling ridiculous and right all at once. In the mirror, we look like royalty. Like the characters we're about to bring to life on screen.

My phone buzzes with messages from the cast:

Zara: *Make us proud, Lambert. Dorothy deserves the world.*

Sophia: *Don't mess this up. We're watching.*

Michael: *The mini-show stage is set. Go big or go home.*

Dante: *About damn time. Good luck, brother.*

Braden: *She's gonna cry. Have tissues ready.*

Daniel: *Rooting for you both. Toto says woof.*

I shove the phone in my pocket before Emily can see. She's focused on getting Mochi into his Toto costume—a little blue gingham vest that matches her dress, complete with a tiny basket.

"There's my good boy." She scratches behind his ears. "Ready to explore Oz?"

I pack her Dorothy backpack with care. Water bottle filled, blue raspberry flavor packets tucked in the side pocket because she hates regular water. An extra dress in case of spills. Lip gloss. Her emergency supplies, including protection for her bladder, hidden in a discreet compartment.

The Felix backpack gets the same treatment, but with one crucial addition—the emerald ring, wrapped in velvet, buried beneath everything else.

"You're being very thorough." Emily watches me zip both bags closed.

"It's a big park." I kiss her forehead, crowns clinking together. "I want to be prepared."

She rolls her eyes but smiles. "My overprotective husband."

Husband. The word still sends electricity through me. Tonight, I'll make it official. Tonight, she'll have my ring on her finger, the world will know she's mine, and we'll start planning a real wedding.

But first, I have to get through an entire day at Starlight Studios without ravishing her. The emerald at her navel peeks out when she moves, and the tiara makes her look like the queen she is. It's going to be the longest day of my life.

"Ready, *deshtari*?" I grasp her wheelchair handles.

"Ready, *zheli*." She tilts her head back to look at me. "Let's go find our yellow brick road."

The elevator doors open to reveal my entire family in the lobby, and I nearly drop Emily's wheelchair handles.

Michelle floats toward us in layers of crimson chiffon that swirl around her legs, ruby jewelry catching the light at her throat and wrists. The dress hits mid-calf, modern but unmistakably Glinda's signature style in Quadling colors. Marcus beside her wears deep burgundy pants and a white shirt with red suspenders, a toy sword hanging from his belt —every inch the Quadling warrior protecting his witch.

"Happy birthday, Emily!" Michelle engulfs her in a hug, careful not to disturb either crown.

Jean approaches in all silver—metallic gray suit with a silver tie, a heart-shaped pin on his lapel that looks suspiciously like it's made from actual tin. Levi prowls beside him in golden browns and tawny oranges, his shirt open at the collar revealing a medallion shaped like a badge of courage.

"We couldn't let you two have all the fun." Jean adjusts his tin heart pin, which catches the light perfectly.

Mum glides forward in an emerald green dress that makes her look twenty years younger, while Ariana rocks head-to-toe purple—violet leather jacket over a plum dress, amethyst jewelry dripping from her ears and neck. Even her lipstick is purple, dark and dramatic against her skin.

"Western witch reporting for duty." Ariana strikes a pose. "Though I promise not to melt."

Grandmère steals the show in a simple blue gingham shirt and denim skirt, her white hair pinned back with clips shaped like tiny farmhouses. She looks exactly like Aunt Em would if Aunt Em shopped at Chanel.

"*Ma petite* Dorothy." She cups Emily's face. "You look perfect."

Dad stands slightly apart in his usual dark suit, but there—on his lapel—sits a silver slipper brooch that must have cost more than most people's cars.

"Pierre Lambert in costume." Emily's voice carries wonder. "Did someone document this?"

"Already done." Marcus waves his phone. "We need the full family shot though."

They arrange us in front of the Starlight Studios logo etched into the marble floor. Emily and I center the group, our crowns catching the light. Michelle and Marcus flank Emily's left, Jean and Levi on my right. Mum and Dad stand behind us with Grandmère between them, while Ariana crouches beside Emily's wheelchair, one hand on Mochi who sits perfectly in his Toto vest.

"Everyone say 'There's no place like Starlight!'" The concierge takes Marcus's phone.

We chorus the phrase through multiple shots—serious, laughing, one where Mochi jumps into Emily's lap and everyone breaks character to coo at him.

"For the 'gram?" I check with Emily before posting. She nods, already uploading her own.

Within seconds, the notifications explode. Comments flood in about the Lambert family's commitment to theme, Emily's crown, our matching costumes. The Wonderful cast account reposts immediately with a string of heart emojis.

"Breakfast?" Levi suggests. "The Emerald Table has emerald waffles today. Literally green waffles shaped like the Emerald City."

"After you, your majesties." Jean makes an exaggerated bow that has his tin heart pin clinking.

Emily laughs, bright and free, surrounded by my family who've dressed as Oz characters just to make her birthday special. Dad offers his arm to Mum, the silver slipper brooch catching light with every step. Even he couldn't resist acknowledging what today means.

"Thank you," Emily whispers, squeezing my hand as I push her chair. "For this. For them."

"They're your family too, *deshtari*." I lean down to kiss her temple, right where the tiara meets her hair. "They just want to celebrate their newest Lambert."

Soon to be official Lambert, if everything goes according to plan.

The Emerald Table lives up to its name—everything shimmers with edible glitter, from the green waffles shaped like the Emerald City's spires to the crystal-clear sparkling juice that catches morning light. Emily gets a birthday button the moment we walk in, bright yellow with "It's My Birthday!" scripted across dorothy slippers.

"First one of the day." The hostess pins it to Emily's bodice. "But it won't be the last. Everyone at Starlight celebrates birthdays."

Emily's smile could power the entire park.

We demolish breakfast—Dad actually laughs when Mochi steals a piece of Grandmère's bacon, and Mum takes approximately four hundred photos of Emily wearing both her crown and her birthday button. Marcus insists on a photo of just Emily, Michelle, Ariana, and himself, captioning it "The girls" before posting to Instagram.

"Ready to conquer the park?" I push Emily's chair back from the table.

"I haven't been to a theme park since I was eight." Her voice carries wonder. "The group home took us to Lagoon once."

"Well, you're about to get the full Starlight experience." Jean unfolds a park map. "And we have VIP access, so no waiting in lines."

"Jean." Emily grabs his wrist. "We are absolutely waiting in at least some lines. That's part of the experience."

Michelle squeals. "I love her so much."

The park sprawls before us, divided into distinct worlds—Wonderful World dominates the entrance with its emerald spires and yellow brick pathways, but beyond that lies Starbound Lagoon, the Phantom's Opera House, Prehistoric Paradise, and the area I've been planning our route around all morning: Starlight Classic Horror.

"Dorothy meet and greet first?" I suggest, steering Emily toward a yellow brick queue.

"There's a meet and greet?" Her eyes go wide. "Of course there's a meet and greet."

The Dorothy working today could be Emily's twin—same blonde waves, same emerald eyes, same blue gingham dress. She actually gasps when she sees Emily approaching in full Dorothy regalia, wheelchair and all.

"Well, if it isn't the real Dorothy!" The character drops to one knee. "I heard you were visiting today."

"You—you know who I am?"

"Everyone at Starlight knows Dorothy herself is here for her birthday." The actress touches Emily's crown. "That's the most beautiful tiara I've ever seen."

Emily's cheeks flush pink. "My husband gave it to me this morning."

My husband. Warmth spreads through my chest at those words, even if they're only Winkie-binding for now.

Dorothy-the-character catches sight of Mochi in his Toto vest. "And who's this handsome fellow?"

Mochi immediately rolls onto his back for belly rubs, tail wagging so hard his whole body wiggles. The character obliges, scratching his white fluffy stomach while Emily laughs.

"That's my service dog Mochi, but today he's Toto."

"Best Toto I've ever seen." Dorothy poses for photos—one with Emily, one with Emily and me, one with the entire Lambert family where Grandmère insists on being called Aunt Em.

We find Felix next, standing near the scarecrow cornfield maze. He takes one look at my costume and breaks character completely.

"Dude. You're Tristian Lambert. You're playing me in the movie."

"Today I'm just Felix." I shake his hand. "This is Emily, the actual Dorothy."

"No way." He kneels beside Emily's wheelchair. "I saw the casting announcement. You're going to be incredible."

Emily blushes again, and I make a mental note to tell her later how beautiful she looks when she's flustered.

Glinda appears in full crimson glory near the Quadling fountain, and Michelle practically vibrates with excitement.

"I'm Glinda too!" Michelle gestures to her outfit.

The character's eyes light up. "A fellow scholar! Most people only know the film version."

They bond over Baum's original descriptions while Marcus and I exchange amused glances.

We find Ellie last—the Wicked Witch of the West, dark-skinned and fierce in purple robes. Before anyone can stop him, Mochi launches himself at her and licks her face with enthusiastic affection.

"Traitor dog!" Ellie cackles in character, but she's laughing as she wipes dog slobber from her cheek. "Even Toto has fallen for my charms!"

"I'm so sorry," Emily stammers, but Ellie waves her off.

"Sweetie, I work in the character department. I've had worse." She scratches behind Mochi's ears. "Besides, how can I stay in character when this fluffball exists?"

We emerge from the meet-and-greet area with approximately seven hundred photos and head toward the gift shop.

"Mochi needs his own Toto," Emily declares.

The shop carries everything Wonderful—silver slippers, emerald jewelry, tin man oil cans, and an entire wall of plush toys. Emily selects a stuffed Toto that's almost as big as the real Mochi, who immediately claims it as his favorite thing by carrying it in his mouth.

"Now he matches you." I kiss Emily's temple. "Everyone in this family has their costume."

"Velocity Underground next!" Marcus consults the park map. "It's a roller coaster based on fast cars and street racing. They've got a handicap transfer system."

The roller coaster screams past us, all neon lights and roaring engines designed to look like an underground racing scene. Emily transfers into the seat while I secure Mochi in one of the climate-controlled crates they keep at every major attraction.

"He gets treats and water while we're gone," the attendant assures me. "And we play music so they don't hear the ride noise."

The coaster launches us into darkness—sharp turns, sudden drops, projection screens showing city streets blurring past. Emily screams with delight beside me, her crown somehow staying perfectly in place. Marcus and Michelle whoop from the row behind us, while Dad actually allows himself to smile during the finale where we "cross the finish line."

"Again!" Emily demands when we exit.

"Bathroom first, water break, then Operator stunt show." I'm not letting her skip her scheduled intervals, even on her birthday.

Michelle insists on accompanying her to the restroom while I make sure Mochi gets walked properly. By the time we reconvene, Emily's downed an entire bottle of water and received birthday wishes from approximately fifteen different Starlight employees.

"Does everyone here know?" she whispers.

"You're Dorothy visiting on her birthday. They probably sent a memo."

The Operator show lives up to Michelle's enthusiasm—practical stunts, real fight choreography, a finale where the hero jumps a motorcycle over a moving car. Emily grips my hand through the whole thing, gasping at every near miss.

Temporal Flux proves gentler, a motion simulator where we travel through film history in a vintage movie projector time machine. Levi narrates every reference, delighted when the ride passes through a French New Wave segment.

"Horror area," Jean announces after we've conquered half the park. "Ariana's been patient long enough."

"Yes!" Ariana pumps her fist. "Classic Horror is calling my name."

Emily's eyes light up. "They have Frankenstein here?"

"They have everything." I push her chair toward the Gothic archway marking the horror section. "Classic literature monsters, modern psychological thrillers, the whole range."

The area transforms into perpetual twilight—gas lamps flicker along cobblestone paths, fog machines create atmosphere, and actors in full monster makeup roam between attractions. A Frankenstein's monster lumbers past, followed by his Bride in full white gown and lightning-struck hair.

"Oh my God." Emily practically levitates from her wheelchair. "They did Mrs. Frankenstein! Mrs. Frankenstein from the novel but Victor didn't destroy her!"

The character catches Emily's enthusiasm and poses for photos, her makeup aged and weathered just like Mary Shelley described. Emily explains the literary differences to anyone who'll listen, and I fall a little more in love watching her geek out over horror classics.

"House of Horrors?" Ariana points to a walkthrough attraction.

"It's got stairs," I check the accessibility guide. "But they have an alternate route with ramps and an elevator."

"Or," Emily suggests, "you could carry me."

"Done." I scoop her into my arms before she finishes the sentence. Mochi gets secured in another crate with his stuffed Toto, and we enter the darkness.

The house winds through classic horror scenes—Dracula's castle, the Werewolf's forest, Dr. Jekyll's laboratory. Emily buries her face in my neck during the jump scares but laughs afterward, demanding to know how they achieved each effect. Her crown stays miraculously perfect through everything.

By the time we emerge, the sun's starting to set, painting Starlight Studios in gold and purple light.

"Dinner?" Mum suggests. "Then evening shows?"

Emily yawns against my shoulder—I'm still carrying her, unwilling to put her down. "Can we do the Phantom ride first? Before I'm too tired?"

The Phantom's Opera House rises before us, all Gothic architecture and gas lamps. Inside, boats wait to carry us through the sewers beneath the Paris Opera House, complete with a recreation of the title song and the chandelier crash.

I settle Emily into the boat, Mochi between us with his Toto clutched in his mouth. As we drift through the Phantom's lair, Emily leans against my shoulder.

"Best birthday ever," she whispers.

"Just wait, *deshtari*." I kiss her crown. "The night's not over yet."

The mini Wonderful stage sits tucked behind the Emerald City courtyard, intimate enough that every seat feels close to the action. A crowd has already gathered—families with kids wearing ruby slippers, teenagers in

Quadling warrior gear, adults clutching commemorative programs.

"Front row reserved seating," the usher checks our names. "Right this way, Mrs. Lambert."

Emily's entire face glows at being called that, even if it's only Winkie-official. I keep her cradled in my arms as we navigate to our seats, refusing to put her down. Mochi trots beside us, stuffed Toto still clamped in his jaws.

The usher helps me settle Emily into the accessible seating area, but I pull her onto my lap instead. She fits perfectly there, crown brushing my chin.

"Comfortable?" I murmur against her hair.

"Always, with you."

The lights dim. Michelle's phone comes out—subtle, angled like she's just checking messages, but I catch the red recording dot. Jean notices too, raising an eyebrow. I shake my head slightly. *Let her.*

The stage explodes into color.

They've condensed everything beautifully—Felix waking as the scarecrow, straw-stuffed and confused, singing about his lost humanity. Glinda appears in crimson robes, working for the Wizard before her redemption, and the actress playing her captures that edge of cruelty beneath beauty.

Dorothy tumbles into Oz via farmhouse. Emily leans forward, completely absorbed as Dorothy meets Ellie for the first time.

"The blocking," Emily whispers. "They're using the film blocking from the test footage we haven't even finished shooting yet."

"Mr. Kellerman has access to everything."

The show rushes through the journey—meeting the Tin Man, the Lion, discovering the Wizard's deception. Then Ellie and Glinda face each other center stage, and the entire theater goes silent.

Emily's breath catches. I feel her hands grip mine as the actresses pour everything into their reconciliation, years of hurt and love tangled together. By the time they reach the final chorus, Emily's crying against my shoulder.

"That's us," she chokes out. "That's what you did for me."

"No, *deshtari*. That's what you did for me."

The show races toward its climax—Felix transforming back to human, the group rallying to save Oz, Dorothy and Felix crowned as the new rulers. The coronation scene unfolds with golden light and sweeping music.

Then the actor playing Felix breaks character, just slightly.

"We have a very special guest in the audience tonight." He shields his eyes from the stage lights. "Dorothy herself, on her birthday."

Spotlights swing to Emily. She freezes in my lap.

"Would you join us on stage? We'd love to crown the real Dorothy."

"I can't—" Emily starts, but Ariana's already bringing her wheelchair closer.

"You can," I whisper. "I'll be right there with you."

I lift her from my lap, settling her into the chair as the audience applauds. Mochi follows us up the accessible ramp, Toto still in his mouth, and suddenly we're center stage under the lights.

This is it.

I drop to one knee.

Emily's hands fly to her mouth. The audience gasps.

"Emily Dorothy Silver." My accent thickens, British bleeding through. "We've been dating eleven months. We've been Winkie married since June ninth, when you accepted my chase at a Metro station and sang your vows back to me."

Her eyes are already streaming tears.

"But I want more than Winkie tradition. I want everything—American marriage, Angoumois marriage, every kind of binding that exists." I pull out the box from my pocket, opening it to reveal the rose gold and emerald ring. "I want to wake up with you every morning for the rest of my life. I want to build our house with ramps and parallel bars and a studio for your designs. I want babies who have your eyes and your creativity. I want to be your Felix, your Nathan, your Erik—whatever you need, whenever you need it."

Mochi drops his Toto and sits perfectly at Emily's side, like he's been trained for this exact moment.

"In Winkie tradition, *Ke deshtari, ke zhitari, ke arini*—you are my heart, my breath, my everything." I slip into the old language, letting it carry the weight of what I feel. "*Wi'ana ke sharari fe'animi*—will you share my name?"

"Yes." Emily's sobbing now, nodding so hard her crown almost falls. "Yes, yes, *zhitari*, yes!"

I slide the ring onto her finger—perfect fit, Madame Laurent knew her craft—and pull Emily from her wheelchair into my arms. The kiss tastes like tears and sugar from breakfast, like eleven months of falling and a lifetime of staying.

The audience erupts. Michelle's definitely filming. Mochi barks once, sharp and celebratory.

And Emily Lambert—my wife, my Dorothy, my *deshtari*—smiles against my mouth like coming home.

The applause crashes over us like a wave. I'm still kissing Emily when Marcus appears beside her wheelchair, reaching for her with tears streaming down his face.

"My baby sister's getting married!" He scoops Emily right out of my arms, spinning her in circles while her crown tilts precariously. "For real this time!"

"Marcus!" Emily's laughing and crying simultaneously. "Put me down before I throw up on your Quadling warrior costume!"

"Worth it." But he settles her back into her chair, kissing both her cheeks. "I'm so happy for you, Em."

Ariana's phone stays trained on us, capturing everything. She's not even trying to be subtle anymore—full vertical video, probably live-streaming to Instagram.

"The proposal of the century," Ariana narrates into her phone. "Emily Lambert said yes, everyone. Our girl's getting properly married."

Mochi trots over with his stuffed Toto, dropping it directly on my feet. He sits, tail wagging, staring up at me with those adoring labradoodle eyes.

"For me?" I pick up the plush toy. "Are you welcoming me to the family, buddy?"

Mochi barks once, then licks Emily's hand before returning to sit between us. My throat tightens. Even the dog knows we're permanent now.

The actress playing Dorothy clears her throat gently. "We have one more request, if the newly engaged couple is willing?"

Emily's still staring at her ring, turning her hand to catch the stage lights on the emerald.

"Would you sing with us?" Felix-the-actor gestures to the small orchestra pit. "We'd love to hear the real Dorothy and Felix perform their duet."

Emily's head snaps up, panic flooding her features. "I—I can't. I've only done special needs theater. In Draper. Small crowds, people who know me—"

"You auditioned for Mr. Kellerman himself." I kneel beside her chair. "You've got the lead role in a major motion picture."

"That's different. That's filming, takes, editing—" Her breathing quickens. "This is live. All these people watching in real time. What if I forget the words? What if my voice cracks? What if—"

"*Deshtari.*" I take both her hands. "You sang Winkie vows to me through a Metro train window with hundreds of commuters watching. You performed your valedictorian speech standing when everyone expected you to stay seated. You just got engaged on a theme park stage in front of strangers."

"That's different too." But her panic's easing, I can see it.

Michelle appears on Emily's other side. "You know every word to every song in *Wonderful*. I've heard you sing them in the shower, while cooking, doing laundry—"

"Even during physical therapy," Ariana adds from behind her phone. "You sang through the parallel bar exercises last week."

Emily looks at me, emerald eyes wet. "What if I mess up?"

"Then we mess up together." I stand, offering my hand. "Just you and me, *deshtari*. Everyone else disappears."

She takes my hand.

The audience settles as I lift Emily from her wheelchair, cradling her against my chest. The orchestra begins—soft strings, building toward the melody. I recognize it immediately. Our song. The one we'll dance to at our wedding.

Emily's voice starts quiet, almost whispered against my shoulder as she sings about moments lasting, about crossing borders and losing resistance. But with each line, she grows stronger. Her hand finds my chest, fingers spreading over my heart.

I pick up Felix's verse, letting my accent wrap around the words. The British lilt Michelle always teases me about bleeds through—it always does when I'm feeling everything too much.

Our voices blend on the chorus. Emily's vibrato wavers on the high notes, not from fear but from emotion. I hold her tighter, swaying slightly like we're already at our wedding reception.

The theater has gone completely silent except for our voices and the orchestra. Even Mochi sits statue-still, watching his humans sing.

When we reach the final verse Emily cups my face with both hands. The emerald on her finger catches stage light, throwing green sparkles across my jaw.

The last note fades. For three heartbeats, nothing.

Then the theater explodes.

Standing ovation. Michelle's sobbing openly in Jean's arms. Marcus has his phone out now too, filming alongside Ariana. Dad's actually smiling—a real smile, not his politician mask.

And Emily Lambert, my fiancée, my wife-to-be, my *deshtari*, buries her face in my neck and whispers, "Best birthday ever."

We claim a spot directly in front of the Emerald Palace, Emily's wheelchair positioned for optimal viewing. The spires gleam green against the darkening sky, promising the fireworks spectacular in twenty minutes.

Jean pulls out his phone first. "Oh bloody hell."

"What?" Michelle leans over his shoulder, then grabs her own mobile. "We've gone viral. Again."

I settle on the ground beside Emily's chair, Mochi immediately claiming my lap. "How bad?"

"Define bad." Levi scrolls through his feed. "Michelle's post from the proposal has two million views already."

Marcus whistles low. "Ariana's livestream hit three million before she even ended it."

Emily's hand finds my shoulder, squeezing. I reach up, lacing our fingers together—the emerald ring pressing against my palm.

"Starlight Studios posted it on their official account," Michelle reports. "Caption says 'Real-life fairytale at Wonderful World.' Twenty thousand comments in an hour."

"Let me see the damage." I hold out my hand for Jean's phone.

The Instagram grid loads. Michelle's posted a carousel —the proposal moment, me on one knee, Emily's face radiating shock and joy, the ring reveal, our kiss, the family celebration. Professional shots, perfectly filtered. Very Michelle.

I switch to comments.

@WonderlandDaily: THE WAY HE LOOKED AT HER IM CRYING

@EmilySilverDaily: she said yes she said YES SHE SAID YES

@LambertWatch: Eleven months. That's it. Eleven months and he's proposing?

@FilmCritique: Career suicide. Wonderful hasn't even started filming.

I scroll faster.

@GabrielleFan2024: Poor Gabrielle. She dodged a bullet with this commitment-phobe.

@AccessibilityAdvocate: A wheelchair user as Dorothy AND Mrs. Lambert? Representation matters!

@ArtemisBlade: bet she's pregnant. only reason men like him marry down.

Emily's fingers tighten on my shoulder. She's reading over me.

"Don't." I close the app, switching to my professional account instead. "They don't know us."

My grid shows Ariana's repost—the singing video. The duet. Emily's voice cracking with emotion on the high notes, my accent bleeding through every word.

The Wonderful cast has invaded the comments section.

@ZaraWashingtonOfficial: I TOLD YALL SOMETHING WAS HAPPENING. Called it last week during table reads!

@SophiaActress: Crying actual tears. This is the most beautiful thing I've ever witnessed.

@MichaelWashingtonActor: Welcome to the family officially, Emily! Can't wait to work with my new sister.

@DanteRiveraOfficial: Felix and Dorothy getting their happy ending before we even film it. Meta.

My phone buzzes. Text from Zara.

Zara: Congratulations!! But we need to talk about what you're planning for the honeymoon because if you break her heart before filming I will END you

I laugh, showing Emily the message.

"She's protective." Emily's voice wobbles. "They all are."

"You're family now." I kiss her hand, the one wearing my ring. "To the Lamberts, to the Wonderful cast, to everyone who matters."

Jean's phone rings. He glances at the screen, grimaces. "Dad's campaign manager. Give me a moment."

He steps away. Levi follows, hand on Jean's lower back.

Michelle slides down to sit beside me. "The political accounts are having a field day. Dad's rivals are calling this a publicity stunt."

"Of course they are."

"But Dad's approval ratings jumped six points in the last hour." She shows me her phone—a news alert. *Lambert Family Values: Pierre's Son Proposes at Theme Park.*

Marcus appears with Dad, both men studying a tablet. "The Associated Press picked it up. So did Reuters. BBC's running it as a human interest piece."

"Angoumois Today posted an editorial," Dad says, his tone measured. "Positive spin. 'Modern Romance Meets Traditional Values.' They're calling Emily the 'American Dream' embodied."

Grandmère settles on a nearby bench, Mum beside her. "Let them talk. A Lambert in love is always newsworthy."

The fireworks countdown begins overhead—five minutes.

My phone explodes with notifications. The cast group chat:

Daniel: Did you really ask permission first?

Tristian: Yes. Month ago in New York.

Braden: Most romantic thing I've ever heard

Carlos: When's the wedding? We're invited right?

Zara: He better invite us. Emily's OUR Dorothy.

Sophia: I'm already designing my outfit

Emily leans down, reading over my shoulder. "They really consider me family."

"You are." I stand, turning to face her. The Emerald Palace glows behind us, the first firework launching into the sky with a boom. "Being a Lambert means the entire world has an opinion about your breakfast choices. Media dissects every decision. Political rivals weaponize your happiness."

Another firework—emerald green sparks cascading.

"But it also means you're never alone. Michelle will fly across oceans when you're hurting. Jean will restructure his schedule around your needs. Marcus will pray over every fear. Ariana will fight anyone who looks at you wrong."

Red and gold bursts overhead.

"And me?" I cup her face. "I'll spend every day proving you made the right choice."

Emily pulls me down, kissing me as the sky explodes in color. Mochi barks approval.

"Worth it," she whispers against my lips. "Every comment, every headline, every camera—worth it."

Day two at Starlight Studios Paris, and Emily's wearing cargo shorts with raptor claw marks across the thighs—her own design—and a tank top that reads *"Specimen 47's Assistant"* in distressed lettering. Mochi sports a velociraptor harness complete with a tail attachment that swishes when he walks.

I've gone full Dr. Nathan Cross. Khaki field pants, torn at the knee. Sweat-stained tank top. Dirt smudges Michelle helped me apply this morning. The leather cuff from the film wrapped around my wrist.

"You look ridiculous," Emily says, but she's grinning.

"You look like you're about to get claimed by a half-raptor paleontologist." I adjust the backpack on her wheelchair. Heavier than yesterday—mine too. I've packed the prosthetic claws and fangs from filming. Tonight, in the cave suite, I'll give Emily the proper raptor claiming she deserves.

The thought makes my accent slip thicker. "Darlin', you have *no* idea what you're in for."

Her cheeks flush. Perfect.

Prehistoric Paradise sprawls before us—towering faux cliffs, jungle vegetation, the distant roar of animatronic dinosaurs. The Raptor Research Center dominates the landscape, all glass and steel designed to look hastily constructed.

"Meet-and-greet with Dr. Cross is at ten," Emily checks her phone. "We're early."

"Good." I kiss her temple. "Gives us time to ride Extinction."

The coaster's already visible—tracks weaving through prehistoric ruins. Emily's eyes light up.

The line for the Dr. Nathan Cross & Maya Reyes Character Experience wraps around the Research Center. Kids in dinosaur costumes. Adults wearing Extinction Protocol merch. A teenage girl spots us, gasps, and immediately starts recording.

"They're Starbounding!" she squeals to her friends.

The cast member managing the queue recognizes me, does a double-take at Emily's ring, and discreetly escorts us through the accessible entrance.

The Research Center's interior recreates the lab from *Extinction Protocol: Rebirth*. Terrariums with moving baby raptors. Computer screens displaying DNA sequences. And in the center, behind a glass partition—

Dr. Nathan Cross leans against a desk, prosthetic claws tapping against metal. The actor playing him—Marcus didn't mention his name, but he's committed—has the posture perfect. Shoulders rolled forward, predatory stillness. Maya Reyes stands beside him, tablet in hand, while a baby Utahraptor puppet chirps from its perch.

The glass slides open. Nathan's head tilts, nostrils flaring.

"Well." My accent bleeds through completely. Alabama drawl thick enough to cut. "Look who wandered into my territory."

Emily laughs, delighted.

The Nathan actor breaks character for half a second, eyes widening as recognition hits. Then he's back, moving with that distinctive raptor gait I spent months perfecting.

"Dr. Lambert." He circles Emily's wheelchair. "Heard you've been studyin' my methods."

"Learned from the best."

Nathan crouches beside Emily, claws retracting slightly. The Maya actress kneels too, both of them examining Emily's outfit with exaggerated interest.

"Custom adaptive wear," Maya observes. "With raptor damage patterns. Clever."

"She's brilliant." I rest my hand on Emily's shoulder, possessive. Nathan's eyes track the movement—approving.

Mochi barks. The baby Utahraptor puppet responds, chirping excitedly.

"Nibbler likes you," Nathan says, scooping up the puppet and offering it to Emily. She accepts it, cradling the animatronic carefully. It nuzzles her neck, purring.

"Can we—" Emily's voice catches. "Pictures? And would you sign our outfits?"

Both characters pull her into a tight embrace—careful of her body, but firm. Claiming her as pack. I snap photos with my phone while Mochi jumps up, licking both actors' faces enthusiastically.

The photographer captures everything. Nathan signing Emily's tank top right across "Assistant." Maya autographing the raptor claw marks on her shorts. Both of them posing with us, Nibbler perched on Emily's lap, Mochi's tongue hanging out mid-lick.

"Cave suite tonight?" Nathan asks, low enough only we hear. He grins, fangs visible. "Gonna claim her proper?"

I tap against Emily's chair. "Every inch."

The Cave Suite sits at the base of Prehistoric Paradise's largest cliff formation. Ariana collects Mochi's leash, shooting me a knowing smirk.

"Remember—she's got physical therapy Monday morning." She scratches behind Mochi's ears. "Don't break your fiancée before filming starts."

"I would never—"

"You absolutely will try." Ariana wheels away with Mochi trotting beside her. "Have fun, you absolute nerds!"

The suite's entrance mimics a cave mouth, complete with dripping stalactites. Inside, the stone walls transition to smooth surfaces embedded with bioluminescent lighting —the same blue-green glow from the underground sequences in *Rebirth*. A massive bed dominates the space, furs draped across it like Nathan's nest in the films.

Emily's already disappeared into the bathroom with the stylist Starlight arranged. I hear water running, quiet conversation.

"Mr. Lambert?" The makeup artist—Colette, according to her name tag—gestures toward the vanity. "Ready for transformation?"

I've been ready since I was seven years old, watching the original *Extinction Protocol* on VHS. Dad thought it inappropriate. Mum smuggled it to me anyway. I must've rewatched it fifty times that summer, memorizing every scene. The horror of losing humanity. The beauty of embracing what you'd become.

The franchise owned me before the Lambert curse even struck.

Colette works methodically. Prosthetic claws first— longer than my fingers, curved and wicked. The adhesive warms against my nail beds. She fits the fangs next, custom-molded to my teeth. Not the full transformation— just enough to show Nathan mid-shift. Accepting both sides.

Foundation darkens around my eyes. Shadows along my cheekbones. She adds subtle scales across my temples, down my neck.

"You filmed these scenes for real." Colette blends the edges. "Most authentic I've seen."

"Spent six months getting the physicality right." I flex my clawed fingers, muscle memory kicking in. The slight forward hunch. Weight balanced on the balls of my feet. "Studied raptor movement patterns. Worked with paleontologists."

"It shows." She steps back, admiring her work. "Emily's a lucky woman."

The bathroom door opens.

Emily emerges in black lace—a corset that showcases the emerald at her navel, matching briefs that sit high on her hips. Her makeup artist has transformed her eyes into smoky shadows, lips painted that perfect poppy red. She's kept her hair loose, blonde waves cascading over bare shoulders.

The tattoo of my initial sits just below her collarbone. My claim.

"Darlin'." The word comes out half-growl. I rise from the vanity, moving with Nathan's predatory grace. "You look good enough to *devour*."

Emily's breath catches. Her pupils dilate.

I circle her wheelchair slowly. Claws tapping against metal. "Been dreamin' about this since I was seven. Before Nathan existed in my head. Before the Lambert curse made me yours." I crouch beside her, fangs visible when I grin.

"Wanted to claim someone like this. Make them *mine* in every way that matters."

"Tristian—"

"You gave me the Winkie wedding night. Sweet. Tender. *Ours*." I trace one claw along her jaw, careful not to scratch. "Now I take what I need. Show you what happens when the raptor stops fightin' and just *accepts*."

Her hand cups my face, thumb brushing the prosthetic scales. "Then take it, Nathan."

The stylists slip out, leaving us alone in the cave's bioluminescent glow.

I freeze mid-claim, claw still hovering near Emily's jaw, as the door nudges open. A familiar chirp echoes through the cave suite.

Nibbler waddles across the threshold, baby Utahraptor puppet moving with startling realism. His head tilts, optical sensors tracking movement as he approaches. Another chirp—higher pitched this time. Questioning.

"No." I rock back on my heels, accent slipping toward genuine disbelief. "No, how did—"

The animatronic chirps again, nuzzling against my leg. His mechanical purr vibrates through the cave suite.

Emily covers her mouth, shoulders shaking with laughter. "Oh my god. He thinks you're actually Nathan."

"Apparently." I crouch lower, examining Nibbler's construction. The joints move seamlessly, scales catching bioluminescent light. "Starlight's engineering team outdid themselves. Motion sensors probably keyed to raptor movement patterns." I tap my claws together. "Which I've been mimicking perfectly."

Nibbler responds to the sound, chirping excitedly. He bumps his snout against my hand, then Emily's knee, then waddles in a circle between us.

"There must be a nursery room for families." Emily reaches down, stroking Nibbler's head ridges. He leans into her touch, purring louder. "They keep him there when they don't need him during meet-and-greets. Part of the kids' amenities, maybe?"

"Cave suites are family-oriented." I scan the space, noticing details I'd missed before. A smaller alcove off the main chamber. Child-sized robes hanging beside the adult ones. "Prehistoric Paradise markets to everyone. Kids get baby raptor companions. Parents get—" I gesture at myself, fangs and claws on full display. "—immersive fantasy fulfillment."

Nibbler chirps again, more insistent. He nudges Emily's wheelchair toward the alcove.

Emily meets my eyes, grinning. "What do you say, Dr. Cross? Let's put our son to bed."

The absurdity hits me sideways. Here I am, full Nathan transformation, prosthetics perfect, ready to claim my fiancée with every ounce of raptor intensity I've spent years perfecting—

And our animatronic offspring needs tucking in.

"Alright." I scoop Nibbler up, his servos adjusting to my grip. "C'mon, little man. Past your bedtime."

The alcove opens into a miniature version of Nathan's research nest. Soft vegetation. Heat lamps casting warm orange light. A charging station disguised as a rocky outcropping. Nibbler's eyes dim slightly as I set him on the pad, his systems recognizing home base.

"Night, Nibs." Emily touches his snout gently. The animatronic's purr softens, settling into sleep mode.

I back out of the alcove, pulling the curtain closed. The cave suite falls quiet again, just bioluminescent glow and Emily waiting in black lace.

"Now then." I prowl toward her, claws tapping rhythm against stone. "Where were we?"

"You were about to claim me." Emily's voice drops, teasing. "Before our son interrupted."

I lean over her wheelchair, fangs catching light. "C'mon, darlin'." The accent bleeds thick, possessive. Pure Nathan. "Let's give Nibs some siblings."

Emily's laugh turns breathless as I lift her from the chair, carrying her toward the fur-draped bed. Her arms loop around my neck, fingers tracing the prosthetic scales.

"You're ridiculous," she whispers against my mouth.

"You're mine." I lay her across the furs, claws framing her face. "Every version of me—Lambert, Nathan, Felix, all of them—completely yours."

I crawl onto the bed, stalking Emily like prey. Her breath hitches, emerald eyes wide beneath the cave's glow. She's seen me like this—raptor posture, scales on my face, fangs bared—but never so close, never poised to claim her completely.

"Tristian—"

"Nathan," I correct, accent dripping with Alabama heat. "Tonight, I'm him. You're Maya. And I'm claimin' what's mine."

Her lips part, inviting. I dip down, capturing her mouth with a growl. Fangs click against her teeth, careful not to cut. She tastes sweet, familiar, *mine*.

I break away, trailing kisses along her jaw, down her throat. Her pulse flutters under my lips, heartbeat quickening. My claws trace the tattoo of my initial, circling it, claiming it.

"Been waitin' for this," I murmur against her skin. "Waitin' to take you proper. Make you understand what you do to me."

Emily arches into my touch, hands grasping at my shoulders. I move lower, nuzzling the swell of her breasts above the corset. Black lace contrasts against her fair skin, emerald glinting at her navel.

My tongue dips into the hollow of her throat, tasting her sweat. Salt and sweetness, all Emily. I nip gently, teeth grazing her collarbone. She gasps, fingers tightening in my hair.

"Gonna mark you," I rasp. "Gonna leave my claim where everyone can see."

Her legs shift restlessly beneath me. I settle between them, claws digging into the furs for control. The scent of her—warm, aroused, *ready*—fills my senses.

I kiss the valley between her breasts, then lower, trailing my mouth over the corset's laces. Each one tugs free under my fangs, loosening the garment until it falls away entirely.

Emily's bare before me, skin flushed pink, nipples hardened to peaks. I lavish attention on each one, sucking, biting gently, circling with my tongue. She writhes under me, breath coming faster.

"Tristian—Nathan—please—"

"Please what, darlin'?" I lift my head, grinning wickedly. "Tell me what you need."

Her cheeks flush darker. "Touch me."

I chuckle, low and hungry. "Where?"

She guides my hand down, pressing it against the heat between her thighs. "Here."

My claws retract slightly, just enough to stroke her through the lace. She's wet, ready, hips lifting to meet my touch. I tease her, slow circles, building pressure.

"Like that?" I ask, knowing the answer.

"Yes—" Her head falls back, eyes closed. "More."

I hook one claw under the waistband of her briefs, tugging them down. She kicks them off, baring herself fully. The scent of her arousal intensifies, driving me wild.

I dip my head, tasting her. Sweet, musky, *Emily*. My tongue delves deeper, exploring every fold, every sensitive spot. Her moans fill the cave, echoing off stone walls.

Her thighs tremble around me. I grip them, steadying her, claws digging into soft flesh. Not hard enough to break skin—just enough to leave marks, reminders of tonight. Of us.

Emily's hands fist in my hair, holding me against her. I feast on her, relentless, until she's crying out, back bowed, coming undone beneath my mouth.

As her tremors subside, I prowl up her body, licking my lips. Her taste lingers, sweet and intoxicating. I capture her mouth again, sharing it with her.

She reaches between us, fumbling with my belt. I bat her hands away, doing it myself. Pants kicked aside, I settle back between her thighs, bare skin against bare skin.

My cock presses against her entrance, hard and aching. I pause there, poised, meeting her gaze.

"Ready, darlin'?"

She nods, breathless. "Yes."

I thrust into her, slow and deep. Her body yields around me, slick and tight. Perfect.

Her legs wrap around my waist, pulling me closer. I brace myself on my forearms, claws sinking into furs. Our bodies move together, rhythm building.

I kiss her shoulder, open-mouthed, then bite down. Gentle, but firm. Marking her. Claiming her.

Emily gasps, nails digging into my back. "Nathan—"

"Mine," I growl against her skin. "All mine."

I thrust harder, faster. Our breaths mingle, ragged and desperate. Sweat slicks our bodies, heat building.

Her inner muscles clench around me, pulsing. Close. So close.

I shift, lifting one of her legs over my shoulder. The angle lets me sink deeper, hit that spot inside her that makes her cry out.

"Give me a clutch, Maya," I rasp, accent thick with need. "Give me babies. Give me *everything*."

Her eyes widen, glazed with pleasure. "Yes—Nathan— yes—"

I feel her peak approaching, see it in the flush of her cheeks, the tremble of her limbs. I chase it, driving into her relentlessly.

Her orgasm hits, fierce and sudden. She screams, convulsing around me. I follow her over the edge, roaring my release, filling her completely.

We collapse together, panting, sweat-slicked. I roll onto my side, gathering her against me. Our hearts pound in sync, slowing gradually.

I trace patterns on her thigh, claws leaving faint red lines. Marks of possession. Of love.

"Mine," I murmur, pressing a kiss to her temple.

She smiles, content. "Yours."

In the alcove, Nibbler chirps softly, settling into sleep mode. Our son, nestled safe in his cave. Our future, bright and full of promise.

I hold Emily tighter, protective, possessive. Tonight, I claimed her fully. Tomorrow, we start our forever. Together.

Morning light filters through the cave entrance, golden and warm. I'm adjusting my cravat in the mirror— Phantom-perfect burgundy against crisp white—when Nibbler waddles over, chirping plaintively.

The little animatronic raptor nudges my ankle with his snout, then Emily's wheelchair. Back to mine. His tail droops.

"Oh, Nibs." Emily sets down her lipstick, the one that matches her Christine gown. She reaches down, stroking his scaled head. "We'll be back."

Nibbler whines, a mechanical keen that sounds heartbreakingly real. He paws at my boot, amber eyes— projection or genuine AI?—blinking up at me.

I crouch, running my fingers along his spine. "We'll bring big brother Mochi tonight. Deal?"

"Tristian!"

"What?" I grin up at her, unrepentant. "I'll tell David Kellerman we're staying in the cave tonight instead of going back to our hotel. He did say it's ours whenever we want."

Emily's blush spreads from her cheeks down her throat. "Careful or David will let us keep him."

"Would that be so terrible?" I glance at Nibbler, who's now sitting expectantly, tail thumping against stone. "He's already claimed us. Look at him."

"We can't adopt an animatronic dinosaur."

"Why not? We adopted a seventy-pound labradoodle." I stand, checking my phantom mask pin—no actual mask today, just the silver symbol at my lapel. "Nibbler's smaller. Quieter."

"Mochi doesn't require an engineering team for maintenance."

"David would provide that." I wheel her toward the alcove where Nibbler sleeps. "Think about it. Our son needs us."

"Our *animatronic* son."

I tuck a curl behind her ear, letting my fingers trail down her neck. "You're thinking about it though."

She swats my hand away, laughing. "You're impossible."

Nibbler follows us to the door, chirping hopefully. I kneel again, scratching under his jaw. "Tonight, little one. I promise."

He settles onto his haunches, accepting this.

"See?" I stand, gripping Emily's wheelchair handles. "He trusts me."

"He's programmed to respond to verbal cues."

"He knows his father when he hears him."

Emily covers her face. "We've been parents for twelve hours and you're already insufferable."

I lean down, kissing her temple. "Wait until I convince David to let us take him home to California."

The Phantom's Mirror maze stretches before us, all silver glass and Gothic architecture. Emily adjusts Mochi's naval coat—Ariana spent an hour getting every brass button perfect on his Raoul costume—while I check my reflection one last time. No mask today, just the silver pin at my collar.

"Ready, mon cœur?" I grip her wheelchair handles.

"Always."

Inside, fog swirls around our ankles. Organ music echoes through the passages. We round a corner and there she stands—Christine Daaé in her white gown, training for a performance that isn't happening.

The actress playing her gasps. "Tristian Lambert?"

"Guilty." I extend my hand. "And my fiancée, Emily Silver."

"Oh my God." Christine's eyes widen. "You're the Dorothy everyone's talking about. The proposal video made me cry."

Emily ducks her head, grinning. "Thank you."

"And Mochi!" Christine crouches, letting the labradoodle sniff her hand. "Perfect Raoul. Can I?"

"He'd love it."

Christine scratches behind Mochi's ears while a figure emerges from the shadows—Erik in full costume, mask gleaming white against black. The actor's voice drops into character. "Another hopeful suitor for my Christine?"

Mochi barks once, tail wagging.

"I think he's claiming her." I laugh. "Though his loyalties lie with Dorothy here."

Erik sweeps into a bow before Emily. "The pleasure is mine, Mademoiselle Silver. Your audition... haunting."

Emily's cheeks flush. "You saw that?"

"The entire cast did. Richard shared it." Christine stands, smoothing her skirts. "We've been betting on whether Tristian could keep up with you vocally."

"She makes me better." I rest my hand on Emily's shoulder. "Always has."

Erik nods approvingly. "As it should be. Will you sing at the wedding?"

"Already planning it." Emily grins up at me. "He doesn't know yet."

"I'm learning my bride has secrets."

"Only good ones."

We take photos—Mochi between Christine and Erik, Emily and I recreating the boat scene pose, all of us together with the chandelier backdrop. Christine slips Emily her personal number before we leave.

"For when you need someone who understands what it's like being cast opposite a Lambert," she whispers loud enough for me to hear.

The Emerald Palace Restaurant gleams like its namesake, all green crystal and gold filigree. Dad stands as we approach, actually smiling.

"There's my future daughter." He kisses Emily's cheeks. "And my son who apparently adopts animatronic children without consulting anyone."

I freeze. "How did you—"

"David called." Mum laughs from her seat. "Something about engineering logistics for transporting Nibbler to Los Angeles?"

"Tristian!" Emily swats my arm.

"I may have sent one text." I pull out her chair—specially positioned at the table's head beside mine. "David was very understanding."

Michelle grins. "You have a dinosaur son now. This family gets weirder every year."

"Says the woman who married a Quadling warrior." Marcus gestures at his own outfit.

Jean leans forward, Tin Man makeup still perfect. "Does this mean Nibbler gets a trust fund?"

"Obviously." I settle into my seat. "He's a Lambert now."

Grandmère taps her wine glass. "I want to meet my great-grandson before we leave Paris."

"He's animatronic, Grandmère."

"Family is family, mon petit." She winks at Emily. "Isn't that right, ma chérie?"

Emily's laughing so hard Mochi noses her hand, checking. "This family is absolutely insane."

"You married into it," Ariana points out.

"Technically not yet," Jean corrects.

Dad raises his glass. "Then we'd better plan a wedding. I'm thinking spring. Grantham Bridge Cathedral."

I grip Emily's hand under the table. "Actually, we were thinking smaller. Just us."

"Nonsense." Mum's already pulling out her phone. "The entire country will want to celebrate."

Emily catches my eye, mouthing *help*.

I kiss her knuckles. "We'll discuss it. Together."

"After dessert," Grandmère declares. "I ordered the entire emerald cake menu."

Mochi barks his approval.

Jean's phone buzzes against the table. Once. Twice. Six times in rapid succession.

"Bloody hell." His accent sharpens—rare for Jean, who keeps his French pristine even when furious. He scrolls, face draining of color. "Dad."

Pierre sets down his fork. "What is it?"

"Hollywood Hype just published." Jean's jaw clenches. "Emily's complete medical history. Foster care records. Everything."

The table goes silent.

Emily's hand trembles in mine. "What?"

Jean passes his phone to Dad, then pulls up more tabs. "The Daily Gossip has it too. Star Tracker. Celebrity Whispers. Someone leaked sealed documents."

My accent fractures, British edges cutting through. "Show me."

The headline screams across Hollywood Hype's homepage: **LAMBERT'S LAME CINDERELLA: Inside Emily Silver's Disability, Abuse, and Desperate Climb to Stardom**.

White noise fills my ears.

They've published everything. Her schizencephaly diagnosis. Surgical history. Martha's abuse reports—the closet, the cigarette burns, foster placements. Her group home psychiatric evaluations after nightmares. Diverticulitis. Kidney stones. Every private medical detail laid bare for entertainment.

"Those absolute bastards." My voice drops to ice. "Every single one of them."

Emily's breathing quickens. Mochi immediately presses against her leg, whining.

"Breathe, mon cœur." I cup her face, forcing her to look at me instead of Jean's phone. "In through your nose. Out through your mouth. With me."

Michelle's already scrolling her own device. "It gets worse. Celebrity Insider is calling her a 'sympathy casting' for Dorothy. Star Watch says you only proposed because Dad's campaign needed positive press."

"Enough." Pierre's voice cuts sharp. He stands, buttoning his jacket. "Jean, contact our legal team. I want every publication named in a lawsuit by morning."

"Dad—"

"Now." Pierre's face hardens into the expression that wins elections. "And draft a statement. We'll give it when we return to Grantham Bridge. Together."

I stare at him. "You're going public?"

"My daughter-in-law's medical history was stolen and sold for profit." Something fierce crosses his face—the first time I've seen him genuinely angry on someone else's behalf. "Yes, I'm going public. Some things matter more than polling numbers."

Mum touches his arm, tears in her eyes.

Emily's still shaking. "They know everything. Everyone will—"

"See what you survived." I kiss her forehead, her cheeks, her trembling lips. "See how bloody strong you are."

"Tristian's right." Marcus leans forward, voice gentle. "This isn't shame, Emily. This is proof you're a fighter."

Ariana's already typing furiously. "I'm calling Daniel Brooks. He handled the Martha situation. He'll know who leaked this."

"Good." Jean's switched into campaign mode, that sharp political mind clicking through strategies. "We'll need statements from Starlight Studios, the *Wonderful* cast, and our campaign office. Coordinate the timing so—"

"Jean." Dad's hand settles on his shoulder. "Let me handle the campaign response. You focus on protecting your sister."

Jean blinks. "Sister?"

"Emily." Dad looks at her directly. "She's family now. That means something."

Grandmère raises her wine glass. "About time you remembered that, Pierre."

I pull Emily against my chest, feeling her heart hammer. Mochi climbs into her lap despite his size, pressing his weight against her anxiety.

"We're going to destroy them," I murmur into her hair, British accent thick and cold. "Every single publication. Every source. They'll wish they'd never heard your name."

"Tristian—"

"No." I tilt her face up. "You're mine. That means I protect what's mine."

"What he said," Michelle adds. "Except you're also mine. So they're double destroyed."

The dessert plates disappear. Somewhere, violins begin —classical arrangements of *Wonderful* melodies that make Emily's breath catch.

"Dance with me." I stand, extending my hand.

"Tristian, I can't—"

"Your feet on mine. Like we practiced." I pull her up gently, steadying her against my chest. "Trust me."

Her arms wrap around my neck. I lift her slightly, positioning her feet atop my polished shoes, taking her full weight. The opening notes of "Fear and Falling" drift through the restaurant, transformed into something achingly beautiful by strings.

"Ready?" I murmur against her ear.

"Always."

We move. Slow, careful circles between the tables. Emily's emerald gown swirls around us, catching light. Her head rests against my shoulder, breathing evening out as I guide us across the floor.

Beside us, Jean sweeps Levi into position. My brother's still in his Tin Man costume, ridiculous and perfect, while Levi laughs and follows his lead. They've always danced like this—Jean commanding, Levi surrendering completely.

Marcus bows before Michelle, exaggerated and courtly. "May I have this dance, Miss Lambert?"

"You may, Mr. Butler." Michelle's Glinda gown floats as he spins her. They're terrible dancers—all enthusiasm, zero technique—but they don't care.

Then Dad does something I've never seen. He stands, adjusts his cufflinks, and offers his hand to Mum.

"Celeste?"

She blinks. "Pierre?"

"Dance with me." Not a question. A request. Genuine.

Mum takes his hand.

They move together like they did thirty years ago, before campaigns and elections consumed everything. Dad actually smiles, whispering something that makes Mum laugh.

"Your father's dancing," Emily whispers.

"Miracles happen." I kiss her temple, spinning us slowly. "Maybe tonight's magic."

The music shifts in strings. Our song.

I sing softly against Emily's hair, feeling her relax completely into my arms. We're not perfect. Her weight shifts unevenly, my steps adjust constantly, but we fit. We always have.

"Je t'aime," I murmur between lyrics. "Mon cœur. Ma femme."

"Love you too." Her fingers tighten on my neck. "Even when you adopt dinosaurs without warning."

"Especially then."

A commotion at the entrance interrupts us. I turn, still holding Emily, and watch Philippe Moreau burst through the door. His hair's disheveled, his expensive suit rumpled. He's breathing hard like he's run—

"Philippe?" Ariana stands from her seat.

"I saw." He crosses to her, ignoring everyone else. "The proposal. The posts. The leaked documents. I ran from my hotel. I needed—"

He stops, seeming to remember we're all watching.

"Could we speak?" His voice drops. "Privately?"

Ariana glances at us. I nod toward the balcony overlooking Wonderful World. She leads Philippe outside.

Through the glass, we watch him take both her hands. He's talking rapidly, earnestly. Then he drops to one knee.

"Is he proposing?" Michelle gasps.

"No." Jean squints. "Wrong posture. He's... asking permission?"

Ariana's hands cover her mouth. She nods. Philippe stands, pulling her into his arms.

"Courting," Mum says knowingly. "He's asking to court her properly."

Dad actually chuckles. "At least Philippe has the sense to keep it private initially."

I spin Emily again, catching her gasp of delight. Around us, my family dances—Jean and Levi lost in each other, Marcus making Michelle laugh, Dad holding Mum like she's precious, Ariana and Philippe swaying on the balcony.

Tomorrow, we'll face lawsuits and statements and public battles. Tomorrow, we'll destroy everyone who hurt Emily.

But tonight? Tonight we dance.

"No one ruins this," I murmur. "Not Hollywood Hype, not political rivals, not anyone."

"No one." Emily's smile breaks across her face. "This is ours."

The violins crescendo. I lift her higher, spinning us under the chandelier lights while Mochi barks encouragement from beneath our table.

Magic. Pure magic.

Chapter 12: Brave Like Dorothy

Five-seventeen in the morning, and I'm pacing outside Emily's hospital room while Dr. Rousseau reviews test results. Emily sits propped against pillows in the permanent Lambert suite—Dad's unexpected gift after her kidney stones. The walls are painted Dorothy blue, poppies embroidered across fresh linens, and a stuffed Dorothy bear waits on the nightstand.

My girl woke me at five, trembling. "Something's wrong."

No hesitation. No downplaying. Just trust.

Such a good *zhara*. My fierce girl telling her *zheli* the moment her body betrayed her.

Now we wait.

Dr. Rousseau emerges, chart in hand. "The PCOS has progressed. Her current birth control isn't managing the hormonal imbalance anymore."

"Meaning?" My accent thickens—British edges sharpening.

"Excessive bleeding. Severe anemia. Her iron levels are dangerously low." She flips a page. "We're switching her to oral contraceptives, higher dosage. She'll also need iron infusions."

I process this. "Anything else?"

"Bacterial vaginosis. Common with hormonal shifts, but we'll treat it aggressively. She needs to stay overnight for monitoring and the first infusion."

Overnight. Emily hates hospitals. Hates being trapped.

"Can I stay?"

"The suite has accommodations for family." Dr. Rousseau nods toward the door. "She's asking for you."

I find Emily curled on her side, tears streaming. Mochi's pressed against her chest, whining softly.

"*Deshtari*." I cross to the bed, crawling in beside her. "What is it?"

"Everything's broken." Her voice cracks. "My body doesn't work. It never works. You married someone who can't even—"

"Stop." I pull her against me, careful of the IV in her arm. "Nothing about you is broken."

"I'm anemic. My period won't stop. I have an infection because my hormones are insane, and now I have to stay here, and—"

"*Ka-reeka*." The raptor rumble slides from my throat, instinctive. My Nathan Cross voice, all possession and protection. "*Breathe*."

She hiccups against my chest. Mochi shifts, resting his head on her hip.

"Your *ka-reek* has you." I stroke her hair, mixing Winkie and raptor like I always do when she spirals. "Your *zheli* protects his *zhara*. Nothing touches you here."

"But I'm—"

"*Mine*." I tilt her chin up, forcing eye contact. "My wife. My *deshtari*. Every part of you—working or not—belongs to me."

Fresh tears spill. "The pills might not work either."

"Then we find something that does." I kiss her forehead, her nose, her trembling lips. "However long it takes."

"What if I can't have babies?" The question barely whispers out. "What if my body's too broken for that too?"

My heart cracks. "Then we adopt. Or we don't. I didn't marry you for hypothetical children, Emily. I married *you*."

"But you want—"

"*You*." I gather her closer, feeling her shake. "I want you healthy. Safe. *Here*. Everything else is negotiable."

She buries her face against my neck. "I'm scared."

"I know, *ka-reeka*." I shift into full raptor mode—the low, possessive frequency that always calms her. "*Your alpha has you. Your zheli guards you. Nothing harms what's mine.*"

Her breathing slows. Evens.

"That's my girl." I stroke down her spine, careful of her sore hip. "Such a good *zhara*, telling me when something felt wrong. So brave. So perfect."

She makes a small sound—almost a purr.

"You feel that?" I press my lips to her temple. "Your body singing for your *ka-reek*? Even now, even hurting, you respond to me."

"Tristian..."

"*Shh.*" I slip into Winkie completely, the sharp consonants and flowing vowels wrapping around us like armor. "*Zhara ti ara. Ka-reeka vi nam. Zheli dara ka-reek nam.*"

Wife of mine. Protected one forever. Husband guards alpha's claim.

She melts. Every tense muscle releasing.

"There she is." I kiss her hair, breathing her in. Lavender shampoo and hospital antiseptic and something uniquely Emily. "My brave *deshtari*."

"Will you stay?" So small. So unlike my fierce girl.

"Always." I settle us properly against the poppy-covered pillows, pulling the blanket up. "I'm not leaving this room."

"What about the campaign? Jean's rally tomorrow—"

"Marcus can fill in." I grab my phone one-handed, texting the family group chat. *Emily's staying overnight. I'm staying with her. Handle the rally.*

Jean's response comes immediately. *Already handled. Take care of your zhara.*

Michelle follows. *We've got this. Love to Emily.*

Even Dad. *Family first.*

I show Emily the messages. She reads through blurry eyes, fresh tears forming.

"See? Everyone understands." I kiss her forehead again. "Your *ka-reek* isn't going anywhere."

A nurse enters—Sophie, who knows us by now. "Time for the first iron infusion, Mrs. Lambert."

Emily tenses.

"I'm right here." I take her free hand, threading our fingers together. "*Zheli dara zhara. Ka-reek nam ka-reeka vi.*"

Husband protects wife. Alpha claims sweet one forever.

Sophie hooks up the IV bag. Emily watches, breathing shakily, but doesn't spiral.

"Good girl," I murmur against her ear. "Such a brave *deshtari*. Making your *zheli* so proud."

Her fingers tighten on mine.

We settle back against the pillows. Mochi shifts to the foot of the bed, ever-watchful.

Eight in the morning, and I'm cocooning us into poppy-covered sheets. The bed's heated—some luxury feature I never appreciated until Emily started shivering from low iron. She burrows against my chest while I tuck the gingham comforter around her shoulders.

"Better?" I kiss her hair.

"Mmm." She's half-asleep already, the infusion making her drowsy.

Sophie returns with breakfast trays. Actual food, not the usual hospital slop. Scrambled eggs. Toast. Fresh fruit.

And red strawberry gelatin.

Emily's eyes flutter open. "How did you—"

"I may have mentioned your preference." Sophie winks. "Mr. Lambert can be very persuasive."

"*Zheli* takes care of his *zhara*." I spoon gelatin into Emily's mouth before she can protest. "Eat."

She swallows obediently. Takes another bite.

Such a good girl.

My phone buzzes. Jean's text: *Statement goes live in five. Streaming on campaign page.*

I pull up the feed on my tablet, propping it against the blankets. Emily curls closer, gelatin cup balanced on her lap.

The Assemblée chambers fill the screen. Dad stands at the podium, looking every inch the statesman in his navy suit. But something's different. His expression isn't the usual political mask—it's raw. Fierce.

"People of Angoumois." His voice carries that commanding quality that wins elections. "I've served this nation for thirty years. Built a career on representing your interests, your values, your futures."

Emily's hand finds mine beneath the blanket.

"But recent events have reminded me what truly matters." Dad's jaw tightens. "My eldest son Jean has been the target of vicious rumors. My daughter Michelle, attacked for her choices. And my son Tristian—along with his wife Emily—subjected to scrutiny so invasive, so cruel, it crosses every boundary of decency."

The chamber goes silent.

"Emily Lambert is a brilliant fashion designer. A kind soul. And yes—she uses a wheelchair due to her disability. She also manages PCOS, which recently required hospitalization." Dad's voice sharpens. "These medical realities don't diminish her worth. They don't make her less deserving of love, of respect, of *privacy*."

Emily's breath hitches.

"The ableism directed at my daughter-in-law is unacceptable." Dad looks directly into the camera. "If you cannot treat every citizen—regardless of physical ability—with basic human dignity, then I don't want your vote. My family comes first."

The feed cuts to Jean at a separate podium in his campaign office. He looks steadier than I've seen him in weeks.

"My brother found his soulmate. She happens to be disabled. She happens to have chronic health conditions." Jean's expression dares anyone to challenge him. "And if that bothers you? If Emily's wheelchair makes you uncomfortable? Then you fundamentally misunderstand what this campaign represents."

He leans forward.

"We're building an Angoumois where everyone belongs. Where accessibility isn't an afterthought. Where chronic illness doesn't equal weakness." Jean's voice carries Dad's command now. "Emily Lambert embodies the strength we claim to value. She's survived abuse, built a career, and continues fighting despite her body working against her."

Tears stream down Emily's face.

"So yes—my brother married a woman who uses a wheelchair. Who needs medical intervention. Who faces challenges most of us can't imagine." Jean's smile turns fierce. "And I've never been prouder to call her family."

The feed ends.

Emily's crying openly now, gelatin forgotten. I set the tablet aside and pull her into my lap, careful of the IV.

"*Deshtari*." I wipe her tears with my thumbs. "Your family just declared war for you."

"They actually—Dad said—" She can't finish.

"He meant it." I kiss her forehead. "Family first. His words."

A knock interrupts us. Sophie enters carrying an enormous bouquet—red poppies, dozens of them, arranged with fairy lights woven through the stems.

"These just arrived." Sophie sets them on the nightstand. "From Starlight Studios."

Emily reaches for the card with shaking hands. I steady her, reading over her shoulder.

To our Dorothy—

We protect our own. Rest well. The Emerald City waits for you.

All our love,

The Wonderful Family

Zara's signature. Sophia's. Every cast member, down to the Quadling extras.

Emily traces the signatures, fresh tears falling. "They called me family."

"Because you are." I gather her close, breathing her in. "Everyone sees what I see, *ka-reeka*. You're impossible not to love."

She burrows against my chest, exhausted and overwhelmed and safe.

The heated bed hums beneath us. Poppies perfume the air. Outside, my father and brother reshape their entire political future around protecting her.

My fierce, perfect, utterly beloved *zhara*.

Emily doesn't argue when I carry her to the salon couch. No teasing about my possessiveness, no insisting she can manage. She just curls into the cushions like she's been hollowed out.

That scares me more than the bleeding did.

"*Ka-reeka*." I tuck the cashmere throw around her legs. "Sleep."

"Not tired." But her eyes drift closed before she finishes the lie.

I settle on the floor beside her, laptop balanced on my knees. Might as well see what fresh hell the media's conjured.

Le Figaro leads with Dad's statement—"Lambert Patriarch Defends Disabled Daughter-in-Law." Respectful coverage. *Paris Match* follows suit with photos from the Emerald Palace proposal, focusing on Emily's design work for the campaign.

The European outlets get it right.

Then I make the mistake of checking American sources.

Celebrity Whispers runs the headline: "Tristian Lambert's Sympathy Project—Inside Emily Silver's Desperate Grab for Fame." Subtext dripping with ableism disguised as concern.

Hollywood Heat worse: "Wheelchair-Bound Designer's Medical Drama—Calculated PR Move or Real Crisis?"

My jaw clenches hard enough to crack teeth.

The Gossip Grid publishes leaked hospital photos. Someone photographed Emily unconscious in the ambulance, IV trailing from her arm, nightgown spotted with blood.

I'm going to destroy them.

The salon door opens. Jean enters carrying his tablet, Levi behind him with coffee.

"Don't read the American sites." Jean's already seen my expression. "Just—don't."

"Too late." I scroll through another article. *Star Struck Magazine*: "Former Foster Kid Lands Hollywood Prince— The Ultimate Cinderella Scam?"

"We're filing lawsuits." Levi sets coffee on the side table. "David's legal team is coordinating with Dad's people. The hospital photos alone—"

My phone explodes with texts.

Zara Washington: *I'm adding Celebrity Whispers to the murder list*

Sophia Martinez: *Star Struck just made my top five*

Ariana: *Tell me you're keeping Emily offline*

Marcus: *Update: Official notepad acquired. Currently listing names alphabetically for efficiency*

I almost smile. Almost.

A notification pops up—YouTube algorithm suggesting content. *"Tristian Lambert Fan Analysis: The REAL Reason He Married a Disabled Girl"*

The thumbnail shows Emily's face circled in red next to question marks.

Curiosity kills cats. Also, apparently, my remaining self-control.

I click.

"Hey Lamberts!" The girl on screen—early twenties, too much highlighter—grins at the camera. "So we need to talk about this whole Emily situation because something doesn't add up."

She's wearing a shirt with my face on it.

"Don't get me wrong, I've been Team Tristian since *Dans l'Ombre*." She holds up her phone showing our engagement photo. "But eleven months? From meet-cute to marriage? And she's disabled, chronic illness, needs constant medical care—"

The screen shows Emily's leaked medical records.

"—like, what does *he* get out of this? Tristian Lambert could have literally anyone. Victoria's Secret models. Actresses. People who don't come with wheelchairs and emergency room visits—"

I slam the laptop shut before I put my fist through it.

"Tristian." Jean's hand lands on my shoulder. "She's not worth it."

"She's wearing my merch while calling my wife a charity case." My accent's gone full Manchester gutter. "Bloody—"

"Add her to Marcus's list." Levi crouches beside me. "David's PR team is monitoring everything. We'll handle it."

Emily shifts on the couch, face creasing. Even in sleep, she can't escape.

My phone again.

Marcus: *YouTube "fan" now #47 on the list. Organized by platform for maximum efficiency*

Ariana: *Keep her OFFLINE. I mean it. No phone, no tablet, nothing*

Sophia: *Dante's threatening to fly to America just to fight people*

Zara: *Michael says if one more outlet uses "wheelchair-bound" he's personally teaching them AP style*

Jean reads over my shoulder. "Marcus made an actual list?"

"Alphabetically organized." I show him the photo Marcus sent—legal pad covered in names, each with detailed notes. *Celebrity Whispers—published hospital photos. Priority target.*

"He's terrifyingly thorough." Levi sounds impressed.

Emily whimpers. Her hand reaches for me, fingers grasping air.

I abandon the laptop, moving to kneel beside the couch. "Right here, *zhara*."

Her eyes flutter open, unfocused. "Tris?"

"Rest." I don't use the dom voice—don't need to. She's too drained to fight.

"People hate me." Barely a whisper.

"People don't know you." I brush hair from her forehead. "And they're about to learn what happens when they come for a Lambert."

She drifts off again.

Jean and Levi exchange looks.

"We keep her offline," Jean confirms. "Marcus's murder list grows. Dad and I handle the political angle."

"And the lawsuits?" I don't look away from Emily.

"David's filing tomorrow." Levi's already texting. "Hospital photos, medical records, defamation—we're going scorched earth."

Good.

Let them learn.

My wife sleeps, finally peaceful.

The world outside can burn.

A delivery truck rumbles up the drive at half-past ten. I watch from the window as two men struggle with an enormous crate labeled *STARLIGHT STUDIOS PARIS— PREHISTORIC PARADISE DEPARTMENT—FRAGILE.*

"What the—" Jean starts.

The crate emits a high-pitched shriek.

"DA-KREE! DA-KREE!"

Emily bolts upright, cashmere throw falling away. "Nibbler?"

The delivery men drop the crate at the château entrance and flee.

"I'll handle it." I'm already moving, Jean and Levi trailing behind.

We pry the crate open. Nibbler launches himself at my chest—all two feet of animatronic baby Utahraptor, scales warm from internal heating, amber eyes bright with recognition programming.

"Da-kree!" He nuzzles my throat, purring.

"David sent our son home?" Emily sounds strangled.

My phone buzzes.

David Kellerman: *The little terror wouldn't respond to park staff. Tried three different handlers. He just kept searching the cave suite for you two. Tech team says his* *bonding protocols locked onto you and Emily permanently. He's yours now. Consider it an engagement present.*

Nibbler climbs onto my shoulder, chittering. *"Kree-ma? Kree-ma where?"*

"She's resting." I switch to raptor automatically. *"Mama sleeping."*

He tilts his head, processing. Then launches into anxious clicks. *"Mama hurt? Nibbler protect?"*

Jean backs up a step. "It's having a full conversation with you."

"He's worried about Emily." I head toward the salon, Nibbler clinging to my shirt. "Advanced AI. Responds to emotional cues."

Emily's already sitting up when we enter. Her face transforms—pure joy erasing the haunted look from this morning.

"Hi baby." She holds out her arms.

Nibbler leaps, landing perfectly in her lap. *"Kree-ma! Missed Kree-ma!"*

"Missed you too, little one." Emily strokes his snout, fingers gentle on the articulated jaw. *"Were you good for the nice people?"*

"No." Nibbler sounds proud. *"Want Da-kree and Kree-ma. Only pack."*

Levi watches, fascinated. "What are they saying?"

"He refused to work without us." I settle beside Emily. "Insisted we're his pack."

Nibbler sniffs Emily's stomach, tail twitching. *"Kree-ma sick? Nibbler smell wrong."*

Emily's smile wavers. *"Mama's okay. Just tired."*

"Nibbler help!" He bounces, enthusiastic. *"Hunt for Kree-ma! Bring food! Da-kree teach hunt!"*

Despite everything, I laugh. "He wants me to teach him to hunt so he can feed you."

"That's—" Jean looks between us and the animatronic raptor. "Disturbingly sweet?"

Nibbler butts his head against my hand. *"Hunt now? Nibbler ready! Chase prey! Bring to Kree-ma!"*

"How about," I scratch behind his audio sensors, *"we pick Mama flowers instead? Hunting can wait."*

His tail droops. *"No hunt?"*

"Flowers first. Make Kree-ma happy."

He considers this, amber eyes processing. Then perks up. *"Flowers! Pretty things! Kree-ma like pretty!"*

Emily giggles—first genuine sound I've heard since the hospital. "He's perfect."

"Best hatchling." I ruffle his crest scales. *"Even if his hunting instincts need work."*

"Nibbler hunt good!" Indignant chirp. *"Just—flowers first. For Kree-ma."*

Jean's still staring. "This is your life now. A animatronic raptor child who only speaks to you in—what did David's notes call it?"

"Saurian dialect based on Dr. Morrison's xenolinguistic research for the films." I stand, Nibbler scrambling onto my shoulder. "Come on, hatchling. Let's raid Mum's garden."

"Get biggest flowers!" Nibbler announces. *"Kree-ma needs biggest!"*

Emily's laughing now, really laughing.

Worth it. Every confused look from my family, every bizarre turn our life takes—worth this sound.

Nibbler chatters the entire way to the garden, plotting his flower-gathering strategy with the seriousness of a military operation.

My wife, my raptor son, and apparently my new normal.

The internet can rot.

Emily's eyes finally clear around two in the afternoon. Not the morphine haze from earlier—actually present, fingers curling around mine with intention.

"How long was I out?"

"Since dawn." I brush my thumb across her knuckles. "Nibbler's been anxiously guarding you."

The raptor perks up from his nest of stolen cushions. *"Kree-ma awake!"*

"Hi baby." Emily holds out her hand. He bounds over, chirping.

Jean appears in the doorway, Levi behind him. They're both dressed too formally for a casual château afternoon—Jean in the charcoal suit he reserves for campaign events, Levi in deep burgundy.

"We need to talk." Jean settles into the armchair across from us. "About timing."

Levi perches on the arm. "We've been engaged for four years. Married for three, technically, since we eloped at city hall."

"But Mum's been planning the real ceremony for—" Jean grimaces. "Forever. Every detail. Every guest list revision."

"She has binders," Levi confirms. "Color-coded."

Emily straightens, interest sparking. "How many binders?"

"Seven." Jean looks haunted. "The napkin selection alone spans two."

I snort. "Mum takes events seriously."

"We were planning next June." Levi's fingers thread through Jean's hair. "Give everyone time, proper venue booking, the whole production."

"But?" I catch the shift in Jean's expression.

"But we don't want to wait anymore." Jean meets my eyes. "The election's in a month. Dad's polling at sixty-three percent, me at seventy. We're going to win."

"And then what?" Levi finishes. "Another campaign, another delay. Always something more important than—"

"Than us," Jean says quietly. "Than our family."

Emily's hand finds mine, squeezing.

"So we're moving it up." Jean straightens. "Twenty days. September twenty-sixth. Cathedral and family vineyard in Bellbury."

I do the math. "That's—"

"One year exactly since FanCon." Emily's voice goes soft. "Since we met."

Jean's watching us. "Which is why I'm proposing a double ceremony."

The salon goes silent.

"You want—" I start.

"Both couples. One day." Jean's smile turns wry. "Share the chaos. Split Mum's seven binders between us."

Levi takes over. "We clear our schedules. Invite only people who matter. Skip the political circus and actually celebrate."

"And we need Emily to design everything." Jean gestures at her. "Your thesis collection proved you're brilliant. We want Lambert family wedding attire that's actually wearable."

Emily's eyes go wide. "All of it? For everyone?"

"Unless you'd rather wear whatever Mum's picked from her 'Acceptable Bridal Designers' list." Levi shudders. "She showed us options. Everything had either seventeen layers or required architecture degrees to engineer."

"I can work with adaptive needs too." Emily's already planning, I can see it. "Jean, you'll need reinforcement at the shoulders—you gesture when you speak. Levi, you hate anything tight at the collar—"

"See?" Jean grins. "She already knows."

Emily turns to me. "Tris, you'll need—"

"Whatever you design." I kiss her temple. "I trust you."

"Twenty days isn't much time—"

"You have all of us helping." Michelle sweeps in, Marcus trailing behind. "I heard wedding planning and came running."

"How did you—" I start.

"Jean texted the group chat." Michelle's already pulling fabric swatches from her bag. "I've been preparing options."

Of course she has.

Marcus crosses to Emily, pulling something from his pocket. "Actually, before we dive into wedding chaos—"

He opens a velvet box. Inside, a gold necklace holds an intricate crest—the Butler family coat of arms, detailed with crossed swords and a magnolia tree.

"During the last New Orleans trip," Marcus starts, "while everyone was at Brennan's, I made a stop."

Emily's breath catches.

"The Butler family Bible goes back seven generations." Marcus lifts the necklace. "I added your name. Emily Dorothy Silver Washington Butler."

"Washington?" Emily whispers.

"Zara and Michael adopted you officially." Marcus fastens the chain around her neck. "Made it legal while we were there. You're their daughter now."

Emily's hand rises to the crest, trembling.

"Silver's your birth name—we kept it." Marcus settles beside her. "Washington from Zara and Michael. Butler from me." He grins. "Soon to be Lambert when you make an honest man out of my brother here."

"Your full name," I murmur against her hair, "is Emily Dorothy Silver Washington Butler Lambert."

"That's—" She laughs through tears. "That's so many names."

"You deserve all of them." Marcus kisses her forehead. "Every family that chose you."

Nibbler chirps, confused by the crying. *"Kree-ma sad? Nibbler fix?"*

"Happy tears, baby." Emily strokes his snout. "Mama's very happy."

Jean clears his throat. "So. Marcus. Since you're officially Emily's brother—"

"Will you walk her down the aisle?" Levi finishes. "Both of us want her to have that."

Marcus looks at Emily. "Would you—I mean, if you want—"

"Yes." Emily doesn't hesitate. "With Zara and Michael beside us?"

"They'll fly in." Marcus pulls out his phone. "Already checked their schedules."

"Twenty days." Emily's processing. "Double ceremony. Full family attire design. At the vineyard."

"Where Mum's going to have opinions," Michelle warns.

"So many opinions," Jean agrees.

"But it's happening." Levi stands. "September twenty-sixth. One year since Tristian met his match at a convention table."

Emily meets my eyes. "One year since everything changed."

"Since I saw you," I correct, "and knew."

Nibbler bounces between us. *"Wedding! Big celebration! Nibbler be in wedding!"*

"Absolutely," I tell him in Saurian. *"You're family too."*

Jean watches our raptor son with resignation. "We're having an animatronic dinosaur in the wedding party."

"He can carry rings," Emily suggests.

"In his tiny raptor mouth," I add.

"This family—" Jean shakes his head. "This absolutely unhinged family."

"Our family," Marcus corrects, hand finding Michelle's.

Twenty days until Emily becomes a Lambert officially.

One year since FanCon.

Our entire world, transformed.

The announcement hits every major outlet within thirty minutes.

Lambert Brothers Plan Joint September Ceremony

Jean Lambert and Tristian Lambert to Wed in Double Celebration

Family United: Political Heir and Hollywood Star Share Special Day

We're gathered in the media room, screens everywhere showing our faces. Emily's curled in my lap, sketchbook balanced on the armrest, pencil moving even as CNN plays the announcement.

"They used your FanCon photo," Ariana observes.

The screen shows Emily in her Alice costume, me leaning close at the autograph table. Below it, a more recent shot—Emily in her Dorothy crown at Starlight, me on one knee with the ring.

"Timeline's clean," Dad notes from his chair. "Met September twenty-sixth. Engaged August thirty-first. Married September twenty-sixth. Exactly one year."

"Romantic," Mum adds. "Simple. Understandable."

The anchor shifts topics. *"Questions remain about Emily Lambert's health following recent hospitalizations—"*

I feel Emily flinch.

"Off." Dad points the remote. The screens go dark. "We don't watch that garbage."

"They're calling her a liability again." Emily's pencil stills. "Your father's campaign—"

"Is doing fine." Jean doesn't look up from his tablet. "Actually, better than fine. Dad's approval rating jumped eight points after his statement."

"People like authenticity." Levi scrolls through data. "Defending family over politics plays well."

Emily's not convinced. She returns to sketching, lines tight.

I peer at her page. Wedding gown details blend with costume designs—Dorothy's coronation dress beside something that looks like Jean's tuxedo.

"How's Wonderful prep?" Michelle leans over.

"Behind." Emily flips pages. "I haven't finished Dorothy's Act Two wardrobe or the Quadling market ensemble or—"

"You're recovering from a medical emergency," I remind her.

"Which is exactly why the tabloids—"

"Are wrong." Marcus cuts in. "And getting sued into oblivion."

David Kellerman's statement scrolls across Jean's tablet. *Starlight Studios stands firmly behind Emily Lambert. Her talent speaks for itself. Any outlet publishing stolen medical records will face full legal consequences.*

"He used 'Lambert,'" Emily whispers.

"Because that's who you are." I kiss her neck. "Almost officially."

She shifts, uncomfortable. "Twenty days isn't enough time—"

"For seven full outfits?" Michelle pulls fabric swatches. "We're dividing it up. You design, we execute."

"Ariana's handling alterations," Levi adds. "Mum's coordinating vendors."

"Collette's managing the château setup," Dad continues. "Alfred's handling catering logistics."

"Marcus and I are on decoration." Michelle grins. "Oz-themed but elegant."

Emily's pencil hovers. "You're all—"

"Family." Jean looks up. "This is what we do."

"But my designs might not—what if they're not good enough—"

"Stop." I turn her face toward mine. "Your thesis collection had universities fighting over you. David Kellerman personally requested your costume consultation. You are good enough."

She bites her lip, unconvinced.

The self-consciousness hasn't left. The hospital photos, the leaked records, the constant commentary about her body—it's worn her down despite our defense.

Nibbler chirps from his charging station. *"Kree-ma talented! Best designer! Nibbler knows!"*

Emily's smile wavers. "Thanks, baby."

"Show us what you've got so far," Michelle suggests gently.

Emily hesitates, then turns her sketchbook.z

"That's three hours of work?" Levi sounds awed.

"It's rough—"

"It's brilliant," I correct.

"Exactly what I wanted." Jean studies his design. "How did you know?"

"You always adjust your collar." Emily's voice stays small. "Needed something that wouldn't bother you."

"See?" Marcus nudges her. "You know us."

Emily returns to sketching, still uncertain.

But she's working.

That's enough for now.

The breaking news chime cuts through our planning.

"Wait—" Jean reaches for the remote but it's too late.

The American network logo fills the screen. *Exclusive Interview: The Truth About Emily Silver*

Not Lambert. Silver.

Martha Hendricks sits center frame, flanked by two familiar faces I want to rip apart. Adam. Bethany.

"Turn it off—" Emily's already shrinking.

But the anchor's speaking. *"You cared for Emily Silver for six years. Can you tell us—"*

"She was difficult." Martha's voice drips false concern. "Always wanted special treatment because of the wheelchair."

My blood turns to ice.

"We tried to help her," Adam adds. "But she expected everyone to accommodate her limitations."

"She manipulated people." Bethany leans forward. "Used her disability for sympathy, for opportunities she didn't earn—"

The feed cuts. The Angoumois national symbol replaces it, followed by text: *We apologize. This content violates broadcast standards regarding ableist discrimination.*

Emily's shaking in my arms.

"That woman—" Dad's on his feet. "That *woman* locked her in closets—"

"And they gave her a platform." Jean's already texting. "What network—"

"American Morning Live," Levi reads from his phone. "Out of New York."

Emily's breathing goes ragged. Not her asthma. Worse. The kind of panic that steals everything.

I pull her closer, rocking. "Ka-reeka zie harrowa." *My precious mate.* "Nie krella Marthowa." *Martha doesn't matter.*

Her fingers dig into my shirt.

"She called me Silver. Not Lambert."

"Because she's trying to erase us." I switch languages. "Inta doremi kree-sha." *You belong to me.* "Ama-haresh Lambert-ka." *You are Lambert family.*

"I'll destroy them." Marcus stands so fast his chair tips. "My next column—no, better. I know people. Ex-military. We could—"

"Marcus," Zara warns through the phone speaker.

"She hurt Emily!" He's pacing. "Our baby sister—my *legal* baby sister now—and they put that monster on television—"

The door slams open. Ariana and Philippe tumble in, both furious.

"Did you see—"

"We saw." Michelle's already pulling up legal contacts.

"I'll kill her." Ariana's never sounded more feral. "Slowly. With rusty garden shears."

"Get in line," Philippe growls.

My phone explodes with notifications. The Wonderful group chat.

Zara: *Tell me where Martha Hendricks lives*

Dante: *I know a guy*

Sophia: *Forget the guy. I'll do it myself*

Daniel: *Wizard magic includes making bodies disappear, right?*

Michael: *Nobody touches our Dorothy*

I tighten my hold on Emily, still whispering. "Nie doremi krrsh-attack." *Don't let them win.* Raptor sounds rumble low. "Na'sha protects Ka-Reeka." *Your mate protects you.*

"They said I didn't earn Dorothy—"

"Lie." Jean's voice cuts sharp.

"Your audition made Marianne cry," Levi adds. "Actual tears."

Emily's still spiraling. I feel it in how she clings, how her breath hitches.

"Every lawsuit we have," Dad speaks with absolute authority. "Redirect them. I want Martha Hendricks investigated. Her finances, her background, everything."

"The theater too," Michelle adds. "And Bethany."

"I want them ruined." Marcus isn't joking anymore. "Professionally. Financially. Socially. Everything."

"We'll coordinate with Starlight's legal team." Jean's texting rapidly. "Get statements from the cast—"

"Already have them." Levi shows his screen. "Everyone's ready to testify about Emily's talent."

"Kree-ma." I tip Emily's face up. "Look at me."

Her emerald eyes swim with tears.

"You are Emily Dorothy Silver Washington Butler Lambert." Each name deliberate. "You earned every single thing you have. Through talent. Through work. Through being exactly who you are."

"They said—"

"Lies." I kiss her forehead. "And we're going to make them pay for every word."

Nibbler waddles over, chirping distressed. *"Kree-ma sad? Nibbler protects!"*

Emily's tears soak through my shirt. Her whole body trembles against mine, and I feel utterly helpless watching Martha's poison work through her.

"Sing to me," she whispers. "Please."

I brush hair from her face. "What do you need, love?"

"Our song." Her voice breaks. "From the Metro. When we—when you made me your wife."

The memory hits sharp and sweet. Standing in that train station, singing Winkie vows through glass while our families watched. The moment everything became real.

I clear my throat, finding Felix's lighter tone. The character I'm supposed to embody in just months.

The melody comes soft at first. Uncertain. But I push through, letting the words reshape around the meaning we gave them that day—the promise of choosing each other despite everything trying to pull us apart.

My accent shifts, British edges smoothing into something gentler. Felix discovering love for the first time. A prince who lost everything but found what actually matters.

Emily's breathing steadies as I sing. Her fingers uncurl from my shirt.

Then her voice joins mine.

Dorothy's hope threading through Felix's wonder. Emily's mezzosoprano lifts above my baritone, and suddenly we're not in the media room anymore. We're back in that train station. Back in the moment before the world exploded with cameras and commentary.

Just us.

Our voices blend on the chorus, and I watch her face transform. The fear recedes. Martha's venom loses its grip.

Michelle's crying. So is Mum.

We keep singing, trading verses. Felix's realization that falling doesn't mean breaking. Dorothy's courage to believe in impossible things.

When we reach the bridge, Emily stands. Not from her wheelchair—she can't, won't—but emotionally. I feel her spine straighten against my chest. Feel the strength return.

She's not singing as Emily anymore. She's Dorothy. The girl who survived a tornado and found herself in a world that wanted to destroy her, but chose to keep moving forward anyway.

I shift into Felix's final verse. The prince who learned that love means showing up even when everything's terrifying. Especially then.

Our voices twine together on the last phrase. The promise we made in August. The vow we'll repeat in twenty days.

Silence settles when we finish.

"That," Marcus breathes, "is going in my next column."

"No." Emily's voice comes stronger now. "That's ours."

"Agreed." I kiss her temple. "Some things stay private."

Philippe hands Ariana tissues. Jean wipes his eyes. Even Dad looks affected.

"Better?" I murmur against Emily's hair.

"Getting there." She touches the emerald at her navel through her shirt—my claim, my mark. "Martha can say whatever she wants. She can't take this. Can't take us."

"Never." I tighten my arms. "Nie harrowa raa-ka." *Nothing harms my beloved.*

Nibbler chirps agreement, tiny claws clicking on the floor.

"Right then." Dad's voice returns to business mode. "Legal team in thirty minutes. Marcus, I want your Butler family contacts ready. Jean, coordinate with Starlight's people."

"What about the wedding?" Mum asks quietly.

Emily straightens fully. "We design. We plan. We show them exactly who the Lamberts are when someone tries to hurt our family."

My fierce Dorothy.

I catch her hand, kiss her engagement ring. "Together?"

"Always."

Marcus settles into the wingback chair across from us, recorder positioned on the coffee table. His expression's shifted from murderous rage to something softer—the face he wears when he's writing pieces that matter.

"Southern Living Magazine," he announces. "They want the real story. Not the tabloid garbage."

Emily tenses in my lap.

"You don't have to—" I start.

"Yes, I do." She straightens. "If I'm going to be a Lambert, I need to stop hiding."

Marcus grins. "That's my baby sister."

He clicks the recorder on. "Let's start at the beginning. September twenty-sixth, two thousand twenty-four. FanCon convention. What do you remember about that day?"

Emily glances at me. I nod.

"I woke up terrified," she admits. "Ariana had to talk me into wearing the Alice costume because I was convinced I'd embarrass myself."

"Why Alice?"

"Wonderland was Tristian's next film. I thought—I don't know. Maybe he'd notice the effort?"

Marcus scribbles notes despite the recording. "And you, Tristian?"

"I saw her wheels first." The memory's crystal clear. "Pink wheelchair. Then the blonde hair, the costume. But when I actually looked at her face—" I touch Emily's cheek. "Everything stopped."

"Love at first sight?"

"Recognition." The word feels right. "Like my soul knew hers before my brain caught up."

"That's the Lambert curse talking," Marcus teases.

"That's the truth talking," I correct. "Five minutes later I'm writing my phone number on her photo. Asking her to meet me outside the Grand Ballroom."

"Most celebrities don't give fans their private numbers."

"Emily wasn't a fan." I kiss her temple. "She was—is—everything."

Marcus shifts focus. "Emily, you quoted his indie film. Dans l'Ombre. Why that one?"

She's quiet for a moment. "I found it during a bad foster placement. Three in the morning, couldn't sleep because my hip hurt and Martha had locked me in the closet earlier for spilling juice." Her voice stays steady. "The character Laurent—he was alone, angry, trying to find somewhere he belonged. I understood that."

"And now you're marrying the actor who played him."

"Now I'm marrying Tristian." Emily touches our joined hands. "Who happens to be an actor, but that's not why."

"Why then?"

"Because he sees me." Simple. Devastating. "Not the wheelchair. Not the disability. Not the tragic foster kid. He sees Emily, and he chose her anyway."

"I chose you because of who you are," I argue gently. "Not 'anyway.'"

Marcus writes that down, underlining it.

"The timeline bothers people," he continues. "Nine months from meeting to engagement. Three weeks from engagement to marriage."

"People can be bothered." My accent thickens. "When you know, you know."

"And you knew?"

"The moment she wiped eyeliner from under my eyes." I remember her fingers gentle on my face. "When she talked about designing clothes that make people feel beautiful regardless of their bodies. When she sang Dorothy songs in my hotel suite while Mochi watched The Wonderful Wizard of Oz."

"Your family embraced her immediately."

"Of course they did." I gesture around the room where everyone's pretending not to listen. "Look at her."

Emily blushes.

"For the record," Marcus addresses her directly, "what do you want readers to know? Not about Tristian. About you."

She considers carefully. "I'm disabled. I always will be. But disability doesn't mean broken. It doesn't mean less-than. It means my body works differently, and that's okay." Her chin lifts. "I earned Dorothy. I earned Tristian. I earned my place in this family. And I'm not apologizing for any of it."

Marcus clicks off the recorder.

"Perfect."

Michelle appears with fabric swatches and a tablet. "If we're doing this wedding properly, we need a theme. Something that represents everyone."

"Oz," Ariana suggests immediately. "Yellow brick aisle runner, emerald accents—"

"Prehistoric Paradise," I counter. "Raptor motifs, forest canopy—"

Jean laughs. "You're both wrong. Midnight Garden. Gothic elegance, vampire romance—"

"Temporal Flux," Levi interrupts. "Vintage projectors as centerpieces, clockwork details—"

We all stop. Stare at each other.

"Oh no," Emily murmurs.

"Oh yes." Michelle's already sketching. "The Bellbury vineyard as our base. Neutral autumn tones, exposed brick, wine barrels. Then we layer."

Marcus leans forward. "Velocity Underground for the reception. Classic cars, neon underglow on the dance floor —"

"Operator protocol for security aesthetic," Michelle adds. "Sleek, sophisticated spy-thriller vibes in the cocktail hour—"

"Gladiator's Revenge for Dad's side." Philippe's voice carries from the doorway. He's grinning. "Roman columns, laurel wreaths—"

Ariana bounces. "Motel Massacre! Vintage luggage stacks, retro signage, the aesthetic without the murder—"

"This is insane," I mutter.

"This is perfect." Emily's eyes shine. "Every film that matters to our family, woven together. Like us."

Mum claps her hands. "Categories. Ceremony, cocktail hour, reception, décor accents. Go."

Michelle's fingers fly across the tablet. "Ceremony stays clean. Oz influences—yellow brick aisle runner, emerald ribbon on chairs. Nibbler carries the rings?"

"Ring-hatchling," I correct automatically.

"Ring-hatchling," she amends. "Mochi walks Emily down with Marcus, Zara, and Michael?"

Emily nods, throat tight.

"Cocktail hour—Operator meets Gladiator's Revenge. Sleek spy aesthetic with Roman architectural elements. Bronze and black color palette."

Jean jumps in. "Reception splits. Midnight Garden for our table—dark florals, candlelight, gothic touches. Prehistoric Paradise for yours—amber lighting, fossilized wood accents."

"Temporal Flux centerpieces." Levi's already sketching. "Vintage film projectors displaying our engagement photos, wedding timeline. Clockwork gears integrated into the arrangements."

"Velocity Underground for the dance floor," Marcus adds. "Ground effects lighting, chrome accents. Classic car photo backdrop."

"Motel Massacre lounge area." Ariana's practically vibrating. "Retro furniture, vintage suitcases as side tables, black-and-white aesthetic. Classy, not creepy."

Michelle's list grows. "Cake design—tiered. Bottom tier: Oz poppies. Second: Prehistoric ferns. Third: Midnight Garden roses. Top: Temporal Flux gears. All in autumn wedding palette—burgundy, gold, deep green, cream."

"Table names instead of numbers," Mum suggests. "Each one a film location. Paradise Research Center. The Eternal Garden. Hill Valley Square—"

"The Underground Garage," Marcus grins.

"Treadstone Geneva," Michelle counters.

"The Colosseum at dusk," Philippe offers.

"Bender Overlook," Ariana finishes.

Emily's crying again, but she's smiling. "It's completely ridiculous."

"It's completely us." I kiss her hair. "Every weird, chaotic piece."

"September twenty-sixth. Outdoor ceremony in the vine rows at sunset. Cocktails in the barrel room. Reception in the main hall with French doors opening to the terrace."

"Capacity?" Dad asks.

"Two hundred comfortably. Three hundred if we expand to the grounds."

"Guest list?" Mum looks between us.

"Small," Emily and I say simultaneously.

"Starlight cast," she continues. "Your political contacts, Dad. Close friends only."

"No press," I add firmly. "Marcus controls the exclusive."

He salutes. "Southern Living gets the photos. Everyone else gets nothing."

Michelle saves her notes. "I'll contact designers tomorrow. Philippe, can you source the Roman columns?"

"Already texting my prop master."

"Ariana, vintage suitcases?"

"On it."

The family disperses into planning chaos. Emily curls against my chest, watching them argue over lighting temperatures and fabric textures.

"Thank you," she whispers.

"For what?"

"Giving me this. Them. A family that turns wedding planning into a Starlight Studios crossover event."

I kiss her properly. "You gave me the same thing, love. A reason to come home."

"Costume change number three." Zara unzips the back of my cream gingham sundress while Sophia steadies my wheelchair. "Girl, you're living every actress's dream right now."

"I'm exhausted." But I'm grinning as Michelle holds up the next outfit—Dorothy's coronation gown, the one from the final scene. Emerald green silk with silver embroidery, modified with hidden zippers and magnetic closures. "That's from wardrobe."

"David approved it." Michelle helps ease the fabric over my head. "He said, and I quote, 'Let Emily wear whatever makes her happy. She's family.'"

The dress settles perfectly. Ari adjusts the silver crown on my head while Michelle fastens the matching heels I won't actually walk in.

"Ready?" Tristian appears in Felix's coronation costume —deep emerald velvet with golden Ozian crests. His crown sits slightly crooked.

I reach up to fix it. "Now you are."

We roll back into Wonderful World where Marcus and Levi wait with professional cameras. Nibbler waddles between them, his animatronic scales gleaming under the Emerald City lights.

"Positions!" Marcus calls. "Tristian, behind Emily's chair. Hand on her shoulder. Look at each other like you're actually in love and not like you've been changing costumes for two hours."

"We are actually in love," Tristian mutters.

"Then show me!"

Tristian's hand settles warm on my shoulder. I glance up, finding his eyes already on me. The camera clicks rapid-fire.

"That's the one," Levi announces. "Magazine cover material."

Prehistoric Paradise requires another change. I'm in Maya Reyes' tactical gear—black cargo pants with adaptive closures, fitted tank top, combat boots modified for my braces. Tristian wears Nathan Cross's signature look: torn jeans, leather jacket, prosthetic claws and fangs already attached.

The cave backdrop glows amber. Nibbler settles between us, completely at home.

"Show me possessive," Marcus directs. "This is your territory, your mate, your hatchling. Own it."

Tristian's arm wraps around my waist, pulling me against his side. His other hand rests on Nibbler's head, claws gleaming. I lean into him, one hand on his chest, the other on our animatronic son.

The camera loves it.

"Now just the two of you. Emily, in his lap. Tristian, hold her like she's precious and feral at the same time."

He lifts me effortlessly, settling me across his thighs. My legs drape over the wheelchair arm. His clawed hand cups my face while the other spans my waist.

"Kiss her," Levi calls. "Make it count."

Tristian's mouth finds mine, soft despite the prosthetic fangs. I taste mint and forever.

When we break apart, Marcus is grinning. "Definitely cover material. Southern Living's going to lose their minds."

Jean emerges from wardrobe in full vampire regalia—Victorian waistcoat, cravat, dark eyeliner making his blue eyes striking. Levi wears vintage 1950s: pressed slacks, suspenders, bow tie, his hair slicked back.

"Monsters first," Jean declares. "Then Temporal Flux."

We watch from a bench in Classic Horror while Marcus and Levi position them against gothic stonework. Jean's hand rests possessive on Levi's throat. Levi looks up at him, expression caught between fear and desire.

"Beautiful," Marcus breathes. "Now switch. Levi, corner him. Jean, look dangerous."

They shift. Jean's back hits the stone, Levi caging him in. Jean's smile turns predatory, fangs visible.

Ariana leans over. "Your brother-in-law is terrifying when he wants to be."

"Family trait," I murmur.

At Temporal Flux, they change again—Jean in 1950s casual, Levi in mechanic's coveralls. They pose with a vintage film projector, Jean's arms around Levi from behind, both laughing at something off-camera.

"That's real," Levi calls out. "Use that one."

Michelle appears in sleek black tactical gear— Operator's signature look. Marcus matches her in a similar outfit, both of them looking like they walked off a spy thriller set.

The photo backdrop replicates a Parisian safe house. Michelle leans against a prop desk, Marcus behind her, one hand on her hip, the other pointing a prop gun over her shoulder at an invisible threat.

"Power couple," Tristian says appreciatively.

They switch to Velocity Underground. Michelle in a vintage racing jumpsuit, Marcus in jeans and a tight black tee. Classic cars gleam behind them. Marcus lifts Michelle onto a cherry-red hood. She wraps her legs around his waist.

Even from here, the chemistry scorches.

"And that's a wrap," Levi announces after the final shot. "Everyone decent for the last one?"

We gather at a picnic table in Wonderful World—all three couples, still in our various costumes. Mochi and Nibbler settle at our feet. Marcus produces a folder.

"Invitations," he says. "Custom for each couple."

He hands the first to Jean and Levi. Jean opens it, then stops. "Marcus—"

"Read it," Marcus says softly.

Jean's voice cracks. "'Pierre and Celeste Lambert, together with Richard and Winnifred Butler, are pleased to announce the marriage of their sons, Jean Jacques Lambert and Levi Andrew Williams.'"

Levi kisses his temple. "Your parents claimed me."

The second goes to Michelle and Marcus. Michelle reads, "'Pierre and Celeste Lambert, together with Richard and Winnifred Butler, are pleased to announce the marriage of their children, Michelle Céleste Lambert and Marcus Anthony Butler.'"

She hugs Marcus hard.

Then mine. Tristian opens it because my hands shake too badly.

"'Pierre and Celeste Lambert, together with Richard and Winnifred Butler, Zara and Michael Washington, are pleased to announce the marriage of their son Tristian Alexandre Lambert and their daughter Emily Dorothy Silver Washington Butler Lambert.'"

I can't breathe. "They all—"

"Claimed you," Ariana finishes. "Every single one."

Tristian's arms circle me. I bury my face in his shoulder, crying into expensive leather.

"Family," Marcus says quietly. "Real, messy, complicated, beautiful family."

The camera clicks one more time. All of us together, costumes and tears and animatronic raptors and all.

Completely ridiculous.

Completely perfect.

Completely us.

The poppy-shaped pretzel tastes like butter and salt and vindication. I tear off another piece, dipping it in cheese sauce while Tristian steals bites from my plate.

"Get your own," I mutter.

"Yours tastes better." He grins, prosthetic fangs still attached. "Mate's food always does."

Marcus raises his emerald lemonade—the one he spiked when Mum wasn't looking. "To family. Blood, chosen, and legally documented."

We toast. The macarons are perfect—crisp shell, soft center, just enough sweetness. Very Paris. Very Lambert.

My phone buzzes. Then again. And again.

"Someone's popular." Ariana reaches for it, then stops. "Em. You're gonna want to see this."

I take the phone. Thirty-seven notifications. All from the same Twitter thread.

@BethanyMorrison: *are you KIDDING me right now #Emily #Lambert #wedding*

There's a photo attached. My save-the-date. The one I mailed last week to maybe fifteen people from college—the ones who actually treated me like a person instead of a charity case.

Cream cardstock with emerald calligraphy:

Save the Date

September 26th

Bellbury Cathedral, Angoumois

Reception to follow at Château Lambert Vineyards

Tristian Alexandre Lambert

&

Emily Dorothy Silver Washington Butler Lambert

That part I knew. What I didn't know—what makes my breath catch—is the embossed letterhead at the bottom.

The families of Pierre and Celeste Lambert, Richard and Winnifred Butler, and Zara and Michael Washington cordially invite you to witness the union of their children.

"I didn't—" My voice cracks. "I didn't know they added that part."

Marcus grins. "Mama and Daddy wanted to make it official. The Washingtons too. You're claimed, baby sister. In writing."

I scroll through Bethany's thread. It gets worse.

@BethanyMorrison: *she's actually doing this. ANGOUMOIS. like she's some kind of princess now*

@AdamTheaterBoss: *Château Lambert Vineyards lmaooo remember when she couldn't afford lunch*

@MarthaHendricks47: *That girl stole from me and now she's living in a castle. This is what happens when you reward lies.*

My hands shake. Tristian takes the phone gently, reads, goes completely still.

"Oh, that's a mistake." His accent thickens. British and sharp. "That's a bloody enormous mistake."

"They're just—" I start.

"Jealous," Michelle finishes. She's reading over Tristian's shoulder. "And about to be sued into oblivion."

Jean pulls out his phone. "I'm texting Dad. This constitutes defamation. Again."

"Wait." Marcus scrolls further. His expression shifts from amused to lethal. "Oh. Oh, they really shouldn't have done that."

He turns the screen. There's another tweet. This one from Adam.

@AdamTheaterBoss: *Emily Silver can barely stand up but sure she's gonna dance at her fancy chateau wedding. Someone check if the groom knows what he's signing up for.*

The table goes silent.

Tristian's chair scrapes back. "I'm going to—"

"Sit." Levi's voice cuts through. "Let Marcus handle it."

Marcus is already typing. "Mama didn't raise me to let trash talk about my sister. Watch this."

He posts a photo—the one from an hour ago. All three couples in our costumes, crammed together at this picnic table. Mochi and Nibbler at our feet. The caption reads:

The Butler-Lambert-Washington family celebrates together. Three weddings. One day. September 26th. Bellbury Cathedral. Family only. If you're confused about who that includes, check the save-the-date letterhead. -Marcus Anthony Butler

Then he tags Richard and Winnifred Butler, Zara and Michael Washington, and Pierre and Celeste Lambert.

Within two minutes, all six parents have reposted.

Pierre's caption: *Our children. All of them. Anyone who has a problem with that can take it up with my lawyers.*

Zara's: *Emily Dorothy Washington. Our daughter. Try us.*

Richard's: *The Butlers stand with family. Always.*

My phone explodes. Bethany's thread fills with replies —people I don't even know defending me, calling out the ableism, demanding apologies.

"There." Marcus drains his bourbon-lemonade. "Now they know."

Tristian pulls me into his lap, careful of my hips. His claws rest gentle on my waist.

"You're a Lambert," he murmurs against my hair. "A Washington. A Butler. You're claimed by three of the most stubborn families in existence. They can't touch you."

I believe him.

For the first time in my entire life, I actually believe it.

"Excuse me?"

The small voice comes from behind Tristian's shoulder. We both turn.

A boy in a navy blue wheelchair sits there, maybe seven years old. His sister stands beside him—pigtails, stimming hands, eyes focused somewhere past us. Both wear Extinction Protocol shirts.

"Sorry to interrupt." The boy's mother hovers anxiously. "They saw you from the churro stand and—"

"No apologies needed." Tristian slides me carefully into my own chair, then crouches to the boy's eye level. "What's your name, mate?"

"Oliver. This is my sister Sage. She doesn't talk much but she loves your movies. We both do." He glances at me, shy. "You're Dorothy. You're gonna be in Wonderful."

My throat tightens. "I am."

"Can we—" Oliver swallows. "Can we get your autographs? And pet your dinosaur?"

Nibbler chirps, tilting his animatronic head.

Tristian's entire demeanor shifts. The accent thickens—pure Alabama drawl. Nathan Cross bleeding through.

"Well now, that there's a Utahraptor hatchling." He beckons them closer. "You gotta approach real slow. Let him smell you first."

Oliver wheels forward cautiously. Sage follows, her hands still flapping.

"That's it. Nice and easy." Tristian guides Oliver's hand to Nibbler's snout. "See how he's lowerin' his head? Means he trusts you. Go on, you can touch."

Oliver's whole face lights up. "He's so soft."

"Nibbler's special." Tristian's voice stays gentle, Southern, completely Nathan. "Most raptors won't let anyone but their pack near the babies. But this one? He knows good people when he sees 'em."

Sage reaches out, fingers brushing Nibbler's scales. She makes a small sound—happy, I think.

"There you go, darlin'." Tristian keeps his movements slow, predictable. "He likes you. See his tail? When it does that little wag, means he's content."

Marcus appears with napkins and a sharpie. I sign Oliver's shirt first—*To Oliver, Keep flying. Emily Lambert*—then Sage's. Tristian adds his signature with a small raptor claw sketch.

"Mr. Lambert?" Oliver's voice goes quieter. "Do you think I could be in movies someday? Even though I can't walk?"

Tristian meets his eyes. "You know who decides if you can be in movies?"

Oliver shakes his head.

"You do. Nobody else. Not them chairs, not what anybody says you can't do. Just you." He taps Oliver's chest. "David Kellerman—man who runs Starlight Studios —he told me somethin' important. Representation matters. That means people need to see kids like you bein' heroes. Solvin' problems. Savin' the day."

"Really?"

"Really. And hey—Wonderful premieres next summer. How'd you and Sage like to come?"

Oliver's mother gasps. "We couldn't possibly—"

"Consider it done." Tristian straightens. "We'll have tickets waitin'. VIP section. Accessible seatin'. The whole thing."

Sage makes another sound, louder this time. Her mother smiles, translating. "She says thank you."

"Anytime, darlin'."

They start to leave, but Oliver wheels back. "Mrs. Lambert? Could you sing something? From Wonderful?"

Everyone at the table goes still. My stomach knots.

"I'm not—I don't have—"

"Please?" His eyes are so hopeful. "Sage loves Dorothy."

Ariana squeezes my hand. "You've got this."

I take a breath. Then another.

The song rises unbidden. The one from Act One's climax, when Dorothy refuses the Wizard's ultimatum—give up the silver slippers, abandon Ellie and her new family, or be declared wicked like her adoptive mother.

My voice starts soft, building.

Sage stops stimming. Turns. Looks directly at me.

My voice cracks on the last note, but I push through.

Tristian moves behind my chair, hands on my shoulders. Grounding me.

The slippers. The family. The choice Dorothy makes—to fly away from the Wizard's threats and return to Felix, to Winkie Country, to the family that chose her.

Silence. Then applause—scattered at first, then building. Oliver and Sage clap hardest of all.

Sage reaches for me. Her mother nods permission. I take the little girl's hand.

"You're brave," she whispers. Clear as crystal. "Like Dorothy."

Something breaks open in my chest.

"So are you," I whisper back.

They leave with promises of premiere tickets and photos with Nibbler. Tristian pulls me into his arms the moment they're gone.

"That," he says, voice thick, "is why you're Dorothy. Right there."

I'm crying. Happy tears this time.

"They needed to see you," Michelle adds quietly. "Kids like them. They needed to know someone like you exists."

Marcus raises his lemonade again. "To Emily Lambert. Who just made those kids' entire year."

"To Emily," everyone echoes.

I bury my face in Tristian's shoulder, overwhelmed and grateful and so, so loved.

The gates open at noon. Two cars—one sleek Mercedes, one practical Honda—roll up the château drive.

I watch from the window, Emily beside me in her chair. Mochi's tail thumps against the floor.

"They're really here," she whispers.

"Course they are, love." I kiss her temple. "You're their daughter."

The doors open. Richard Butler steps out first—tall, silver-haired, wire-rimmed glasses. Lawyer to the bone. Winnie follows, shorter, round-faced, warm brown eyes. Nurse scrubs visible under her cardigan.

Emily makes this small sound. Vulnerable. Scared.

"I've got you." I wheel her toward the foyer.

Mum's already there, Grandmère beside her. Dad hovers near the salon entrance. Jean and Levi descend the stairs.

The doors swing open.

"Emily." Winnie's voice breaks.

Then Emily's rolling forward, and Winnie's on her knees, arms wrapped around my fiancée. Richard crouches too, one hand on Emily's back, the other cupping her face.

"Our girl," he says quietly. "Our brave, beautiful girl."

I step back. Give them space.

Marcus appears, grinning. "Ma. Dad."

"Baby boy." Winnie releases Emily long enough to hug him. "Look at you. All grown up and married."

"To the prettiest girl in Europe," Marcus confirms, pulling Michelle close.

Richard straightens, extends his hand to me. "Mr. Lambert."

"Tristian." I take it. Firm grip. Assessing eyes. "Thank you for coming."

"Family doesn't thank family." His gaze shifts to Emily. "She's ours now. That means you're ours too."

Winnie stands, wiping her eyes. "Now where's this boy causing my daughter so much trouble?"

I blink. "I—"

"Relax, honey. You're good people. I can tell." She pats my cheek, then surveys the room. "Celeste, Pierre. Thank you for having us."

Mum steps forward. "It is our honor."

Grandmère embraces Winnie like they've known each other for decades. "Come. We have tea prepared."

The afternoon blurs—introductions, laughter, stories. Richard and Dad disappear into the study with Jean and Philippe. Something about legal strategy.

I stay close to Emily. She's glowing, surrounded by both families, Mochi sprawled across her lap.

Then her phone rings.

Everyone goes silent.

Emily glances at the screen. Goes pale.

"Martha."

"Don't answer it," Ariana starts.

"Let her." Richard's voice cuts through. "Put it on speaker."

Emily obeys, hands shaking.

"Emily, darling." Martha's voice drips false sweetness. "I've been trying to reach you. We need to talk about this wedding nonsense—"

"Mrs. Hendricks." Richard's lawyer tone is ice. "This is Richard Butler, Emily's first legal father. You're on speaker with the Lambert and Butler families, as well as Philippe Moreau, legal counsel to Pierre Lambert."

Silence. Then—

"She doesn't have a—"

"I have adoption papers that say otherwise. Notarized, filed, legal. Emily Dorothy Silver is now Emily Dorothy

Silver Washington Butler Lambert. Anything you say to her, you say to us."

"This is ridiculous. Emily was my foster daughter. I have rights—"

"You have nothing." Philippe's accent sharpens. "You pawned her mother's belongings. You locked her in closets. You filed false reports claiming she stole family heirlooms that never existed."

"That's not—"

"We have hospital records," Winnie adds quietly. "From every emergency room visit during Emily's time in your care. Malnutrition. Dehydration. Untreated infections. Shall I continue?"

Emily's crying now. I pull her against me.

Richard leans closer to the phone. "Here's what's going to happen, Mrs. Hendricks. You, Adam, and Bethany Morrison are going to retract every statement made to the press. You're going to issue public apologies. And you're going to disappear from Emily's life permanently."

"Or what?"

"Or I bury you." Richard's voice doesn't rise. Doesn't need to. "Criminal charges for child abuse. Civil suits for emotional damages. I'll tie you up in court until you can't afford groceries. Your choice."

Another call beeps through. Bethany.

"Answer it," Richard says.

Emily does, still crying.

"Emily, oh my God, I didn't mean—" Bethany's voice is frantic. "The network edited what I said, I swear, I never called you a—"

"Save it." Marcus takes the phone. "We have the raw footage, Bethany. You called her a 'crippled gold-digger' on camera. You laughed about it."

"I was upset! Adam said—"

"Adam's next." Richard again. "But first, you. Retraction. Apology. Or litigation. Ten seconds."

"I—okay. Okay. I'll do it."

The line goes dead.

Adam calls thirty seconds later. Gets the same treatment. Agrees within five minutes.

Richard ends the call, sets Emily's phone down. "Done."

Emily's shaking. I hold her tighter.

"Come on, honey." Winnie stands. "Let's get you comfortable. Where's your bedroom?"

"Upstairs," I manage. "I'll—"

"You'll carry her. I'll show you the stretches that'll help."

We move through the château—me carrying Emily, Winnie beside us, Mochi trotting behind. Jean opens doors. Levi grabs pillows.

In our room, I lay Emily on the bed. She's still crying, but quieter now.

Winnie perches on the edge, brushing Emily's hair back. "Baby girl. You're safe now. All of us—Lambert, Butler, Washington—we've got you."

"I know," Emily whispers. "I just—I can't believe—"

"Believe it. You're ours." Winnie kisses her forehead, then turns to me. "Her hips. They seize up when she's stressed, right?"

"Yeah. Left worse than right."

"Mm-hmm. Come here. I'll show you." She guides Emily onto her side. "Pressure points. Here—" Her fingers find the spot just above Emily's hip. "Firm but gentle. Fifteen seconds."

I watch, memorizing.

"Now here." Base of her spine. "This releases the sciatic nerve. You'll feel her relax."

Emily sighs as Winnie works.

"And stretches." Winnie demonstrates—knee to chest, gentle rotation. "Never force it. Let her body tell you when to stop."

I kneel beside the bed, hands replacing Winnie's. Emily's muscles loosen under my touch.

"Good." Winnie nods approval. "You're a natural."

"I just want to help her."

"You do. Every day." She squeezes my shoulder. "Now I'll let you two rest. We'll be downstairs when you're ready."

The door closes softly.

I keep working—pressure points, stretches, the rhythm Winnie showed me. Emily's breathing evens out.

"Tristian?"

"Yeah, love?"

"I have parents now. Real ones."

My throat tightens. "You do."

"And they made Martha go away."

"They did."

She turns her head, green eyes finding mine. "This is real. All of it. I'm really yours. Really theirs."

I lean down, kiss her softly. "Really ours. Forever."

Emily's lips find mine, soft and needy. Her fingers curl into my shirt, pulling me closer.

Heat floods through me. The scent of her—vanilla and something uniquely Emily—fills my senses. My hands tighten on her hips, careful even as want surges.

But she's been crying. Been through hell today. Needs rest more than—

The shift happens without conscious thought. My accent bleeds south, rougher around the edges. Predator recognizing prey.

"No time for that, darlin'." I ease back, watching her eyes widen as she catches the change. "When you wake up, I promise."

Her breath hitches. Pupils dilate.

"Though maybe—" I trail one finger along her jaw, down her throat. "—a little pleasure to help you sleep, huh?"

"Tristian." Her voice wavers between plea and protest.

"Shh." I press my thumb against her lower lip. "Let me take care of you."

I shift her onto her back, mindful of her hips. Her body's already relaxed from Winnie's massage techniques, pliant under my hands. Good. Makes this easier.

"Arms up." I tug her shirt over her head, toss it aside. She's wearing one of those adaptive bras—front clasp, easy access. I flick it open.

"We shouldn't—the family's downstairs—"

"Family knows to leave us be." I kiss the hollow of her throat. "And you're gonna be quiet for me, aren't you?"

She nods, already breathless.

I work methodically. Jeans next—carefully, watching for any wince of discomfort. Her body knows mine now, trusts me. Nine months of learning every response, every trigger point.

"Beautiful." The word comes out with that Alabama drawl Nathan carries when he's hunting. When he's found his mate and needs to claim, possess, protect.

I slide my hand between her thighs. She's already wet, ready. Always is when I slip into this headspace, this rougher version that still worships her.

"That's my girl." I circle slowly, watching her face. "Gonna make you feel so good, darlin'. Gonna chase all those bad thoughts right out."

Her hips lift, seeking more pressure. I give it, adding another finger, finding the rhythm she needs.

"Eyes on me." I catch her chin when her gaze starts to drift. "Right here, Emily. Just you and me."

She trembles, biting her lip to stay quiet. The flush spreads down her chest, across those perfect breasts. I lean down, take one nipple in my mouth while my hand continues its work.

"Tristian—" My name breaks on a gasp.

"That's it. Let go." I increase the pressure, curl my fingers just right. "I've got you. Always got you."

She shatters quietly, muffling her cry against my shoulder. I work her through it, gentling as she comes down.

When her breathing settles, I clean her up with a warm cloth from the bathroom. Dress her in soft pajamas—the Dorothy ones she loves. Settle her under the covers.

"Sleep now." I kiss her forehead, accent still lingering. "I'll be right here when you wake."

"Promise?"

"Promise, darlin'. Not going anywhere."

Her eyes drift closed. Within minutes, she's out.

I strip down to boxers, slide in beside her. Pull her against my chest where she fits perfectly.

Downstairs, I hear voices. Family gathering, probably planning our defense strategy.

But right now, in this moment, my world is just this. Emily safe in my arms. Finally believing she belongs.

Finally home.

The scream rips me from sleep at two-seventeen.

Emily thrashes beside me, tangled in sheets. Her hands push against my chest, eyes wild and unseeing.

"No—please—you said—"

"Emily." I catch her wrists gently. "Love, wake up. It's just a dream."

She fights harder. "Don't—don't leave me for her—"

Ice floods my veins. "Who?"

"You promised—" She's sobbing now, still caught in whatever hell her mind's created. "You promised it was real —"

I pull her against me. She struggles, but I hold firm, stroking her hair. "Emily Dorothy Silver Washington Butler Lambert. Wake. Up."

Her breathing hitches. Those green eyes finally focus on my face.

"Tristian?"

"Right here." I kiss her forehead. "Always right here."

She collapses against my chest, shaking. Mochi jumps onto the bed, whining as he nuzzles her arm.

"Sorry," she whispers. "I'm sorry, I just—"

"Don't apologize." I tilt her chin up. "Tell me what you saw."

She shakes her head, pulling away. "It's stupid. Just—just a nightmare."

My jaw tightens. I know that deflection. That self-protective curl of her shoulders.

The shift happens instinctively. My voice drops, gains that commanding edge she responds to. The tone that says husband, protector, the one who knows what she needs even when she won't ask.

"Emily." Not harsh, but absolute. "Look at me."

Her gaze snaps to mine. I see it there—the submission she gives only me, the trust beneath her fear.

"What. Did. You. See."

She swallows hard. "You—you were at the theatre. With Bethany."

My stomach drops. "And?"

"You said—" Her voice cracks. "You said you made a mistake. That you wanted someone who could give you normal. Someone who wasn't—" She gestures at her legs, her wheelchair beside the bed. "Broken."

"Christ, Emily—"

"She was standing. Dancing with you. And you looked so happy, and I was just—I was in my chair watching, and you didn't even see me—"

I pull her into my lap, cradling her like she weighs nothing. Because to me, she doesn't. She's everything, and that makes her weightless and infinite all at once.

"That's not real," I say firmly. "That will never be real."

"But what if—"

"No." I catch her face between my palms. "Listen to me. Bethany Morrison is nothing. A bitter girl who couldn't handle that you got everything she wanted. The role. The recognition. Me."

Emily's breath shudders. "She's had a crush on you since she saw Dans l'Ombre. She told everyone—"

"Don't care." I kiss her hard, possessive. "She's not my wife. She's not wearing my ring. She's not carrying my name or my claim or my heart."

"But I can't dance like—"

"You danced with me. At the park." I soften my grip, thumbs stroking her cheeks. "Your feet on mine, your arms around my neck. Most perfect dance of my life."

"That's not the same—"

"It's better." My accent thickens, British bleeding through. "Because it's ours. Because when I hold you like that, I'm holding all of you. Your strength, your brilliance, your body that fights every damn day and still shows up."

She's crying again, but different now. Quieter.

"I chose you," I continue, voice dropping to that dominant register that makes her shiver. "The moment you rolled up to my table in that Alice costume. Before I knew your name, before I knew anything except that you were mine. You understand me?"

"Yes," she whispers.

"Say it properly." The command isn't harsh. Just absolute.

Her spine straightens slightly. "Yes, husband."

"Good girl." I kiss her temple. "Now tell me you believe me."

"I—" She falters.

"Emily."

"I'm trying. It's just hard to believe someone like you would choose—"

I silence her with another kiss, this one slower. Reverent.

"Someone like me," I murmur against her lips, "waited twenty-seven years to find someone like you. I'm not giving that up for anything."

Tristian's thumb traces circles on my hip at seven in the morning. I'm still curled against him, that nightmare clinging like cobwebs I can't quite shake.

"What are you planning?" I ask, because I know that look. The one that says he's already three steps ahead, fixing problems I haven't even voiced.

"You'll see." He kisses my shoulder. "Get dressed. Something comfortable."

"Tristian—"

"Trust me?"

I sigh. "Always."

Two hours later, I'm staring at Zara, Sophia, and Ariana in our sitting room. Levi lounges on the sofa beside Ariana, grinning like he's in on whatever scheme my husband's cooked up.

"What's happening?" I ask.

Zara wraps me in a hug. "Spa day, baby girl. Tristian's orders."

"He called us at midnight," Sophia adds, adjusting her gorgeous curls. "Said you needed your sisters."

My throat tightens. "He told you about—"

"The nightmare?" Ariana crouches beside my wheelchair. "Yeah. And we're gonna make sure you know exactly how gorgeous you are."

"I don't need—"

"Emily." Zara's voice carries that mom-tone I can't argue with. "When someone offers you a day of pampering at the most exclusive spa in Angoumois, you say thank you."

"Thank you," I mumble.

Levi stands, stretching. "Come on. Train leaves in twenty minutes."

"You're coming?"

"Jean's buried in campaign stuff." He shrugs. "Figured I'd keep you ladies company. Plus, Tristian promised me a massage that'll make me forget politics exist."

The train station in Grantham Bridge buzzes with morning commuters. Tristian guides my wheelchair through the crowd, one hand possessive on the handlebar. He's dressed down—jeans, white t-shirt, leather jacket— but still turns heads.

"You have a meeting," I say as we board the first-class car.

"In Bellbury. Convenient, that." He lifts me into a plush seat, folding my chair. "I'll be done by two. Meet you after?"

"You planned this entire thing around your schedule?"

He kisses me slow, thorough. "Planned it around yours. You deserve to feel as beautiful as you are."

Heat floods my cheeks. "I look fine—"

"You look stunning." His accent thickens, British and commanding. "But you don't believe it. So today, we fix that."

The train pulls away from the station. Angoumois countryside blurs past—vineyards, stone cottages, rolling green hills. Zara and Sophia claim seats across from us while Ariana and Levi settle nearby.

"So what's this spa like?" Sophia asks.

"Best in the country." Tristian scrolls through his phone. "They just created something called the Silver Slipper Package. Exclusively for Emily."

I blink. "They what?"

"Named it after you." He shows me the website. There's my name in elegant script, alongside photos of treatment rooms and gorgeous models. "Full body massage, facial, mani-pedi, hair, makeup. The works."

"That's—that's too much—"

"It's not enough." He pockets his phone. "But it's a start."

Bellbury appears through the window forty minutes later. The coastal town gleams white and blue, boats bobbing in the harbor. Salt air rushes in when the doors open.

Tristian wheels me down the platform. The spa sits on the waterfront—a converted manor house with flowering vines climbing stone walls.

"I'll be back at two," he murmurs, kissing my temple. "Have fun. Please?"

"Okay."

He leaves for his meeting. Levi holds the spa door open as we enter.

The interior takes my breath. Marble floors, crystal chandeliers, the scent of lavender and eucalyptus. A woman in crisp whites approaches, smiling.

"Mrs. Lambert?" She extends her hand. "I'm Genevieve. We're honored to host you today."

"Thank you for—for creating that package—"

"Our pleasure." Her eyes are kind. "Your husband was very specific about your needs. We've prepared everything."

They lead us to private changing rooms. Mine has a robe in the softest fabric I've ever touched, slippers with grips for stability, even a shower chair.

Ariana helps me change. "You good?"

"Yeah." I touch the robe. "This is incredible."

"You're incredible." She kisses my cheek. "Now let's get pampered."

The massage room glows with candlelight. My therapist—a gentle woman named Claire—works magic on muscles that haven't relaxed in weeks. She knows exactly where I hold tension, where my body fights itself.

"Your husband sent detailed notes," she says softly. "About your hip, your legs. I'll be careful."

Tears sting my eyes. Of course he did.

After the massage comes the facial. Then mani-pedi in a room overlooking the ocean. Sophia holds my hand while technicians paint my nails rose gold.

"He really loves you," she says.

"I know. I just—sometimes I can't believe it's real."

"Girl." Zara leans forward from her chair. "That man flew us across an ocean because you had one bad dream. It's real."

"Besides," Ariana adds, grinning, "Philippe says Tristian won't shut up about you. Ever."

Heat creeps up my neck. "He talks about me?"

"Constantly. Philippe says it's adorable and annoying in equal measure."

We dissolve into giggles. Levi wanders over from the men's section, looking blissed out.

"I need Jean to stress less," he announces. "So I can do this weekly."

The final stop is hair and makeup. The stylist—Océane—runs her fingers through my waves.

"Gorgeous texture," she murmurs. "What are we thinking?"

"I don't know. Something that doesn't look like I tried too hard?"

She smiles. "Leave it to me."

An hour later, I barely recognize myself in the mirror. My hair falls in perfect beachy waves, subtle highlights catching light. The makeup is natural but flawless—my eyes bigger, lips fuller, skin glowing.

"Oh my God," Ariana breathes. "Emily."

I stare at my reflection. That's me. That girl who looks confident, beautiful, put-together.

That's actually me.

Océane appears beside me. "Your husband will lose his mind."

"I—" My voice cracks. "I look—"

"Stunning," Zara finishes firmly. "You look stunning."

We're admiring our reflections when Sophia gets that look. The one that means trouble.

"What time did Tristian say he'd be back?" she asks.

I check my phone. "Two. We have forty minutes."

"Perfect." She grins. "There's a tattoo parlor two blocks over."

Ariana's eyes light up. "Oh, I like where this is going."

"What?" I wheel back slightly. "We can't just—"

"We absolutely can." Zara pulls out her phone, already searching. "Bellbury Ink. Five-star reviews. Walk-ins welcome."

"But Tristian—"

"Will love it," Levi finishes. He's way too invested in this plan. "Trust me. Possessive husband energy for days."

My stomach flips. "We'd need permission from David. Contract stuff—"

Sophia's already dialing. "Mr. Kellerman? Hi, it's Sophia Martinez. Quick question about our contracts..."

She puts him on speaker.

"—as long as it's tasteful and relevant to the film," David's voice crackles through. "What are you planning?"

"Matching silver slippers," Sophia says. "Dorothy's iconic shoes. On our wrists."

Silence. Then David laughs. "Marketing will eat that up. Do it. Send me photos after."

He hangs up.

I stare at my friends. "We're really doing this?"

"Hell yes," Ariana says. "Sisters of Oz, making it official."

Bellbury Ink smells like antiseptic and possibility. The artist—a woman named Margot with full sleeve tattoos—sketches the design in ten minutes. Delicate silver slippers, small enough for our inner wrists, detailed enough to recognize instantly.

"Four matching?" she asks.

"Four matching," Zara confirms.

Levi films everything for posterity. I go first because I'm terrified I'll chicken out. The needle buzzes, sharp and stinging.

"Breathe," Margot says gently. "Almost done."

Fifteen minutes later, we're wrapped in plastic film, grinning like idiots. The slippers gleam silver against our skin—permanent proof that we're family now.

"Post it," Sophia urges. "Instagram. Tag everyone."

My fingers shake as I type: *Got matching ink with my sisters. Dorothy's silver slippers for the girls who helped me find home. @SophiaMartinezActress @ZaraWashington @AriTattooQueen#WonderfulFamily #SistersOfOz*

I add a photo of our four wrists together, the fresh tattoos bright against varied skin tones.

The post goes live.

My phone explodes within seconds.

Ariana laughs, reading comments. "Michael just commented: 'My girls! So proud!'"

"David shared it," Sophia adds. "Official Wonderful account reposted."

Zara's grin turns wicked. "Tristian just liked it. Wait—he's typing—"

My phone vibrates with a text.

Tristian: *Zhara. Where are you?*

Heat floods through me. He only uses Winkie when he's feeling very possessive or very turned on.

Usually both.

"Oh, we're in trouble," I whisper.

Me: *Bellbury Ink. We got lunch plans.*

Tristian: *Cancel them. I'm two minutes away.*

Me: *Too late. Already walking to the restaurant.*

It's not entirely a lie. We're moving toward the door.

Tristian: *Emily Dorothy Silver Washington Butler Lambert.*

Full government name. In Winkie. My thighs clench involuntarily.

Me: *Gotta go, Zheli. Love you!*

I silence my phone. Levi's filming again, cackling.

"Last time I ran from Tristian," I announce, wheeling fast down the sidewalk, "I ended up married on a Metro train."

"Then we better move quickly," Ariana laughs, pushing my chair faster.

We duck into a café three doors down—Le Petit港. French-Asian fusion, according to the sign. The host seats us immediately at a corner booth.

My phone lights up with notifications. I don't check them.

"He's going to lose his mind," Sophia says, delighted.

"Good." Zara raises her water glass. "To Dorothy and her silver slippers. To the sisters who found each other."

"To family," I whisper.

We toast. My wrist throbs pleasantly under the bandage—permanent proof that I'm not alone anymore.

That I never will be again.

My phone buzzes one more time. I peek.

Tristian: *When I find you, Zhara, we're having words. The possessive kind.*

I bite my lip, grinning.

Can't wait.

The café serves these incredible shrimp dumplings that melt on my tongue. I'm halfway through my second plate when Sophia snorts, scrolling her phone.

"Oh no. Oh, this is gold."

"What?" I lean over.

She shows me Bethany's Instagram. There's a photo of Tristian from the premiere—close-up, intense eyes, that smoldering expression he does for cameras. The caption makes my stomach turn.

Still thinking about meeting @TristianLambert at FanCon. A real gentleman. Some people get lucky, but true class recognizes class. #HollywoodRoyalty #LambertAppreciation

"She did not." Ariana grabs the phone. "Is she seriously —"

"Thirsty," Zara finishes. "So desperately thirsty."

Levi reads over my shoulder. "Oh, we're destroying her. Publicly."

"We shouldn't—" I start.

"Baby girl." Zara's already typing. "She called you a scam on national television. We're razzing her a little."

I watch as Zara comments: *Funny, my husband says Tristian only has eyes for his WIFE. You know, Emily Lambert? The one you tried dragging through the mud? #TryAgain*

Sophia adds: *True class recognizes true love. Tristian found his in Emily. Stay pressed.* 🦢

Ariana goes brutal: *Imagine being this desperate for a married man who literally roared at you through a phone. Could not be me.*

Levi's contribution makes me choke on tea: *As Tristian's brother-in-law, I can confirm he thinks you're pathetic. His words, not mine. Well, mostly his words. I agree though. #LambertFamilyOfficial*

"Levi!" I gasp.

"What? It's true. He said it last week."

My phone buzzes. Multiple notifications. I open Instagram.

Michael Washington commented: *My daughter Emily is CLASS. You wouldn't recognize it if it bit you.*

Dante added: *Sophia and I stand with the Lamberts. Emily earned her place. You earned a lawsuit. Choose wisely.*

Philippe Moreau, always diplomatic: *Mademoiselle Morrison, perhaps focus on your own life rather than coveting another woman's husband. It is unbecoming.*

Then Tristian's comment appears, and my entire body heats.

Miss Morrison. I warned you once. Consider this your final warning. My wife—my ZHARA—is off-limits. As am I. Respect that, or face consequences. The Lambert kind. The

Winkie kind. The raptor kind. All three are significantly unpleasant when protecting what's MINE.

"Oh my God," I whisper.

"He went full possessive," Ariana crows. "All three modes activated."

Sophia fans herself. "That's the hottest threat I've ever read."

"Bethany's crying somewhere," Zara says. "Guaranteed."

Levi's phone rings. He grins. "It's Michael. Hey—"

I hear Michael's laugh through the speaker. "—that girl needed taking down. Dante and I are flying to Bellbury with Philippe. Jean's chartering something. Where are you?"

"Bellbury. About to relocate."

"Don't tell Tristian where you're going. Make him work for it."

Levi's grin turns feral. "Oh, I like how you think. Jean needs to chase me anyway. He's been too comfortable."

He hangs up. Turns to us. "Ladies. We're running."

"What?" I blink.

"Traditional bride hunt," Zara explains, standing. "Winkie custom. The men chase, we evade. First to catch their bride wins bragging rights."

"But we're already married—"

"Doesn't matter." Sophia tosses bills on the table. "It's about the game. The pursuit."

"Levi has a handicap van Tristian can't track," Ariana adds. "Company rental. No GPS."

My heart pounds. "We're seriously doing this?"

"Hell yes." Levi's already moving. "Van's two blocks over. Move, move!"

We burst onto the street. Levi pushes my wheelchair fast, Sophia and Zara flanking us. Ariana runs ahead, laughing.

The van waits in a parking garage—white, unmarked, completely nondescript. Levi loads my chair while I transfer to the passenger seat.

"Where are we going?" I ask as he peels out.

"Ferry terminal," Zara says from behind me. "We're not staying on the mainland."

"We're not?"

She grins. "Nope. Private island. My family's place. Middle of nowhere, forty minutes by boat."

"They'll never find us," Sophia adds gleefully.

"Oh, they'll find us." Levi floors it toward the coast. "But they'll have to work for it."

My phone explodes with texts.

Tristian: *Emily. Where are you.*

Tristian: *ZHARA.*

Tristian: *I can track your chair—*

Me: *Chair's in a van you don't know about. Good luck, Zheli.* 😘

Tristian: *You're running from me?*

Me: *Isn't that the point of a bride hunt?*

Three dots appear. Disappear. Appear again.

Tristian: *When I catch you—and I WILL catch you— you're not moving for a week.*

Heat floods through me. I bite my lip, grinning.

Me: *Promises, promises.* 💋

I silence my phone.
Let the hunt begin.

The ferry cuts through blue-green water, salt spray misting my face. I've never seen ocean this color—like someone melted emeralds and sapphires together.

My phone buzzes against my thigh. I pull it out.

Tristian: *Found the ferry terminal. Worker said four women and a man boarded fifteen minutes ago.*

Tristian: *You're on water, Zhara. Running to an island.*

Tristian: *That won't save you.*

I grin, typing back.

Me: *Maybe I don't want saving.*

Three dots. Then a message that makes my breath catch.

Tristian: *Good. Because when I find you—and I will—I'm stripping that gorgeous dress off with my teeth. Slowly. While you beg.*

Heat pools low in my stomach.

Tristian: *Then I'm taking you on whatever surface is closest. Floor, table, wall. Doesn't matter. You ran from me, love. That has consequences.*

Tristian: *The Lambert kind. Remember?*

My thighs clench involuntarily.

Me: *You're very confident for someone who has no idea where I am.*

Tristian: *I tracked Phantom across three countries when he escaped the stables. You think I can't find my own wife?*

Tristian: *I'm going to taste every inch of you. Make you come on my tongue until you forget your own name. Then maybe—MAYBE—I'll forgive you for this.*

I drop the phone in my lap, face burning.

"Oh my God," I whisper.

Sophia glances over from her seat. "Tristian?"

"He's—he's threatening to—" I can't finish.

She grins. "Let me guess. Very detailed descriptions of what he plans to do when he catches you?"

"How did you—"

"Dante's doing the same thing." She shows me her phone.

I read the screen. Dante's texts are somehow both romantic and absolutely filthy. Something about rose petals and restraints and making Sophia scream his name loud enough the neighbors complain.

"Oh wow."

"Yeah." She fans herself. "He gets creative when I run."

Ariana snorts from across the aisle. "Philippe just sent me a voice memo in French. I don't speak French but I'm pretty sure it's illegal in several countries."

"Levi?" I ask.

He's staring at his phone, neck red. "Jean is—Jesus Christ—he's describing things I didn't know he knew about."

"Let me see," Zara demands.

Levi shows her. Her eyebrows shoot up.

"Damn. Your husband has a mouth on him."

"Usually he's so proper!" Levi's accent thickens—pure Ohio now. "Where did he learn—"

"Marcus," Zara says. "Definitely Marcus. That man corrupts everyone."

My phone buzzes again.

Tristian: *Silent now? Thinking about it?*

Tristian: *About my hands on your hips. My mouth between your thighs. How I'll make you ride me until you're shaking.*

Tristian: *You're wet right now, aren't you, Zhara? Just from reading these.*

I squeeze my legs together. He's not wrong.

Tristian: *That's what I thought. My good girl, getting ready for me.*

Tristian: *But you still ran. So when I catch you, I'm edging you. For HOURS. Until you're begging, crying, promising never to run again.*

Tristian: *Then maybe I'll let you come.*

Holy shit.

Sophia leans over, reading. "Oh, he's good."

"He's evil," I correct.

Me: *Bold threats from someone still on the mainland.*

Tristian: *Jean chartered a boat. We'll be there in twenty minutes.*

Tristian: *Run faster, love. It'll make catching you more satisfying.*

I look up at Zara. "They chartered a boat. Twenty minutes out."

She grins, pulling out her phone. "Perfect timing then."

"For what?"

"We're not going to Michael's place." She shows me a real estate listing. "Bought this last month. Smaller island, completely private. Full accessibility features—ramps, roll-in shower, the works. Michael doesn't even know yet."

The photos show a gorgeous stone cottage overlooking cliffs. Gardens, a private beach, modern interior with wide doorways and smooth floors.

"You bought an island?" I breathe.

"Technically a very large rock with a house on it." She shrugs. "But yes. Wanted somewhere for us. Family getaways. Plus—" She winks. "—good for hiding from overprotective husbands."

Levi laughs. "They're going to search Michael's island for hours."

"Exactly." Zara texts someone. "Captain's rerouting. Ten minutes to my place."

Ariana's phone rings. She answers, putting it on speaker.

"Where are you?" Philippe demands. His accent is thicker than usual—always happens when he's worked up.

"Wouldn't you like to know," Ariana purrs.

"Ma chérie, when I find you—"

"If you find me."

"—I am going to bend you over the nearest surface and remind you exactly who you belong to."

Heat flashes across Ariana's face. "That's quite a promise, Moreau."

"It is not a promise. It is a guarantee." His voice drops lower. "Run all you want. It only makes the chase sweeter. And the punishment longer."

"Punishment?" she challenges.

"You think you can tease me, run from me, and face no consequences? Non, mon coeur. You will learn."

They're all completely unhinged, I decide. Every single one of them.

My phone buzzes.

Tristian: *Docking now. Where are you hiding, Zhara?*

Me: *Check Michael's island. Maybe I'm there. Maybe not.* 😇

Tristian: *You're playing with fire.*

Me: *Good thing I like getting burned.*

I silence my phone as the ferry approaches a small dock. The cottage sits above us, all stone and charm and accessibility features I didn't know I needed.

"Welcome to Paradise Point," Zara announces. "Population: us. For now."

Levi helps me transfer to my chair. "How long until they figure it out?"

"Hours," Sophia says confidently. "Michael's place is huge. They'll search every room."

"Then what?" I ask.

Zara grins. "Then they find us. And we see who caught their bride first."

My phone lights up with one final text.

Tristian: *You're going to regret this, love. In the best possible way. I promise you that.*

I smile, tucking the phone away.

Can't wait.

"Water's gorgeous," Levi announces, emerging from the waves in nothing but a navy speedo that leaves very little to imagination.

"Jesus Christ," Sophia mutters. "Jean's a lucky man."

"Damn right he is." Levi grins, wringing out his hair. "You ladies coming in?"

"In a bit," Zara says. "We're staging a photo shoot first."

I've changed into a blue gingham bikini—tiny triangles of fabric that show off the silver slipper tattoo on my wrist and Tristian's 'T' on my shoulder. The belly ring he gave me catches sunlight, emerald winking between the gingham triangles covering my chest.

"Lay out on the towels," Ariana directs, already in photographer mode. She's wearing a purple string bikini that shows off every single one of her sixty-plus tattoos. "Emily in the middle. Levi, you too. Zara on the left, Sophia on the right."

We arrange ourselves on the sand. The warmth seeps into my hip immediately, loosening muscles that have been tight for days.

"Oh my god," I breathe.

"Warm hip is a happy hip," Zara says knowingly. "Why do you think I bought a Mediterranean island?"

Ariana snaps photos from above. "Okay, now everyone on your sides. Emily, prop up on your elbow—perfect. Levi, flex a little. Not that much, we're going for sexy not showing off."

"I contain multitudes," he says.

"You contain ego," Sophia corrects.

More clicks. Ariana circles us, getting different angles.

"These are amazing," she announces. "Post-worthy?"

"Absolutely," Zara confirms.

Ariana uploads the best shot to Instagram—all of us stretched out on jewel-tone towels, ocean in the background, looking like we're in a travel magazine spread.

Caption: *Paradise Point. Population: Enough.*

My phone explodes within seconds.

Tristian: *EMILY DOROTHY SILVER WASHINGTON BUTLER LAMBERT.*

Tristian: *WHAT ARE YOU WEARING.*

Tristian: *That is NOT enough fabric.*

Tristian: *WHO APPROVED THIS.*

Tristian: *I'm getting on that boat RIGHT NOW.*

I giggle, showing the others.

Sophia's phone buzzes. She reads, face going pink. "Dante wants to know if I'm trying to kill him. Says he's already hard and they're still searching Michael's wine cellar."

"Jean just sent me twelve texts in French," Levi reports. "The gist is 'get your ass to a room' and something about christening every surface when he finds me."

Ariana smirks at her screen. "Philippe's threatening to tie me to the bed for a week. Pretty sure that's supposed to be punishment but—"

"Sounds like a vacation," Zara finishes.

My phone keeps buzzing.

Marcus: *Em. EMILY. That is my BABY SISTER in a BIKINI on the INTERNET.*

Marcus: *I'm getting Zara to delete that RIGHT NOW.*

Marcus: *Never mind Zara won't answer her phone.*

Marcus: *EMILY ANSWER ME.*

Tristian: *I see your tattoo. My initial. Right there on your shoulder for everyone to see.*

Tristian: *And my emerald. In your belly button. Claiming you.*

Tristian: *Do you have ANY IDEA what that's doing to me?*

Tristian: *I'm supposed to be searching this mansion but all I can think about is peeling that blue gingham off with my teeth.*

Me: *Then maybe you should find me faster.* 😘

Tristian: *You're EVIL.*

"Ariana," Zara says suddenly, "what if we did individual shoots? Like beach boudoir?"

"Oh hell yes." Ariana sits up. "Emily first. We'll use the waterline, get that sunset glow—"

"I'm not leaving this sand," I interrupt.

They all look at me.

"My hip," I explain. "It hasn't felt this good in weeks. I'm staying right here until someone forcibly moves me."

Understanding crosses Zara's face. "The warmth."

"It's perfect." I stretch out fully, letting heat soak into muscles and joints. "Like natural physical therapy."

Levi lies back on his towel. "Then we bring the shoot to you."

"Exactly." Ariana repositions. "Okay, Emily. Roll onto your stomach—can you do that?"

I manage it, propping my chin on my hands.

"Gorgeous. Now look at me like Tristian just walked in."

I think about him in the shower this morning. Water on his skin. His accent thickening as he—

"Perfect!" Ariana clicks rapidly. "That's the one. That's the 'I'm going to destroy my husband' look."

More photos. Different angles. The sand is still warm beneath me, working magic on my chronically tight hip.

My phone buzzes beside my head.

Tristian: *The warm sand helps your hip, doesn't it, my darling?*

I blink. How did he—

Tristian: *I know you. Know that you've been hurting more than you admit. Know warmth helps.*

Tristian: *For our honeymoon, I'll find you the warmest beach in the world. Hell, I'll buy you one if I have to.*

Tristian: *Somewhere you can lay in the sun every day. Somewhere your pain eases just from existing.*

Tristian: *You deserve that. Deserve everything.*

Tears prick my eyes.

Me: *You can't just say things like that when you're supposed to be sexually frustrated.*

Tristian: *Who says I'm not both? I'm extremely sexually frustrated AND planning our accessible beach honeymoon.*

Tristian: *I contain multitudes, love.*

I laugh, pressing my face into the towel.

"What?" Sophia asks.

"He's talking about buying me a beach."

"Of course he is," Ariana says. "That man would buy you the moon if you asked."

"Wouldn't even have to ask," Levi adds. "He'd just do it. Then act like it's normal."

My phone buzzes again.

Tristian: *We found the wine cellar empty. You're not at Michael's, are you?*

Me: *Took you long enough to figure out.* 😏

Tristian: *WHERE. ARE. YOU.*

Me: *Paradise Point. Zara's new place. Come find me, husband.*

Tristian: *I'm commandeering the boat. Be there in fifteen minutes.*

Tristian: *And Emily? Don't you DARE move from that sand. I want to find you exactly like you are in those photos.*

Tristian: *Warm. Happy. Mine.*

Heat floods through me that has nothing to do with the sun.

"They're coming," I announce. "Fifteen minutes."

"Better make these last shots count then," Ariana says, grinning wickedly. "Because once they arrive, we're all getting thoroughly claimed."

The ocean sparkles. The sand works its warmth into my bones. And somewhere across the water, my husband is racing to find me.

I smile into the camera.

Can't wait.

I wake to water droplets hitting my face.

My eyes flutter open. Tristian looms above me, dripping wet, swim trunks clinging to every defined muscle. His chest heaves. Hair plastered to his forehead. Eyes absolutely feral.

"Hi," I manage.

He growls—actually growls—and drops to his knees in the sand. His mouth crashes against mine, fierce and claiming. I taste salt water and possession.

"Swam," he pants against my lips between kisses. "Put my phone in a waterproof case and swam because I couldn't wait another bloody second."

His accent is pure British rage and desire. Hands frame my face, thumbs stroking my cheekbones while he devours my mouth.

"The island," he breathes. "Next door. It was for sale."

I blink. "Was?"

"Bought it." Another kiss. "Thirty minutes ago. Wire transfer while I was swimming. And one next to Hawaii."

My brain short-circuits. "You bought two islands while —"

"Already paid for renovations." His forehead presses to mine. "Having the Felix bed from Starlight copied. One for every property we own."

The coronation bed. Sunflower yellow comforter, carved headboard with Ozian crests, the bed where Dorothy and Felix—

"You'll sleep in emerald elegance," Tristian continues, voice dropping lower. "Like the Queen of Oz you are. Everywhere we go. That bed. That reminder of who you've always been."

My throat tightens. "I like our Regency bed at home."

The one in LA. Where he first made love to me. Where I became completely his.

"Then we'll keep it." He kisses my nose. "Everywhere else though—"

A splash interrupts. Jean has tackled Levi into the shallows. They're both laughing and cursing in French.

"Lasted longest," I observe.

"Clearly trying to avoid punishment," Tristian agrees. "Jean's going to make him pay for that."

Marcus has Zara pinned against a palm tree. Dante has Sophia over his shoulder, marching toward the beach house. Philippe and Ariana have already disappeared.

"I'll never run again," I promise. "Well, not for a while at least."

"Good." Tristian's smile turns predatory. He brushes sand off my shoulder, fingers trailing over his tattooed initial. "Finish your nap, my darling. This sand is working magic on your hip and I want you relaxed."

"And then?"

His thumb traces my lower lip. "Then I'm going to carry you to that beach house. Find the bedroom with the softest mattress. And make you scream my name until everyone on this island knows exactly who you belong to."

Heat pools low in my belly.

"The boys will hear."

"Let them." He kisses the corner of my mouth. "Let the whole Mediterranean hear. You're my wife. My queen. Mine."

The possessiveness should probably bother me. Instead it makes me feel safe. Wanted. Chosen.

"How long do I have?" I ask.

"Twenty minutes." Another kiss. "Then you're mine for the rest of the afternoon."

I settle back onto the warm sand, letting heat continue working into my hip. Tristian stretches out beside me, still dripping, one hand resting possessively on the small of my back.

Jean drags a laughing Levi from the water. "You're in so much trouble."

"Worth it," Levi gasps.

"We'll see if you're still saying that in an hour."

They disappear toward the house, leaving wet footprints.

Tristian's fingers draw patterns on my spine. "I love you."

"Love you too." I close my eyes. "Even when you're feral and buying islands."

"Especially then," he corrects.

The ocean whispers. Sand radiates warmth. And my husband waits beside me, patient and possessive in equal measure.

Twenty minutes.

Then I'm his.

Again.

Always.

Chapter 13: Every Stitch Counts

Fifteen days.

Fifteen bloody days until I marry Emily Dorothy Silver Washington Butler Lambert in front of God, three countries' worth of press, and everyone we've ever loved.

"Sit still," Emily orders from her wheelchair. She's got pins in her mouth, measuring tape around her neck, and that look—the one that means even my most commanding raptor voice won't move her.

"You've been working for six hours straight."

"Almost done with Jean's waistcoat." She doesn't look up, fingers flying across burgundy silk. "Then I need to finish Michelle's bodice before—"

"Before you collapse from exhaustion?"

"Before I lose the light." She finally meets my gaze. Those emerald eyes flash with determination and creative fever. "This is my family's wedding, Tristian. I will not send anyone down the aisle in anything less than perfection."

Can't argue with that. Won't even try.

I retreat to the salon where chaos reigns. Mum and Winnie hunch over fabric swatches while Nibbler chirps happily from his cushion in the corner. Michelle drapes herself across the chaise, scrolling her phone.

"Engagement photos dropped," she announces.

My phone explodes immediately.

The first set—Emily and me at the Emerald Palace, her in that stunning green dress, me in Felix's coronation costume. Her crown catches the light. My hand rests on her shoulder, thumb brushing my tattooed initial on her skin.

We look like royalty. Like we've always belonged exactly here.

Next come Marcus and Michelle on the Operator stage set. All sleek black tactical gear and dangerous grace. Marcus has Michelle pinned against a concrete wall, both laughing at some private joke. The shot captures them mid-motion—alive, electric, absolutely perfect for each other.

Then Jean and Levi in the Monsters area. Jean's got Levi pressed against stone archway, mouth against his neck like he's about to bite. Levi's face shows mock terror and real desire. They're both in vintage evening wear—Jean in classic Dracula black, Levi in Victorian waistcoat and cravat.

"Jean's going to love that one," I mutter.

"Already sent it to the Assemblée campaign manager." Michelle grins wickedly. "Nothing says 'vote for progressive values' like your candidate's brother publicly claiming his husband in full vampire cosplay."

The photos flood every major outlet within minutes. *Variety, People, Elle, Southern Living*. Even French and British publications pick them up.

Hollywood's Favorite Couples: A Starlight Studios Love Story

Lambert Family Double Wedding: September 26th

From FanCon to Forever: Tristian Lambert and Emily Silver's Fairy Tale

My phone buzzes with texts from the Wonderful cast, the Extinction Protocol crew, even Christine from the Phantom experience.

David Kellerman calls. "The publicity is gold. Absolutely gold. Keep doing whatever you're doing."

"Getting married," I tell him.

"Perfect. Don't stop."

Jean appears in the doorway, looking harassed. "Ariana and Philippe just went Instagram official."

"About bloody time."

"They're calling themselves 'Philiana' on Twitter. It's trending. Dad's campaign manager is thrilled because apparently Philippe's family has serious political connections in Marseille."

Everything is spinning faster now. The wedding. The publicity. Three couples navigating tabloids and trending hashtags and the relentless hunger for content.

Ariana bounces past with fabric samples. "Emily needs the sapphire organza. Where did Mum put the sapphire organza?"

"Third drawer," Celeste calls from somewhere deep in the château.

"Found it!"

I check the time. Eight-thirty. Emily hasn't eaten since breakfast.

Back in her studio, I find her hunched over Jean's waistcoat, nearly finished. Her shoulders curve forward with exhaustion. Hands tremble slightly.

"Food," I announce.

"Almost done—"

"Now, my darling." I crouch beside her wheelchair. "You're shaking."

"Fine in five minutes—"

"Emily Dorothy." The raptor voice. Low and commanding.

She doesn't even flinch. Just keeps stitching.

Well. That's new.

"The dress won't be perfect if you faint," I try instead.

"Won't faint."

"Your hands are trembling."

"Almost. Done."

Emily finally smiles. Sets the waistcoat carefully aside. "Two down. Four to go."

"After food."

"After food," she agrees.

Victory tastes sweet.

I carry her downstairs where Alfred has prepared her favorite—chicken piccata with angel hair pasta. She eats curled against my chest while I read her wedding RSVPs on my phone.

Dante and Sophia—yes. Zara and Michael—yes. Daniel Brooks—yes. Half of Hollywood—yes.

Bethany Morrison sent a gift. Emily had me return it unopened with a firm decline.

"Fifteen days," Emily murmurs against my shoulder.

"Fifteen days until you're legally, officially, irrevocably mine."

"Already yours."

"Then fifteen days until everyone else accepts that fact."

She laughs softly. Kisses my jaw.

Fifteen days.

I can wait fifteen days.

Barely.

The dining room overlooks the eastern gardens. Sunlight cuts through leaded glass, throwing geometric patterns across the table where I'm meant to be reviewing seating charts for the reception.

Can't focus worth a damn.

Emily's been locked in that studio for nine hours today. Nine. Even for her obsessive perfectionism, that's excessive.

Footsteps approach—rapid, purposeful.

Winnie appears in the doorway, face tight with concern. "Tristian."

I'm on my feet before she finishes my name.

"Emily?" The word comes out sharp. Dangerous.

"She won't leave the atelier. Been crying for the past twenty minutes. Won't tell us what's wrong, just keeps working." Winnie's accent thickens with worry. "Michelle and Ariana are holding her hands together so she can't drive the wheelchair. I drove her out myself."

Bloody hell.

"Where is she?"

"Hallway. Near the stairs." Winnie catches my arm as I move past. "Tristian, put our stubborn girl to bed, please. Maybe make love after. Or before. Or both. Just—relax her somehow."

"What's wrong?" Ice floods my veins. "Is she—"

"Might be developing a cyst. She's crying in pain. Collette is already calling the doctor."

The raptor wakes instantly. Protective. Possessive. Mine is hurt.

I find Emily in the hallway, Michelle and Ariana flanking her wheelchair like guards. Emily's face is blotchy, tear-streaked. She clutches her lower abdomen with both hands.

"Felix," she whispers. Voice broken.

The sound destroys me.

"Zheli has you, zhara." I crouch before her. Wipe tears from her cheeks. "Tell me."

"Hurts."

"I know, my darling. I know." I stand, lifting her from the wheelchair in one smooth motion. "Michelle, leave the chair here."

"Tristian—" Emily starts.

"No." The word comes out in Felix's voice—that low Midwestern command he uses when Dorothy puts herself in danger. When she exhausts her magic healing wounded villagers while the Wizard's soldiers patrol the streets. "Not this time, Dorothy."

Emily's breath catches. Recognizes the shift.

Good.

I carry her upstairs, each step deliberate. She doesn't fight, just curls against my chest. Trembling.

In our bedroom, I settle her on the bed. She tries to sit up.

"Lie down." Still Felix. Still commanding. "Zheli is taking care of you now."

"I need to finish Michelle's bodice—"

"What you need is rest." I move to her wardrobe, pulling out the Wonderful Wizard of Oz nightgown—soft cotton, worn from washing. Comfortable. "And proper care."

"Felix, I don't feel good."

The admission cracks something in my chest.

"My poor Dorothy." I return to her, voice softening just slightly. "Shhh, zhara. Zheli has you."

I help her undress carefully. No underwear—nothing to put pressure on where the cyst might be forming. The nightgown slides over her head, falls to her knees.

Her right wrist catches my attention. Swollen. The brace she usually wears sits discarded on the nightstand.

"Emily Dorothy." I lift her hand gently. The MP joint of her middle finger is inflamed, angry red. "How long?"

"Just today. I was sewing—"

"For nine hours straight." I retrieve the brace, fasten it carefully around her wrist. "Without breaks. Without eating. Without telling anyone you were in pain."

She has the grace to look ashamed.

"Your punishment," I tell her quietly, "is bedrest."

Her eyes widen. "Tristian—"

"Do you remember our Winkie wedding night? What I promised if you ever pushed yourself to illness again?"

Pink floods her cheeks. "Yes, but—"

"Dad took Mum's credit cards away just yesterday for the same offense." I cup her face, thumb brushing her bottom lip. "Every Lambert husband employs discipline when necessary, zhara. I warned you."

"How long?"

"Until the doctor says otherwise."

"The wedding—"

"Is fifteen days away. Michelle's bodice can wait until you're well." I settle beside her on the bed, pulling her against my chest. "Nothing matters more than your health."

She's quiet for a long moment. Then: "Zheli, I have to pee."

I carry her to the bathroom, wait while she handles what she needs, carry her back.

"Read to me?" Small voice. Seeking comfort.

Perfect.

I grab *Wonderful: The Life and Times of Dorothy Mae Gale* from the nightstand—the novelization written in first-person from Dorothy's perspective. We're halfway through, right at the part where they meet Nick the Tin Man.

Settling against the headboard, I arrange Emily carefully in my lap. Open to our bookmarked page.

"'Why do you wish to see the Wizard?' Nick asked, his voice echoing hollowly in his metal chest."

Emily relaxes against me as I read. Felix will ask for a brain

Then Dorothy speaks.

"'I want a grand house in the city,' I told them. 'For me and Felix.'"

I feel Emily smile against my shoulder.

The text continues with Felix's reaction—how thrilled he becomes, immediately dragging Dorothy down the yellow brick road with renewed enthusiasm.

"'Felix, slow down!' I protested, stumbling in my silver heels. 'I'm wearing—'"

Emily joins me for the next line, both of us reading together: "'—heels!'"

I continue in Felix's voice, letting the accent thicken: "The sooner we see the Wizard, the sooner we can marry. The sooner we marry, the sooner I'm human again. The sooner I'm human, the sooner I can ravish you into oblivion."

"Makes me blush every time," Emily murmurs.

"Makes virgin Dorothy blush too." I kiss her temple. "Felix kisses her with his burlap lips right after. Scandalous."

The scene shifts to the magic cabin that appears each night for shelter. Felix rubs Dorothy's aching feet, massaging away the pain from walking all day.

Emily's breathing evens out. Pain medication Dr. Rousseau prescribed earlier finally kicking in.

"Tomorrow," she whispers, "read the Emerald Cathedral wedding."

"Tomorrow," I promise. "The most beautiful chapter in the entire book."

"Alright." Her eyes drift closed. "Sleep, zhara. We'll make love once you wake."

"Zheli..."

"Shh." I hold her closer, one hand resting protectively over where the cyst might be forming. "Rest now, my Dorothy. Your Felix has you."

She falls asleep within minutes, breath soft against my neck.

I text the family group chat with my free hand:

Emily's resting. Doctor coming shortly. Wedding prep continues without her until she's cleared.

Jean responds immediately: **Good. She'll work herself to death otherwise.**

Just like someone else I know, Levi adds.

Pot, kettle, Michelle contributes.

Mum sends a heart emoji.

Dad's response surprises me: **Take care of our daughter.**

Our daughter.

I stare at those words until they blur.

Emily shifts in her sleep, curling tighter against me. The emerald belly ring catches light from the window—my claim, my mark, my forever.

Fourteen days.

Fourteen days until I marry this brilliant, stubborn, extraordinary woman who pushes herself too hard and loves too fiercely and somehow chose me out of everyone in the world.

Fourteen days until she becomes my wife in every legal, binding sense.

But she's already mine.

Has been since that first moment at FanCon when green eyes met mine and the Lambert curse struck like lightning.

I stay exactly where I am—holding her, protecting her, keeping her safe.

Always.

Dr. Rousseau finishes examining Emily's hand, expression grave. "No hand sewing for seventy-two hours minimum. After that, perhaps an hour or two, but—" She pauses, meeting my eyes over Emily's sleeping form. "Mr. Lambert, if she continues at this pace, she risks permanent joint damage. She may never embroider again."

The words land like bullets.

Emily stirs, blinking awake. "What?"

"Your MP joints are severely inflamed," Dr. Rousseau explains gently. "The repetitive motion, combined with your arthritis—"

"No." Emily's voice cracks. "No, I—embroidery is everything. It's why I became a designer. I can't—"

"Emily—" I start.

"No!" Tears spill down her cheeks. "You don't understand. The beadwork, the crystals, the embroidery—

that's what makes my designs special. That's what got me into Starlight. That's—" Her breath hitches. "That's the only thing I'm actually good at."

"That's not true—"

"It is!" She's sobbing now, whole body shaking. "Anyone can sew a seam. Anyone can draft a pattern. But the embellishment, the detail work—that's mine. That's the only thing that makes me worth—"

"Stop." I pull her against my chest, heart shattering. "Just stop, zhara."

Dr. Rousseau quietly packs her supplies. "I'll return tomorrow to check on her. Ice the joints every few hours. The medication should help."

She slips out, leaving us alone.

Emily cries into my shoulder. Deep, wrenching sobs that tear through both of us.

"Zheli, hold me. Please just—hold me."

"I've got you, Em. I've got you."

I cradle her like something precious and broken, one hand stroking her hair while she mourns. This isn't pain I can fix with medication or money or commands. This is loss—the potential death of something she loves.

My phone buzzes after twenty minutes. Emily's still crying, quieter now but no less devastated.

I text Zara with one hand: **Emily's specialist says minimal hand sewing or risk permanent damage. She's heartbroken. Don't know what to do.**

The response comes immediately: **Let her grieve. Sometimes that's all you can do.**

There has to be something—

There is. You're already doing it. Hold her. Be present. The rest will come.

I set the phone down. Return full attention to Emily, who's gone silent against my chest.

"I'm sorry," she whispers finally. "I'm being dramatic—"

"You're mourning." I kiss her forehead. "That's allowed."

"Michelle's bodice—"

"Will be finished by someone else."

"The wedding—"

"Matters less than your hands." I tilt her face up gently. "Emily Dorothy, look at me."

Those green eyes—red-rimmed, devastated—meet mine.

"You are worth everything to me," I tell her fiercely. "With embroidery skills or without. With perfect hands or damaged ones. Every version of you is the woman I chose. The woman I married. The woman I will love until my last breath."

Fresh tears spill over.

"But zheli—"

"No buts." I wipe her cheeks carefully. "Rest now. We'll figure out the rest tomorrow."

She nods, exhausted from crying.

I settle her back against the pillows, mind already spinning.

$100 million in personal assets. The Lambert trust that'll come eventually. Connections spanning three continents and every major industry.

Somewhere in the world exists technology that can translate Emily's artistic vision into reality without destroying her hands. Embroidery machines. Computer-aided beading systems. Something that preserves her creativity while protecting her body.

I'll find it.

I'll commission it if necessary.

Whatever it costs, whoever I need to hire—Emily will have the tools to continue her art.

But for now, I let her mourn.

Hold her while she grieves what might be lost.

Tomorrow, I'll start making calls.

Tonight, I'm just zheli—her Felix, her protector, her husband—keeping her safe while her world threatens to crumble.

"Sleep, zhara," I whisper against her hair. "I've got you."

She drifts off within minutes, exhausted.

I stay awake, already planning.

Jean spreads the seating chart across the dining table while I stare at names without actually seeing them.

Three hours.

Emily hasn't spoken in three hours.

Just lies upstairs curled around Mochi, eyes open but empty. I've checked on her four times. Each time she manages a small smile that doesn't reach her eyes.

"Tristian." Jean taps the chart. "Focus. Do we seat Dante's family near the Washingtons or—"

My phone rings.

David Kellerman.

I answer immediately. "David."

"Tristian." His voice carries warmth—that particular tone he uses when he's being paternal rather than professional. "Zara called me. Told me about Emily's hands."

Course she did.

"Dr. Rousseau says if she continues at this pace, she'll lose the ability to do detail work permanently." The words taste like ash. "She's devastated. Won't talk. Just—lies there."

Jean glances up sharply.

"I'm sorry, son." David sighs. "I know how much her art means to her."

"There has to be something. Some technology, some machine—anything that lets her continue designing without destroying her joints."

"Actually," David says slowly, "that's why I'm calling. Well, partially."

My heart stutters. "Partially?"

"First—the premiere for *The Phantom of the Opera* is October second. I need you and Emily there. Red carpet, press, the works. Marianne's already planning to interview you both about *Wonderful* since filming starts October third."

October second. A week after the honeymoon.

"We'll be there."

"Good." Papers rustle on his end. "Second reason—I've been in touch with the head of Starlight's costume department. She works with several adaptive technology companies that create computer-aided embroidery systems for designers with mobility issues."

I'm on my feet. "What?"

"Tablet-controlled. The designer creates the pattern digitally, and the machine executes it with precision matching hand-embroidery. Beading attachments, crystal settings, even French knots." He pauses. "The entire *Wonderful* cast heard what happened. Everyone chipped in. The machine's being delivered tomorrow morning."

The room blurs.

"David—"

"Emily's family now, Tristian. We take care of our own." His voice roughens slightly. "That girl auditioned for Dorothy with more courage and raw talent than I've seen in thirty years. She's going to change this industry. A little thing like inflamed joints won't stop her—not if we have anything to say about it."

Tears spill over before I can stop them.

"Bloody hell." I press my free hand over my eyes. "I'm—Christ, David—"

"I know, son. I know." Warmth floods his tone. "Tell Emily we love her. Tell her she's stuck with all of us now."

"She's going to cry."

"Good tears this time, I hope."

"Yes." I laugh wetly. "Good tears."

We discuss premiere details—what Emily should wear, accessibility arrangements, interview topics. By the time we hang up, I'm still crying.

Jean's beside me instantly, pulling me into a hug.

"What happened?"

"The cast." I can barely get the words out. "They bought Emily an embroidery machine. Tablet-controlled. Being delivered tomorrow."

"Oh, Tristian." Jean holds me tighter. "That's—God, that's perfect."

"She's going to—" My voice cracks. "She's been so broken all day and tomorrow she'll—"

"Tomorrow she'll have hope again." Jean pulls back, hands on my shoulders. "Because you have people who love you both. Who see her worth. Who want her to succeed."

My phone buzzes.

Emily: more blue raspberry water please? the wonderful bottle

Relief crashes through me. She's asking for something. Communicating.

Small victory.

"Go." Jean waves me toward the kitchen. "I'll finish the seating chart."

I grab Emily's water bottle from the counter—green with Dorothy and Felix dancing, silver slippers glittering, the Oz family crest prominent. Fill it with blue raspberry sparkling water from the fridge. No ice. She hates ice in her bottles.

Upstairs, I find her exactly as I left her—curled on her side, Mochi's head resting against her chest, Nibbler nestled by her face making soft mechanical purring sounds.

But she's singing.

The new song. The one written specifically for Emily's Dorothy.

Her voice wavers, raw with emotion. Mochi's eyes track her face adoringly—he's heard her sing since he was eight weeks old, knows this means comfort and safety.

I set the water bottle on the nightstand. Lower myself carefully onto the bed behind her.

Emily doesn't stop singing. Continues through the devastating second verse—Dorothy realizing Aunt Em's cruelty, Uncle Henry's indifference, Hiram's violent possession aren't normal. Aren't love.

Her voice breaks on the final chorus.

The last note dissolves into quiet sobbing.

I pull her against my chest, careful of her inflamed joints. She turns in my arms, burying her face against my shoulder.

"The song's about ignoring the abuse," she whispers. "Until Hiram tries to—to force himself on her. Until she can't ignore it anymore. Until the cyclone comes and takes her away."

"I know, zhara."

"Sometimes I feel like Dorothy. Like I spent years in a bubble, pretending foster care was normal. Pretending the pain was normal. Pretending I didn't deserve better." She pulls back, meeting my eyes. "Then I met you. My Felix. My cyclone."

"Best bloody cyclone you'll ever have."

That gets a watery laugh.

"Make love to me, zheli." Soft. Seeking comfort in the only way she knows I can give it right now. "Please."

I cup her face gently. "You're sure?"

"Need you. Need to feel—" She swallows hard. "Need to feel worth something."

"Emily Dorothy—"

"Please."

The desperate edge to her voice decides me.

"Mochi," I call. The labradoodle lifts his head. "Nibbler. Go play with Uncle Levi."

Mochi bounds off the bed immediately, tail wagging. Nibbler chirps once before scampering after him, claws clicking on hardwood.

The door closes behind them.

Emily reaches for me with trembling hands—the left one still braced, the right one swollen at the knuckles.

"Not those hands." I catch her wrists gently. "Let zheli do all the work, Dorothy."

She nods, surrendering.

I undress her slowly, reverently. The Wonderful Wizard of Oz nightgown pools on the floor. Nothing underneath—Dr. Rousseau's orders to avoid pressure on her abdomen where the cyst formed.

Perfect access.

I strip quickly, then settle beside her. She's already breathing faster, pupils dilating with need.

"Roll onto your back, zhara. Let me see all of you."

She obeys, and I take a moment just to look—blonde hair fanned across the pillow, emerald eyes locked on mine, my belly ring catching light in her navel, my initial tattooed on her shoulder, the silver slipper on her wrist.

Mine.

Completely, irrevocably mine.

I start at her wrists—kissing the inflamed joints carefully, worshiping the hands that create beauty even when they hurt. Work my way up her arms, across her collarbones, down to breasts that fit perfectly in my palms.

"Zheli—" She arches into my touch.

"Patience, my Dorothy." I circle one nipple with my tongue. "Let me take care of you."

By the time I settle between her thighs, she's trembling with need. I take my time, using mouth and fingers until she's crying out, hands fisting in the sheets because she can't grip my hair without pain.

When I finally push inside, slow and deep, she sobs with relief.

"There you are, zhara." I rock into her gently. "There's my brave girl."

"Love you—" She gasps as I angle differently. "Love you so much—"

"Show me." I capture her mouth. "Show zheli how much."

We move together, slow and intimate, until she breaks apart beneath me. I follow seconds later, burying my face in her neck as we shatter together.

Afterward, I hold her while our breathing evens out.

"Tomorrow," I whisper against her hair, "you're getting a gift."

"Hmm?"

"From the *Wonderful* cast. Something that'll let you continue your art without destroying your hands."

She stills. "What?"

"David called. The entire cast chipped in for an adaptive embroidery system. Tablet-controlled. Being delivered in the morning."

Silence.

Then she's crying again—but these tears are different. Lighter.

"They did that? For me?"

"You're family, zhara. We take care of our own."

She kisses me fierce and grateful, tasting like salt and hope.

"Thank you," she breathes. "For everything. For being my cyclone."

"Always, my Dorothy." I pull her closer. "Always."

Michelle sprawls across the chaise in the media room while Jean claims the oversized armchair. I settle on the floor, back against the sofa, remote in hand.

"Triplet time?" Michelle grins at me upside-down, dark hair cascading over the edge.

"Triplet time," I confirm.

Jean groans. "Again? We watched it three days ago."

"Emily watches it weekly. I need to keep up."

"You've seen it seventeen times since meeting her." Jean counts on his fingers. "You basically have it memorized."

"Eighteen after tonight." I pull up the Starlight Studios classics menu. "And I don't care. It's her favorite."

The 1940 title card fills the screen—*The Wonderful Wonderful Wizard of Oz* in elegant silver script against black velvet. Starlight's logo glimmers beneath.

"Fine," Michelle sighs dramatically. "But I'm reciting every line."

"You always do," Jean and I say together.

The film opens on sepia-toned Kansas. Young Dorothy —played by Frances Gale in her breakout role—runs down a dirt road toward home, boots gleaming in sunlight.

"Those shoes are perfect for farm work," Michelle observes for the eighteenth time.

"Hush." I throw a pillow at her.

The familiar story unfolds. Cruel Aunt Em. Distant Uncle Henry. Then the cyclone, violent and sudden, carrying Dorothy's house into vivid Technicolor Oz.

Maxime appears first—the Witch of the North, tall and elegant in silver robes. His voice carries warmth and wisdom as he explains the silver slippers' power.

"Maxime's accent is perfect," Jean murmurs. "That upper-class Parisian delivery."

Then comes the Wicked Witch of the West.

The camera pans up slowly—revealing long, dark legs. A willowy frame draped in black. Finally, a face of striking beauty—dark skin, high cheekbones, eyes burning with intelligence and rage.

Ellie. The witch who will become Dorothy's mentor, mother, everything.

Dorothy trembles but stands tall. Frances Gale's performance still gives me chills—twenty-two years old playing sixteen, every emotion raw and real.

The Yellow Brick Road begins.

First companion—Felix, the Scarecrow. Played by Robert Chen in the performance that made him a legend. He tumbles off his pole with practiced clumsiness, landing at Dorothy's feet.

"'Well now,'" I recite softly, "'aren't you a vision in gingham.'"

Michelle kicks my shoulder. "Nerd."

But I am. Because Emily loves this film. Loves how Dorothy and Felix bicker through three scenes before their first real conversation. How he makes her laugh despite the danger. How she sees past the straw to the brilliant prince cursed by Glinda years ago.

The Tin Man joins them next—heart stolen by the eastern witch, searching for what was taken. Then the Lion, courage stripped away, desperate to reclaim his roar.

They travel together. Face trials. Grow close.

The film's centerpiece arrives an hour in—Dorothy's first lesson with Ellie.

The witch finds them camped in her forest. Demands Dorothy remove the silver slippers immediately.

Dorothy refuses.

"'Those slippers,'" Frances Gale delivers with perfect defiance, "'are mine by right. The house fell because of the cyclone. I didn't ask for any of this.'"

Silence.

Then Ellie laughs—genuine, surprised. "'You have fire, little one. Perhaps you're worth teaching after all.'"

Jean shifts forward in his chair. This scene always gets him. The moment Ellie sees something of herself in Dorothy. Decides to protect rather than destroy.

The dynamic shifts. Ellie becomes mentor. Dorothy becomes student. Felix watches with growing concern as Dorothy learns magic—power that changes her, darkens her, makes her dangerous.

"'I'm losing you,'" Robert Chen whispers on screen, straw fingers touching Dorothy's face. "'To her. To the magic. To whatever you're becoming.'"

"'I'm becoming strong,'" Frances Gale replies. "'For the first time in my life, I'm not helpless. Don't take that from me.'"

Michelle's quiet now. Even Jean's stopped making commentary.

Because this is where the film transcends its fantasy roots. Becomes something deeper.

Dorothy discovering agency. Felix loving her enough to let her grow even when it scares him. Ellie protecting her adopted daughter while teaching her the truth about the Wizard's manipulation.

The climax builds—Dorothy turning Felix human again through true love's kiss. The four of them plus Glinda confronting the Wizard. The revelation that he's a fraud.

That he cursed Felix and corrupted Glinda because they questioned his power.

The final scene shows all five ruling Oz together. Dorothy in silver, Felix in gold, Ellie in black, Glinda in red, the Lion as their general.

Not one ruler. Five.

Shared power. Shared responsibility. Shared love.

The credits roll.

"Emily cries every single time at the coronation," I tell my siblings quietly. "Says it's everything she ever wanted as a kid in foster care. A family that chose her. A place where she belonged. Power to protect herself."

Michelle's eyes glisten. "Well now I'm crying."

"Me too," Jean admits.

I stand, stretching. "Thanks for watching with me."

"Anytime." Michelle hugs me tight. "You're good for her, you know. Your Dorothy finally got her Felix."

We laugh together, triplets united.

Upstairs, I find Emily awake, sketching on her tablet—the new embroidery software already loaded, courtesy of tomorrow's delivery.

"How was triplet time?" she asks without looking up.

"Perfect." I kiss her temple. "Watched your favorite. Again."

"'My favorite'?" She finally meets my eyes, smiling. "Tristian, you've seen it more than I have lately."

"Good." I settle beside her. "Someone needs to keep track of how many times Felix saves Dorothy."

"Thirteen."

"Fourteen, actually. You always miss the forest scene."

She laughs—bright and clear and everything I need.

"Love you, my Felix."

"Love you, my Dorothy."

Always.

Six days.

Six days until Emily becomes my wife before God, family, and Angoumois witnesses.

Six days until we're legally bound in every jurisdiction that matters.

I'm already hers in every way that counts—Winkie marriage, raptor claim, soul-deep certainty—but the paperwork will make it official.

Emily sits in the salon, left wrist braced, surrounded by garment bags and tissue paper. The Cyclone dominates the center table—industrial-grade adaptive embroidery system, named after Oz's tornado but looking more like something from Extintion Protocol control rooms.

"Ready?" She grins despite obvious exhaustion.

"Always."

She wheels to the largest garment bag. Unzips it with her right hand, movements careful.

My wedding suit emerges.

Christ.

The jacket's deep purple—not garish but rich like twilight settling over Prehistoric Paradise. Blue threading catches light across the shoulders, subtle as raptor scales. The waistcoat beneath shifts between purple and pink depending on angle, iridescent like Nathan Cross's eyes mid-transformation.

"Em..."

"Try it on." She's bouncing slightly. Excited.

I strip to boxers right there—we're past modesty—and reach for the white silk shirt first.

It glides over my skin like water. French cuffs. Mother of pearl buttons.

The waistcoat next. Purple-pink shimmer, cut perfectly to my torso. I fasten it while Emily watches with professional assessment.

Then the jacket.

It fits like it was molded to my body—which, knowing Emily's attention to detail, it essentially was. The purple deepens near the lapels, where tiny embroidered DNA helixes spiral in thread so fine you'd miss them without looking closely.

"Extinction Protocol?" I trace one helix.

"Your favorite Starlight franchise." She wheels closer. "Look at the pocket."

A pocket square in shimmering blue—exactly the shade of Nathan's raptor form. Folded to suggest scales.

"Emily."

"Cufflinks next."

I fumble them from the box she offers.

Silver T-Rexes. Tiny sapphire eyes.

My hands shake fastening them.

"Boots," she prompts.

Patent leather. Victorian style but sleek, modern somehow.

"Hidden zipper," Emily explains. "Victorian aesthetic but I'm not making you deal with twenty buttons when we're trying to leave for our honeymoon."

I laugh, sliding them on. Perfect fit.

"Belt."

Even the belt has a custom buckle—a subtle T interwoven with an E that looks like abstract art unless you know what you're seeing.

Our initials. Claimed.

I stand before the mirror.

The man looking back is someone I barely recognize. Not Hollywood Tristian or rebellious Lambert son or Nathan Cross.

Just... me. Emily's husband. Wearing armor she designed.

"You're beautiful," she whispers.

"This suit—" My voice cracks. "Emily, this is..."

"Check the inside." She's crying now. Happy tears.

I slip the jacket off carefully, turn it.

There.

Hand-stitched despite the pain, despite doctor's orders, despite everything—

A raptor track. Perfect detail. Purple thread on purple lining so it's nearly invisible.

And beneath it, tiny letters I have to squint to read:

To my Nathan. Forever your Maya. -E

The Cyclone sits silent on the table. Did ninety percent of the work. Saved her hands from permanent damage.

But this one detail—this claim, this love note, this promise—she did herself.

Knowing it would hurt.

Doing it anyway.

"Em." I kneel beside her wheelchair, jacket clutched in both hands. "You didn't have to—"

"Yes I did." She touches my face with her braced hand. "Everything else the machine can do. But claiming my raptor? That's mine."

I kiss her. Slow and deep and reverent.

When we break apart, she's grinning.

"So it fits?"

"Like scales."

"Good." She wheels back slightly. "Because I'm not altering anything six days out."

"Wouldn't dream of asking."

I stand, admiring the suit again in the mirror. The purple catches light. The DNA helixes shimmer. The pocket square suggests feathers or scales depending on how I move.

And inside, against my heart—

My mate's claim.

Forever.

I change back into regular clothes while Emily wheels to the mannequins arranged near the windows. Three suits stand like silent wedding party members.

"Jean's?" I cross to the first one.

"Midnight Garden tribute."

Of course.

The suit is midnight black—so dark it almost drinks light. But when I lean closer, roses bloom across the fabric in thread just barely darker than the base. You'd miss them entirely from five feet away.

"The vest." Emily's voice holds pride.

Deep crimson. Fresh blood color. Perfectly Jean.

The shirt beneath has pinstripe patterns that resolve into thorn vines when I focus. Victorian gothic but modern somehow.

Then I notice the collar.

"It stands higher." I touch it carefully.

"Like Count Valdris's signature look." Emily wheels closer. "But formal rather than predatory. Jean wanted to honor the film without looking like he's attending a costume party."

The cufflinks catch lamplight. Tiny silver stakes crossed like an X.

"He's going to lose his mind when he sees this."

"Already did. Cried for fifteen minutes when I showed him the collar." She grins. "Now look at Levi's."

The second suit makes me blink.

Silver at the shoulders. Gradually shifting to white at the hem. A gradient effect that seems to shimmer as I circle it.

"Temporal Flux." I recognize the 1950s-meets-future aesthetic.

"The vest." Emily prompts.

I lean in. Circuit board patterns embroidered in metallic thread so fine they look like abstract art unless you know what you're seeing.

"And the fabric's heat-reactive." Emily's bouncing slightly now. "When someone touches it, the silver briefly shifts to pale blue before fading back. Like the time projector activating."

"Emily, this is—"

"Wait until you see Marcus's."

The third suit stops me cold.

Purple. My color family but darker, richer.

Then I see the pinstripes. Racing stripes. Speed lines built into the fabric itself.

"Velocity Underground," I guess.

"His favorite franchise. The vest has a gear shift pattern —" She wheels closer to point. "See? Subtle enough he won't look ridiculous but detailed enough Marcus will notice every time he looks down."

The shoes sit beside the mannequin.

"Tire tread pattern on the soles." Emily's grinning full-force now. "He's going to leave racing marks on the vineyard's dance floor."

I laugh, imagining Marcus's face when he discovers that detail.

"Michelle's dress?"

Emily gestures toward the garment bag hanging slightly apart from the suits.

I move closer but don't touch. Wedding party viewing rules still apply.

"Operator tribute. Structured like a tactical dress but in burgundy silk." Emily wheels alongside me. "Hidden pockets everywhere because she insisted—and I quote—'you never know when you need to store evidence at your own wedding.'"

"That's very Michelle."

"The belt buckle doubles as an actual USB drive." Emily says it casually.

"You're joking."

"Functional. Encrypted. Thirty-two gigabytes." She's absolutely serious. "Michelle said if she's wearing a spy-film tribute, it should have operational capability."

I stare at the garment bag. My sister—model, fashionista, occasionally terrifying Lambert triplet—will carry classified-level storage at her own wedding reception.

"And yours?" I turn back to Emily.

Her expression shifts. Secretive.

"You're not seeing my dress until I'm walking toward you at that cathedral."

"Em—"

"No." Firm. "Bad luck. Groom rules. Absolutely not."

I know better than to push.

"But you can see my shoes."

She wheels to a box I hadn't noticed before. Opens it with her right hand.

The shoes inside make my breath stop.

Dorothy's silver slippers. The ones from the cast announcement sketch. Made real.

Crystals cascade down the sides and top in intricate curving patterns. The embellishments catch light like water, like magic, like everything Emily is.

The heels aren't typical—they're part of the same artistic design, embellished with patterns that match the upper construction.

"You made these for the film," I manage.

"And for the wedding. Same design. Same crystals." She lifts one carefully. "I don't usually wear heels—"

"Because they hurt your hips."

"—but I'd wear these everywhere if I could." She turns it, letting light play across the surface. "They're perfect."

Dorothy's slippers. Made by my Dorothy.

For our wedding.

For her coronation as Mrs. Lambert.

For clicking together three times and making dreams come true.

I kneel beside her wheelchair, touching the shoe with reverent fingers.

"Six days," I whisper.

"Six days," Emily agrees.

And I can't wait.

"Ariana's?" I spot another garment bag across the room.

Emily's grin turns wicked.

"Motel Massacre. Her favorite horror franchise."

I approach carefully. The bag reveals a dress that makes me pause.

Innocent. That's the first word that hits me.

Pale pink like strawberry milkshakes and vintage postcards. Full skirt that would look perfect spinning on a dance floor. Nipped waist. Sweetheart neckline.

1953 vintage perfection.

Then I notice the details.

The hem embroidery resolves into tiny motel room keys when I crouch to examine them. Scattered across the pink fabric like they fell from someone's pocket.

Room 12. Room 7. Room 3.

The kill sites from the film.

"Christ, Em."

"Look at the bodice."

I lean closer.

The stitching suggests blood spatter if you know what you're looking for—but reads as abstract floral from five feet away. Delicate. Pretty.

Absolutely terrifying once you see it.

"Ariana cried when she saw it," Emily says quietly. "Said it was perfect. Feminine and fierce and everything she wanted."

"You gave her a murder dress."

"I gave her Norma Bender's Sunday best." Emily wheels closer. "The dress she wore when police finally arrested her. Pink and proper and covered in evidence nobody saw until too late."

The fabric shifts in lamplight. Innocent. Deadly.

Just like Ariana herself.

"Philippe's?"

Emily gestures toward the final mannequin.

The suit makes my actor brain immediately catalog details.

Roman-inspired but modern. Deep crimson—blood color, arena sand color, victory color.

The jacket has subtle quilted patterns that suggest gladiator armor without being costume-y. Leather accents at the shoulders. Bronze threading that catches light like metal in sun.

"Gladiator's Revenge tribute," I guess.

"The buttons are actual bronze. The belt buckle is modeled after Roman military insignia." Emily's voice holds satisfaction. "And the vest—"

I lean in.

Embossed patterns. Tiny swords crossed with olive branches.

Victory and peace.

Death and honor.

Everything the Gladiator's Revenge franchise built its empire on.

"The boots have hidden tread patterns." Emily's almost laughing now. "Footprints shaped like gladiator sandal marks. Philippe's going to leave ancient Rome all over the vineyard."

I straighten, looking at all six outfits arranged before us.

My purple raptor suit. Jean's midnight roses. Levi's time-traveling silver. Marcus's racing stripes. Michelle's tactical burgundy. Ariana's innocent pink murder dress. Philippe's Roman crimson.

A wedding party wearing their souls on their sleeves—or vests, or hems, or embroidered linings.

Film tributes. Love letters. Family claims.

All created by the woman in the pink wheelchair who sees people clearly enough to dress them in their dreams.

"Emily."

"Hmm?"

"This is the most extraordinary work I've ever seen."

She ducks her head. Pink climbing her cheeks.

"It's just clothes."

"It's art. It's identity. It's—" I kneel beside her again. "It's everything we are, visible."

She looks up. Green eyes bright with unshed tears.

"I wanted everyone to feel seen."

"You succeeded."

A yawn catches her mid-smile. She tries to hide it.

"Come on." I stand, already reaching for her. "Nap time."

"I should put these away—"

"Collette can handle it when she brings dinner." I scoop Emily from her wheelchair easily. "You're exhausted."

"Only a little."

Another yawn betrays her.

"Alright," she admits. "Only because I'm sleepy."

I carry her toward the bedroom, but Emily twists suddenly.

"Wait—the scarecrow."

"What?"

"From Kellerman. The plush. I need—" She points.

Sure enough, a Felix scarecrow plush sits on the side table. Gift from David after our engagement photos released.

I detour, letting Emily grab it one-handed.

She clutches it against her chest like a child with a beloved toy.

My heart cracks open.

This woman. My wife. My Emily.

Creating masterpieces while battling chronic pain. Dressing our entire wedding party in their souls. Falling asleep with a scarecrow plush because it reminds her of me.

I carry her to our room, where afternoon sun streams through windows.

Six days until she's legally mine.

But she's already home.

Three days.

Seventy-two hours until Emily becomes legally mine in front of God, family, and the entire Angoumois press corps.

But first—medical clearance.

I check my watch. Eight-seventeen in the morning.

Seven appointments scheduled back-to-back at Grantham General. Every specialist Emily sees.

Because I'm thorough. Possibly paranoid.

Definitely not risking my bride collapsing mid-ceremony.

"Ready, love?" I wheel Emily toward the car where Peter waits.

She clutches her medical binder. Pink tabs mark each section.

"This feels excessive."

"It's necessary."

"Tristian—"

"Emily." I stop walking. Crouch beside her wheelchair. "Please. Let me have this."

Her expression softens.

"Okay."

Physical therapy first.

Dr. Chen runs Emily through range-of-motion tests, checks her hip flexibility, examines the way her hands grip and release.

"Swelling's improved significantly," she notes. "The adaptive embroidery system made a real difference."

Relief hits my chest.

"So she's cleared?"

"For the wedding? Absolutely. Just remind her to take breaks during the reception. No marathon dancing." Chen grins at Emily. "Even with those fancy shoes."

Next comes occupational therapy.

More hand tests. Fine motor skills. Grip strength.

"Looking good," Dr. Mills declares. "The cyst drainage helped tremendously. Keep icing after any detailed work."

Emily nods, taking notes.

I photograph every page of instructions.

Urology appointment runs smooth. Dr. Beaumont confirms Emily's kidney function remains stable. No new stones detected. Hydration levels acceptable.

"Champagne in moderation at the reception," she advises. "Stick with water mostly."

"Noted," I say, already texting Alfred to stock Emily's preferred sparkling water.

Gynecology takes longer.

Dr. Laurent does a full exam while I pace the waiting room like a caged animal.

Thirty minutes feels like thirty hours.

Finally Emily emerges, looking tired but smiling.

"Cyst's completely resolved," she reports. "Birth control's working. Everything looks normal."

My shoulders drop three inches.

"Thank Christ."

Gastroenterology next.

Dr. Moreau reviews Emily's food diary, checks for inflammation markers, discusses the wedding menu I sent him last week.

"You've done excellent work avoiding triggers," he tells Emily. "The customized menu should pose no issues. Just eat slowly at the reception. Don't let excitement override your body's signals."

Emily promises to be careful.

I make mental notes anyway.

The nutritionist appointment feels redundant after gastro, but I insist.

Madame Fontaine weighs Emily, checks her vitals, reviews meal plans.

"Down one pound from last month." She frowns slightly. "Underweight, but not dangerously so. The wedding stress?"

"Probably," Emily admits quietly.

"Let's get calories up this week. Focus on nutrient-dense foods." Fontaine hands me a list. "Make sure she's eating regularly."

I fold the paper into my jacket.

Consider it done.

Finally—Dr. Rousseau.

Five-thirty. Last appointment of the day.

Emily looks exhausted. Dark circles shadow her eyes despite makeup.

But she straightens when Rousseau enters, determination written across her face.

"Well." Rousseau reviews charts from every specialist we've seen today. "Quite the gauntlet you've run."

"Tristian wanted thoroughness," Emily says dryly.

"Tristian wanted reassurance his bride won't faint at the altar," I correct.

Rousseau's mouth twitches.

"Understandable." She continues reading. "Physical therapy clears you. Occupational therapy clears you. Urology, gynecology, gastroenterology, nutrition—all clear with minor notes."

My heart hammers.

"So she's—"

"Cleared for the wedding. Yes." Rousseau sets down the files. "You're underweight by one pound, Emily, but nothing alarming. The hand swelling has decreased significantly. The cyst has resolved completely. Your chronic conditions remain stable."

Emily's breath catches.

"I can get married?"

"You can get married." Rousseau smiles. "Just pace yourself at the reception. Rest when needed. Stay hydrated. Listen to your body."

"I will."

"And you—" Rousseau points at me. "Stop hovering quite so intensely. Stress affects her symptoms."

Guilty as charged.

"I'll try."

"Try harder." But her tone gentles. "She's stronger than you think, Monsieur Lambert."

I look at Emily.

Green eyes bright with unshed tears. Silver slipper necklace catching light. Pink wheelchair decorated with raptor stickers from Nibbler.

Strong doesn't begin to cover it.

"I know," I say quietly.

Outside the hospital, Emily grabs my hand.

Pulls me down.

Kisses me.

Soft. Sweet. Tasting like relief and gratitude and three days until forever.

When she pulls back, she's smiling.

"Thank you."

"For what?"

"For caring this much." Her thumb brushes my knuckles. "For the appointments and the lists and the paranoia."

"I'm not—" I stop. "Alright. Maybe a little paranoid."

"A little?"

"Moderately paranoid."

She laughs.

The sound fills the parking lot like music.

Three days.

Then she's mine legally, officially, irrevocably.

But watching her laugh in evening light, medical clearance confirmed, wedding dress waiting—

She's already everything.

I stare at the suitcases spread across our bedroom floor.

Marcus sits cross-legged beside Mochi, inventory list in hand.

"Wheelchair charger?"

"Packed," I confirm, tucking the cord into Emily's pink travel case.

"Diapers?"

I grab the discreet black bag from the closet. The nighttime ones. The long-travel kind.

Emily doesn't talk about the accidents. Morning bladder control gets worse when she's stressed. Around her period. When her body simply gives up fighting.

But I notice the laundry. The quiet shame in her shoulders after particularly bad nights.

So I pack extras without comment.

"Got them."

Marcus nods, checking his list. "Pain meds?"

I line up bottles on the bed. Hydrocodone. Ibuprofen. Naproxen sodium.

"Check."

"Birth control? PM dose?"

Into the travel pill organizer. Purple compartment.

"Check."

"Anxiety meds, muscle relaxers—both PM?"

Same purple compartment.

"Check and check."

Marcus continues down the list while I sort medications like a pharmacy tech.

Proton pump inhibitors. Green compartment for morning. Prevents the diverticulitis flares.

Metformin. Purple again. Evening dose for PCOS management.

Probiotics. Green. Morning prevention against yeast infections and bacterial vaginosis.

Cranberry pills. Lemon extract capsules. Both green. UTI and kidney stone prevention.

"Inhaler?"

I grab three. One for Emily's purse. One for my jacket. One backup in luggage.

"Covered."

"Peppermint pills for nausea?"

"Already in her purse."

Marcus sets down his list, surveying the organized chaos.

"You're terrifyingly prepared."

"She needs—"

A crash from down the hall.

Then Emily's voice, shrill with panic.

"ZHELI!"

I'm running before conscious thought catches up.

Marcus follows, Mochi barking frantically.

I find Emily surrounded by fabric samples, sketches scattered like confetti, her wheelchair surrounded by wedding binders and color swatches and—

Tears streaming down her face.

Hands shaking violently.

Breathing too fast.

"Can't—everything's—the flowers don't match the napkins and the shoes need breaking in and I still haven't finished Michelle's dress alterations and the seating chart makes no sense because—"

I scoop her from the chair.

Ignore her protests.

Carry her straight to the bathroom while Marcus quietly starts cleaning up behind us.

"Zheli, I need to—"

"You need to breathe." I set her on the counter. Turn on the tub. Hot water, lavender salts.

Her whole body trembles.

"There's so much—"

"I know, love." I strip her methodically. Gently. "But right now, you're going in the tub."

"The napkins—"

"Don't care about napkins."

I lift her into steaming water, watching tension start bleeding from her shoulders.

She hiccups. Sobs quietly.

I grab my phone, text Alfred.

Light meal. No tomatoes. Something gentle. Five minutes.

"Zheli." Emily's voice breaks. "I can't do this."

"Yes, you can."

"Everything's falling apart—"

"Nothing's falling apart." I kneel beside the tub. Brush wet hair from her face. "You're overwhelmed. There's a difference."

Tears keep falling.

Alfred knocks softly. Enters with a tray.

Plain rice. Grilled chicken. Steamed vegetables—carefully selected, no triggers. Ginger tea.

Bless that man.

I dismiss him with grateful nod.

Fork a small bite of chicken. Hold it to Emily's lips.

"Eat."

"I'm not—"

"Emily."

She opens her mouth. Chews mechanically.

I feed her slowly. Rice. Vegetables. Sips of tea between bites.

Her breathing gradually steadies.

"Good girl," I murmur. "Good girl for calling Zheli."

Something shifts in her expression. The panic receding.

"You dropped everything."

"Always will." Another bite of chicken. "That's what Zheli means, remember? I'm yours. You're mine. When you call, I come running."

She accepts more rice.

Swallows.

"The wedding—"

"Is handled. Marcus is organizing your workspace. Alfred's coordinating with the vineyard. Mum has the seating chart under control."

"But Michelle's dress—"

"Can wait until tomorrow. After you've slept." I cup her face. "You don't have to carry everything alone, Ka-reeka."

Wife.

She leans into my palm.

"I'm sorry."

"Don't apologize for being human." I kiss her forehead. "Just let me help."

We sit in steam and silence.

I feed her the rest of the meal.

Watch color return to her cheeks.

When she finishes, I wash her hair. Massage her scalp until she melts.

"Better?"

"Yeah." Barely a whisper. "Thank you, Zheli."

"Always, love."

Two days.

Then she's officially mine.

But watching her finally relax—

She's already everything.

Five in the morning.

Emily emerges from the bathroom, jaw set in that stubborn line I know too well.

I hold up the travel pad.

Her eyes narrow.

"No."

"Yes."

"Tristian, I'm not—I don't need that." Pink floods her cheeks. "I'm an adult. I can hold it."

"Six hours to Bellbury." I keep my voice gentle. Firm. "And your period starts in three days."

"I'm fine—"

"Your bladder's unpredictable this close to your cycle." I step closer. "The birth control makes it worse. You know this."

"I can make it six hours—"

"Ka-reeka." The raptor rumble slides into my voice. Low. Possessive. "Don't fight Zheli on this."

Her breath catches.

But that stubborn chin lifts.

"I'm not a child."

Time to switch tactics.

I let Nathan's Alabama drawl curl around the words, thick as molasses.

"Now darlin', nobody said you were." I crouch beside her wheelchair. Meet those defiant green eyes. "But your Ka-reek knows your body. Knows how that birth control messes with your bladder control. Knows you'll be miserable an hour in if you don't wear protection."

"Tristian—"

"And I know—" The drawl deepens, protective edge sharpening. "—my wife's too proud to admit when she needs help. Too used to handlin' everything alone."

Her lower lip trembles.

Got her.

"But you ain't alone anymore, sweetheart." I brush my thumb across her cheek. "You got a husband who's gonna take care of you whether you like it or not."

"It's embarrassing—"

The raptor growl cuts her off.

"*Nekh-tha Ka-reeka.*" Mine. Wife. The possessive trill vibrates in my chest. "*Ka-reek ta-nek kree-sha.*" Husband protects mate.

Emily's eyes widen.

I switch back to Nathan's drawl, gentler now.

"Baby, there ain't nothing about you that embarrasses me. Not your wheelchair, not your meds, not your bladder." I hold up the pad. "This is just another way I take care of what's mine."

Her resistance crumbles.

"You're incredibly bossy."

"Lambert trait." I grin. "Possessive, protective, and completely unreasonable when it comes to our mates."

She huffs.

But wheels closer.

Victory tastes sweet.

I help her transfer to the bed, sliding the pad into her underwear with practiced efficiency.

She won't meet my eyes.

"Hey." I tip her chin up. "Look at me, love."

Green eyes shimmer with unshed tears.

"I hate needing this."

"I know." I kiss her forehead. "But I love that you trust me enough to let me help."

"Do I have a choice?"

"Technically yes." I lift her back to the wheelchair. "Practically? Not when your Ka-reek's this stubborn about keeping you comfortable."

A watery laugh escapes.

"You're impossible."

"You're marrying me in two days." I crouch again, hands on her armrests. Cage her in. "So you're stuck with impossible."

The raptor rumble surfaces again.

"*Ka-reek ta-nek Ka-reeka. Ta-kree, ta-sha, ta-mekh.*" Husband protects wife. Always, forever, completely.

Emily's hand finds my cheek.

"I love you."

"Love you too, darlin'." Nathan's accent bleeds through. "Now let's get you dressed and fed before Marcus starts yellin' about schedules."

I pull out the outfit I selected last night.

Soft leggings. No waistband to irritate. Dorothy-blue tunic—loose, comfortable. Sneakers already broken in.

Everything chosen for six hours in a car.

Everything designed to keep my Ka-reeka comfortable.

Because that's what Zheli means.

I'm hers.

She's mine.

And I'm going to take care of her whether she thinks she needs it or not.

That's not just a Lambert thing.

That's a Tristian thing.

She's everything.

And everything deserves protection.

Even from pride.

I survey the château courtyard like a general preparing for battle.

Three SUVs. Luggage already loaded. Emily's medical supplies triple-checked.

Six hours to Bellbury.

Should be simple.

Except nothing's simple with the Lamberts.

"Everyone knows the groupings?" Jean consults his tablet. "First car—Mum, Dad, Grandmère. Second—Ariana, Philippe, Michelle, Mochi. Third—"

"Us." I finish, hand on Emily's shoulder. "Me, Emily, you, Levi, Marcus."

"And Nibbler." Emily glances at our animatronic son, currently chirping anxiously by the fountain.

Right.

Nibbler.

This should be interesting.

"Let's get you settled first, love." I crouch beside Emily's wheelchair. "Ready?"

She nods.

But I catch the tension in her jaw.

The drive worries her.

I kiss her temple. "You'll be fine. Promise."

Marcus opens the third SUV's door. The bench seat's already configured—center section clear for transfer, extra cushions positioned.

"Alright, darlin'." Nathan's drawl surfaces as I lift Emily. "Nice and easy."

She wraps her arms around my neck.

Trusts me completely.

I settle her on the bench seat, arranging pillows behind her back. Extra support for her hips.

"Comfortable?"

"Yeah." She shifts slightly. Tests the position. "Actually really comfortable."

"Good."

Now for the chair.

I collapse the footrests, lock the wheels. Switch to manual mode.

Three hundred pounds of pink wheelchair.

"Need help, brother?" Levi appears beside me, already reaching for the frame.

"Grab that side." I position the portable ramp against the SUV's cargo area. "Marcus—"

"On it." Marcus takes the other side.

Robert Butler materializes from the second car. "Let me —"

"Philippe too." The man joins our little assembly line.

Five men.

One wheelchair.

This is either going to be smooth or a complete disaster.

"On three." I grip the frame. "One, two—"

We lift.

The chair rises. Steady. Controlled.

Robert and Philippe guide it up the ramp while Levi, Marcus, and I push.

Metal scrapes against metal.

"Left—no, your other left—"

"I know my bloody left, Marcus—"

"Would everyone shut up and push?" Jean calls from inside the car.

We push.

The chair slides into the cargo area. Perfect fit.

I collapse the ramp, secure the chair with tie-downs.

Done.

"Teamwork." Marcus grins, slightly winded.

"More like controlled chaos." But I clap his shoulder. "Thanks."

Mochi barks from the second car where Ariana's already buckled in.

The labradoodle wears his travel harness, tail wagging.

At least someone's excited about this trip.

I turn to Nibbler.

Our animatronic baby Utahraptor sits by his travel crate, amber eyes fixed on Emily through the car window.

Chirping.

Distressed chirps.

Oh bloody hell.

"Nibbler, in." I point to the crate.

The raptor's head tilts.

Chirps louder.

Backs away.

"Nibbler—"

More chirping.

Insistent. Upset.

Emily leans out the car door. "He doesn't want to be separated."

"He's an animatronic." But even I don't believe that anymore. Not after watching him bond with us at Starlight. "He has to ride in the crate for safety."

Nibbler's tail lashes.

The chirping becomes a keening sound.

Distress call.

For his Kree-ma.

Marcus whistles low. "That's... surprisingly heartbreaking for a robot."

It is.

Damn it.

I crouch in front of Nibbler. Let the raptor biology David programmed into him recognize dominance.

Authority.

"*Kree-ta.*" The command rumbles from my chest. Young one.

Nibbler's chirping quiets.

Amber eyes lock on mine.

"*Da-kree ta-nek.*" Daddy protects. "*Kree-ma nekh-sha.*" Mama is safe.

The raptor's head tilts the other way.

Considering.

Time to pull out the big guns.

I shift into full Nathan Cross mode. Alpha raptor. Pack leader.

Da-kree.

The growl that emerges carries every ounce of protective dominance the character demands.

"*Ta-kree, ta-sha. Kree-ma nekh-tha in kree-den.*" Always, forever. Mama is mine in protection. "*But Kree-ta ta-nek kree-sha. In kree-den. Kree-sha.*" Young one must obey. In protection. Obey.

Nibbler's posture shifts.

Submissive.

He chirps once. Soft.

Then walks into the crate.

Curls up.

Those amber eyes stay fixed on me.

"*Kree-sha ta-nek.*" Good boy obeys.

I secure the crate door. Lift it into the cargo area beside Emily's chair.

Nibbler chirps again.

Quieter now.

Resigned.

"You're terrifyingly good at that." Jean observes from the driver's seat.

"Method acting." I climb into the back beside Emily, pull her against my side. "Ready?"

She nestles into me. "That was impressive."

"Nathan's basically my personality turned up to eleven." I kiss her hair. "The alpha thing comes naturally."

"Possessive, protective, completely unreasonable—"

"Lambert trait." Marcus settles in beside Levi. "We've been over this."

Jean starts the engine.

The convoy begins to move.

Six hours to Bellbury.

Two days to forever.

I hold Emily close as the château disappears behind us.

Almost there, love.

Almost there.

Twenty minutes into the drive, Jean pulls into our usual café—Le Bon Matin—on the edge of Grantham Bridge.

"Coffee stop." He announces. "Last chance before we hit the motorway."

Emily perks up immediately. "My mocha."

I help her into the manual chair while Marcus and Levi unfold the portable ramp. The power chair stays secured in the cargo. Too much hassle for a quick stop.

Inside, the barista recognizes us immediately.

"Miss Emily!" Margaux beams. "The usual?"

"Please." Emily wheels to the counter. "Lactose-free whole milk, fall mocha."

"Extra whipped cream?"

"Obviously."

I order my espresso. Jean gets his pretentious pourover. Marcus wants some complicated latte with four modifications.

Levi just asks for black coffee.

Sensible.

We claim the corner table while Margaux prepares our drinks.

Jean settles across from me, that insufferable smirk already forming.

Here we go.

"So, Tristian." He leans back. "Remember when you swam from the boat to Paradise Point?"

"I was pursuing my bride." I keep my voice level. "Winkie tradition."

"You didn't pursue. You stalked." Jean's grin widens. "Emily posted a photo in a bikini and you literally abandoned the charter boat."

"The captain understood."

"The captain charged you double."

Emily giggles beside me.

Traitor.

"At least I didn't propose in a closet." I fire back.

Jean's expression falters.

Perfect.

"A *broom* closet," I continue. "At a political fundraiser. During dessert service."

"It was romantic."

"You locked yourselves in and forgot Levi's mic was still on. The entire ballroom heard everything."

Levi chokes on his water. "We agreed never to mention that."

"Everything," I repeat. "Including the part where you cried because Levi said yes."

"I had something in my eye—"

"For fifteen minutes?"

Marcus cackles. "Oh, this is brilliant. Continue."

Emily's shoulders shake with suppressed laughter.

Jean narrows his eyes. "Fine. Remember the train station wedding?"

Bloody hell.

"You sang Winkie vows through a *departing train window.*" He's enjoying this far too much. "With half of Grantham watching."

"It was spontaneous."

"You climbed onto the platform railing. Security had to physically restrain you from jumping onto the moving train."

"I wanted to kiss my wife properly."

"You screamed 'THAT'S MY WIFE' at random passengers."

Emily's laughing openly now. No longer even pretending to side with me.

Margaux brings our drinks, clearly eavesdropping.

She's grinning too.

I take a long sip of espresso. Regroup.

"Right then. Let's discuss the time you commissioned a thirty-foot portrait of Levi."

"That was a gift—"

"For your *office*." I lean forward. "At the Assemblée. Where you conduct official government business."

"It's tasteful."

"It's Levi. Shirtless. On a horse. In the rain."

Marcus nearly spits his latte. "What?"

"The horse is symbolic," Jean protests.

"Of what, exactly?"

"Strength. Nobility—"

"Thirst." Levi supplies helpfully. "It symbolizes thirst."

Even Jean laughs at that.

"You're all ridiculous." Emily wipes her eyes. "But Tristian wins."

"What? How—"

"He bought two islands while swimming." She sips her mocha, whipped cream coating her upper lip. "Mid-hunt. That's peak Lambert insanity."

I kiss the whipped cream away. "That's peak *devotion*."

"That's peak *unhinged*."

"Lambert trait," we all say in unison.

Marcus raises his complicated latte. "To being absolutely unhinged about the people we love."

"Hear, hear."

We clink cups.

Jean's phone buzzes. "Dad says stop embarrassing the family name at public cafés."

"How does he—"

"Margaux posted us on Instagram." Levi shows his screen.

Sure enough. The four of us. Mid-laugh.

Caption: *The Lambert brothers being completely normal. #NotACult #LambertCurse #WeLoveIt*

Two thousand likes already.

Emily snorts. "We're never living any of this down."

"Wouldn't want to." I kiss her temple. "Ready to continue?"

She nods.

I help her back into the manual chair, and we load up for the final five and a half hours.

Almost to Bellbury.

Almost to forever.

Forty minutes later, Emily shifts in her seat.

Again.

"Love." I keep my voice gentle. "You alright?"

"Mmhm." She doesn't meet my eyes.

Another ten minutes. More shifting.

She's gripping the armrest now.

"Emily—"

"I'm fine." Too quick. Too defensive.

Jean catches my gaze in the rearview mirror. Raises an eyebrow.

I text him: *She needs to stop.*

His response: *Third service station. Ten kilometers.*

"We're stopping soon anyway." I announce casually. "Levi needs a break."

Levi doesn't miss a beat. "Yeah, all that coffee went straight through me."

Emily relaxes slightly.

Smart man, my brother-in-law.

When we pull into the service station, I don't wait for protests. I'm out of the vehicle, unfolding the power chair while Levi lowers the lift.

"I can use the manual—"

"Power chair." I keep my tone firm. "Bathroom's on the other side of the building. You need the range."

She wheels forward without further argument.

Good.

Levi and I walk several paces behind while Jean stretches by the vehicle.

"Her period's coming." I say quietly.

"How do you know?"

"She can't sit still. Keeps shifting. That means her bladder's acting up."

"Ah." Levi nods. "Winnie gets migraines before hers. Throws up everything."

We reach the accessible toilet.

Emily wheels inside. Locks the door.

I lean against the wall outside, checking my phone.

Marcus texts: *All good?*

Me: *Bathroom stop. She's fine.*

Marcus: *Fourth one. Period incoming?*

Me: *Less than a week, probably.*

Marcus: *After the wedding then. Thank God.*

Marcus: *Can you imagine dealing with that AND wedding stress?*

Me: *Don't.*

I pocket my phone.

Levi returns from the men's room, drying his hands on his jeans.

"Still in there?"

"Yeah."

"Want me to check on her?"

Before I can answer, the door unlocks.

Emily wheels out, face slightly flushed.

"Better?" I ask.

"Fine." She won't look at me. "Can we go?"

I crouch beside her chair. "How many times did you go?"

"Tristian—"

"How many?"

"...twice."

Bloody hell.

"Your period's less than a week out." I stand, push her chair toward the vehicle. "Probably four or five days."

"I know my own cycle—"

"Your bladder goes mental right before. You know this."

Levi wisely stays silent, walking ahead to give us space.

"It's embarrassing." Emily mutters.

"Why?"

"Because we have to stop every hour—"

"Forty-five minutes." I correct. "And I don't care."

"Everyone else—"

"Also doesn't care." We reach the SUV. "Jean's prostate means he pees constantly. Levi drinks a gallon of water daily and needs breaks anyway. Marcus has IBS. Nobody's judging."

I load her into the vehicle, secure the chair in cargo.

When I slide in beside her, I take her hand.

"The birth control makes it worse before your period." I say quietly. "Dr. Laurent explained. Your bladder capacity drops by almost half."

"I hate it."

"I know." I kiss her knuckles. "But we plan around it. That's what we do."

She leans against my shoulder.

Jean starts the engine. "Everyone good?"

"Yeah." Emily calls forward. "Sorry for the delays."

"Please." Levi twists in his seat. "Jean stops every thirty minutes to 'check the route' which means pee. You're fine."

"I have a small bladder—"

"You have an *old* bladder." Marcus chimes in from the lead vehicle via our open phone line. "Face it, Jean. You're ancient."

"I'm twenty-seven."

"Exactly. Ancient."

Emily laughs.

I kiss her temple, settling her more comfortably against me.

Four more hours.

Then Bellbury.

Then our wedding.

Then forever.

Worth every single bathroom stop.

Jean parks at the next service station—bigger than the last, with proper picnic tables under shade trees.

"Lunch break." He announces. "Forty-five minutes."

I help Emily into the power chair, grabbing the cushion and resistance band from cargo.

"Where are we going?" She wheels beside me.

"Picnic table." I nod toward the shaded area. "You need stretches."

Her face falls. "Tristian, I'm fine—"

"Your right hip's been clicking for the last thirty kilometers." I keep walking. "I can hear it every time you shift."

"It always clicks."

"Not like that."

We reach the furthest table. Most private.

I spread the cushion across the bench, pat it. "Up."

Emily transfers from her chair with practiced ease, settling onto the cushion.

I kneel on the grass, unlace her left trainer first.

"Start with the bad one." She says quietly.

"Always do."

I peel off her right sock, set it aside.

Her ankle's slightly swollen. The dysplasia causes fluid buildup when she sits too long.

I press my thumbs into her heel chord, working upward with firm pressure.

She hisses.

"I know." I keep my voice low, soothing. "Breathe through it."

Marcus appears, settling on the bench beside Emily with his tablet.

"Right then." He pulls up something on screen. "Pop quiz time."

"What?" Emily's attention shifts.

"Winkie law." Marcus grins. "Specifically, Article Seventeen, Section Four. What does it say about wedding night protocol?"

"That's not real—"

"It absolutely is." I work deeper into her heel chord, feel the knot start to release. "Answer the question, love."

Emily glares at me. "The groom must present—ow—his bride with—*Tristian*—"

"Keep going." I move to her calf, stretching the gastrocnemius.

"—with tokens representing his—bloody hell—his intention to provide."

"Correct." Marcus scrolls. "What are acceptable tokens?"

"Food, clothing, shelter—*Ahhh*—" She grips the table edge.

I ease back slightly. "Too much?"

"No. Keep going."

Stubborn woman.

I continue working up her calf, feeling every tight band of muscle.

The dysplasia means her right leg compensates constantly. Everything stays contracted.

"Additional acceptable tokens?" Marcus prompts.

"Livestock." Emily breathes through another stretch. "Precious metals. Land deeds."

"What about animatronic dinosaurs?"

She laughs despite the pain. "That wasn't in the original text."

"Should be." I move to her hamstring, supporting her knee. "Bend."

She complies.

I push her knee toward her chest, stretching the entire posterior chain.

Her hip pops audibly.

"There it is." I hold the position. "Thirty seconds."

"I hate you." But she's smiling.

"Liar."

Marcus keeps reading. "Section Eight covers gift-giving etiquette. The bride must present her groom with something handmade."

"Like embroidered vows?" Emily asks.

"Exactly like that." I ease her leg down, start on the hip rotations. "External first."

I guide her knee outward, opening the hip joint.

The arthritis makes this the worst part.

Her breathing quickens.

"Marcus." I nod.

"Right." He switches topics immediately. "So, Nibbler."

"What about him?" Emily focuses on Marcus instead of the pain.

"He's definitely your child now." Marcus shows his phone. "Look at this."

Instagram post. Nibbler in his travel crate, looking absolutely dejected.

Caption from Michelle: *When your father becomes an alpha and you have to obey. #NibblerSulks #RaptorDrama*

Eight thousand likes.

Emily laughs. "Oh, poor baby."

I continue the rotation, pushing slightly deeper.

She grips Marcus's arm.

"Almost done." I promise. "Internal rotation, then we switch sides."

I guide her knee inward. Feel the joint resist.

Bloody dysplasia.

"Section Twelve." Marcus scrolls frantically. "Wedding night positions approved by Winkie tradition—"

"MARCUS." Emily's face flames.

"What? It's educational."

"It's mortifying."

"It's comprehensive." He grins. "Very illustrated."

"Stop showing her that." I finish the rotation, lower her leg gently. "Left side now."

The left hip cooperates better. Milder dysplasia means less resistance.

I work through the same sequence—heel chord, calf, hamstring, rotations.

Emily talks with Marcus about absolutely nothing. Wedding flowers. Nibbler's diet. Whether Mochi needs a tuxedo.

Anything to distract from the discomfort.

When I finish, I help her sit up properly.

"Better?"

She rotates both hips experimentally. "Yeah. Actually."

"Good." I kiss her knee. "Ice packs in the cooler. Twenty minutes on each hip before we drive again."

"Tristian—"

"Non-negotiable."

Jean approaches with sandwiches. "Lunch is ready. Nice timing."

Levi carries drinks, sets them on the table.

I retrieve the ice packs, wrap them in towels, position them against Emily's hips.

She doesn't protest this time.

Progress.

We pull through the vineyard gates at seventeen minutes past five.

Three hours late.

The villa sprawls before us, cream stone glowing in the late afternoon sun. Temporary wooden ramps angle up to both entrances.

"They're not finished." Emily stares.

"They're functional." I unbuckle her seatbelt. "That's what matters."

Marcus parks beside Michelle's Range Rover. Jean's Audi sits near the fountain.

The others beat us by over an hour.

I help Emily into her chair while Levi and Marcus handle luggage.

Mochi barrels out the front door, Nibbler close behind.

Both animals make straight for Emily.

Mochi presses against her leg. Nibbler chirps frantically, nudging her arm.

"I'm okay." Emily strokes both. "Just stiff from the drive."

Nibbler chirps again. Higher pitched.

He knows she's lying.

"Inside." I position myself behind her chair. "We'll do stretches before dinner."

"Tristian—"

"You've been sitting six hours with one break." I push her toward the ramp. "Your hips are screaming."

Michelle appears in the doorway, wine glass in hand.

"Finally." She kisses Emily's cheek. "We were starting to worry."

"Bladder breaks." Emily says flatly.

"Say no more."

Inside, the villa smells like fresh paint and lavender. Open floor plan, massive windows overlooking rows of grapevines.

Mum emerges from the kitchen. "Emily, darling. Your room is ready."

"Thank you, Celeste."

Dad nods from his position near the fireplace. Reading glasses perched on his nose, tablet in hand.

Probably campaign analytics.

Some things never change.

Grandmère sits in the corner armchair, knitting something purple.

"There's my boy." She sets the needles aside. "And his beautiful bride."

I kiss her cheek. "Grandmère."

"Your room is the large one." She gestures down the hall. "Main floor. We thought—"

"Perfect." I squeeze her shoulder. "Thank you."

Emily wheels herself down the corridor. I follow with Mochi and Nibbler trailing behind.

The bedroom is enormous. King bed faces windows overlooking the vineyard. Ensuite bathroom through the door on the left.

Roll-in shower. Grab bars. Everything Emily needs.

"Wow." She wheels to the window.

I close the door behind us.

Mochi immediately claims the dog bed near the bathroom. Nibbler settles beside him, watching Emily with those disturbingly intelligent eyes.

"Bed." I point. "Now."

"I should unpack—"

"Stretches first. Then dinner. Unpacking can wait."

She transfers to the mattress without arguing.

Too tired to fight.

I grab the massage oil from my bag—always packed—and kneel beside the bed.

"Right hip first."

She rolls onto her left side, draws her right knee up.

Mochi lifts his head, watching.

Nibbler chirps softly.

Both animals know the routine by now.

I pour oil into my palm, warm it between my hands.

Start at her greater trochanter, work deep into the hip flexors.

She hisses.

Nibbler chirps again. Anxious.

"Shh." I keep my voice low. "I've got her."

Emily's muscles resist. Six hours of sitting has everything locked tight.

I work slowly, methodically. Psoas, iliacus, tensor fasciae latae.

Every trigger point gets attention.

Mochi whines.

"It's okay, boy." Emily reaches toward him.

He licks her fingers.

I continue working, feeling the gradual release.

Her breathing deepens. Evens out.

Twenty minutes on the right hip before I switch.

The left cooperates better. Always does.

Nibbler settles his head on his claws, still watching.

Good boy. Learning to trust the process.

When I finish, Emily's half asleep.

"Done." I kiss her temple. "How do you feel?"

"Like jelly."

"Perfect."

Mochi stretches, shaking himself.

Nibbler chirps questioningly.

"She's better now." I tell him in raptor. "Good watching."

He trills, pleased with the praise.

Emily rolls onto her back. "What time is dinner?"

"Seven." I check my phone. "You've got ninety minutes."

"I should shower."

"Want help?"

"Please."

I lift her easily, carry her toward the ensuite.

Mochi and Nibbler remain in the bedroom.

Standing guard.

Our boys know exactly what Mama needs.

And so do I.

I wake to the scent of buttermilk and sage.

Alfred's here.

Emily stirs beside me, nose wrinkling.

"Is that—"

"Biscuits and gravy." I kiss her forehead. "Your favorite."

She's up and in her chair faster than I've seen her move all week.

Mochi trails behind as she wheels toward the kitchen. Nibbler chirps from his charging station—battery's low this morning.

Alfred stands at the stove, apron tied around his waist. The same one he wore when I was eight.

"There's my girl." He doesn't turn from the pan. "Figured you'd need proper fuel before tomorrow."

Emily stops beside him. "You flew out just to cook breakfast?"

"I flew out because you're family." He plates golden biscuits, ladels sausage gravy over top. "Besides, Collette's handling the château. She insisted."

Tears shine in Emily's eyes.

Alfred sets the plate in front of her. "Eat."

She does.

The scale sits in the corner of the kitchen.

Dr. Rousseau's orders—daily weigh-ins until the wedding.

"After breakfast." I catch Emily's glance toward it. "Enjoy your food first."

Twenty minutes later, she transfers onto the scale.

Digital numbers climb.

Stabilize.

"You did it." I lift her off, spin her in a circle. "Healthy weight. Official."

Emily buries her face against my shoulder.

Relief, not tears.

"Told you those midnight snacks would work." Marcus appears in the doorway, already dressed. "Southern Living wants a follow-up interview before the wedding. You two available at ten?"

"Sure." Emily's voice is muffled against my shirt.

Philippe's voice carries from the garden.

Then Ariana's gasp.

We exchange glances.

Outside, Philippe kneels in the grass.

Ariana's hands cover her mouth.

Purple velvet box open between them.

"Will you marry me?" Philippe's voice shakes. "I know it's only been three months, but—"

"Yes." Ariana drops to her knees. "Yes, you ridiculous gladiator. Yes."

He slides the ring on her finger.

The family erupts from various doors. Michelle crying, Mum clapping, Dad actually smiling.

Marcus lifts Ariana, spins her. "Welcome to the family circus, officially."

Jean hugs Philippe. "About time."

"Tomorrow's a wedding." Grandmère announces. "Today we celebrate two."

A familiar whinny echoes from the front drive.

Phantom.

I wheel Emily around the house.

Robert leads my stallion down the ramp. Emerald follows, noticeably rounder than last month.

Foal's due in spring.

Phantom spots Emily, tosses his head.

Trots straight to her chair.

Emerald waddles behind, protective.

"Hey, handsome." Emily strokes Phantom's nose.

He lowers his head, breathing warm air across her face.

Claiming scent.

Emerald nudges Emily's shoulder. Gentle but insistent.

My human. Mine.

"I see you, beautiful girl." Emily touches Emerald's muzzle. "How's our baby?"

The mare huffs contentedly.

Phantom circles behind Emily's chair. Plants himself between her and the house.

Guard position.

No one approaches his mate without permission.

"Want to ride?" I ask Emily. "We've got four hours before the cousins descend."

Her face lights up. "Really?"

"Phantom's been asking for you since we left Grantham."

Marcus helps me lift Emily onto Phantom's back. The stallion stands perfectly still, muscles tense with focus.

I mount behind her, arms bracketing her waist.

"Ready?"

She leans back against me. "Go."

Phantom moves smoothly into a walk. Emerald follows, matching pace despite her bulk.

We ride through the vineyard rows. Morning sun warm on our shoulders.

Emily's hands rest on Phantom's neck, fingers tangled in his mane.

The path slopes gently upward.

Phantom breaks into an easy lope.

Emily laughs. Full and genuine.

"I'm flying!" Her voice carries across the vines.

Emerald trumpets beside us. Happy sound.

Phantom's ears flick back, checking on Emily.

I tighten my arms around her waist.

Tomorrow she becomes my wife.

Legally.

Officially.

But right now—

Right now she's just Emily.

Free.

Flying.

Mine.

We're halfway back to the house when chaos erupts from the driveway.

"TRISTIAN!"

Seven bodies barrel toward us.

I dismount quickly, help Emily down.

Too late.

The Lambert cousin horde arrives.

"You got married without us!" Nine-year-old Henri crashes into my legs.

"The wedding's tomorrow." I catch him before he bounces off.

"But the Metro wedding—" Seven-year-old Sophie tugs my sleeve. "Jean showed us the video."

"That was—complicated."

Two-year-old Jules toddles over, arms up.

I scoop him into one arm, balance him on my hip.

"Oggie!" He pats my face. "Oggie home!"

"Yeah, buddy. Oggie's home."

Mochi bounds from the house, tail helicopter-spinning.

The kids shriek.

Dog pile ensues.

Literally.

Mochi accepts his fate, lying down while seven children swarm him with pets and kisses.

Nibbler emerges next, freshly charged.

Complete silence.

Then—

"IS THAT A DINOSAUR?" Henri whisper-screams.

"Utahraptor." Emily wheels closer. "His name's Nibbler."

"Does he bite?" Sophie creeps forward.

"Only bad guys." I set Jules down. "Be gentle."

Nibbler chirps, head tilting.

The kids approach slowly.

Margot reaches out first.

Nibbler bumps her palm with his snout. Soft trill.

Friend.

"He's purring!" She giggles.

Four-year-old Luc touches Nibbler's flank. "Soft."

"He's family." Emily explains. "Like Mochi. Like all of you."

The kids swarm Nibbler next. Gentle pats, careful touches.

Jules hugs Nibbler's leg.

The animatronic lowers his head, nuzzles the toddler's hair.

My phone buzzes.

Robert's name flashes.

I step away, answer. "Yeah?"

"Martha Hendricks called the main line." Robert's voice is ice. "Demanding to speak with Emily."

Every muscle tenses. "What did she want?"

"To 'apologize' for the media statements. Offering to come to the wedding as a guest."

"Absolutely not."

"Philippe's handling it. Thought you should know."

I hang up, turn.

Philippe stands near the garden, phone pressed to his ear. His gladiator posture radiates controlled fury.

Emily's face has gone pale.

She heard.

The kids notice immediately.

"Auntie Emily?" Henri touches her hand. "You okay?"

"I'm fine, sweetheart."

"You're sad." Margot climbs into her lap, careful of Emily's legs. "We can fix sad."

Sophie starts singing. Off-key, enthusiastic.

The other kids join in. Chaotic harmony.

Jules conducts with a stick he found somewhere.

Emily's tears fall, but she's smiling.

Philippe returns, jaw tight.

"Handled?" I ask quietly.

"She won't call again." His eyes promise violence if she tries.

Robert appears beside him. "Already contacted the security team. Martha Hendricks, Adam Morrison, and Bethany Morrison are officially banned from Lambert properties. Their names are flagged."

"Good."

Henri tugs my sleeve. "Can we ride the horses?"

"After lunch—"

"Please?" Seven voices chorus.

Emily laughs. Genuine sound. "How can you say no to that?"

I can't.

Twenty minutes later, we're all in the paddock.

Henri and Sophie ride Phantom together, my hands steadying them.

Margot sits with Emily with Emerald, chattering about the foal coming in spring.

Luc and the twins take turns on the old mare.

Jules rides in the saddle with Marcus on Philippe's gelding.

Robert supervises from the fence, camera ready.

"Say cheese!" He calls.

The kids yell. The horses whinny.

Mochi barks.

Nibbler trills.

Emily beams, crown crooked on her head, Margot's arms around her waist.

My family.

All of them.

Tomorrow we make it official.

But right now?

Right now we're just us.

Chaotic.

Loud.

Perfect.

Martha Hendricks can rot.

This—

This is what matters.

The paddock gate creaks.

Aunt Brigitte appears with a baby carrier.

"Emily, *chérie*—" She switches to English mid-sentence. "Could you hold Océane? I need both hands to help Jules with the saddle."

Before I can answer, she's placing a three-month-old bundle in my arms.

Océane.

The littlest Lambert cousin.

Downy dark hair. Enormous brown eyes. Perfect tiny fists.

She blinks at me.

Then her face scrunches.

Oh no.

The wail starts soft. Builds to full-volume distress.

I freeze. What do I—

"Here." Tristian's already there, scooping Océane from my lap with practiced ease. "Hey, *ma petite*. What's wrong?"

He settles her against his chest. One hand cradles her head. The other supports her bottom.

Océane's cries shift to whimpers.

Tristian sways. Gentle rocking motion.

Starts humming. Something French. Probably the same lullaby Collette sang to him.

The baby quiets.

Stares up at him with absolute trust.

My ovaries *detonate*.

Gone.

Reduced to ash.

Because Tristian Lambert—Hollywood star, raptor shifter, my possessive Winkie husband—is standing in golden afternoon light with an infant cradled against his chest like she's made of spun glass.

"There we go." His voice drops to that soft rumble he uses when I'm hurting. "Better?"

Océane yawns. Tiny fist curls into his shirt.

I'm going to *die*.

Actually expire.

Right here in this paddock.

"Em?" Tristian glances over. "You okay?"

"Fine." My voice cracks.

His eyes narrow. Reading me.

The corner of his mouth lifts.

Bastard knows exactly what he's doing.

Océane makes a soft sound. Tristian adjusts his hold, drops a kiss to her forehead.

Nope.

Dead.

I'm dead.

Gone.

RIP Emily Lambert.

Cause of death: fiancé holding baby.

"Jules! Wait for me!" Henri's shout breaks the moment.

Tristian hands Océane back to Brigitte, who's returned with Jules successfully saddled.

But the image is *burned* into my brain.

Those gentle hands.

That soft expression.

The way he swayed without thinking.

Natural.

Easy.

Like he was born to—

Stop.

I can't think about this.

Not now.

Not when we're getting married tomorrow and I'm still processing everything and my body already hates me and—

Tristian wheels me toward the house while the kids continue their riding lesson.

"Talk to me." He crouches beside my chair once we're alone in the garden. "What's going on in that beautiful head?"

"Nothing."

"*Mon cœur.*" His thumb brushes my cheek. "Don't lie."

I swallow hard. "You looked good with her."

Understanding flashes in his eyes. Then heat.

Dangerous heat.

"Yeah?"

"Don't—" I shake my head. "We can't. I'm not—we talked about this. PCOS means—"

"I know what PCOS means." He cuts me off gently. Cups my face. "But when you're ready? When *we're* ready?"

His accent thickens. British bleeding through.

"I'm not leaving our bed until you're pregnant."

My breath catches.

"I'll take however long it takes." His forehead presses to mine. "Months. Years. However many specialists, treatments, procedures you need. We'll do it together."

"Tristian—"

"But when you're ready." He kisses me soft. Sweet. "Not before. This is your choice, love. Always your choice."

Tears prick my eyes.

Because he means it.

Every word.

No pressure. No expectations.

Just—possibility.

Someday.

When I'm ready.

If I'm ready.

"I love you." The words tumble out.

"Love you more." He grins. Kisses me again. "Now stop looking at me like you want to jump my bones when there are twelve children fifty feet away."

I laugh despite myself.

He wheels me inside where Celeste has tea ready.

But I can't stop seeing it.

Tristian with Océane.

Tristian with our hypothetical someday-maybe child.

Tristian as a father.

My hand drifts to my stomach.

Someday.

When I'm ready.

When we're ready.

Together.

The convoy of vans pulls up the vineyard drive at four.

Dust clouds kick up behind six vehicles.

I'm already moving down the steps before they fully stop.

Emily wheels beside me, Mochi trotting at her side.

The first van door slides open.

Chaos erupts.

"EMILY!"

Six boys pour out like they've been spring-loaded.

Ages three to sixteen. All shouting over each other.

Zara appears from the second van, laughing as her sons swarm Emily's wheelchair.

"Boys—*boys*—give her space to breathe!"

Too late.

The youngest—three-year-old Jasper—climbs straight into Emily's lap.

"We missed you!"

"You look like a real princess!" Eight-year-old Marcus Junior adds.

Zara reaches us. Pulls Emily into a hug over Jasper's head.

"Look at you. Glowing."

"Exhausted." Emily laughs. "But yeah."

Sophia emerges next, twin girls on her hips.

Four months old. Identical except one's in pink, the other purple.

"These are Luna and Stella." Sophia passes purple-clad Stella to Emily. "Say hi to Auntie Em."

Stella gurgles.

Drools on Emily's shoulder.

Emily doesn't even flinch.

Michael rounds the van. Grins at me. Pulls me into a back-slapping hug.

"Congrats, man. Tomorrow's the big day."

"Tomorrow." The word tastes surreal.

Dante appears with Sophia's older daughters—ten-year-old Mia, seven-year-old Grace, and four-year-old Violet.

The girls immediately start petting Mochi, who accepts the attention like the professional he is.

"Uncle Tristian!" Violet latches onto my leg. "Is Nibbler here?"

"In the house. But he's in sleep mode right now."

"Can we wake him?"

"After you get settled."

Braden—our Nick the Tin Man—climbs out of the third van with his boyfriend Carlos, who plays Roar the Cowardly Lion.

Daniel follows, adjusting his glasses.

Our Wizard.

The oldest member of the cast at seventy-two.

"Tristian." He clasps my hand. "Beautiful property."

"Wait till you see the venue." I gesture toward the cottages. "Six guest houses. Take your pick."

Jean appears from inside the main house with Levi, Marcus with Michelle.

Ariana bounces down the steps with Philippe.

Introductions blur together.

Kids running everywhere.

Babies being passed around.

Adults laughing, hugging, talking over each other.

Margot, Henri, Jules, and the younger Lambert cousins stare wide-eyed at the film stars in their midst.

"Is that really Carlos Martinez?" Margot whispers to me.

"Yeah. Want to meet him?"

She nods so hard I'm worried about whiplash.

I wave Carlos over. Make introductions.

Within minutes, the Lambert cousins and the Wonderful kids are playing some elaborate game involving racing around the vineyard rows.

Mochi supervises.

Emily sits surrounded by Zara, Sophia, and Michelle.

Stella still in her lap.

Looking radiant despite her exhaustion.

My chest tightens.

Tomorrow.

Tomorrow she becomes my wife.

Legally.

Officially.

Not just Winkie tradition but actual law.

Michael claps my shoulder. "You good?"

"Yeah." I swallow hard. "Yeah, I'm good."

"Because you look like you might pass out."

"Just—processing."

Dante joins us. Hands me a beer from the cooler someone dragged out.

"Breathe, man. You've already done the hard part."

"What hard part?"

"Falling in love." He grins. "Everything else is just paperwork."

I laugh despite my nerves.

Watch Emily lean down to kiss Stella's fuzzy head.

Zara says something that makes her throw her head back laughing.

God, she's beautiful.

"Bachelor party starts at eight," Michael says. "Jean's planned something."

"Should I be worried?"

"Probably."

Great.

"Bachelorette party's at the same time," Dante adds. "Sophia and Michelle are handling it."

I glance at Emily again.

She catches my eye.

Mouths: *I love you.*

Fourteen hours.

Fourteen hours until she's legally mine.

Until I can call her my wife without qualifiers.

Until the world recognizes what I've known since FanCon.

She's it.

My everything.

My always.

Tomorrow can't come fast enough.

The vineyard's lower terrace glows with string lights.

Eight o'clock sharp.

Michael hands me a whiskey as I settle into one of the Adirondack chairs arranged in a circle.

Jean drops into the seat beside me, already nursing a beer.

Marcus, Daniel, Dante, Philippe, Michel, and Braden complete the circle.

No Levi.

No Carlos.

"Where's—"

"With the girls." Jean grins. "Honorary Dorothy Squad member. Has been since the island bride chase."

"Carlos too," Dante adds. "They're doing the full bachelorette experience."

I blink.

"Levi's the one going down the aisle," Marcus explains. "Makes him an honorary bride."

Fair enough.

Daniel raises his glass. "To tomorrow. To new beginnings."

We drink.

The night unfolds easy.

Stories about Emily and Jean.

How I knew after five minutes at FanCon.

How Jean proposed to Levi in a Paris closet after dating for three weeks.

"Lambert curse," Marcus says, shaking his head. "Still can't believe it's real."

"Believe it." Jean's smile goes soft. "Tomorrow I marry the love of my life."

"Same." The word comes out rough.

Philippe leans forward. "Twenty-three days. I knew after twenty-three days with Ariana."

Daniel says. "My grandfather was the same. Saw my grandmother across a dance hall. Married her six weeks later. Sixty years they had."

Dante nods. "My parents. Two months from meeting to wedding. Thirty-five years strong."

The conversation shifts to wedding day logistics.

Venue setup at noon.

Ceremony at four.

Reception until midnight.

My phone buzzes.

Instagram notification.

Dorothy Squad posted a photo.

I open it.

Emily, Michelle, Ariana, Sophia, Zara, Levi, and Carlos.

All in face masks and robes.

Getting manicures and pedicures.

Emily's nails are blue gingham with tiny silver slippers on the accent fingers.

Levi's are deep vampire red.

The caption: *bride prep with the squad* 🦢

"They're posting content," I mutter.

Jean checks his phone. Grins. "Levi looks good in red."

Another notification.

Video this time.

I tap play.

Emily's voice: "So we're about to do something extremely brave—"

Camera pans to show her lying on a table in one of the guest cottages.

Sophia holds her hand.

"—full body hard wax. Including Brazilian."

My eyebrows shoot up.

"Emily, you don't have to—"

"Shh. I want to look perfect for my husband."

The video cuts.

Next clip shows Emily mid-wax.

Swearing in Winkie.

Rapid-fire words I've only heard during our most intense moments.

Sophia and Zara are dying laughing.

Another cut.

Levi on the table now.

Also swearing.

Jean chokes on his beer beside me.

Final clip.

Emily and Levi on the couch.

Both pouting.

Tears streaming down their faces.

"We want our husbands," Emily whimpers.

"It hurts," Levi adds.

They're hamming it up.

Definitely know what they're doing.

The video ends.

I'm already standing.

"Excuse me." I set down my whiskey. "I'm going to make love to my wife."

Marcus jumps up. "Tradition! The night apart!"

"Screw that." I'm already walking toward the house. "I have skin to soothe. With my tongue. All night."

Jean's right behind me.

"Jean—your wedding—tradition—" Marcus sputters.

We ignore him.

Lambert romantic possessiveness flaring hot in both of us.

The house comes into view.

Through the French doors, I spot them.

Emily and Levi curled on the sectional.

Still in their robes.

Michelle rubbing Emily's shoulders.

Sophia bringing them water.

I push through the door.

Emily's head snaps up.

Those green eyes lock on mine.

"Tristian—"

I cross the room in four strides.

Bend.

Scoop her into my arms.

She squeaks.

Wraps her arms around my neck.

"What are you—"

"Taking care of my wife."

Jean mirrors my movements with Levi.

Lifts him easily despite his protests.

"Jean! The tradition—"

"Don't care."

Michelle grins. "Called it. Told you they'd last an hour."

Ariana holds up her phone. "I got it on video."

"Post it," I say over my shoulder.

Already heading for the main floor bedroom.

Our room.

The one with the accessible bathroom and the king bed and blackout curtains.

Emily buries her face in my neck. "You're supposed to be drinking with the guys."

"The guys can wait."

"It's bad luck—"

"We're already married. Remember? Metro station. Winkie vows."

She laughs.

That beautiful sound that makes my chest tight.

I shoulder open the bedroom door.

Kick it closed behind us.

Lower her onto the bed.

She looks up at me.

Flushed.

Hair slightly mussed.

Robe slipping off one shoulder.

"Hi."

"Hi yourself." I kneel beside the bed. "Let me see."

She bites her lip.

Slowly parts the robe.

The wax job is—

Christ.

"Emily."

"Too much?"

"Perfect." My voice drops. "You're perfect."

I lean in.

Press a kiss to her hip.

She shivers.

"Tristian—"

"I'm soothing. Like I promised."

Her laugh turns into a gasp as I kiss lower.

Tomorrow she becomes my wife.

Legally.

Officially.

But tonight?

Tonight she's already mine.

And I'm going to worship every inch of newly smooth skin.

All.

Night.

Long.

Chapter 14: Butterfly Gown, Cathedral

I Do

Sunlight cuts through the curtains.

I blink awake.

Emily's sprawled across my chest.

One leg hooked over mine.

Her breathing soft and even.

My wedding day.

Our wedding day.

The thought makes my chest tight.

Emily stirs.

Then bolts upright.

"Bathroom—"

I'm already moving.

Scooping her into my arms before her feet touch the

floor.

Naked.

Both of us.

We didn't bother with clothes after—

Well.

After.

I rush her across the cool hardwood.

She squirms. "Tristian, hurry—"

Five steps to the bathroom.

I kick the door open.

Lower her onto the toilet just as she—

"Made it," she breathes.

Relief floods her face.

I lean against the doorframe.

Watch her.

Even now.

First thing in the morning.

Completely exposed.

She's the most beautiful thing I've ever seen.

"Stop staring at me while I pee."

"Can't help it." My accent thickens. British bleeding through. "You're stunning."

She rolls her eyes.

But she's smiling.

When she finishes, I carry her to the clawfoot tub.

The one Jean had installed specifically for this weekend.

Deep enough for her to soak.

Wide enough for both of us.

I set her on the edge.

Turn on the taps.

Steam rises immediately.

"Bath before chaos?" Emily asks.

"Bath before chaos," I confirm.

The tub fills.

I add lavender oil.

Her favorite.

When it's ready, I lift her in.

She sighs.

Sinks into the water.

I slide in behind her.

Pull her back against my chest.

My hands find her legs.

Smooth.

So incredibly smooth.

"Worth the pain?" I murmur against her ear.

"Ask me tomorrow when I'm not still tender."

I laugh.

Press a kiss to her shoulder.

Run my palms up her thighs.

Appreciating every inch of silky skin.

She worked hard yesterday.

Both waxing sessions—legs and Brazilian.

Levi complained for an hour after.

Emily cried.

Then demanded we come soothe them.

Which we did.

Thoroughly.

"Tristian." Her voice goes breathy.

"Mm?"

"We have a wedding in"—she checks the waterproof clock on the shelf—"seven hours."

"Plenty of time."

My hand drifts higher.

She catches it.

Laces our fingers together.

"People are probably already awake."

As if on cue, footsteps pound past our door.

Children's laughter.

Mochi's excited bark.

Marcus's voice: "C'mon, boy! Let's burn off that energy before you knock over the flower arrangements!"

The front door slams.

Emily giggles. "Marcus is taking Mochi for a run."

"Good." I nuzzle her neck. "Keeps him occupied."

"You're terrible."

"You love it."

"I do." She tilts her head back. Looks at me upside down. "I love you."

The words hit different this morning.

Heavier.

More real.

In seven hours, she'll say them in front of everyone.

Our families.

Friends.

The Wonderful cast.

Half the film industry, probably.

"I love you too." I kiss her forehead. "My almost-wife."

"Almost-wife," she echoes.

We soak in silence.

Her back against my chest.

My arms wrapped around her.

The water warm.

Perfect.

More footsteps outside.

Jean's voice: "Levi, have you seen my—"

"Bathroom counter!"

"Thank you, mon cœur!"

Emily traces patterns on my forearm. "Your family is chaos."

"Our family," I correct.

She smiles.

That brilliant, luminous smile.

"Our family."

I hold her tighter.

Seven hours.

Then she's legally mine.

Emily Dorothy Silver Washington Butler Lambert.

The woman who saved me from a life of empty relationships and hollow performances.

Who sees past the fame.

The name.

The accent and charm.

Sees me.

Just Tristian.

The boy from Grantham Bridge who never felt like he belonged anywhere.

Until her.

"What are you thinking?" she asks softly.

"That I can't wait to marry you."

"Again." She grins. "Technically marry you again."

"This one counts for taxes."

She laughs.

The sound echoes off the tile.

I capture it.

Store it in my memory.

Along with every other perfect moment.

"We should probably get out," Emily says eventually. "Before someone comes looking."

"Five more minutes."

"Tristian—"

"Please, love."

She melts back against me.

"Five minutes."

I hold my bride.

In the quiet morning light.

Before the ceremony.

The photographs.

The celebration.

Just us.

Exactly how it should be.

I trail my fingers along Emily's thigh. Her skin, freshly waxed, is smooth as silk. She shivers at my touch, a soft gasp escaping her lips. I can feel her heartbeat quicken against my chest.

"Need help relaxing, love?" I murmur, my voice low and husky. My fingers drift higher, tracing patterns on her inner thigh. Her breath hitches, but she doesn't respond. Not with words, at least. Her body, though—that's a different story. The way she leans into my touch, the slight arch of her back... it's all the answer I need.

My fingers inch closer to her center, and I can feel the heat radiating from her. She's already wet, her body ready for me. I appreciate the smooth skin, the result of yesterday's waxing session. It was worth the pain, she said. And I agree. Every inch of her is perfect.

"You're so soft, love," I whisper, my voice a mix of English and French. The British accent bleeds through, thicker with my growing arousal. "So smooth."

She moans softly, her head falling back against my shoulder. I take advantage of the exposed skin, pressing kisses to her neck, her collarbone. My fingers continue their exploration, tracing the outer lips of her pussy, teasing.

"Tristian," she breathes, her voice barely a whisper.

"Mm?" I hum against her skin, my fingers dipping between her folds, gathering her wetness.

"Please," she begs, her hips lifting slightly, seeking more friction.

I chuckle, low and deep. "Please what, love?" I ask, my voice a dirty rasp. I switch to Winkie, the language of our people. The language of our love. "Tell me what you need, ma chérie."

She whimpers, her body squirming against mine. "Touch me," she pleads, her voice a mix of English and Winkie. "Please, touch me."

I grin, victorious. My fingers find her clit, circling the sensitive bundle of nerves. Her moan is music to my ears, her body arching beautifully against mine. I hold her tighter, my other hand splayed across her stomach, keeping her flush against me.

"Like this, love?" I ask, my voice a dirty growl. I switch to French, the language of my heart. "Is this what you need, mon amour?"

She nods, her breath coming in quick pants. "Yes," she gasps. "Yes, please."

I increase the pressure, my fingers moving in quick, tight circles. Her moans fill the bathroom, her body writhing against mine. I can feel her tension building, her muscles coiling tight.

"That's it, love," I encourage, my voice a mix of English, French, and Winkie. "Let go for me. Let me feel you come undone."

Her body obeys my command, her orgasm ripping through her. She cries out, her body convulsing against mine. I hold her through it, my fingers drawing out every last wave of pleasure.

As she comes down, I turn her in my arms, capturing her mouth in a fierce kiss. She melts into me, her body boneless and sated. I pull back, resting my forehead against hers.

"Better, love?" I ask, a smirk playing on my lips.

She laughs, a soft, breathless sound. "Much," she admits, a smile tugging at her lips.

I help her from the tub, wrapping her in a fluffy towel. I can't help but steal kisses as I dry her off, my body already aching for more. But we have a timeline to keep. A wedding to prepare for.

So, with one last kiss, I sweep her into my arms and carry her back to the bedroom. Where her wedding dress awaits. Where our future awaits.

And I can't wait.

A knock interrupts our moment.

"Emily? It's Levi."

She stiffens against me.

Wedding mode.

"Coming!" she calls.

Her voice only shakes slightly.

I help her from the tub, wrapping her in a plush towel. Support her weight as she stands on unsteady legs.

"I've got your dress," Levi says through the door. "It's time."

Time.

The cathedral.

Our wedding.

Emily's hands tremble as she dries off.

I steady them with my own.

"Breathe, love."

"I'm okay." She inhales deeply. "Just... nervous."

"About marrying me?"

"About tripping down the aisle."

I cup her face.

"You won't trip. Levi will have you."

"What if—"

I kiss her.

Soft.

Gentle.

Silencing her doubts.

"No what-ifs," I whisper against her lips. "Just us."

Levi waits in the hallway.

Emily's wedding dress hangs in a cream garment bag draped over his arm.

He grins when I open the door.

Takes in my towel-wrapped state.

Emily's damp hair.

"Cutting it close, aren't we?"

"Shut up," I mutter.

"Sophia's already at the cathedral with Zara. Michelle and Adele are loading the van." He turns to Emily. "Celeste has Mochi in his tux. He looks extremely distinguished."

Emily laughs.

That nervous, breathy laugh.

"We'll meet you there," Levi continues. "Jean's having a minor crisis about his boutonniere."

"Of course he is," I say.

Levi disappears down the hall.

The garment bag floating behind him like a ghost.

Emily watches it go.

Her eyes wide.

Uncertain.

"Hey." I tilt her chin up. "Seven hours. Then you're mine."

"I'm already yours."

"Legally mine."

She smiles.

That small, secret smile.

The one just for me.

Bellbury Cathedral rises above the city like a monument to history itself—Gothic spires reaching toward heaven, flying buttresses that echo Notre-Dame, the intricate rose window that rivals Westminster Abbey. Every Lambert since the founding of Angoumois has married here.

My parents.

My grandparents.

Generations stretching back two hundred years.

Now Emily and me.

I'm still in jeans and a t-shirt when I slip inside through the side entrance. The vast interior swallows sound—every footstep echoes against stone floors worn smooth by centuries of worship. Sunlight streams through stained glass, painting the pews in jewel tones.

"Tristian."

Father Benedict emerges from the sacristy.

Eighty-three years old.

White hair.

Kind eyes behind wire-rimmed glasses.

He married my parents thirty-two years ago in this very cathedral. Christened Jean, Michelle, and me when we were three days old, our screams probably echoing off these same walls.

"Father." I embrace him carefully. "Thank you for doing this."

"I wouldn't miss it." He grips my shoulders, studying my face. "Your Mum showed me photos of Emily. She's lovely."

"She is."

"And strong, I think. To have survived what she has."

My throat tightens.

"Stronger than me."

"Perhaps you both needed strength for different battles." He gestures toward the altar. "Come. Let me show you the arrangements."

We walk down the center aisle together.

The altar gleams with fresh flowers—poppies and emeralds, Dorothy's colors and mine woven together. The unity candle sits on a pedestal, flanked by silver candlesticks that belonged to my great-grandmother.

"Your mother requested the harp," Father Benedict says. "And the string quartet will play during the processional."

I picture Emily coming down this aisle.

Levi supporting her.

Every Lambert cousin watching.

The Wonderful cast.

Philippe and Ariana.

Marcus and Michelle.

Jean waiting at the altar beside me.

My wife.

Legally.

Finally.

"Father," I say quietly. "Can I ask you something?"

"Of course."

"Do you..." I pause, searching for words. "Do you think she knows what she's getting into? The scrutiny, the media, the Lambert name?"

Father Benedict smiles.

That same gentle smile from my childhood.

"I think," he says carefully, "that Emily Silver knows exactly what she's choosing. And more importantly, *who* she's choosing."

"She could have anyone."

"But she chose you." He taps my chest. "Not the actor. Not the Lambert heir. You."

I swallow hard.

"I want to be worthy of that choice."

"Then love her well. Protect her fiercely. Honor her always." He pauses. "The rest will follow."

"I will."

"I know." Father Benedict's eyes twinkle. "Your mother already informed me I'll likely be christening your children within a few years."

Heat floods my face.

"Mum is..."

"Hopeful?"

"Pushy."

He laughs.

That rich, warm laugh that filled Sunday masses throughout my childhood.

"She's excited. All mothers are when their children marry." He squeezes my shoulder. "Now go. Get dressed. I expect you at this altar in your finest suit, ready to make your vows before God and witnesses."

"Yes, Father."

I turn to leave.

"Tristian?"

I glance back.

"She's lucky to have you too," he says softly.

Outside, the cathedral bells begin to chime.

Three hours until the ceremony.

I pull out my phone.

Text Emily.

Father Benedict is ready. The cathedral is perfect. Can't wait to see you walk down that aisle.

Three dots appear.

Disappear.

Appear again.

I love you.

I smile.

I love you too. See you at the altar, Mrs. Lambert.

The dressing room smells of cedar and expensive cologne.

Jean stands before the full-length mirror, adjusting his collar for the third time. The midnight black suit transforms him—makes him look less like a politician and more like the aristocratic vampires from *Midnight Garden*.

I watch him smooth invisible wrinkles from the vest.

Deep crimson against black.

Like fresh blood.

"Stop fidgeting," I tell him.

"I'm not fidgeting."

"You've touched that collar five times."

"It's higher than I'm used to." He tilts his chin. "Does it look like Count Valdris?"

"That's the point, isn't it?"

The roses bloom across the fabric when sunlight hits the pattern. Subtle enough for a wedding, dramatic enough to honor his favorite film. Emily's genius—translating cinema into wearable art.

Jean turns.

Studies the tiny silver stakes crossed at his wrists.

"She got the cufflinks perfect," he murmurs. "Down to the engraving."

Through darkness, light.

Count Valdris's motto.

I've seen *Midnight Garden* enough times to recognize it.

"Where's Dad?" I ask.

"Arguing with his tie." Jean smirks. "He's been in there twenty minutes."

The bathroom door opens.

Dad emerges in charcoal gray with burgundy accents—traditional compared to our suits, but Emily added her touches. The tie pin shaped like the Angoumois crest. Cufflinks that match his Assembly ring.

He stops.

Takes in Jean's vampire-inspired suit.

My extinction purple.

"You both look..." Dad pauses. "Distinguished."

"Emily designed them," Jean says.

"I gathered." Dad crosses to the mirror, finally getting his tie straight. "She has remarkable talent."

I shrug into my jacket.

The purple deepens as I move, blue threading catching light like raptor scales. The DNA helixes spiral along the lapels—so fine you'd miss them unless you looked closely. My pocket square shimmers blue against purple fabric.

The T-Rex cufflinks wink sapphire at my wrists.

Emily embedded Dr. Nathan Cross into every detail.

Even the Victorian boots have hidden zippers because she knows I'll want them off fast tonight.

The custom buckle catches my eye when I fasten the belt.

A T interwoven with an E.

Abstract unless you know.

Our initials.

Our marriage.

"Extinction Protocol," Dad observes. "Your breakout role."

"My favorite character," I correct.

He almost smiles.

Almost.

"She designed Marcus's suit too?" he asks.

"All of them." I adjust my collar. "Marcus has *Velocity Underground*—purple pinstripes like speed lines, gear shift patterns on the vest. Even tire treads on the shoe soles."

Jean laughs.

"That's perfect for him."

"Philippe's is *Gladiator's Revenge*," I continue. "Levi has *Temporal Flux*. Michelle and Ariana both have dresses based on their films."

Dad straightens his own jacket.

Studies us in the mirror.

Two generations of Lambert men.

"Your mother will cry when she sees you," he says quietly.

"Mum cries at everything," Jean mutters.

"Today she has reason." Dad meets my eyes in the reflection. "You're getting married, Tristian. Both of you are."

The weight of it settles.

This cathedral has witnessed Lambert weddings for two centuries.

Today it witnesses ours.

A knock interrupts.

"Five minutes," Marcus calls through the door. "Michelle just texted."

My heart kicks.

Emily.

In her dress.

Coming here.

To marry me.

"How's she doing?" I call back.

"Sophia says she's terrified and trying not to throw up."

Jean grins.

"Same as you then."

"I'm not terrified."

"You've checked your phone sixteen times in the last hour."

"That's—"

"Terrified," Dad finishes.

They're both right.

I pull out my phone.

Text Emily one more time.

Almost time, love. Can't wait to make you legally mine.

Three dots.

I'm shaking so hard Zara had to redo my lipstick twice.

You'll be perfect. See you at the altar.

Love you.

Love you more.

I pocket my phone.

Turn to face Dad and Jean.

"Ready?" Jean asks.

"Ready," I confirm.

Dad crosses the room.

Grips my shoulder.

The same way he did when I was seven and terrified before my first school play.

"You chose well, Tristian," he says softly. "Emily will be good for you. For all of us."

My throat tightens.

"Thank you, Dad."

"Now go." He releases me. "Father Benedict is waiting. And your bride will be here soon."

We file out of the dressing room.

Down the corridor toward the cathedral proper.

Marcus waits near the side entrance in his purple-striped suit, gear shift patterns catching light.

He grins.

"Looking good, Cross."

"Shut up, Racer."

Jean straightens his vampire collar.

Dad adjusts his Angoumois crest pin.

And together we walk toward the altar where Emily will become my wife.

The cathedral doors open.

Michelle enters first, burgundy silk moving like water. The tactical dress from *Operator* fits her like armor—structured, precise, deadly elegant. She catches my eye and pats her hip where I know at least three hidden pockets conceal God knows what.

"Evidence storage," she mouths.

I bite back a laugh.

The USB belt buckle glints as she takes her position.

Sophia follows in emerald green, carrying Luna while Dante holds Stella. The twins wear matching dresses with tiny golden slippers embroidered on the hems. Sophia winks at me before settling beside Michelle.

Then Ariana appears.

Pale pink.

Innocent.

Deceptively so.

The full skirt swishes as she walks, sweetheart neckline demure. But I see what Emily embedded—motel room keys along the hem, blood spatter disguised as abstract florals on the bodice.

Motel Massacre hidden in strawberry sweetness.

Ariana grins at me like she knows exactly what I'm thinking.

Takes her place as maid of honor.

The music shifts.

My breath catches.

Dad escorts Levi down the aisle.

The silver-to-white gradient suit shimmers with each step, heat-reactive fabric briefly flashing pale blue before fading back. Circuit board patterns gleam on the vest underneath. Jean's hand flies to his mouth, eyes bright with tears already.

Levi's barely holding it together either.

When they reach the altar, Dad kisses Levi's cheek before placing his hand in Jean's.

My brother's fingers tremble.

The music swells again.

Marcus and Zara appear at the cathedral entrance.

Between them—

Emily.

My wife.

My Dorothy.

The strapless gown takes my breath. Sweetheart neckline edged in delicate diamonds. The bodice fits her perfectly, smooth fabric highlighting every curve. But it's the skirt that destroys me—layers of flowing fabric scattered with golden butterflies that catch light as she moves.

Ethereal.

Dreaming.

Real.

Her silver slippers gleam beneath the hem.

The tiara of diamond poppies crowns her head, veil trailing behind like mist.

Michael joins them on Emily's left, and together—Marcus, Zara, Michael—they walk my girl down the aisle.

All three.

Claiming her.

Loving her.

Emily's hands shake on their arms.

Her eyes find mine.

Lock.

Hold.

I mouth *I love you.*

She mouths it back.

Mochi trots beside the wheelchair Marcus pushes—golden bowtie perfectly tied, service dog vest gleaming. He takes his position near the altar, tail wagging gently.

Behind them comes Nibbler.

Our animatronic son wearing a purple bowtie that matches my suit exactly.

The raptor chitters softly.

Carries the ring pillow in his mechanical jaws.

Several guests gasp.

Emily laughs—bright, clear, perfect.

The sound fills the cathedral.

Marcus, Zara, and Michael bring Emily to the altar steps.

Father Benedict smiles.

"Who presents this woman?"

"We do." Marcus speaks for all three. "Her family."

They each kiss Emily's cheek.

Marcus whispers something that makes her eyes shine.

Zara squeezes her hand.

Michael adjusts her veil tenderly.

Then they step back.

I move forward.

Kneel before Emily's wheelchair.

Take both her hands in mine.

"Hi," I whisper.

"Hi," she whispers back.

Her fingers tremble.

I kiss her knuckles.

Stand.

Marcus locks Emily's wheelchair.

I lift her into my arms.

She weighs nothing.

Everything.

Her dress cascades over my purple suit—gold butterflies against extinction blue, emeralds against DNA helixes.

Dorothy and her Scarecrow.

Maya and her raptor.

Emily and Tristian.

I carry her to the altar.

Set her gently on the cushioned bench Father Benedict prepared.

Settle beside her.

Jean and Levi take their places at the second altar position.

Father Benedict opens the ceremony book.

"Dearly beloved—"

The cathedral doors crash open.

Heads turn.

Martha Hendricks storms down the aisle.

Adam beside her.

Bethany trailing behind, somehow squeezed into a white dress that screams *bride*.

My hands fist.

Marcus moves first—already halfway down the aisle before I process what's happening.

"This is a farce!" Martha's voice echoes off stone walls. "That girl manipulated everyone with her wheelchair act—"

"Ma'am, you need to leave." Marcus blocks their path.

Two hundred guests stare.

Security converges from the sides.

"She's a liar!" Adam shouts. "Playing victim for attention—"

"We have a restraining order." Philippe appears beside Marcus, phone already raised. "You're in violation."

Martha ignores them both.

Eyes locked on Emily.

"You think you deserve this? A cripple playing dress-up with a movie star?"

The word hits Emily like a slap.

Her shoulders curl inward.

"Get them out." Jean's voice cuts ice-cold through the cathedral.

But Bethany pushes past security.

Reaches the altar steps.

"Tristian." Her voice drips honey-poison. "You can't actually want *her*. Look at her. She can't even stand on her own—"

Something in Emily shifts.

I feel it.

The trembling stops.

Her spine straightens.

"Marcus." Emily's voice rings clear. "Tristian. Help me up."

I move without thinking.

Marcus mirrors me from the other side.

We lift Emily between us—supporting her weight, her hands gripping our arms.

Standing.

Emily faces Bethany.

"You're right." Emily's words carry through the cathedral. "I can't stand on my own. But I've done things I never thought I would. New York. Los Angeles. Europe. I ride horses with Tristian and Marcus. I'm going to play Dorothy Gale in a *film*. I'm not a virgin anymore."

Gasps ripple through the crowd.

I should stop her.

Can't.

Won't.

"And Bethany?" Emily's smile turns razor-sharp. "You've had fantasies about Tristian. News flash—you're not the girl he wants."

"Emily—" I try.

She keeps going.

"Want to know how good he is in bed? His tongue. His fingers. His cock buried so deep—"

"*Mon étoile*—" My accent thickens involuntarily.

"How possessive he gets. The *voices*." Emily's eyes never leave Bethany's face. "The raptor growl when he claims me. The Winkie commands. The accent when he's —"

"*Nae'mora deshtari*." The Winkie dom voice escapes before I can stop it. *Enough, beloved.*

Emily doesn't even pause.

"—when he's inside me. When he makes me scream his name. When he—"

David Kellerman stands from his pew.

"Security. Remove these trespassers. Now."

Zara's already on her phone.

Michael moves toward Martha with Dante flanking him.

The entire Wonderful cast rises as one.

A wall of protection.

Sophia holds up her phone.

"Livestreaming everything. Try us."

"I'm calling my cousin at the *Times*." Marcus doesn't release Emily. "You'll be front-page news for all the wrong reasons."

Guards converge.

Grab Martha's arms.

Adam struggles.

Bethany stares at Emily like she's seeing her for the first time.

"How did you even—" Emily's breathing stays even. "How did you know? How did you get here from Utah?"

"Your little friend Ariana posted the location." Bethany spits the words. "Easy enough to book a flight when you're desperate."

"Desperate." Emily laughs. "That's you. Coming to my wedding. Wearing white to someone else's ceremony. Pathetic."

Her lungs hold steady.

No wheeze.

No panic.

No inhaler.

Just Emily.

Standing between Marcus and me.

Claiming her space.

Her voice.

Her life.

"You think Tristian wants someone like you?" Bethany makes one last attempt. "Someone who needs help with everything?"

"I think—" Emily's grip tightens on our arms. "I *know* Tristian wants his wife. The one he married on a Metro train. The one he swam to an island for. The one he renovated his entire house for. The one he's standing beside right now."

She turns to me.

Eyes blazing emerald fire.

"The one who just publicly detailed their sex life in a cathedral full of his family and friends because she was tired of being told she doesn't deserve happiness."

Heat floods my body despite everything.

Absolutely wrong response to this situation.

Father Benedict clears his throat loudly.

Security drags Martha, Adam, and Bethany toward the exit.

Martha screams protests.

Adam threatens lawsuits.

Bethany just stares back at Emily with pure hatred.

The doors slam shut behind them.

Silence fills the cathedral.

Two hundred guests stare at us.

At Emily still standing between Marcus and me.

At the aftermath of her explosive declaration.

Emily's face drains of color.

Realization hits.

"Oh God." Her voice drops to a whisper. "Father Benedict. I'm so sorry. I just—in your cathedral—I said—"

Father Benedict's lips twitch.

"My child." He steps closer. "I've married Lamberts for forty years. Trust me when I say I've heard worse."

"But I talked about—"

"Your intimate relationship with your husband." Father Benedict's eyes crinkle. "Whom you married months ago. Whom you're renewing vows with today. And whom you just defended your choice to love in front of two hundred witnesses."

He gestures to the pews.

"I'd say that's rather biblical, actually. Cleaving to one's spouse. Forsaking all others."

Nervous laughter ripples through the crowd.

Marcus helps me lower Emily back onto the cushioned bench.

She's trembling now.

Adrenaline crash.

I settle beside her.

Take her hands.

"Breathe, love."

"I just told everyone about your—"

"I know."

"In detail."

"I noticed."

"At our *wedding*."

"Also noticed."

Her eyes meet mine.

"Why aren't you mortified?"

I brush her veil back.

Kiss her forehead.

"Because you stood up for yourself. No inhaler. No panic attack. Just my fierce, brilliant wife telling the world exactly where they can shove their ableist bullshit."

"Tristian!" Father Benedict protests.

"Sorry, Father."

Not sorry.

Emily laughs.

Watery but real.

"Can we please get married now before I ruin anything else?"

Father Benedict opens his book again.

"Dearly beloved—*again*—we are gathered here today..."

Father Benedict recovers his composure.

"The couples have chosen to exchange personal vows."

He gestures to me. "Tristian?"

I turn to Emily.

Clear my throat.

"Emily Dorothy Silver Washington Butler Lambert." Her full name tastes like home. "In the world of *Extinction Protocol*, Dr. Nathan Cross spent thirty years believing himself a monster. Unworthy of love. Too damaged, too dangerous, too *other* to deserve his mate."

I shift into Nathan's Alabama drawl.

"*Then Maya Reyes walked into his lab with coffee and terrible puns about DNA sequencing.*"

Laughter from the Wonderful cast.

Emily's eyes shine.

"She saw past the scales. Past the claws. Past every defense mechanism he'd built." My voice drops. "She touched his raptor face and called him *beautiful*."

I reach for Emily's hand.

Press her palm to my cheek.

"*Kree'sha nae'tara.*" The raptor language rumbles from my chest. *My chosen mate.*

Emily's breath hitches.

"You see me, *mon étoile*. Not the actor. Not the Lambert heir. Just Tristian. The boy who ran from his father's expectations. The man who found his purpose in your emerald eyes."

I switch to Nathan's voice completely.

"*So I'm claimin' you, Dr. Reyes. Before God and two hundred witnesses and our mechanical raptor son. You're mine. I'm yours. No take-backs.*"

The growl escapes.

Possessive.

Claiming.

Emily shivers.

"I love you," I finish in my own voice. "In English, French, Winkie, and raptor. Forever."

Father Benedict nods to Emily.

She swallows hard.

"Tristian Alexandre Lambert." Her voice steadies. "Dorothy Gale spent her whole life being told she was too much of a dreamer. Too fragile. Too *different* to belong anywhere that mattered."

She shifts into Dorothy's Kansas accent.

"*Then she met a scarecrow who didn't have a brain but somehow understood every dream she'd ever dreamed.*"

My throat tightens.

"A man who was king but chose to be her partner. Who saw her silver slippers and didn't see a cripple—he saw *magic*."

Emily's fingers tighten on mine.

"*Mora'kesh ti'nara.*" The Winkie flows like water. *My heart's home.*

"You renovated your house for my wheelchair.. You carried me across continents and never once made me feel like a burden."

Her free hand touches my face.

"So I'm choosin' you, Mr. Lambert. Before the Wizard and Glinda and all of Oz. You're my yellow brick road. My emerald city. My home."

She drops the accent.

"I love you. In every language we've created together. Always."

Father Benedict gestures to Jean and Levi.

Jean speaks first.

"Levi Williams." His voice carries that careful politician's precision. "In *Midnight Garden*, Lord Ashford spent centuries watching others fall in love while he remained frozen. Beautiful. Eternal. Alone."

Jean's accent thickens—proper British aristocracy.

"Then a mortal stumbled into his garden at midnight, smelling of sunshine and absolutely terrible coffee."

Levi grins through tears.

"He was everything I wasn't. Warm. Alive. Impossibly brave enough to love a creature of darkness."

Jean takes Levi's hand.

"You chose me when I was my father's puppet. You stayed when I couldn't promise you children or political safety. You loved me when I didn't love myself."

His voice breaks.

"So I pledge myself, mon coeur. In darkness and daylight. In this life and whatever comes after."

Levi wipes his eyes.

"Jean Pierre Lambert." His American accent contrasts Jean's British. "In *Temporal Flux*, Claire Chen spent his whole life chasing the past. Trying to fix mistakes with his grandfather's projector. Never living in the *now*."

Levi shifts into Claire Chen's determined tone.

"*Then she met an antique dealer who told her the best moments aren't the ones you rewrite—they're the ones you choose to stay in.*"

Jean's composure cracks completely.

"You taught me that love isn't about perfect timing. It's about choosing each other every single day. In every timeline. Every possibility."

Levi squeezes Jean's hands.

"You're my present tense, Jean. My right now. My forever."

He smiles through tears.

"*So I'm choosing this moment. This man. This life we're building together.*"

Father Benedict clears his throat.

"The rings?"

Nibbler chirps.

Waddles forward with the pillow in his jaws.

The cathedral erupts in laughter.

I retrieve both rings.

Slide the rose gold band with its emerald onto Emily's finger.

She places my matching band—purple sapphires embedded in silver—on mine.

Jean and Levi exchange their rings.

Simple platinum bands engraved with coordinates.

Father Benedict beams.

"By the power vested in me, I now pronounce you— married. Again." He looks at Emily and me.He nods to Jean and Levi.

"You may kiss—"

I don't wait.

Pull Emily into my arms.

Kiss her like I did on that Metro platform three months ago.

Like I will for the rest of our lives.

She tastes like forever.

The vineyard transforms.

Café lights strung between posts flicker to life as dusk settles. Each table tells a story—Jean's midnight roses twining with Levi's vintage clock centerpieces, Emily's golden brick pathways meeting my raptor claw place settings.

But there's more now.

Michelle's sleek racing flags draped across the bar. Marcus's tactical operator gear mounted on the far wall like art installations.

I freeze mid-stride.

"When did—"

"Last night." Michelle appears at my elbow, stunning in her burgundy tactical dress. "While you were busy worshipping your wife."

Wife.

The word still hits different.

I scan the crowd until I find Emily.

She's changed into Maya's science gala dress—black silk with strategic cutouts, adaptive closures hidden in the draping. The emerald at her navel catches light through the sheer panels.

Mochi sits at attention beside her wheelchair.

Nibbler curls at her feet.

My family.

I cross to Emily.

Drop a kiss on her bare shoulder.

"*Mora'kesh.*"

She shivers.

"Stop making me want to skip our own reception."

"Who says we have to stay for the whole thing?"

Her laugh draws Marcus over.

He's shed the purple suit jacket. Rolled his sleeves to reveal tactical watch straps that definitely weren't part of Emily's design.

"Dinner's served." He grins. "Hope you're hungry, brother."

Mum's ratatouille arrives in covered copper pots.

The tomato-free version of what I learned to make for Emily that first night at FanCon.

Twelve months ago.

A lifetime.

Alfred ladles portions while servers pour vineyard wine—the non-alcoholic blend Dad commissioned specifically for tonight. Deep burgundy in crystal glasses, tasting of oak and blackberries without the bite.

Emily takes a sip.

Makes a small sound of approval.

"This is dangerous."

"Why?" I cut her zucchini into manageable pieces without thinking. Muscle memory from months of shared meals.

"Because I could drink an entire bottle and not realize it's missing the alcohol."

Levi raises his glass from across the table.

"To Emily Lambert. Fashion designer. Dorothy Gale. Raptor tamer. The woman brave enough to marry into this chaos."

"To Emily!" The chorus echoes.

Heat floods my chest.

Pride.

Possession.

Mine.

Jean stands next.

"To Tristian. Who swam across open water like an unhinged romantic. Who bought *two islands* because one wasn't enough. Who somehow convinced the universe to give him everything he didn't know he needed."

"To Tristian!"

Emily's hand finds mine under the table.

Squeezes.

I bring her knuckles to my lips.

"*Je t'aime.*"

"Love you too." She switches to raptor. "*Kree'sha nae'tara.*"

The growl escapes before I can stop it.

Low.

Possessive.

Marcus kicks me under the table.

"Save it for the honeymoon, Cross."

Emily flushes scarlet.

But she doesn't let go of my hand.

Dinner dissolves into laughter.

Stories.

Marcus recounting how Michelle made him wait six months before their New Orleans elopement. Jean describing Levi's terrible coffee addiction. Philippe demonstrating proper gladiatorial stance while balancing a wine glass.

The children race between tables.

Jasper claims Nibbler as his personal mount.

Mochi herds them like sheep.

I watch Emily.

The way she leans into conversation with Sophia and Zara. How she signs to little Sage who sits cross-legged at her feet. The automatic check of her phone for blood sugar alerts that never come because she ate exactly what her body needed.

Healthy.

Happy.

Home.

"Five minutes."

Emily wheels toward the house.

Michelle and Ariana flank her like tactical escorts.

I lean against the bar.

Wait.

Jean appears beside me. "She's changing."

"I gathered."

"Into something you'll recognize."

My pulse kicks.

The string quartet shifts into position near the makeshift dance floor—weathered boards laid over grass, lights strung overhead like stars.

Four minutes.

Three.

The vineyard quiets.

Everyone turns toward the house.

And there she is.

Blue gingham dress.

Simple cotton that somehow looks like poetry against her skin. The bodice fitted, the skirt full enough to accommodate her seated position. White eyelet trim at the collar and sleeves.

But it's the details that gut me.

One braid over her shoulder.

Tied with a piece of golden straw.

Felix's straw.

From the sketches she showed me months ago. The costume she designed for Dorothy.

Her feet—

Silver slippers.

The ones from the ceremony. Crystal-adorned, catching every flicker of café light.

She wheels herself across the grass.

Mochi walks beside her. Nibbler chirps from where Jasper's abandoned him by the cake table.

The quartet begins.

Soft strings.

A melody I know.

Our melody.

I cross to Emily.

Kneel.

"May I have this dance, Mrs. Lambert?"

Her smile breaks like dawn.

"Always."

I stand. Lift her from the chair in one smooth motion. Her arms circle my neck, legs wrapping my waist as I settle her weight against me.

Her feet rest on mine.

Silver slippers atop black leather.

"Ready?"

She nods.

I move.

Slow.

Swaying more than dancing, really. But her head tilts back, eyes closed, and she's *flying*.

The music swells.

I hum against her temple. The words Emily sang that night at the karaoke bar. When I kissed her for the first time and accidentally recorded it for my entire family.

She joins me.

Soft at first. Then stronger.

Her voice carries across the vineyard—pure, controlled, *Dorothy's* voice breaking through Emily's shyness.

Guests form a circle around us.

I spin. Gentle. Keeping her secure.

Her braid swings. The straw catches light.

"You planned this." I murmur it against her ear.

"Maybe."

"The straw—"

"From your collection. The prop department sent it when I told them what I needed."

My chest tightens.

She tied herself to me.

Literally.

Dorothy claiming her Scarecrow.

Maya marking her raptor.

Emily choosing Tristian.

I dip her. Support her spine with one arm while her hair nearly brushes the boards.

She gasps.

Laughs.

Glows.

When I pull her upright, her forehead presses mine.

"Love you." She breathes it. "So much it scares me sometimes."

"Good." I turn us again. Her silver slippers flash. "Because I'm never letting you go."

"Promise?"

"*Kree'sha nae'tara.*" The raptor growl rumbles through both our chests. "Forever mine."

"Forever yours."

The music builds.

I lift her higher. She throws her arms wide like wings.

Dorothy soaring over Oz.

The crowd applauds but I barely hear it.

Just Emily.

Her heartbeat against mine.

Her weight in my arms.

Her *trust*—absolute and unwavering—that I'll keep her safe.

Always.

The final notes fade.

I lower her slowly. Press my lips to hers.

She tastes like vineyard air and vanilla buttercream and *home*.

When we break apart, she's crying.

Happy tears.

I know the difference now.

"Ready for cake?" I ask.

She shakes her head.

Points to the dance floor where Jean and Levi have taken our place. Then Michelle and Marcus. Philippe sweeping Ariana into an elaborate dip.

"One more song," Emily whispers. "Just us."

So I hold my wife.

Her silver slippers resting on my feet.

And we dance.

Epilogue: Silver Screen Miracles

March in Los Angeles.

Eighteen months since Emily walked down that vineyard aisle.

Well.

Wheeled.

Same difference.

I adjust my bow tie in the limo's tinted window. Purple—Emily's design, naturally. The fabric shimmers with microscopic film reels stitched into the weave. Only visible when light hits just right.

Beside me, Emily fidgets with her gown.

Emerald silk. Adaptive construction hidden beneath couture perfection. The bodice features hand-embroidered poppies—her adaptive machine's first major project after the wedding.

She's stunning.

Also terrified.

"Breathe, love."

"I'm breathing." She's not. Her inhaler sits in Zara's clutch three seats away, just in case. "Totally breathing."

"Emily."

"What if—"

I take her hand. Press it against my chest so she feels my heartbeat. Steady. Calm. "You designed the accessibility protocol yourself. Remember?"

She did.

Three months of meetings with the Silver Screen Board. Ramps. Designated seating. ASL interpreters. Closed captioning on all montages.

Dorothy changing the rules.

Her breathing slows.

Matches mine.

"Better?"

She nods.

Across from us, Jean scrolls through his phone. Levi reads a book—some political thriller Dad recommended. Michelle examines her nails, burgundy polish catching the streetlights. Marcus grins like he knows something we don't.

Probably does.

He always does.

"You look beautiful, Emmy." Zara leans forward. Adjusts one of Emily's emerald clips. "Absolutely radiant."

"Listen to Mama Washington." Michael winks. "She's never wrong about these things."

Emily flushes.

Still not used to having parents who show up.

Three sets of them now.

Mum called this morning from the château. Dad too— brief, gruff, but *proud*. Said Jean's policy reforms are gaining traction. Said Emily's accessible design advocacy opened doors he never thought possible.

Said he's glad Tristian found someone who fights as hard as he does.

I'll take it.

Philippe texted from Santorini. He and Ariana extended their honeymoon another week. Something about "Greek islands" and "finally understanding why Tristian became feral."

Fair.

The limo slows.

Outside, the Dolby Theatre blazes.

Cameras. Lights. The red carpet stretching like a river of expectations.

Emily's hand tightens in mine.

"We don't have to do this," I murmur. "Say the word and we're gone."

"You're nominated for Best Actor."

"Don't care."

"*Tristian.*"

"I mean it." I do. "You. Me. Mochi and Nibbler. We disappear to Paradise Point and never look back."

She laughs.

Soft at first. Then genuine.

"You'd really skip the Silver Screens?"

"*In a heartbeat.*"

The limo stops.

Door opens.

Sound crashes in—screaming fans, rapid-fire camera clicks, someone shouting questions about Emily's dress.

Marcus exits first. Then Michelle. Jean and Levi.

Zara and Michael.

Then us.

I step out. Turn. Offer my hand.

Emily takes it.

Transfers from seat to wheelchair in one practiced motion. Her gown pools perfectly around her legs—exactly as she designed.

The crowd *erupts*.

Not polite applause.

Roaring.

Signs appear. "DOROTHY FOR BEST ACTRESS." "LAMBERT POWER COUPLE." "EMILY WE LOVE YOU."

One girl—maybe twelve—holds a poster.

Emily in her Alice costume from FanCon.

Full circle.

I crouch beside Emily's chair. Press my forehead to hers.

"Ready to show them what a real leading lady looks like?"

She grins.

"Let's go make history, Mr. Lambert."

So we do.

Emily wheels forward.

I walk beside her.

Cameras flash.

Reporters shout.

And my wife—

My Dorothy—

Faces them all with her chin up and emerald eyes blazing.

Behind us, the family follows.

Jean texting Dad updates.

Levi already planning post-ceremony drinks.

Michelle coordinating with our stylist about after-party looks.

Marcus documenting everything for the Southern Living exclusive.

Zara and Michael beaming like Emily just won already.

The red carpet stretches ahead.

Endless.

Overwhelming.

Perfect.

Because Emily's hand finds mine.

Squeezes.

And I know—

Whatever happens tonight—

We've already won.

The first reporter shoves a microphone toward us.

"Tristian! Emily! How does it feel returning to the Silver Screens as a married couple?"

I open my mouth.

Emily beats me to it.

"Like coming home." Her voice carries. Strong. Clear. "Just with better shoes this time."

She lifts one foot.

Custom silver heels peek from beneath emerald silk.

Dorothy's slippers.

The crowd loses it.

I grin.

Pull her chair closer as we navigate toward the next cluster of press.

Jean would approve of her deflection technique. He's gotten brilliant at it over the past year—steering conversations away from controversy, toward policy substance.

Reelection does that.

Six-point lead in November. Dad's too, though his margin was tighter. Twelve percent.

Not that Dad minds.

He told Jean last month this is his final term. Wants to "focus on legacy." Which apparently means hovering over potential grandchildren like some sort of political fairy godfather.

Jean and Levi started the adoption process in January.

Paperwork everywhere. Home studies. Background checks that made even *my* security clearance look casual.

Levi's scaling back his acting schedule. Already turned down two films. Says he wants to be present—actually *there*—when they finally bring their son or daughter home.

Jean cried when Levi said that.

Dad almost did too.

Almost.

Progress.

Another flash. Another question.

Emily handles it.

I watch her work the carpet like she was born to this.

Maybe she was.

Just took her twenty-three years to find the right stage.

My phone buzzes.

Text from Philippe.

The sea is gorgeous but we're coming home early. Ari misses Mochi. (I miss decent coffee.)

I snort.

They've been in Santorini three weeks. Meant to stay five.

Marriage changes people.

Another text.

Michelle.

Stop reading your phone on the red carpet you absolute disaster. Also I'm craving pickles. Why am I craving pickles?

Because she's fourteen weeks pregnant and refuses to admit morning sickness exists.

Marcus knows.

We all know.

Michelle thinks she's being subtle.

She's not.

She cried at a diaper commercial last Tuesday.

Lambert grandchild number one incoming.

Dad's already planning the nursery at Grantham Bridge.

Mum's knitting.

Knitting.

I didn't know she *could* knit.

Emily squeezes my hand.

"You okay?"

"Perfect."

I am.

Mostly.

There's this... *thing*.

This desperate, gnawing, utterly *feral* need that's been building for months.

Get Emily pregnant.

It's not logical.

Not rational.

It's pure Winkie instinct crossed with raptor biology and Lambert family madness.

Every time we make love, I feel it.

That primal urge to *claim*. To *mark*. To put a baby in my wife and watch her grow round with our child.

Nathan would understand.

So would Felix.

Hell, every character I've ever played who had a possessive streak would understand.

Because Emily is *mine*.

And I want everyone to know it.

Want her wearing my ring—*check*.

Want her carrying my name—*check*.

Want her body sheltering our baby—

Working on it.

We've been trying since Christmas.

Four months of—

Well.

Trying.

Emily tracking cycles. Me coordinating filming schedules around ovulation windows. Both of us pretending it's spontaneous when really I've got her fertility app memorized better than my shooting schedule.

Her PCOS makes it harder.

Dr. Laurent warned us.

Could take six months. A year. Maybe longer.

Maybe fertility treatments.

I don't care.

I'll wait.

I'll do whatever it takes.

But that doesn't stop the *wanting*.

The way my hands gravitate to her stomach when we're alone.

The dreams where she's swollen and glowing and *ours*.

The raptor part of my brain that sees Michelle's pregnancy and *snarls*—not with jealousy, but with pure determined *I'm next*.

Emily hasn't said anything.

Hasn't mentioned if we're close.

Her period's due...

She handles that.

I just show up with heating pads and chocolate when needed.

Good husband behavior.

Another reporter.

Another question.

Emily laughs at something.

Touches her stomach briefly.

Probably adjusting her dress.

Probably nothing.

Probably.

But my heart kicks anyway.

Because—

What if?

"Tristian?" Emily looks up. "They're asking about *Wonderful*."

Right.

Focus.

I'm nominated for Felix.

She's nominated for Dorothy.

We're here for the film.

Not potential babies.

Not family planning.

The film.

"*Wonderful* changed everything," I tell the reporter. "Gave us both roles we'd dreamed of. Gave Emily a platform she deserves."

"And gave Hollywood its first wheelchair-using lead actress to earn a Best Actress nomination," the reporter adds.

Emily beams.

There she is.

My Dorothy.

My wife.

Maybe—*maybe*—mother of my future child.

God, I hope so.

But tonight?

Tonight we walk this carpet.

We smile for cameras.

We celebrate Emily's brilliance.

The rest?

We'll figure it out.

Together.

Always together.

The ceremony stretches.

Awards. Montages. Speeches that blur together.

Emily's category comes first.

Best Costume Design.

She's up against legends—fifty-year veterans with decades of nominations.

She's twenty-four.

The envelope opens.

"And the Silver Screen goes to... Emily Dorothy Lambert, for Wonderful!"

The theater *detonates.*

Standing ovation.

Immediate. Thunderous.

I'm on my feet before my brain catches up.

Beside me, Marcus whoops. Jean grips Levi's hand. Michelle's crying—hormones, probably, but still.

Zara and Michael embrace.

Emily freezes.

Just for a heartbeat.

Then she's moving—wheeling herself toward the stage with Sophia and Zara flanking her like honor guards.

The accessible ramp she designed herself.

Making history.

She reaches the podium.

Daniel Brooks hands her the statuette—silver film reel catching stage lights.

Emily stares at it.

"I..." Her voice cracks. "I dreamed about this moment in foster care. Late nights when I couldn't sleep. When I felt invisible."

The audience quiets.

"I designed clothes for my dolls because I couldn't afford real fabric. Practiced acceptance speeches into hairbrushes because I didn't think anyone would ever actually *see* me."

She looks down.

At the award.

At her hands.

"But my husband saw me. At a comic convention, of all places. And he didn't see my wheelchair. Didn't see someone who needed fixing. He saw *me*. The designer. The dreamer. The woman who could create magic with needle and thread."

Her gaze finds mine across the theater.

"Tristian believed before I did. Before Hollywood did. Before anyone thought a disabled girl from Logan, Utah could stand on this stage."

You're standing on it now, love.

"So this—" She lifts the statuette. "This is for every kid who feels invisible. Every designer told they're not 'right' for the industry. Every dreamer who thinks their body disqualifies them from greatness."

Beat.

"You belong here. I promise."

The applause builds.

Crashes.

Emily wheels offstage.

And I can barely *breathe* from pride.

Best Actress comes during the second hour.

Four nominees.

Emily against three powerhouses—women with awards already lining their shelves.

The presenter opens the envelope.

Pauses.

Dramatic effect.

I hate him.

"*Emily Dorothy Lambert, Wonderful!*"

If the costume design reaction was loud, this is *apocalyptic.*

Everyone standing.

The *Wonderful* cast section screaming.

Dante hoisting Jasper onto his shoulders.

Sophia sobbing into Michael's chest.

Braden and Carlos chanting "DOR-O-THY! DOR-O-THY!"

Emily doesn't freeze this time.

She wheels forward like she *owns* this moment.

Because she does.

Zara and Sophia escort her again.

The presenter—Dame Catherine Wright, living legend herself—places the second statuette in Emily's lap with visible emotion.

"I told you," Emily says into the microphone. Voice steady now. Certain. "I told you resilient hearts win."

She looks at the camera.

At America.

At every kid watching who sees themselves in her.

"Disability doesn't disqualify dreams. It just means you dream *louder*. Fight *harder*. And when someone tells you that you can't—you prove them catastrophically wrong."

Grin.

"Also? Marry someone who believes you can fly even when your legs don't work. Helps."

Laughter.

Applause.

My wife.

She wheels off.

Two awards.

Both deserved.

Both hers.

Best Actor comes last.

Of course it does.

They save the major categories—build suspense.

I'm not nervous.

Not really.

Emily's already won.

That's what matters.

But then the montage plays.

Clips of Felix.

My performance.

The transformation from entitled prince to humbled scarecrow to man who *chooses* love over power.

Chooses Emily—Dorothy—over everything.

The presenter takes the stage.

Opens the envelope.

"Tristian Alexandre Lambert, Wonderful!"

The roar returns.

I stand.

Kiss Emily hard and fast.

Taste salt—she's crying again.

Happy tears.

I make my way to the stage.

Each step surreal.

The statuette heavy in my hands.

Real.

I reach the podium.

The theater quiets.

Waiting.

"Funny thing about playing Felix," I start. "He's a character who loses everything—crown, identity, memory—and discovers he never needed any of it."

I turn the award over.

Study the engraving.

Tristian Alexandre Lambert, Best Actor.

"Because what he needed was standing right in front of him. In a blue gingham dress. With emerald eyes and a heart that refused to quit."

I find Emily in the audience.

Third row.

Silver statuettes in her lap.

"I met my wife at a comic convention. She was in a pink wheelchair, dressed as Alice, and she asked me about a French film I made when I was nineteen. A film barely anyone saw."

Beat.

"But she saw it. Saw *me*. Not the actor. Not the Lambert heir. Just... Tristian."

My voice catches.

Steady.

"Emily taught me what Felix learned—that strength isn't about power or perfection. It's about showing up. About choosing love even when it's hard. Especially when it's hard."

I lift the award.

"So this belongs to resilient hearts. To people who fight chronic illness and ableism and a world that says they don't belong. To my wife, who proved she belongs *everywhere*."

The applause builds.

I should leave.

Exit stage left.

But Emily's *looking* at me.

Hand pressed to her stomach.

Something in her expression—

Oh.

Oh God.

She nods.

Barely perceptible.

But I see it.

I see it.

My legs go weak.

"I—" Into the microphone. Voice cracking. "Sorry, I need—"

I'm moving.

Off stage.

Down the ramp.

Ignoring protocol and producers and probably several million viewers.

I reach Emily.

Drop to my knees beside her wheelchair.

"Tell me."

"Tristian, you're supposed to be backstage—"

"*Tell me.*"

She bites her lip.

Glances at Zara.

Sophia.

They're both crying.

They know.

Emily takes my hand.

Places it on her stomach.

Flat now. Won't be forever.

"Eight weeks," she whispers. "Twins."

The world *stops*.

Twins.

Our babies.

The Winkie determination worked.

The raptor biology worked.

We worked.

I press my forehead to her stomach.

Right there.

In front of God and Hollywood and international television.

Don't care.

"*Mavi ne doreni,*" I murmur. Winkie. *My little fighters.*

Then raptor.

Low clicks and purrs that vibrate against Emily's dress.

Mama. Daddy. Safe. Protected. Ours.

"Tristian—" Emily's laughing. Crying. Both.

"Everyone's watching."

"Don't care."

I don't.

Let them watch.

Let them see a man utterly wrecked by joy.

Jean's hand lands on my shoulder.

"*Mon frère*..." Wonder in his voice.

"Twins," I choke out. "She's—we're—"

"*Twins?!*" Michelle shrieks.

Marcus drops to his knees beside me.

Hands lifted.

"*Thank you, Jesus.*" Voice shaking. "Thank you, thank you, *thank you*—"

He's praying.

Right here.

While the cameras roll and the ceremony continues somewhere behind us.

"Two more Lambert babies," Levi breathes. "Oh my God."

"Best. News. Ever." Michelle hugs Emily from behind. Careful. Gentle. "They're going to have a cousin so close in age—"

"*Cousins,*" Jean corrects. "We got the call yesterday. Our daughter comes home in May."

What.

I stare.

"You—*what?*"

Levi grins.

Pulls out his phone.

Shows a photo.

Little girl. Maybe two. Dark curls and huge brown eyes.

"Amélie," Jean says softly. "Our Amélie."

Marcus makes a sound.

Somewhere between laugh and sob.

"God is *showing off* right now."

He is.

Three Lambert babies.

All arriving within months of each other.

Family.

I turn back to Emily.

To my wife.

To the mother of my children.

"*Je t'aime,*" I whisper. "More than anything."

"I love you too." She cups my face. "Even when you talk to my uterus in fake languages."

"*Our* uterus."

"Not how biology works."

"Don't care."

I kiss her.

Deep and claiming and utterly inappropriate for live television.

Still don't care.

Behind us, someone clears their throat.

The show's producer.

Looking very stressed.

"Mr. Lambert, you're supposed to be—"

"With my wife," I finish. "Exactly where I'm supposed to be."

Emily laughs.

The sound wraps around my heart.

Squeezes.

This.

This is everything.

Not the awards.

Not the fame.

This.

Family surrounding us.

Babies growing inside Emily.

My Dorothy.

My resilient heart.

My *everything*.

"Come on," Emily says. Wheels herself toward the exit. "Let's go home."

Home.

The Hills House.

The nursery we'll build.

The life we'll create.

Together.

Always together.

I stand.

Take her hand.

And we leave.

Awards clutched.
Babies protected.
Family behind us.
Lambert strong.
Lambert proud.
Lambert complete.